Praise for

A DISTANT GRAVE

"The result is a fast-paced, tension-filled yarn filled with twists the reader is unlikely to see coming. Taylor tells the story in a lyrical prose style that is a joy to read. She excels in vividly portraying both the rural Ireland and Long Island settings and in developing memorable characters, including D'arcy's partner, Dave Milich, and her troubled daughter, Lilly." —Associated Press

"Taylor combines complex layering of plots with depth of characterization, lovely Emerald Isle color, and prose that often rises to lyricism. . . . Taylor further burnishes her bona fides as a practitioner par excellence of literary crime fiction."
—*The Free Lance-Star*

"Complex, slow-burning . . . Taylor has crafted another believable and intriguing installment of Maggie's story." —*BookPage*

"[*A Distant Grave*] is as intricately plotted as *The Mountains Wild*."
—*Library Journal*

"Taylor pulls out all the stops—subplots, threats, red herrings, warning bells—to keep the pot boiling till the end." —*Kirkus Reviews*

"Tana French fans will be eager for the next series entry."
—*Publishers Weekly*

"The Irish setting takes center stage. . . . A solid series."   —*Booklist*

"Lyrical, haunting, and impossible to put down . . . Absolutely do not miss this."   —Hank Phillippi Ryan

"Sarah Stewart Taylor commands the most complex of emotions— grief, guilt, love—with ease to deliver a story that, like a chill off the water, gets in your bones."   —Tessa Wegert

Praise for

THE MOUNTAINS WILD

"Taylor has sculpted *The Mountains Wild* as a valentine to Ireland, delving into its beauty, history, and varied landscape. . . . *The Mountains Wild* is a terrific series launch."
                                   —Oline Cogdill, *South Florida Sun Sentinel*

"Gripping."   —*The Christian Science Monitor*

"Sarah Stewart Taylor has written a beautiful, bittersweet novel about loyalty and loss and how they can blind us to the truth."
                                                           —*Star Tribune*

"Maggie is a first-class protagonist—an ace investigator and appealing everywoman with smarts and heart. Suspense fans are sure to welcome her to the crime scene."   —*BookPage*

"This fantastic novel has something for everyone: mystery, murder, police work, family drama, and even romance. Fans of strong

women protagonists and crime drama will love this chilling page-turner."
—*Mystery Scene*

"The atmospheric, intricately plotted story builds to a stunning, unforgettable conclusion. . . . This outstanding book will please fans of mysteries set in Ireland and readers of police procedurals."
—*Library Journal* (starred review)

"This mystery, evocative of the Irish diaspora, interrogates both a young woman's disappearance and the meaning of homeland."
—*Kirkus Reviews*

"Taylor, a mystery veteran, shifts into noirish territory after her humorous Sweeney St. George series, and it works just fine." —*Booklist*

"Fans of Elizabeth George should take note." —*Publishers Weekly*

"Lyrical, moody, *The Mountains Wild* unfolds like an Irish ballad, at turns stirring, tender, and tragic. . . . A triumphant return to the genre."
—Julia Spencer-Fleming

"Atmospheric and lyrical, *The Mountains Wild* is that rare thing—a riveting thriller with a beating heart." —Lisa Unger

"*The Mountains Wild* should top everyone's must-read lists this year!"
—Deborah Crombie

A
Distant
Grave

Sarah Stewart Taylor

MINOTAUR BOOKS
NEW YORK

Published in the United States by Minotaur Books, an imprint of St. Martin's Publishing Group

A DISTANT GRAVE. Copyright © 2021 by Sarah Stewart Taylor. All rights reserved. Printed in the United States of America. For information, address St. Martin's Publishing Group, 120 Broadway, New York, NY 10271.

www.minotaurbooks.com

The Library of Congress has cataloged the hardcover edition as follows:

Names: Taylor, Sarah Stewart, author.
Title: A distant grave / Sarah Stewart Taylor.
Description: First Edition. | New York : Minotaur Books, 2021.
Identifiers: LCCN 2020057562 | ISBN 9781250256447 (hardcover) |
    ISBN 9781250799227 (ebook)
Classification: LCC PS3620.A97 D57 2021 | DDC 813/.6—dc23
LC record available at https://lccn.loc.gov/2020057562

ISBN 978-1-250-84718-8 (trade paperback)

Our books may be purchased in bulk for promotional, educational, or business use. Please contact your local bookseller or the Macmillan Corporate and Premium Sales Department at 1-800-221-7945, extension 5442, or by email at MacmillanSpecialMarkets@macmillan.com.

First Minotaur Books Trade Paperback Edition: 2022

10 9 8 7 6 5 4 3 2 1

For Maura

Brother, I come o'er many seas and lands
To the sad rite which pious love ordains,
To pay thee the last gift that death demands;
And oft, though vain, invoke thy mute remains:
Since death has ravish'd half myself in thee,
Oh wretched brother, sadly torn from me!

And now ere fate our souls shall re-unite,
To give me back all it hath snatch'd away,
Receive the gifts, our fathers' ancient rite
To shades departed still was wont to pay;
Gifts wet with tears of heartfelt grief that tell,
And ever, brother, bless thee, and farewell!

—Catullus, translated by George Lamb

A
Distant
Grave

The cold was different here.

It got inside you, the raw knife edge of it slipping beneath your clothes at your collar and your cuffs, taking your breath and setting your nerves to alarm. The skin on his face and neck stung; his hands and feet were going about the business of going numb, but until they did, they were going to do their best to warn him.

He turned his face away from the wind coming off the water, rubbed his upper arms and hopped in place to try to generate a little body heat. If she didn't appear soon, he'd have to go back and wait in the car; otherwise he was going to get frostbite. For the third time, he pulled up the sleeve of his blazer and checked his watch. He'd been waiting thirty minutes now. He'd give it another ten and then he'd have to assume she was standing him up.

Cursing, he jogged from one end of the narrow little strip of sand and rocks to the other, then stopped to watch the streetlights from the marina play on the surface of the water. Behind him, the masts and hulls of sailboats wrapped in white plastic for the winter rose like mountains. Ahead of him, the expanse of the Great South Bay lapped the rocks. Beyond it were the barrier beaches. Yesterday, he'd driven over the two long bridges to the west to stand on the sand at the edge of the Atlantic and listen to the roar and rush of the waves coming in. He'd felt a moment of awe, as he always did standing at the edge of the sea. He had grown up deep inside his own country, near lakes and rivers and water that played at the shore, rather than raged at it. The sea represented freedom to him, joyous movement, a bridge between places, something that couldn't be contained. The countries where he'd worked, so many of them already in his life, were mostly dry and barren places, deserts, plains, or humid jungles, far from the ocean. When he got home, he always went for a walk by the sea first thing, to remind himself that he was free.

Where was she? He hopped around some more.

Suddenly, it seemed obvious she wasn't coming. The disappointment felt like a blow. He wanted this, wanted to see her, wanted to tell the story, wanted it over with so he could be free of it. He searched for an out. Maybe there'd been some sort of delay—traffic, a late train. Ten more minutes. He could wait that long.

Jesus, the cold. It reminded him of the cold in the blue house, the way it came through the concrete and seeped through your skin and into your bones, the way you could never get on top of it. He had always thought of warmth as an intangible, a state of being, but he had learned the truth: that it was something that could be taken away, then given back; something that could be handed to you, like a blanket.

Or a story.

He hadn't understood, before the blue house, that a story could be a gift, too. When you told someone your story, you were sharing a piece of yourself. That was why there was also a cost to telling your story. Once it had been heard, it couldn't be unheard. You took on *the burden of the story when you heard it. He knew what he was asking of her, to listen to his story, to have to take it in and reckon with what it meant.*

He turned back toward the parking lot, the water at his back, and felt the shimmer of awareness he had become used to over the years, the animal sense that someone was there and meant him harm.

No face appeared, but he was sent back to the blue house, to the cold and the darkness and the voices coming through it, those gifts of the inner thoughts and histories of other human beings. He had told his story. They had all told their stories, made offerings of them. He had wanted to tell this story, but when he heard the voice, saying his name, he knew he never would.

Of course. Of course death would look like this. It made perfect sense, as logical as the conclusion of a well-told tale. Of course this was it.

The end.

And it was then that the bullet found him, so quickly that when he died, he was still thinking of stories, and endings, and of the sea, the sound of it, how it filled your head so you couldn't think of any other thing.

1

Marty is waiting for me in the parking lot. I know he's nervous because he can't keep his hands off the buttons of his coat and from across the parking lot I can see that his forehead is creased with worry. He's wearing one of his beige suits that looks like it time-traveled from 1972, and he's even got a tie on, brown, with rust-colored flowers, ugly as sin.

Martin Cascic is the commander of the Suffolk County Homicide Squad, and my boss. He's also my friend and I feel a little guilty prick of conscience that he has to take this meeting because of me. I've brought him a danish to make up for it. "Here you go," I say handing it over. "It's pineapple."

He nods. Pineapple danish from a deli on New York Avenue is his favorite, for some reason I can't even begin to fathom, and he takes a giant greedy bite of it, knocks a few crumbs off his chin, then opens his car door and puts the rest of the pastry on the dash. "Ready?" he asks me.

"As I'll ever be." We look up at the front of the county building. The district attorney's office is in the Suffolk County office building complex in Hauppauge. The building looks like a concrete egg carton;

it's hard to believe anyone ever thought people would want to work in a building like that.

We do the ID-and-metal-detector routine, check our service weapons, and head to the second floor. District Attorney John J. "Jay" Cooney Jr. steps out to greet us, a big smile on his face. He's an objectively nice-looking man, no way around it, with a squared-off head; full, thick hair that's still mostly light brown though he's past fifty now; a narrow, aristocratic nose; and eyes a startling shade of blue. If his mouth were a different shape, he'd look like a Kennedy, and he's got a little of that charisma. There's something robust yet elegant about him; his suits fit perfectly, his shoes are perpetually shiny, and he always looks like he's just had a fresh shave. I once saw him running an electric razor over his face in the back of a car just before a press conference. I've never been inside his house, but I suspect the décor involves a lot of whales. He's a Republican, but a moderate one, and before this past November, he usually got a lot of Democrats to vote for him, too. It's dicier now. But the fact that his father, John J. Cooney Sr., known as Jack, was a longtime Suffolk County judge and then DA before him doesn't hurt; voting Cooney for DA is a habit around here.

"Please sit down," Cooney says. "Do you want coffee?"

Marty does, but he shakes his head. I shake my head, too, because I've had the coffee here before and know it's bad. Cooney even once told me he knows it's bad, which made me like him a tiny bit more than I did before, which still wasn't much.

He doesn't say anything else, so Marty gets us going. "Jay, thanks for agreeing to meet with us. As you know, Maggie has some questions about your decision not to charge Frank Lombardi. Maggie, do you want to explain the new information you have?"

I've been practicing all morning. I know I need to keep my voice even, my emotions in check. But the office is too warm, the old furnace chugging away in the basement of the building.

I fix my gaze on the family photo behind Cooney's desk to try to keep myself calm. It shows Cooney and his wife with their three children, two teenage girls and a boy of about ten, all wearing matching white outfits on a beach somewhere. Right in the middle are an older couple, also wearing white. I focus on the black Lab sitting in front of them, its tongue lolling. The frame around the picture is polished sterling silver, simple, masculine. Cooney's office is drab, painted beige, standard-issue desk and chair from the '90s, and the frame and the picture clash with their surroundings. *Jay Cooney's not your average civil servant,* I think they're meant to convey.

"I know the statute of limitations on the rape charge is up," I say. "But I've been thinking about something. I think we might have a good case against Frank for impeding a criminal investigation. Even though the case was being investigated in Ireland, there was an initial report made by my uncle to the Suffolk County P.D. and later to the FBI. The Garda told him to do it. Now, that case was never closed and so any actions by Frank over the past twenty years would be within the scope of what we could charge." I hand him a folder filled with typed notes. "I had a conversation with someone who is willing to testify that Frank asked someone who had been at the party to keep quiet about it as recently as five years ago, and I can—"

Cooney's been sitting on his desk, leaning back and pretending to listen, but now he stands and says, "Maggie, let me just stop you there. I know this has been a hard time for your family, and I know you want to see justice, but we made the decision not to pursue any charges against your ex-brother-in-law here and I don't want to waste your time. It's not here. The evidence, the legal basis, none of it." He waves the folder in the air. "Too much time has passed, and pursuing something so . . . uncertain takes resources away from the cases we *can* win."

I try to keep my voice upbeat, *collaborative,* as they say. "But if you'll just read what I have. I talked to one of Erin's classmates, who was at the—"

He smiles sadly. "Maggie. Please. We have limited resources, limited manpower. We need to focus it on more recent crimes. The MS13 threat is growing in Suffolk County. You know that better than anyone. And there are bad people out there, people who are committing crimes now. Let's work together to direct our resources toward getting those people."

Marty clears his throat next to me.

"You don't think people are in danger?" I ask Cooney. "You have no idea whether Frank Lombardi is a danger to anyone right now or not. He's a sociopath, Jay. I found diaries in my basement, in Brian's things. Frank was awful to him when they were kids. He was controlling and abusive. And what's the message to the women of Suffolk County here? Are we telling them we couldn't give two shits about them, about what happens to them?"

Marty puts a hand on my arm and says in a low voice, "Maggie."

But Cooney rises to the bait. His face is red now, his upper lip curling in anger. If I'm honest, I get a thrill of satisfaction when I see how rattled he is, when he gathers up all of his six feet one inch and looms over me, trying to scare me, trying to make me shut up.

"Maggie, we don't have a legal basis to charge. We just don't. There's not enough here and it's been too long to go out on a limb on this. And your connection to the case—you know this, I don't need to tell you—it taints everything. It just does. I told Marty this. I don't know why—" He looks at Marty, whose discomfort radiates from him like a fever.

"You have everything you need," I say. "You know you do. I saw Marty's wrap-up. The interview with Devin O'Brien. It was corroborating. It was!" Marty's grip on my arm is firmer now, telling me *stop*.

Cooney says, "It was twenty-seven years ago! I'm not going to risk the good reputation of this office in order to satisfy some personal grudge. I know this has been an incredibly difficult time for your family, but I'm done. I'm done talking about this. Marty, take care of it."

The air in the room feels thick and hot, crackling with tension.

Marty looks right at Cooney and says, "She's not a child to be managed, Jay. She's a lieutenant on the homicide squad and she has every right to lodge a complaint about a case. But I think she's done that, so we'll be going now. Thank you for your time. We appreciate you being willing to hear us out."

The *us* makes my throat seize up. Marty didn't want to do this. I had to convince him to ask for the meeting. He must have known it was going to go like this. But he did it for me.

"Okay. Goodbye." Cooney's hands are in fists at his sides, and as we leave the room, I can feel him waiting to release all his anger. Something's going to get knocked over or thrown once we're out.

Marty's silent all the way back through security and out to the cars. I try to break the awful quiet by saying, "That went well."

Marty looks at me, doesn't smile. He's sixty-two, wiry and compact. He looks more like a high school wrestling coach than a cop. He's a small guy, only five feet seven or so, with a gray buzz cut and a slightly elfin face that's usually set in a judgmental frown. But he and I are close now, and I get to see his truly face-transforming smile more than a lot of the other detectives on the squad. He was right there with me after my ex-husband Brian's suicide. And Marty was the first person I told about Brian's brother Frank and his friends raping my cousin Erin when she was in high school and about what actually happened all those years ago in Ireland.

Marty took statements from my ex-brother-in-law, Frank, from Frank's friends. He gathered all the evidence to present to Cooney's office, even though he must have known they weren't going to do anything with it. Marty sat in my living room with me and my daughter, Lilly, for hours in the days afterward, as the whole thing unspooled here and over in Ireland. I shiver, remembering.

But his smile isn't there right now.

"Listen, Mags. I've got something to tell you," he says. He's worried, chewing at his lip as he fiddles with his key fob.

"You firing me?"

The edges of his mouth turn up, just a little. "Nah, not today. No, it's about, uh, Anthony Pugh."

Adrenaline surges through my veins. My vision goes starry. Anthony Pugh is a suspect in the killing of at least four women on Long Island's South Shore between 2011 and 2014. Three years ago, I tracked him down, and we arrested him as he was driving toward the beach with a woman named Andrea Delaurio in the back of his car. He'd been assaulting her for days. I believed with every fiber of my being that he was taking her to the beach to kill her. So did she. We saved her life, but, tormented by what Pugh had done to her, she killed herself before we could charge him. We weren't able to get him on the murders, for lack of evidence, and he only served a year in prison on related charges. He lives in Northport now, about ten miles from my house.

"What?"

"The guys from the Second Precinct who we have checking in on him once in a while called me up just as I was leaving. A couple times, last month or so, they followed him into Alexandria. Seemed like he was just cruising, you know, maybe nothing to it. Then, last Thursday, he drove by your house." He reaches up to scratch his forehead. He's nervous.

"What the fuck? Why didn't they tell me?"

"They weren't sure he meant to drive by. He didn't stop, didn't look at your house." He pushes the unlock button. We both hear the beep. But he waits. There's something else. He doesn't want to say it. "This morning, five a.m., he did it again. Except this time he slowed and looked up at your house, sat there ten or fifteen seconds, then drove away."

I look out across the parking lot, toward Veterans Memorial Highway. It's one of those February days where you might be fooled into thinking spring is on its way. The sun is down low in the sky, shining up a scrubby, empty field across the way. "What should I do?" I ask Marty.

"You don't have to do anything. We can have someone on the house, if you want. We'll definitely keep an eye on him. You'll know if he's coming your way, if he's anywhere near the high school. You and Lilly are heading over to Ireland soon for vacation, right?"

"Sunday. But, what the fuck, Marty?" An image of Anthony Pugh's face when I arrested him flashes into my head. Pale gray eyes, grayish-blond hair; the kind of guy you'd never notice, the kind of guy who looks completely harmless. Even then, when I had him down on the pavement on a shoulder of the LIE, my handcuffs around his wrists, he looked so innocent, so normal, like the battered, drugged-up woman in the back of his car was there by accident. He should be in jail. I shouldn't have to think about him at all.

Marty opens the passenger door for me. "I know. You going on vacation is good, buys us some time. We can try to figure out if he has anything up his sleeve."

"Okay," I say, but I'm still agitated, angry at Cooney.

Marty knows it. "You did your best," he says. "We need to let it go. Let's get back."

I nod, get into my car, tell him I'll see him back at headquarters. I have a ton of paperwork to do today and then I have to go get Lilly from school. I'm exhausted from working and managing her grief over her father's death. The sun goes behind a cloud and once more, it looks like what it really is: a dreary mid-February day, with many more dreary winter days to come. I crank the heater, not sure if I'm cold because of the chill or the idea of Anthony Pugh, out there waiting for something, waiting for me.

The LIE is packed for a couple of exits, then starts emptying out the farther east I drive.

I'm almost back to headquarters when my phone rings. Seeing Marty's number, I answer on the car system and say, "I know that was fun, but come on, Marty."

He snorts. "Ha, no, Mags, we got a body. Just heard from dispatch. The pleasure of your company's required down on the South Shore. Guy got shot on the beach near that water park in Bay Shore Manor. You'll see the cars. Third Precinct got the call. Lab's already on the way."

I feel my stomach drop. *Shit.* "Okay. I'll get off and head down there. They tell Dave?" My partner, Dave Milich, lives in Port Jefferson, on the North Shore.

"Yeah, when they couldn't get us. He's on the way already."

"I'll give you an update later. Bye, Marty."

I swing into the right lane, get off in Holbrook, and, feeling like I haven't gained any ground at all this morning, head back the way I came.

2

Bay Shore, Long Island, is a prosperous town on the South Shore, part of the bigger town of Islip, and this narrow handlebar of sand with a little park and a pier on one side and a marina with boat slips and access to the bay on the other is sandwiched strangely between a homeowners' association filled with big waterfront houses with views to the west, and a tight little neighborhood of rentals and smaller ranches to the east. The wind coming off the Great South Bay is stiff and chilled; the waves out beyond Fire Island and the barrier beaches are tall and dangerous on days like this.

They've got the marina entrance blocked off already, and the parking lot is full of marked and unmarked cars, a crime lab van, and a mobile operations unit trailer. Dave is talking to some of the uniforms from the Third Precinct, but he detaches from the group when he sees me and comes over. Dave's a decade younger than me, a startlingly good-looking guy with dark hair and big brown eyes, fully aware of his effect on women. Dave was adopted in Florida when he was a baby. His birth parents were teenagers from Mexico and he loves when people up here eye him up and ask him where he's "from" and he can say, "Coconut Grove. How about you?" He's in a leather jacket he wears year-round, and I'm cold just looking at him. I once offered to buy him a parka and he said, "No thanks, Mom." Now I let him shiver.

"Hey," he says. "Dog walker called it in, six ten this morning. They secured the scene and looked for ID, but haven't found any yet. No witnesses they can find so far. Looks like it must have happened overnight."

I point to the busy parking lot. "Any cars here that aren't ours?"

"Nope." He's holding a lidded paper cup of coffee that still has a whisper of steam coming out of the hole in the top. It smells sweet and milky.

"Give me some of that," I say. I tug the cup out of his hand and take a slug. He frowns and I hand it back. "Let's look at the body."

There's a kids' water park next to the entrance that looks like it's under construction, and a run-down playground. Along the water is a thin strip of sand and chunks of asphalt piled for a breakwater, a few wooden benches here and there, and then a narrow boardwalk leading to the pier, which is named after some local dignitary. The white-plastic-wrapped boats loom behind us like ghost ships.

Our victim is lying on his back on the sand, right next to the rocks. He's a middle-aged white man in jeans and a gray tweed blazer. The only thing that explains the unique stillness of his torso, the unnatural way his legs and arms have arranged themselves on the beach, is a coin of congealed blood on his right temple. There's some blood on the sand beneath him and his skin is already waxy and bluish. It was in the thirties last night. He would have cooled down fast.

The latex gloves Dave passes me go on rough over my cold hands. I hold back one side of the guy's blazer and pat the empty breast pocket, then check the side pockets and the pockets of his jeans.

Nothing. No cough drops. No crumpled receipts. No phone. No wallet. No keys. Nothing except a small, smooth pebble from the beach, the kind that looks prettier when it's wet.

"He got robbed," I say.

Dave nods.

But it's more than that. I think he's lying where he fell. He wasn't running away, wasn't fighting. Whoever killed him just . . . shot him. It feels like an execution to me. I look at the man's face, the part of it I can see, anyway. He's slender, my age—forty-six—or a bit older, I think. His hair is dark, going gray, as is his neatly groomed beard. No wedding ring, and no tan lines to tell me if the ring was there before the robbery. His eyes are brown, and he's staring up at the gray winter sky with a placid, almost peaceful look on his face. It isn't true that the last expression on someone's face gets frozen there when they die; rigor mortis can do strange things to people's faces. But he doesn't look like he was fearful or in pain. He looks . . . resigned, almost beatific. I think of martyred saints in paintings, their bodies in pain but their faces calm.

A final look at the guy's face and then I nod to the lab techs so they can start setting up the tent and collecting evidence. A deputy medical examiner will get a body temp and make initial observations before they take him back to Hauppauge for the autopsy. "I don't see any shoeprints in the sand," Dave says. "It's wet enough they'd show. What do you think? They were standing right there and he fell onto the sand after he was shot?"

"Yeah, I think that's it. Look at the depression the body made. There was some force behind that."

Dave puts a hand out to represent the bullet. He brings it toward his right temple and hits it hard with his index finger. I watch as he lets his body fall, then catches himself.

"It came more from that direction," I say, pointing to the east. "He fell on his back."

"Yeah, we'll get something better from the firearms division at the lab, but I think you're right," Dave says. "The shooter was over there." He gestures toward a spot on the ground. "They were standing here." He does a little shuffle to the side to show where the victim was standing. "And the shooter was here." *Shuffle, shuffle.* "The shooter held the gun right about here, and *bam*." He's holding his hand up about a foot from his forehead. He's probably right. Dave's got a nose for firearms evidence, always has. He's a vet; he was in Afghanistan before he became a cop, and he knows guns.

"Bullet casing and autopsy will tell us," I say.

Dave nods. I look up. The marina is full now, people suddenly spread out across the parking lot. A TV van is trying to get in and the Third Precinct uniforms are talking to the driver through the window, explaining that they can't be on the scene.

"It was a cold night for a walk on the beach," Dave says, emphasizing *walk* just a little. I know exactly what he's saying. This guy was here to meet somebody. Chances are, he was here to buy something. Top two things people buy on cold beaches late at night: drugs and sex.

I look down at the body again. His clean brown leather shoes, heathery blue sweater, blazer, and fashionable jeans are high-quality stuff. He's dead, and still I can tell he was a handsome guy when he was alive. But handsome guys in nice clothes buy drugs and sex, too, I remind myself. They buy them all the time.

Dave tucks his head and neck down into the collar of his leather jacket and, from deep inside the collar, says what I'm thinking: "Could be a drug thing, could be a sex thing." Dave's growing a moustache for a fundraiser—cops with cancer, I think—and the moustache sits on top of his collar like a small animal. Normally I'd mention this, but we're at a crime scene, so I save it for later. *You gonna bring your little friend with you? You wouldn't want to leave him alone out here. There might be predators.*

I shrug. "Drug thing, more likely. Something went wrong here and he got shot. Little cold for a sex thing."

"Yeah," Dave says, shaking his head. "I wouldn't want to take my pants off with that wind coming off the water."

"First thing is, we need an ID. Maybe get them out doing door-to-doors and looking for the car?"

"Yeah, car is the first thing."

I'm looking down the beach, trying to remember what I know of the neighborhood. "He could live around here. Let's make sure no one's been reported missing this morning." I point to the seafood place down by the marina. "We should check and see if that restaurant was open last night. They might have seen something. And then check all the bars and restaurants on Main Street. Let's get the description out to the employees who worked last night. See if he was out last night in town."

"Sounds good." Dave waves the Third Precinct uniforms over so we can give instructions.

They get moving, fanning out to arrange the canvassing, assign the restaurant jobs. I stand there for a moment, fixing the scene in my mind: the stillness of the body, the water stretching out away from the rocks.

Dave comes up behind me, touches me gently on the shoulder.

"You okay?" he asks. Dave and I both have our things. His is loud noises, explosions. Mine is bodies on beaches. For a couple of reasons now. We check in with each other when they come up.

"I'm okay," I say, though I'm not really. I take a deep breath. "I was just thinking how odd it is, nowadays, to not be able to identify someone right away. No phone, no wallet. It's like he fell out of the sky, you know?"

Dave looks out at the water. "Or like he washed up from the ocean," he says. "Like some kind of mermaid."

3

....

With a bit of sputtering and chugging, the machine kicks into action and everyone goes off to do their jobs. The techs don't find anything on the beach. None of the cars are obvious marks. We'll have to go deep into the surrounding neighborhoods and get residents to account for their own vehicles before we start breaking into them, but I'm hoping we'll get something before we have to start doing that. I feel tired suddenly, exhausted by all of it. If this case drags out too long or there are developments just before we're supposed to go, I'll have to cancel my trip to Dublin.

And I don't want to cancel the trip. I haven't seen my boyfriend, Conor, since he came and stayed with us early last November. Conor and I reconnected last year in Ireland, twenty-three years after the first time I went over there, when my cousin Erin disappeared. I went back over to work on Erin's case in May and blew up my daughter's world in the process.

I've been counting on these two weeks with him, two weeks when we can continue to see just what this improbable thing between us is, this long-ago connection that's come roaring back to life in the middle of tragedy and trauma. We've been trying to tend it long distance but we need the two weeks to figure out what our next steps are, to let Lilly and Conor's son, Adrien, get to know us and each other.

I've also been looking forward to getting off Long Island, getting away from the looks that I know follow me and Lilly everywhere. It feels like every single person on the island knows about what happened to our family.

And then there's my feud with Cooney. This morning's argument in his office was the second or third one we've had. Cooney is tight with the Suffolk County police commissioner, Pat Messenger, who's being treated for lung cancer right now and, according to the gossip around headquarters, isn't going to live much longer. Marty's my boss, but Pat holds my career in his hands, and right now he's not holding on very tightly.

I need a vacation.

By eleven, the deputy ME's done what he needs to do and they're getting ready to take the body. Dave and I watch them get it into a bag and lift it onto a stretcher. Everyone stops while they take it to the van. It'll go back to the ME's office and they'll do a quick examination, just to make sure our victim doesn't have his name and phone number conveniently tattooed on his thigh or something. Given the ME's workload, the autopsy will probably have to wait until Monday or later, which means I won't know anything before I'm supposed to get on a plane. But the cause of death seems pretty clear here. Maybe it won't matter.

I look up to see one of the Suffolk County assistant district attorneys, Alicia Piehler, striding toward us in black heels so high it hurts just watching her. "Got anything good?" she asks.

"No. Looks like he was robbed, gunshot wound to the head, but no ID, no car here."

"Do you think he lives around here?" Alicia asks me. ADAs always respond to homicide scenes, just so they're in the loop, but it's mostly routine at this point. Once we start to get some good evidence, once Alicia can see a charge starting to take shape, that's when she'll really engage. She's smart, one of the best ADAs Cooney's got in his office, and everyone seems to think that he's grooming her for bigger and better things.

"Yeah, that's my bet. He walked here to meet someone. I'm thinking we'll be hearing from whoever he didn't come home to last night pretty soon."

"Let me know, okay?" Alicia's eyes shift to the phone in her hand, which is alive with lights and sounds I didn't even know an iPhone could make. I know she's involved with a big MS13 gang case going to federal court. Over the last couple of years, there have been a bunch of murders of civilians by members of MS13 from Central America. The FBI task force, which Alicia is part of, has had some good solves, and the word is that they'll be getting a lot of new resources from the incoming administration. I don't like some of the messages that are coming down along with those resources, though, and a few Latino cops, including Dave, have told me they've felt a real shift since November with the MS13 cases being pulled into the immigration debate. That's all just nasty background noise to what we do every day, but it's there and you can't ignore it.

Alicia's on the front lines of all of it, and she probably has about a hundred things on her plate. Not to mention the fact that Cooney is running for reelection next year and got slapped with a vague accusation of ethics violations the same day a Democratic county legislator announced he's going to run against him.

She taps on the phone's screen for a second, and then her eyes, green, lined with shadow and dark eyeliner, flick up to meet mine. "You know who lives just down there, don't you?"

I look down the shoreline. It takes me a minute. Cooney and his wife own one of those houses in the nice neighborhood that gazes out at the sea. Someone pointed it out to me once. "Your boss. He know yet?"

"Oh yeah. He hates when anything happens down here. It's like it reflects badly on him or something. He was in a really crappy mood this morning, so keep me in the loop, right?"

"He's not going to like me being on it, then," I say. "You hear about our meeting? I think I'm the reason for the crappy mood."

She shrugs. "He understands it's personal for you, even if it doesn't seem like he does." She smiles. "He thinks you're a good cop, at the end of the day." But her smile disappears quickly and her eyes dart away from mine. Her phone buzzes again; she looks at it and says, "I gotta go. I'll catch up with you in an hour or two."

Dave and I take stock. In a few hours there will be more details from the medical examiner, and my instinct is that someone's going to report this guy missing. In the meantime, it's a waiting game, and I hate waiting games. I want to talk to possible witnesses. We walk over to the seafood place by the marina but no one's there yet. Then we walk around the neighborhood, looking for people out walking or getting into their cars. We'll have to arrange a more organized canvass later, but I want to know if there's anything obvious.

There isn't. No one heard anything or saw anything last night.

I look up and down the street and then at Dave. "Let's get some lunch," I say. "You know any places here?" Dave's been doing a lot of online dating lately around the island. And he has good taste in food. He's like a one-man restaurant recommendation app.

He thinks. "There's a new taco place on Main Street," he says. "The decorations are weird, but the food is good." We take his car and head down to Bay Shore's Main Street, a couple-block stretch of shops and restaurants running parallel to the shore.

He's right. The inside of the restaurant is decorated with huge Andy Warhol–inspired paintings of puppies, but the tacos are great and I polish them off, along with an iced tea, while keeping an eye on my phone. I'm hoping someone's filed a missing persons report by now, or that someone in the neighborhood heard something last night, saw the police presence, and put two and two together.

But my phone stays quiet. "I gotta get Lilly at four," I tell Dave. "I hope we have something by then."

"We should. This guy's got to have come from somewhere, right? How's she doing, anyway?" He has the look on his face that people get when they aren't sure whether to ask me how we're doing. It's starting to annoy me, that look—part compassionate, part afraid I'm going to break down in tears. But Dave's different. Dave was on the scene an hour after my ex-husband, Brian, died. He helped out a lot in the days that followed. He knows how bad it was for Lilly, how all the emerging, sparkling, shining parts of her disappeared in the well of her grief.

"A little better, I guess. Her friends have been great. You know. It sucks. She lost her dad, but it's more complicated than that. She's still embarrassed. There's all the shit going on with Brian's family. She hasn't seen either of his parents since June because they won't agree not to talk about Frank with her. You know. It sucks. It's going to take time. And . . ." I take a deep breath. "Dave, Marty told me something this morning." I tell him about Pugh.

"Shit. You want me to start driving by at night?"

"No. I don't think he's dumb enough to try anything. I can handle him if he does. It'll be fine. They're keeping an eye on him." I'm conscious of my face, of putting on a smile for him.

"Should be good for you to get away for a bit," he says.

"If I can." I haven't said it out loud yet. "This case, Dave. We're supposed to leave Sunday."

"We'll get something," he says. "And if we don't, the team can handle it."

I know he's right, but the truth is that I don't want the team to handle it. I took three months' leave after Brian's death. I was just getting back in the groove of my job when I lost it on Cooney, and now it feels like I'm fighting to get my career back. I want to see Conor and I want this case, too. I want to crush it, want to find whoever pulled the trigger and put that handsome guy on the beach in a body bag.

It's only been a few hours but it's already starting to feel off, something about it hitting me as foggy and strange, a hard one to solve. I'm signing the credit card receipt when my phone rings and I look down to find the number of the Suffolk County Medical Examiner's office.

"Hey, it's Maggie D'arcy," I say, standing up, gesturing to Dave.

"Maggie." It's Constance Fuller, the assistant ME. "I think you're going to want to come up and see something on this body they just brought in."

"What is it, Connie? He got his name tattooed on his ass?"

"No," she says. I can hear the worry in her voice. She hesitates, about to tell me, then settles on, "I'm going to let you see it for yourself."

Traffic's light on the Sagtikos and we're in Hauppauge in twenty minutes. The medical examiner's office is in a dreary complex with other county government buildings, including the DA's office, and as we get out of the car, we see Cooney's black Lexus parked in his spot. It's always quiet out here, the landscape thinning as it heads toward the East End. If any part of Long Island feels rural, this is it; there's a gun shop down the road, next to the deli where we get our morning bagels and chicken cutlet sandwiches, and more trucks and baseball hats than you'd think. People from the city were surprised by how Long Island voted in November, but I could have told them. The sky feels big out here, open, like the island is running out of land.

Inside, they have the body laid out on the table for us, facedown, a white sheet pulled up over his head. Connie's all business, but the distress that I heard in her voice over the phone is visible on her face.

"I won't do the full autopsy until next week, but I wanted you to see this in case it helps with the ID," she says. She nods and one of the techs gently pulls the sheet down to the victim's buttocks. His skin is pale and mottled, typical of a corpse that's been outside in the cold after death. But that isn't why Connie wanted us to see him.

"Jesus Christ," Dave says quietly.

"Yeah," she says. "That's quite an identifying mark. I thought you might be able to do something with that."

The scars that cover our victim's back are like folded wings, four or five deep gouges that healed long ago but look like rope laid across his skin. They're raised, pink and white, and I feel sympathetic pain flash across my own shoulders.

"What the fuck?" Dave says under his breath. "How would you get something like that?"

"Not by accident," Connie says. "Someone drew a knife across his back, deliberately, slowly."

"Torture," I say, then look up. "Could it be self-inflicted?"

"I don't think so."

"How old?"

"Five to ten years," she says. "I think."

"Jesus. I need photos of those," I say. "We can use them to confirm the ID. Thanks, Connie."

"Will do." She nods to one of the techs, who goes to get camera equipment.

"You have any thoughts about who and why?" Dave asks her. He looks shaken, too, and it takes a lot to shake Dave.

"There's something really methodical about these," Connie tells us, her eyes serious behind her glasses. "The scars are very even. The knife was sharp. It feels sadistic to me, maybe ritualistic, as though the person who did it knew exactly what he or she was doing. But that's more my emotional instinct, and as you know I am not a fan of emotional instinct." She gives us a wry smile. "That won't be in my report."

I stare at the scars, horrified at the thought that one human being could do that to another. Somehow, it seems so much worse than the bullet hole in his head.

"What about the gunshot wound? You got any ideas about a range for us?" Dave ventures.

"Not a chance I'll give you a range until we've autopsied him and recovered the casing and the firearms division has had a chance to do its thing." She glares at him.

"Okay, okay." Dave puts his hands up. "Sorry, Connie."

She nods. "Well, I might have something else for you," she says. "I don't think the guy's underwear and T-shirt were bought in the United States."

"What?"

She pushes over printouts of photographs showing a pair of men's boxer briefs and then a close-up of a label. It reads "M&S." Then she shows us the label from the T-shirt: also M&S. "Marks and Spencer," she says.

"That's a British brand. They have stores in Ireland, too."

"Yes, it is. You can order it here—I checked—but it wouldn't be very widespread."

"Connie, thanks so much, you're amazing," I say. I'm already walking fast out of the room, talking to Dave over my shoulder.

"Airlines, rental cars, and hotels," I tell him, breaking into a jog. "And we need the uniforms to start looking for cars in the neighborhood. Anything with a rental company sticker or papers on the dash. We're gonna get him, Dave."

4

....

It doesn't take long to find the car.

We're nearly back to the scene when Dave gets a call from the Islip cop coordinating the search. They've found something, a new Ford Focus, red, with Jersey plates and an Enterprise map left on the dash, on the residential street just outside the marina entrance. They've asked at all the houses on the street and it doesn't seem to belong to anyone.

"They've got one of the techs coming with the tools to get the car unlocked," Dave says. The Third Precinct patrol officers have blocked off the street. When we pull up, they let us through and point to the Ford.

"Here we go," I tell Dave. I can feel my energy returning. We've got something. The car's going to have a registration; we're going to trace him through the rental company. It'll take ten minutes to get his name and address. Maybe he left his phone and wallet in the car. If this is the car our victim drove to the scene, we're going to get our ID. It's entirely possible that we'll find a phone with a text message identifying who he was meeting last night and we'll have that person in custody by tonight. I can do cleanup tomorrow and head off Sunday morning with the satisfied feeling of knowing I put a bad guy in jail.

"Car's too new for the slim jim, but we got in with a wedge," the tech says, opening the driver's-side door with a little flourish.

We put on booties and new gloves to avoid contaminating evidence in the car. It's almost completely clean, smelling strongly of whatever chemicals rental companies use to make it seem like you were never there. I use one finger to drop the glove box door and carefully pull out the Enterprise document folder inside. The rental agreement is on top. "Gabriel Treacy," I call out. *Treacy*, I think. *Irish spelling.*

There's an address just below: 237 King Street, Dublin 7 Ireland.

Dave and I look at each other. I remember seeing a Marks & Spencer in Dublin. The odds just went up that this is our guy's car.

"What's the date on the rental docs?" Dave asks.

I look. "Uh, three days ago at Kennedy airport." Gabriel Treacy's signature at the bottom is an elegant scrawl.

I hand the rental documents over to the tech for bagging. "We gotta call Berta," I tell Dave. "Tell her to get on to the rental desk, the airlines, immigration, everybody. I want to know who this guy is, why he was here. We'll have to get the embassy involved. I'll call my friend Roly Byrne in Dublin to make the family notification." Roly's a senior detective with the Garda Síochána, Ireland's national police service, and an image of his face comes to me, his blue eyes narrowed in humor. *Jaysus, D'arcy. You had to be making more work for me.*

"What else have we got?"

Dave's doing a quick search to see if there's anything else in the car. There's not. The trunk is empty and the back seat doesn't look like it's been touched by anyone since the rental agency's cleaner. "Nothing," he says. "There's a phone charger here, though, which means he had a phone at some point."

I'm already starting a text to Berta Stanos, the research expert on the homicide squad. She'll make quick work of Gabriel Treacy. We'll have his entire life history by the time Dave and I get back to headquarters in Yaphank.

"Got something else," one of the techs calls out. "It slid under the seat, like it fell out of his lap or something." We all wait and watch as he holds it up, a rosary, with a Saint Christopher medal attached. The beads are black against white latex. "Patron saint of travelers," he says. "Didn't work very well, did it?"

"Nope."

Dave and I step back from the car as the guys from the lab get ready to tow it. There are a bunch of uniforms from the Third Precinct standing around, guarding the scene. "Who can organize some door-to-doors for me?" I call out. A young woman in uniform peels away from the crowd and comes over.

"I can do it."

"Okay. I want you to organize more door-to-doors in all these neighborhoods." I point to the rooflines off to the east and then the line of oceanfront houses to the west. "Anything they saw yesterday or last night, anything at all. Did anyone see him parking the car? Did they see him walking over to the water? Was anyone with him? I want to know if anyone was here earlier so we can start to create a window. Keep it nice and broad—what were they doing last night, anything out of the ordinary, did they hear anything? Let me know as soon as you get something good. Let me know if you get a whole lot of nothing. That's important too."

I zip my jacket all the way up and turn away from the salty wind. "Dave and I are going to check hotels."

I call up the map app on my phone, type in "hotels near me," and a mid-range chain motel on the other side of Main Street pops up, the only one really close. Dave and I drive up there. It's on the edge of a residential neighborhood, the low-slung motel complex packed in between apartment buildings and a shopping center; the trees planted by whatever development company built this block are skeletal against the gray-white sky. It's quiet in the small lobby, and when we ring the bell on the reception desk, it takes a few minutes for an elderly man in a beige wool sweater and black scarf to come out through the door behind the desk. I introduce myself, show him my identification, and tell him we're looking for a man named Gabriel Treacy. The old man stares at me for a moment, then yells something back toward the door in a language I don't recognize. A few seconds later, a young man in glasses, early twenties maybe, comes out. He says something to the old man, who shakes his head, then he turns to us and says, "How can I help you?"

I show him my identification. "I'm Detective Lieutenant Maggie D'arcy, with the Suffolk County P.D. Did you have someone named Gabriel Treacy staying here over the last couple of days? Guy with a beard, about forty-five years old, may have had an Irish accent?"

He raises his eyes to meet mine. "May I ask why you need to know? Normally I wouldn't give out information about a guest." Bingo. He's just told me that Gabriel Treacy was staying here. The old man hovers behind him, looking nervous.

"There's been an accident," I say. "We need to identify the person involved in the accident."

"Is he, is he all right?"

I give him a smile that I hope is reassuring. "I can't really talk about it. Right now, the priority is learning about him. When did he check in?"

The younger man studies me for a long moment, trying to read me. "Has he died?"

"Sir, we need more information about him. We'll need to get into the room."

"He might not want you to go in his room."

"Sir, I think he would," Dave says from behind me, a little bit of menace in his voice.

The old man says something and the younger one translates. "Okay, but my grandfather says that if he's angry, we're sending him to you when he comes back." He looks back down at the computer screen. "Room one-oh-four. Mr. Treacy checked in on Tuesday. He was supposed to check out today."

Dave and I exchange a glance.

I push over a Post-it with the rental car's license plate number. "This the plate on file?" The younger man checks and nods. "Okay, thank you," I say. "We need to see the room. I assume it's been cleaned today?"

"Not yet. We've been short on cleaning help." He takes a key card out of a drawer and sticks it into the little coding machine. We follow both men outside and around the corner to room 104.

"We'll go in ourselves," Dave says authoritatively.

The younger man hesitates at the threshold and then says, "He spoke Bengali, when he checked in, after he heard me speak it to my grandfather. He's not Bangladeshi, like us, but he spoke very good basic Bengali and he was very kind to my grandfather, complimenting him on the cleanliness of the room and so forth. We hope he's well." There's a tiny uplift at the end of the sentence, half a question mark. "We have never had a guest who, who wasn't from Bangladesh or India, who spoke any Bengali."

I give him a small smile, but don't say anything. There's nothing to say. I think he must know that the man in room 104 is dead.

The room smells neutral. Gabriel Treacy didn't spend enough time here to leave his mark. Dave shuts the door behind us and we look around. The bed is hastily made, the covers pulled up over the pillows; only one side looks slept in. We'll get the techs in to check the sheets for biological material, but I'm betting they won't find any that didn't belong to Gabriel Treacy.

We both slip off our shoes, just in case this is a crime scene, and Dave hands me latex gloves from his coat pocket. I put them on and cross the room to the desk. There's a printed map of Bay Shore, but no marks on it, a receipt from Enterprise, a receipt from a Chinese restaurant, and one for a meal at the restaurant with the puppy décor and good tacos.

Nothing else.

I take as few steps as I can to reach the bathroom. The sink is clear of any personal belongings and the wastebasket contains a few tissues and, on top, an empty travel-size tube of toothpaste.

"Closet," I say. Dave opens it up and sure enough, there's a small, black, hard-sided carry-on. I carefully lift the luggage tag. It's got Gabriel Treacy's name and the same Dublin address on it.

Dave unzips the front pocket. "Bingo." In a little sleeve, there's a passport with a dull red cover. There's a gold harp on the front and the words "Éire" and "Ireland" in the center.

The picture inside is of our victim. The dead guy is Gabriel Treacy. No question about it.

"Geez, he liked to travel," Dave says. He shows me the open passport, flipping through pages covered with stamps and visas. "India, Kabul, Japan, Hong Kong, Beirut, Istanbul, Addis Ababa. What the fuck did he do for a living?" There's a page of stamps in Cyrillic script, papers stapled in. I find the stamp from Kennedy airport: February 14, 2017. Valentine's Day. And there's an emergency contact listed in the passport: *Stella Treacy, Carraghmore, Sixmilebridge, County Clare, R. of Ireland.*

"Conor's from County Clare, too," I say. Dave looks up at me. "It's kind of in the middle of the country, and over toward the west coast."

A tiny smile and what I know to be a smartass remark twitch on Dave's lips, underneath the moustache. But he doesn't say it, whatever it is.

We check the rest of the room. The only other thing of any interest is a piece of lined paper on the bedside table, next to a ballpoint pen. It's a messy to-do list, just for himself, like the ones I make for *myself.* It's dated at the top—*15/2/17*—in the Irish and British style, with the day listed before the month. There are three items:

> *Ring N. to see about legal implications*
> *Gill account ?*
> *H. T. notes*

I take a picture of the paper with my phone. Once we locate his family, we can have them make sense of the list, figure out who N. and Gill and H. T. are.

Back in the lobby, I tell the younger man and his grandfather that we'll wait for someone to come keep an eye on the room until the crime lab can process it. "I'm sorry to have to tell you," I say gently, "but as you probably suspected, Mr. Treacy is deceased. Thank you for helping us to learn more about him. Can I get your names?"

The younger man nods, his eyes wide. "I'm Sabbir Ahmed. My grandfather's first name is Uddin. He's the owner." He pushes a business card over so we have the spelling.

"When was the last time you saw Mr. Treacy?"

"Last night. I saw him drive into the parking lot around six, go into his room, and then he went out again not long after."

"Did you have any conversation with him at any point in his stay? Did he say anything about why he was visiting Bay Shore?"

"No," Sabbir Ahmed says. "He asked me how to get to the ocean and I told him to put Robert Moses State Park into his GPS. That was the day after he arrived. He told me later he'd gone out there and walked to the Fire Island Lighthouse. He said it was beautiful, that he loved the sea." He translates the question for his grandfather, who shakes his head, but says something in Bengali. "He said they only spoke about the weather, and the man, Mr. Treacy, told him he should be proud of having such a successful and well-maintained business. That was all."

"He didn't ask directions to any other locations in Bay Shore?"

Sabbir Ahmed shakes his head, but his grandfather says something and I wait for the translation. "My grandfather says that he wishes the man an easy and pleasant journey. He does not know the man's faith, but he has said that he wishes him to return to his God, if he had a God."

"That's very kind. I will pass that along to his family when we locate them. He didn't have anyone visit him, did he? Did you see any strange cars in the parking lot during the time Mr. Treacy was staying here?"

Uddin Ahmed says something and his grandson nods a few times, then shakes his head. Finally Sabbir Ahmed says, "No, I didn't see anyone staying here. My grandfather thought there was a strange car parked yesterday morning, but we had some painters working, so . . ."

"Do you remember the color and make?" I ask.

"It was a white SUV," Sabbir Ahmed says after conferring with his grandfather. "New." I write that down so I can check it later.

"Security footage?" I ask. I can see the camera mounted over the door. It looks like it's pointed at the parking lot. "Maybe we can get the plate."

"Yes, it's on the computer in the back."

"Thanks, we'll send someone to copy it. Please let us know if you have any troubles with the police presence here, Mr. Ahmed. I'm sorry that your business will be interrupted for a bit. We may need to talk to you again, and we need to ask you not to talk to anyone about Mr. Treacy."

Sabbir Ahmed nods, and his grandfather holds up a hand in farewell.

We hang around until officers from the Third Precinct arrive to secure the scene and the crime scene techs get there to process the room, then head out to the parking lot. Once we're back in my car, I look over and find Dave watching me, the little smile twitching on his face.

"What?" I ask.

My car got really cold while we were inside and he's hunched down into his jacket again. But he twinkles at me from somewhere inside the collar. "Irish guy? Dublin? Jeez, Mags. You didn't have to kill someone so you could justify going to visit your boyfriend and getting a little action."

I give him the finger and pull out of the parking lot.

5

....

Dave doesn't let it go. "So, you gonna go do the notification?" he asks me once we're heading back to Suffolk County P.D. "Combine business with pleasure, right? Wink. Wink."

"You are way too interested in my love life."

"Just happy for ya," he says. And he is, which is why I let him get away with it.

It's three thirty now. I'm not going to make it. I call Uncle Danny and ask him to pick Lilly up from school. He acts like he's been waiting around for me to ask: "'Course, Mags. I was just about to head out anyways. It's quiet today. I can bring her home and make her something to eat." I say a little silent thank-you for him, for his willingness to help us out. After I hang up, I remember Anthony Pugh and send him a text saying, "Set the alarm once you're inside. I'll explain later." He won't think it's too strange. My job means we need to be extra careful a lot of the time.

At headquarters, I pull us into an incident room and get the team together.

"Okay, Gabriel Treacy. That's T-R-E-A-C-Y. Forty-five-year-old male, Irish national, flew into Kennedy three days ago. Stayed at a motel in Bay Shore. Motel is owned by Mr. Uddin Ahmed. His grandson is point of contact. His name is Sabbir Ahmed. Gabriel Treacy checked in on the fourteenth. He was supposed to check out today. We don't know how he spent the day or evening yesterday, but he left the motel around six and at some point he drove to Bay Shore Manor Park and parked just outside the entrance to the marina. He may have been meeting someone, it may have been a chance encounter, but whichever, someone shot him in the head and left him there. We believe his phone and wallet were stolen. No electronics that we've found so far. We didn't uncover anything indicating why he was here but we may get something more from the suitcase. I'm going to call my contact in Dublin. They'll notify and interview the family. One strange thing—he had marks on his back that seemed to indicate he was ritually injured or . . . tortured at some point. We'll get more information on that from the autopsy." I can see them all taking that in. "Oh, and someone needs to get on to the airlines, find out when his return ticket was. Berta, what have you got for us?"

Berta Stanos is the tech expert on our team, a tall, gray-haired woman who looks like a retired gym teacher and who people usually peg as just an especially fit and active Greek American grandmother until she starts telling them about the "online sickos" she's so good at tracking in her job on the homicide squad. She's getting close to mandatory retirement age, but she came to the work late, after raising five kids, and she's still at the top of her game, which is tracking down electronic records, using cell phone data and records in investigations, and combing the internet and social media for information about crime suspects and their victims. She has contacts at every government agency we work with, and she finds things that no one else can find. Everyone's already trying to figure out how we might be able to keep her on as a consultant. Berta brings the skepticism of someone who didn't grow up with the internet, doesn't trust anything she reads unless she's confirmed it in four or five places, and isn't afraid to get on the phone and interview people by using her voice and asking actual questions, which is one of the biggest problems with anyone younger than thirty-five, I've found. Her skepticism has saved me more than once, and when Berta tells me something, I generally feel like I can run with it.

"Here's what I've got so far. He worked for an international aid organization called Global Humanity," she says. "Based in Dublin, Ireland. They do a lot of good stuff in the world, people. Feeding starving kids in Africa, setting up refugee camps in Syria. I found his LinkedIn page and a professional résumé. He's done this kind of work his whole adult life—UNICEF, CARE, Irish Aid, now this place. There's an editorial he wrote for the *Irish Times* a couple years back about Yemen. Another one about . . . uh"—she looks down at her screen—"private military contractors and aid organizations. I'll keep at it, try the social media stuff, but I don't see any reference to family members. Nothing obvious, anyway. You'll probably have to get the police over there to run that. I gotta do some more, but that's the obvious stuff."

"That explains the passport," I say. "Thanks, Berta. According to the guy at the motel, he spoke some Bengali, which is the language they speak in Bangladesh and parts of India. That's probably why. I'll get on to my contact in Dublin. As soon as I do that, we need to try to get into all of his accounts. Berta, can you get on to the phone company and see if the phone is still registering anywhere? And try to get the call record if you can, though they may give you a hard time—it's going to be an Irish account and there may be some issues with getting access. Can you work on that and liaise with the consulate in the city if necessary?" She nods.

"Cause of death was gunshot wound to the head?" someone asks. I look up and see Bill Trillio, one of the detectives on the squad, waiting for my answer. Bill is Long Island from way back, the son of a retired and legendary Suffolk County homicide detective. He's ten years older than me, a barrel-chested guy with a boxer's nose and an attitude, and I have the sense he feels like I leapfrogged over him to make lieutenant, even though it's his own adherence to outdated techniques and prejudices that's stalled his career. He's never liked me and he's tight with Pat Messenger and, for reasons I've never understood, with Cooney, too. I'm always careful around Bill.

"Yeah," I say. "Single GW, looks like. No weapon at the scene."

Bill says, "Single GW? Robbery? Bay Shore? Sounds like MS13, right? Might be an initiation killing or connected to Bollina or one of the others."

"Eh, maybe, but don't get hemmed in by that until we hear from the ME," Dave tells him. Bill's been our point person on a lot of the MS13 cases the last couple of years. He's been on a lot of murders connected with the gangs—senseless, awful things that stay with you for months. To be fair, with what he's seen, that's where Bill's mind is going to go. He and I worked a murder last year, the killing of a seventeen-year-old named Juan Bollina that was probably a gang initiation killing tied to the international criminal gang founded in Los Angeles and now operating across Central America and the US. Recently, Long Island has seen a lot of MS13 activity and Juan Bollina's won't be the last murder we have to investigate. He was a good kid from Islip who made the mistake of developing a crush on a girl who was somehow related to a member of MS13. Bollina's body was found behind a dumpster in Central Islip last year. He'd been beaten badly and shot in the head. The gang task force had an idea about who killed him and we interviewed some witnesses and persons of interest, but in the end the case stayed open and it's still on Bill's mind. To be honest, that could be where this thing is going to end up. But it doesn't help anyone to get locked into a theory too soon, and something's telling me to be cautious here. We go over the basic details again and I give out assignments. I tell Bill to head back to Bay Shore to check on the status of the door-to-doors. I tell Dave to coordinate with the medical examiner and the crime lab so we'll get more results as soon as they have them.

Berta's going to work on getting into the accounts and tracing Gabriel Treacy's movements online. Now I need to call Roly and have Marty contact the Irish consulate in New York.

The energy in the room is good, everybody ready to go. Detectives spend a lot of time waiting for something to happen, and when it does, we settle into our routines with the satisfaction of old dogs jumping up on a couch.

I recognize my moment and seize it.

"Oh, Dave," I say, real serious, concerned, waiting until I've got everyone's attention. Dave looks up, innocent as a lamb to the slaughter.

"Yeah?"

"Hey, make sure to give your pet hamster something to drink. Little creatures like that, they get thirsty really easily, especially in a warm room like this."

Everyone laughs. Dave grins and gives me the finger. "Love ya, Dave," I say as everyone files out.

Dave and I didn't get along when we first started working together. He was too macho, too full of himself. But we got to like each other over the years. As he became comfortable with me, as I challenged the ideas he had about what women could do, and as the shit he went through in Afghanistan leached out of him like a thin stream of poison, he turned into someone I can say "love ya" to and mean it. Moustache notwithstanding. The truth is, he wears it well. He's got a little Tom Selleck vibe going on, and it's not the worst thing to take him down a peg as often as possible.

I head to the canteen, get a cup of coffee, and sit down to call Roly Byrne.

It's nine in Dublin. I picture Roly sitting in his elegant house in a Northside suburb, surrounded by his beautiful family and his wife Laura's impeccable interior decorating. I can almost see the sky outside his house, an Irish sky, blue-black, smudged with stars, salt water on the air. In the middle of it all is Roly, lean, rangy, his tailored suit and thinning gray-blond hair and his nervy energy, a foot or index finger always tapping, always moving. He answers fast, with a booming, "D'arcy! How are you, then?"

"Good, except I've got an Irish guy who got himself shot on a beach here last night. He's from Dublin. Arrived three days ago. We've got the passport and everything. Someone's going to have to notify the family. I believe that someone may be you." Roly works for the Garda Síochána, the Irish police service. The Garda National Bureau of Criminal Investigation offers technical support and investigators to local jurisdictions across Ireland. After years on the NBCI's cold case squad, Roly recently got moved over to investigating major crimes, like homicides. Normally, a local guard (as they call their cops) would do the next-of-kin notification, but I'm betting they'll let Roly do it because of his connection with me. That connection is going to cut through a ton of red tape for everyone.

"You serious? What are the chances of that? Irish fella?"

"I don't know. I get a lot of guys who get shot, America in 2017, you know. But you're right, not a lot of 'em are Irish. My partner asked if I knocked him off to justify going to visit Conor. My partner's an asshole."

"Ah, good one. All right. What's his name? Your victim?"

"Gabriel Treacy. Worked for an international aid organization called Global Humanity. Home address is King Street, Dublin 7."

"Hmmm. Smithfield. Old neighborhood with a lot of new development, fancy flats and that. Okay, I'll get it sorted and see if we have anything. Was there a phone on him?"

"Nope. No electronics anywhere. We're thinking he was robbed. There's an emergency contact in the passport, though. Stella Treacy, address in County Clare. I'm assuming not a wife, because of the different address, but maybe an ex-wife or mother or sister. I'll send you a scan of the passport. He was quite a traveler. Stamps from all over the world. Goes with the line of work, I guess. Oh, and here's something weird." I tell him about the scars on Gabriel Treacy's back. "Thanks, Roly."

"I'll be seeing you soon enough, right? You and Lilly still coming over?"

"Yeah, we're on a ten a.m. flight Sunday."

"This case gonna banjax your holiday?" Roly's caught a case two days before a family vacation more times than he wants to count. He knows what it's like to want to see the case through and at the same time not want to let his family down.

"I hope not," I say. "But, you know."

"All right, I'll get on it over here and ring you back. What are you thinking? Just a random thing? Robbery?"

"Yeah, his wallet and phone are gone, so probably." He can hear my hesitation, the space after "probably," and he sends something down the line that makes me go on. "Yeah, I don't know. Doesn't feel like a straight robbery to me. Maybe a drug thing, but I don't know. Maybe some kind of gang initiation thing. We've got a lot of that going on here right now."

"Okay. I'll speak to you in the morning."

"Thanks, Roly."

By the time I get off the phone, Dave has sent everyone else off to their various tasks. He says they're working on scheduling the autopsy, which is good, though we have to wait until the family notification is made. That's the first thing. I'm hoping Roly can do it quickly and we can get on this. Tomorrow's Saturday. We've got all day to find something. I'll have to work tomorrow, which I wasn't planning on doing, but maybe we'll have something by the end of the day and I can still leave Sunday morning. Roly should be back in touch tomorrow and we'll know for sure what Gabriel Treacy was doing in Bay Shore. His family will have text messages from him. He may even have talked to someone just before he was killed.

My brain is slowing down. I can feel it. "Okay, I'm out of here," I tell the team. "Everyone finish up what you've got and then go home and get a good night's sleep. We'll be notifying the family. Something's going to break tomorrow, I can feel it. I want you all rested and ready, 'kay?"

Everyone nods and I head out to my car, feeling their energy behind me, lifting me up, reminding me it's not all on me. They've got their jobs and they're going to be working away at them while I go home and tend to my daughter. There are about a thousand things to be cynical and anxious about right now, but tonight, as I stand in the parking lot fumbling for my keys and feeling the salty, late-winter air blowing across Long Island, I feel grateful, thinking of them all in there, working together, and I smile to myself, and to the setting sun, before getting in the car and taking off toward the west.

Gabriel loved stories.

His nan told him stories sometimes, about naughty animals she had known, scratching cats and biting dogs and runaway cows. There was a story about a cat that gnawed on a barmbrack and a lamb that went to school with one of Nan's friends, so she could feed it from a bottle.

His mother didn't tell stories. But she would hand him a book if he asked, and he wanted to know the stories so badly that he taught himself to read when he was four. His mother liked that. She would tell everyone about his reading, as though he'd done something miraculous. Sometimes she even made him perform for whoever it was she was telling, made him open a book and read a passage. Gabriel hated that.

"Aw, the dote," the old ladies would say. "Isn't he clever?" And his mother would smile.

They had Gulliver's Travels and a book with all the plays of Shakespeare and a book of stories about Cú Chulainn. And they had a Bible on a shelf in the sitting room.

There were loads of stories in the Bible. His mother didn't like to go to mass but sometimes she would read the Bible and leave it out, and once Gabriel could read he flipped through the pages, looking for words he recognized. One day, he found his name. He saw the G-A-B-R-I-E-L and he read, "Gabriel, make this man to understand the vision," and he stopped there and read about Daniel and a ram with two horns and a goat with one horn smiting him, and he asked his granddad what "smite" meant and his granddad said, "Where did you get that, now?" but he told Gabriel it meant kill.

For years, he had dreams about the goat who killed the ram. It came to him from his subconscious like a monster, the one horn sharp and dangerous, the goat's head down for the smiting. And then the four horns growing where only one had been, and the goat raising its head, its eyes yellow and glittering with evil.

Years later, a nun explained to him about Daniel's vision, about how the ram was the Persian and Median kings, how the goat was Alexander the Great, who would conquer the Persians and Medians, and how, after he died, his kingdom would be divided into four. The nun explained about how the angel Gabriel had told Daniel to try to forget about the vision, to save it for another time.

But Gabriel never outgrew the dreams, and he knew that once you had heard a story, once you had seen a vision of the future, it wasn't as simple as putting a book back on the shelf.

6

Uncle Danny is stirring something on the stove when I get home. He's wearing an old New York Jets sweatshirt, from before they left the island, and he leans down so I can kiss him on the cheek. He's lost weight, stopped smoking, and I'm still not quite used to this new Uncle Danny. He smells different, feels different when I hug him. When I point to the ceiling and raise my eyebrows, he whispers, "She's talking on her phone. She seemed okay when I picked her up, quiet, ya know?" He nods to the front door, the alarm console. "Everything okay?"

"Yeah, just a few extra precautions. Anthony Pugh drove by this morning. Maybe he's been checking out the house. Maybe not. Let me know if you see anything, right?"

"I will." He scowls a little. He'll keep an eye out now.

I look into the pot. "Whatcha got in there?"

"That curry you had in the fridge. Lilly said that sounded good for dinner."

"You want to stay?" I get a bottle of white wine out of the fridge, pour some into a glass, wave it at him to see if he wants some, but he's already getting his coat on.

"Nah. I'm meeting Eileen at the bar," he tells me. "We're gonna go do some shopping."

Uncle Danny was bashful when he first told me he was dating a retired teacher he'd met online. "I've been spending time with a lady called Eileen," he said when I stopped by the bar one night at the beginning of November. "I thought I could ask her to come have Thanksgiving with us. That okay with ya?" He couldn't look at me when he said it. I had to work hard not to burst into nervous giggles.

"Of course," I said. "We'd love to have her."

Eileen has six adult children, a bunch of grandchildren, and a house in Port Washington that's the same house she raised all those kids in with her late husband. Danny loves the grandchildren, keeps buying them too many plastic toys, which means they love him, too. I'm so happy for him I can barely stand it, but I also feel a little pang of jealousy. Me and Lilly, just the two of us, we seem so small and quiet next to Eileen's family. There's no way we can compete.

"Tell her I say hi," I say. "And thanks, Uncle Danny. I really appreciate you picking up Lilly."

"'Course, baby. This new case gonna get in the way of your trip?"

"I don't know. Weird thing—the victim's an Irish guy. We don't know why he was over here."

"Yeah? What happened to him?"

"Probably a robbery, just a random thing," I say. "We don't know."

But the image of those scars on Gabriel Treacy's back comes to me and I must shiver a little because Uncle Danny says, "You okay, Mags?"

"Yeah, just tired. You go see Eileen." I give him a half hug. "Love ya."

"Love ya too, baby." He grins at me and takes a cellophane-wrapped chocolate out of his coat pocket. "Give it to Lilly after she has a good dinner." He's started eating better since Eileen, goes for walks with her around her neighborhood, but he still carries chocolates in his pockets.

"You spoil her, you know that?"

"That's what uncles are for." He winks at me and then he's gone and it's up to me to go up and drag Lilly down for dinner.

"How was the last day of school?" I ask her once we're sitting across from each other at the kitchen island. She looks up from her bowl of rice and chicken curry, her long dark hair falling across her face, her eyes huge and sad. She's lost weight in the eight months since June; her face is more angular, more adult. Of course, with what she's been through in the past eight months, it's no wonder she looks older. She *is* older. We both are, in some fundamental way that I can barely quantify. Her therapist says she's still at the denial/pain stage of grieving her father, that because of the complexities of his death, she may be stuck here for a while, that it's my job to just be there for her, to not ask too much, to take my cues from Lilly and, above all, make sure she knows I'm not going anywhere, that I'm a steady presence, there in the background when she's ready to talk. Her therapist says she's going to start lashing out, trying to share her pain with the one person who won't reject her. It's why I've made arrangements to go off-duty at four most days, let my team handle details that come up after that. It's mostly worked. When Marty approved it, he told me I'd never be sorry for putting family first and I had to choke down my gratitude so he wouldn't see me cry.

"Okay. We didn't do much, since it was the last day before vacation. I got work from my teachers for the second week we're over there."

"Good job remembering to do that. Any of your friends going anywhere nice?"

"Chloe's going to Club Med in the Bahamas. Mia's mom is taking her to look at colleges."

I feel a little flash of guilt. "Wow. It doesn't seem possible it's time for you guys to do that already. We'll have to start thinking about that. Maybe we can do a trip this summer."

"Yeah," she says, but listlessly, and I have to push down a pang of annoyance. I'm trying so hard and she can't even pretend to be interested. I feel the sense of exhaustion from earlier wash over me again. I've been waiting for months for Lilly to show some interest in life again, to acknowledge how hard I've been trying, even though I know that isn't her job. But it doesn't seem to be happening, and I'm just . . . weary. I force myself to smile and reach out to touch her hand.

"Are there any clothes you want to get before we leave for Dublin?" I ask her. "I don't think we're going to anything too formal, but it might be fun to have some new outfits."

"I don't know." She shrugs. "I think I'm good."

I hesitate. "Are you feeling okay about going over there?"

She looks up at me with Brian's eyes, wide, brown, liquid, sad. "I guess. It's better than being here."

"Conor said they cleared out and painted the extra bedroom so you'll have your own space." When we visited Conor and his son, Adrien, in Dublin, Lilly had to sleep in a room cluttered with Conor's books and research materials. She made some bratty comments about it that Conor overheard, and when I apologized he said that of course it bothered her and they'd do better before we came back.

She gets up to drop her bowl in the sink and she's about to head for the TV when I say, "Lil? One thing I need to tell you. Marty wants us to be a bit careful the next few days, until we go. So that means keeping doors locked and alarms on. You know the drill. Okay?"

"What happened?" Lilly's used to periodic upgrades to our home security because of something going on with my work. She's not overly concerned.

"Nothing specific. Just a precaution, okay?" She nods and pushes her hair out of her face.

We drift into the living room and she curls up on the couch to watch a cooking competition. I've gotten lax about television-watching during the week this winter. She settles in under a blanket my mom crocheted in the '80s, neon orange and royal blue that clashes with the pale blue and gray rug and curtains I chose when I redid the downstairs a few years ago. My cell phone rings, and I look down to see Alicia Piehler's number. I take it out into the hallway. "Hey, Alicia," I say.

"Hey, Maggie. I just wanted to check in on this Treacy thing. The boss wants to know if there's anything yet?"

"Seriously? We got the body this morning. He really must be running for reelection, huh?"

Alicia laughs, then lowers her voice. "You know it. He's really worried about Lizza, now that he's said he's definitely running." Ken Lizza is a former cop and Suffolk County legislator, a Democrat who's going to challenge Cooney in the election next year, and he's making Cooney nervous. "I told him it was going to be a while but he said he wanted an update."

"Well, the guy seems to have been involved in humanitarian work around the world. We're not sure yet why he was here. I was thinking he was meeting someone to buy drugs, maybe sex, but . . . maybe, maybe not. It's a weird spot for it. We can't count out MS13. I have a call in to Dublin. I'll check in as soon as I get anything. We're going to hear from Connie tomorrow about the autopsy. Dave's coordinating, but probably not until Monday or later, and the consulate will probably get involved, too, so who knows." For some reason, I don't tell Alicia about the scars. "I'm supposed to be taking vacation, but we'll see what happens tomorrow."

She's done. I can feel her attention shut down. "Okay, thanks, Maggie. Talk to you tomorrow."

I have a text from Conor when I get off the phone. *I'm off to bed. Talk in the morning? Two days . . .* I text back, *I'll call when I'm up. Can't wait,* and push down the little sliver of guilt I feel; he doesn't know what's going on and how it could affect my trip. But maybe we'll know something by tomorrow. I make sure the alarm system is on, grab my laptop, and curl up on the couch next to Lilly to go over what Berta gave us and see what else I can find.

I do my own search first, just to make sure, and it doesn't take long online to get the basics. "Gabriel Treacy Dublin" delivers a whole bunch of references to Global Humanity. It seems to be a humanitarian aid nonprofit with programs in India, Sri Lanka, Bangladesh, Afghanistan, Pakistan, Syria, Rwanda, and other countries. Their main office is in Dublin. The landing page of their website says that they "Partner with other international NGOs and hundreds of local organizations to provide disaster aid, refugee assistance, and hope for the future for people of the world displaced by conflict, oppression, and climate change." They seem to both solicit donations for their programs and the partners they work with and also to actually provide direct assistance in places where terrible things have happened or are happening. I find Gabriel Treacy's photograph and bio on the "About Our Team" page. He's listed second in the lineup; at the top is the organization's CEO, Gillian Gleeson. There's my "Gill" from the list in Gabriel Treacy's hotel room. Her portrait shows her in front of a mosque in a desert landscape, her brown hair in a pixie cut and her direct gaze challenging and serious. Gabriel Treacy's portrait is professional, but casual. He's posed in front of a brick wall, his hands in the pockets of his blazer, a khaki safari shirt with a slightly rumpled collar underneath it. He's smiling, but only slightly, and there's something about his eyes that makes me linger on the photo, thinking of the scars. His title was "Senior Partner and COO," which probably means he did a bit of everything.

Beyond that, I find some photos of him at various events in Dublin. It looks like he made the circuit at fundraisers for other humanitarian organizations. The editorial Berta mentioned is one of three I find alerting the Irish public to various humanitarian crises unfolding around the world. I wonder what Gabriel Treacy's mental health was like; after an hour of looking at pictures of starving children and destroyed cities, I can feel my heart rate rising, a sense of horror washing over me.

He's got a Facebook account and a Twitter account. The Twitter account seems to have been used more recently, mostly retweets of articles and tweets about international development issues and humanitarian crises. All business. Nothing the least bit personal. The Facebook page has a few photos posted by other people, including one of him with a woman, both of them dressed in formalwear, but he has the page locked down so I can't see any more. The woman is tagged in one of the public pictures and when I click on her name—Abena Tekle—I get her Facebook page and a number of photos of her in different locations around the world: Paris, London, what looks like Kyoto, Moscow. She's not as conscious of privacy as Gabriel Treacy was. Her bio section says she was born in Addis Ababa, went to Yale, and now lives in Dublin. That's it. Gabriel Treacy's wife or girlfriend, I'm assuming, from the way they're standing next to each other and from a few comments on her page—"Bonsoir, beautiful Abena. XXOO to you and Gabriel!" and so forth. I write her name down.

That's enough for tonight. Roly will have some more for me tomorrow and we should get some good breaks in the case.

I snuggle back in next to Lilly and she leans against me, letting me stroke her hair, something I'm usually not allowed to do. The cooking competition comes to an end, a young woman with purple hair is sent home and starts crying as she says it's okay, really, it's been the best experience of her life, and then suddenly, Lilly's sobbing, her shoulders heaving, her breathing ragged and violent. She buries her face in my chest, burrowing into me as if she's trying to hide in my flesh.

"Oh, Lil." I wrap her tight in my arms, letting her pain run into me, wishing there was something I could do to take it away. But there isn't, so I just soak up all I can, holding her close against my body until she stops crying and I can lead her up to bed.

7

Sunrise is at quarter to seven, a slash mark of nearly fuschia pink sky. I go down to stand on the beach with my coffee, the steam from my cup mingling with my breath as I watch the pink fade and the golden edge of the sun peek above the line of the horizon to the east. When my phone buzzes and the screen reads "Conor," I answer with, "I was just watching the sunrise and thinking about you!"

"Great minds," Conor says, from across the very water I'm looking at right now. "I was thinking about you, too, but unfortunately, I'm watching it rain outside the windows. No sun at all. Just lashing rain. It's pretty grim." I see him then, his smile and the *movement* of him, the way his shoulders slope, the way his hair curls at the back of his neck, the way he turns his head. When he talks, he pitches forward a little, leaning on his elbows or the balls of his feet, his dark eyes intense, looking right at you, a gleam of cynical humor always there. For so many years, I held that idea of him in my mind, pining for . . . something intangible, a sense of his energy, and it's very strange now, having access to it at the end of a phone.

"Ah, I'm sorry for you. Here, I'm taking a picture. I'll email it. Check it out."

"That is beautiful," he says after a second. "And just think, it will be setting again in about twenty minutes."

"Don't be so negative. Unlike you, I am filled with wonder at the majesty of the natural world. I think I understand now why our ancestors built all those winter solstice thingies. This time of year, it's like you've got to capture the sunlight and hold it while you can. And the days are getting longer now, you know."

"I didn't realize I'd fallen in love with a Druid. Are you going to make me go and sleep rough at Newgrange?"

"I just might. Actually, I do really want to go there sometime, and the other one, too. What's it called?"

"The Hill of Tara?"

"Yeah. Will you take me?" I start walking back up to the house.

"Maybe. We could drive up, I suppose. Though I should warn you that standing out in a field with a bunch of new age lunatics wasn't exactly part of my vision for this holiday." Conor and Adrien have been planning on taking us on a road trip down to Cork and then up the west coast to Galway when we're over there.

I nod to my next door neighbor Mrs. Yaktitis, who's out getting her paper. "Mmmmm. All right, we'll see. I'll save the Druid activities for another trip."

"You and Lilly all set for your holiday?" he asks. I can hear the hesitation in his voice, the nervousness. He knows that my job's special super power is blowing up plans without thinking twice, like a movie villain walking away from an explosion.

I hesitate. "Well, I got a case yesterday. I think it's going to be okay, though. Victim was an Irish guy, actually. Looks like he might be from Clare, like you. Town called Sixmilebridge?" I know he can hear my forced breeziness.

"The Bridge. Yeah, that's not far from Broadford. My da used to buy sheep from a man in the Bridge. We had some family over that way for a while. Do you know who killed him yet?"

"No. We just got the ID. But the team can handle it, I think. Probably a robbery. I'll know more soon. Roly is coordinating the notifications for me."

"I'll cross my fingers it's all wrapped up today," he says. There's a new coolness in his voice that I can hear, even across the ocean. "We're really looking forward to seeing you." When he was here in November, I was so sure of the weight of what's between us. It felt real, solid. But the distance has slowly drawn away my certainty.

"I know. Can't wait to see you too," I say. "I'll call this afternoon and let you know what's going on." I take a deep breath. I have to say it. "It might be we come a day or two later if I need to clean up some details, but I'm really hoping we can fly tomorrow. Okay?"

"Okay, so. I should get Adrien up," he says. "I'll speak to you later." He's gone before I can say goodbye and I stand in the driveway as the whole of the sun clears the shore and the little slivers of stone in the asphalt come alive with light. When I turn to look back at the water, it's Erin I'm thinking of, and I wish I could call her down to see the way the sun touches the frosted tops of the waves.

I'm trying to help Lilly lay out the clothes she wants to take on the trip when Roly calls.

He's all business. "D'arcy. It was too late for me to get to Sixmilebridge last night, so I had the local lads do it. Stella Treacy was his mother. She died about a year ago and the house has been sold already. They gave me the number of a neighbor. Helen Reid. Treacy's not married, no kids. The mammy's neighbor said he had a fairly serious girlfriend until recently."

"Thanks. I think I found her Facebook page," I say.

"Abena Tekle. She lives in Dolphin's Barn now. I got her name from Treacy's landlord. She used to live there with Treacy, so she was on the lease. I guess she does the same kind of work. The landlord said they both traveled frequently for their jobs. There's his boss, too. I'm going to see if we can locate her, but it's Saturday. Unless the girlfriend has her number, we may not get her until Monday and sure, you'll be here yourself then, won't you?"

"Yeah, I think so. And I should interview them properly, or someone should, get statements and everything. Can you get that rolling for me?" My mind is racing with details. There are all kinds of protocols that have to be followed when you're investigating a crime in two countries. We may have to involve the FBI and the Irish government, but Roly's senior position in the Garda should help smooth the way. "We should get more from the medical examiner today so I'll know pretty soon if I have to delay. Thanks, Roly. Anything else? I can't get those scars out of my head."

"I'm sure the girlfriend will know. I also put his name out to a few of my contacts here. I'll get back in touch as soon as I have anything good."

"Great, thanks. I'll talk to you soon."

Lilly's going to spend the day at her friend Chloe's house, just to be safe, so I drop her there, check to make sure I wasn't followed, then drive down to Bay Shore.

The wind has come up since I was here yesterday and the water is choppy, frosted with little whitecaps. There are two Third Precinct guys in uniform guarding the scene, and a tech is taking samples of sand from around the spot where Gabriel Treacy died. We're in a race against time to preserve evidence before it gets soaked beyond recognition.

"Anything?"

"They got your casing," the tech says.

That's good. We'll get all kinds of information from the bullet casing: the angle, the kind of firearm that fired it, whether that firearm has been used to kill anyone else. "Oh, perfect. That should give us something. Anything else?"

"Maybe a scrap of a receipt." Before I can ask, he says, "CVS, the fifteenth."

"One of the really long ones?" I ask.

"Ha. No, just a scrap, but there are a couple numbers. You may be able to get something from it."

"Okay. I'll get someone on it. Nothing else?" He shakes his head and goes back to his work.

Dave arrives and we walk over to the spot where Gabriel Treacy was found, just above where the techs are working. "So he's standing there," I say, pushing Dave into position. "And whoever it is comes from there." I point to the east, toward the pier. "They could have come across the rocks and those chunks of asphalt. Wouldn't be any footprints in the sand that way, right? We should make sure they checked carefully for evidence there, too. You'd have to be pretty sure-footed, though."

"Yeah. Treacy looks up. Maybe they talk, maybe they don't. And the shooter kills him, takes his phone and wallet, whatever else he might have, then heads back to wherever he came from."

"So what's Treacy doing here?" I ask. "Who's he meeting?"

Dave plays the game with me. "He arranges to meet up with some girl—or guy—here. He meets her and her job is to talk to him so he's in position and someone else robs him. Or maybe whoever he's meeting gets him talking, makes him feel at ease and then robs him herself or himself."

"I don't know. For a wallet and a phone? They could have just held him up or punched him, right? Why would they kill him?"

"Something went wrong. He fought back."

"Yeah. But it didn't look to me like he fought back. It looked like someone just came up and popped him, you know?" I'm thinking about what I just said, though. Maybe it wasn't just a wallet and phone. Maybe he had something else. Something that was worth killing him for. His laptop wasn't found in the rental car or his motel room. Maybe he had a backpack or laptop bag that seemed worth killing him for. But still, it didn't look like he was fighting. I can't help coming back to my first impression of the scene. "It felt like an execution to me, Dave."

"So maybe Bill's right? MS13? Initiation killing?"

"Maybe." I'm thinking back to the Juan Bollina case last year. Our assumption was that the murder of Juan Bollina was an initiation killing, that some kid had been forced to shoot him to prove his loyalty to his new friends. I remember responding to the scene with Bill. I'd felt desperation and chaos in the air, a raw, nervy displacement of energy.

I can't put into words why this one felt different, but it did. This felt organized, efficient. Professional.

We look around. I can just see the rooflines of the fancy waterfront houses along the shore to the west, like faraway white mountains. Dave says, "What are the chances any of those houses have security cameras pointed in this direction?"

I put a hand up to my eyes. "Not good. Angle's wrong. They'd want to point them straight out at the beach, where someone could walk up, or the road. You want to go look, though? We're gonna have to drive over there. The road doesn't go through."

"Yeah." We nod to the techs and take Dave's car out of the marina, making a left off Main Street to get into the neighborhood to the west. It's a classic wealthy Long Island neighborhood, a warren of streets proceeding to dead ends and cul-de-sacs to keep out non-residents, big houses on big lots, mature trees and well-tended lawns, the older colonials unrenovated, the ones closer to the water mostly new construction, enormous glass-fronted mansions for extra-lucky bankers and tech executives. I park and we walk up and down the streets, looking for cameras. Closer to the water, there's a lot that was most likely a tear-down, and a mostly constructed but still unpainted monstrosity with columns out front and a strong *Gone with the Wind* vibe. As we walk toward the beach we see a gazebo and a sign reading "Manorhaven Residents Only. 24-Hour Video Surveillance."

"There you go!" Dave says. "I'll have the Islip guys get the footage."

"Yeah, don't get too excited. The camera's probably pointed at the road so they can catch illicit sunbathers on their private beach. But make the call."

He does, while I pull my running gloves out of the pockets of my parka and pull my hood up around my face. The wind is stiff and I'm turning away from it, toward the north, when I have a strong feeling of being under surveillance, the sense of a pair of eyes somewhere near, tracking me. I look up quickly and catch movement out of the corner of my eye, but when I turn, I can't tell where it came from. I'm still scanning the houses and the beach when Dave comes up, sticking his phone back in his pocket. "What?"

"Felt someone's eyes on me," I say. "Probably just the sun flashing in one of those windows."

Dave turns and looks. He's got the same hypervigilance I do, for some of the same reasons, and he always believes me when I say I felt something. "All the neighbors are probably inside watching through the windows," he says finally. "Trying to figure out what's going on."

We start walking, looking back toward the marina. It's all man-made here, rocks hauled in to create the breaker, sand from somewhere else dumped to make a beach. I like beaches with shells and long stretches of dark and light sand, emerald seaweed balancing on the water, little shiny rocks like diamonds. I like real beaches, made by time. This isn't that kind of beach. A seagull calls overhead but doesn't bother looking for mussels. We find a couple of discreet cameras high on the rooflines, but just like I thought, they're all pointed in the wrong direction. The almost-finished Tara wannabe would have had a good view of the site of Gabriel Treacy's murder and as we walk past I can hear machinery inside. A young guy in a hat and construction mask comes out, carrying buckets of paint, and I stop and ask him if anyone was at the house Thursday night. "The owner don't live here yet," he says.

"No, I know. I'm just wondering if anyone was here working Thursday night." He stares at me blankly, then turns and yells something in Spanish back into the interior of the house. It's mostly complete, with shiny wood floors covered with clear plastic, but only half the windows are up and there are piles of construction debris everywhere.

The man who comes out seems to be the foreman because he orders the other worker to keep doing what he's doing and tells me that he usually sends his crew home by five. "And the owner's not here in the evenings obviously?" Dave asks him.

"No, no. The owner he is living somewhere else. I am not sure where."

"Your men, they haven't said they've seen anything strange, have they? Anything they were concerned about?"

He misunderstands. "No. My guys, they are all honest."

"Okay. Thanks," I tell him. Someone will have to check out all the men working on the house, but I don't tell him that right now. We turn around and head back to Dave's car on the labyrinthine residential streets around the canal.

"That one's Cooney's," I say, pointing to a big midcentury colonial at the back of an austere stretch of lawn. Next to it is a much newer, nicer house, modern, with a lot of glass and stone. It makes Cooney's look a little shabby, from another time.

Back at the scene, we discover that the press has arrived; a *Newsday* reporter comes jogging over from the other side of the parking lot.

"Detective Lieutenant D'arcy, Detective Sergeant Milich," he calls out. "Eric Coombs from *Newsday*. Do we know anything more about the man who was killed here?"

"No, *we* don't," Dave says.

"Well, is it fair to say a tourist was randomly shot here Thursday night?" Coombs says. "Should the public be concerned?"

"We have nothing to report right now," I say. "There will be a press conference once we know more."

"But in terms of alerting the public? Should people be careful walking on South Shore beaches? Is there any reason to believe the killer could strike again? Could this be an MS13-related killing, given the area?"

"We have nothing to report right now," I repeat, hustling Dave into the car before he gives anything away. Both of us want to tell

Coombs not to write his story so it sounds like people need to panic, but the truth is that we can't say there's no need to be worried. We don't know that people shouldn't go walking on the beaches.

I want to go back to the spot where Gabriel Treacy died, but I'm not going to do that now the press is here. We just sit there for a few minutes, not saying anything. We're both antsy now, waiting.

"We're probably not going to get anything today," Dave says. He's right. Medical examiners and crime lab techs have their own timelines.

"I know," I say. "Fuck. My time's running out on this. We're supposed to fly tomorrow morning. If we don't have anything by then, how am I gonna go?"

"Even if we get something good from the casing, we still need to know why he was here, right?" Dave says. "Someone needs to take statements from his contacts. Maybe you going to Ireland to interview his family and everything, maybe that's the best thing you could do?"

He has a point. Even if he's just trying to make me feel better.

My phone buzzes with a text from Roly.

"Look," I say to Dave, holding my phone out to him. He reads along with me.

Here ya go, D'arcy. Girlfriend's in Germany for her job. They split last year. She was pretty upset. She's flying back to Dublin and can talk to you on Monday. Rang the boss as well. She was driving. Said he wasn't over on a work trip. He didn't tell her he was going out of the country. She was very surprised. Couldn't think why he'd be in the States. She can talk to you Monday too.

We're silent for a long moment, watching Eric Coombs try to get the uniformed officers to talk to him.

"What you said, Dave, you may be right," I say. "If he wasn't over here on a work trip, then why was he here? What was he doing in Bay Shore?"

Dave watches as the officers shut Coombs right down. His head is hanging a little as he walks back to his car. "And what was he doing at the marina?" Dave asks. "That's what we've gotta figure out."

8

Saturday at headquarters usually feels skeleton, but when we have a big case—which this is, on account of the nice neighborhood, the mystery about what exactly we're looking at—it's as busy as a weekday. Dave and I update everyone once we get back from the scene and make sure they know what they're working on. Then I go to talk to Marty. But when I poke my head into his office, he's not alone.

Cooney and Pat Messenger are there, Cooney sitting in a chair too small for him and looking much too elegant for Marty's plain office and Pat leaning awkwardly against the heating unit at the back of the room. He's pale, his eyes sunken; Pat is six feet three, built like a quarterback, but now his blue jacket is hanging off his shoulders, his belt cinched tight in the loops of his too-loose pants.

"Detective D'arcy," Cooney says, nodding at me from across the room.

I stand up a little bit straighter, straighten my blazer over my hips. I nod to Pat.

"Marty gave us the update," Cooney says quickly. "Sounds like you're all working hard here on this. Anyway, keep us in the loop,

Marty. The press is going crazy on this thing." He stands up, nods at me again, and brushes past me into the hallway.

"Maggie," Pat says, wincing, and follows Cooney out.

Marty waits until they're gone, then says, "Okay, I gave them an update, but tell me what you really got. Anything?" He gestures vaguely at the chair Cooney just vacated.

Marty must have had a fresh buzz cut this morning; his precise silvery crew cut contrasts with the messy room and his rumpled polyester-blend dress shirt and navy tie.

"Nothing, really. Apparently, it wasn't a work trip and his boss didn't know he was coming over here, either. The girlfriend and boss can both talk on Monday. Hopefully one of them can get us access to his phone and email accounts."

"So, you still want to head over there tomorrow?"

"That's the plan, but I can cancel if you think I need to stay here for this. I don't want to leave Dave in it."

Marty studies me for a long moment. I have the sense he hasn't made up his mind yet. He's thinking hard and I can see the exact moment he decides. The tension in his face relaxes and he sits up, ready for whatever's coming. "Dave and your team can handle things here. Might be good for you to do some poking around over there. You can come back though, right? If there's a development here and I need you on it? Lots of flights from Ireland and so forth."

I nod. "Yeah, I can come back anytime. You sure?"

"I'm sure. Dave's got it. It might be good for you to get away for a bit." Something about his voice puts me on my guard. Does Marty think I've been off my game? I've been working all my cases hard since I came back from leave. I've had two solves and I know I've put in some good police work. So why does he think I need a break?

He knows me well enough to know what I'm thinking. "Maggie, don't get me wrong. You're A-plus. It's not that. It's just . . . with Anthony Pugh up to whatever he's up to and . . . when your boyfriend was here back in November, you had a lightness to you. It was nice. You gotta get that back a little. Not for me, not for . . ." He spreads his arms around him, at the squad's offices. "For you. You know what I mean?" He smiles, and I feel a rush of gratitude.

I'm running out of time, but we work away at it, starting to fill in the holes.

Berta's got all of Gabriel Treacy's travel information and she's working on tracking down his credit card and phone records.

"Plane reservations, Maggie," she says, dropping a printout on my desk. I scan the reservation. Treacy was due to fly back to Dublin the day after he was killed, on a seven p.m. Icelandair flight through Reykjavík. He made the reservations for the plane tickets and motel on the same day, a week before the trip. That makes me think it was sudden, whatever it was that brought him across from Ireland.

"I'm getting a wall from the phone company and the bank that issued his credit card," she says. "They want the death certificate, which we don't have yet. You may need the embassy to authorize it. You'll have an easier time getting it once you're over there, I bet."

"Yeah. I'll see if my friend can grease the wheels. We need those phone records ASAP."

I hold a case meeting at three, ask for updates from the Islip cops who have been doing door-to-doors. Bill Trillio's got the compiled interviews the Third Precinct officers did in the neighborhood this morning. They found an elderly lady in an apartment off Bayview

Avenue who said she thought she heard a gunshot Thursday night, but it's not very specific. A middle-aged couple who lives just outside the marina said they stepped outside to smoke around ten p.m. and saw someone they thought was a woman running away from the marina, and the officers who interviewed them found them credible. Less credible was the guy who said he heard a loud whooshing sound and saw very bright lights in his window Thursday night and who the interviewing officer told us has made ten reports of unidentified flying objects in Bay Shore over the past three years. They did find a rent-a-cop who was coming home from a security job and stopped at the marina for a smoke around nine p.m. He swore there was nobody there then, so we've got a narrower window now, since the body was found at six a.m.

I tell the team that I'm heading over to Ireland and that Dave's in charge now. "I'm just a phone call away. Any time of day or night. And I'll give Dave regular updates on what I get over there. We're going to solve this. I know it. Thanks for your hard work." Everyone nods and says they hope I have a great trip, but I can feel already that the power's shifted. Cops are essentially military: We feel most comfortable in hierarchical structures where we know the chain of command and we know who's just above us. I've stepped out of the chain and Dave's stepped in to take my place. It's good everyone's adapted so quickly, but it stings a little, too.

I shut down my laptop and let Dave walk me out to my car. He gives me a quick hug.

"It's gonna be fine, Mags," he says. "Looks like we've got a good lead here and I think you're gonna be able to figure out why he was over here. I got a feeling about it. And I'll keep you in the loop." He opens the car door for me, lets me get settled, then leans in and gives me an awkward hug. "Safe travels," he says, before he shuts the door, carefully, not slamming it, and giving it a final pat as I drive off, like he's carefully tucking me into bed.

I'll think about that later, Dave's feeling, and wonder if it really was a feeling about the case, or if he was bullshitting me to get me to go to Dublin. If it was a feeling, I'll always wonder if he got it from me, if I knew something then that was hidden even from myself, that was there all along but I just couldn't see it.

9

I go for a long run in the morning, getting ready for the plane.

The dawning day is cold and bright, the sun catching frost on the rocks and shells along the beach. My legs feel nice and loose and I keep going once I hit my usual halfway point, following the residential roads all the way into Centerport and then back around again. By the time I'm showered and finishing the packing for me and Lilly, who can't be bothered, I feel better, more centered, confident that it's all going to be okay.

Lilly's apathy doesn't help, though. She gets dressed, eats a little breakfast, half-heartedly throws some toiletries in a bag. Her phone's been acting up, so, without asking, she uses my laptop to send something to Chloe and her other friends on one of her social media sites, and when I sign on to my email to see if there's anything more from Roly, my settings are all messed up and there's one of those scammy messages about cleaning my Mac's hard drives. She knows it drives me crazy when she messes with my computer, but I can't get mad at her just before we get on the plane, so I keep my voice calm and ask her not to borrow it again without asking.

Uncle Danny takes us to Kennedy, the radio tuned to the '80s station, the skies gray and cold outside the windows of his Nissan. I'm feeling nostalgic for some reason, going to the airport, I suppose, and I remember driving through Queens with my parents once, going to visit my mom's uncle, my cousin Erin next to me in the back of the car, counting Christmas lights on the houses along the Belt Parkway. I can almost feel the pressure of her hand in mine, hear the excitement in her voice when she'd say, "That's the prettiest one so far, Maggie. *That's* the winner."

"Thanks for driving us, Uncle Danny," I say, reaching out to cover his hand with mine on the steering wheel when he pulls up at departures. He's wearing his old Jets sweatshirt again and a purple ski hat, and he looks over at me and smiles. "You guys have a great trip, now, and make sure to call me," he says, getting our bags out. He hugs Lilly a little too hard and she gives me a funny smile over his shoulder. "Lil, you be good and send me a postcard, right?" He winks at me as he gets our bags out of the trunk. An airport cop is lurking so I kiss Danny one more time and say, "Get going before you get arrested." He winks again and then he's gone. Something about the swiftness of it, of his profile through the car window disappearing around the turn in the departures lane, makes me gasp.

"What?" Lilly asks, staring at me.

I take a deep breath and force a smile. "Nothing. Sorry. Let's go find our gate, love."

We get in after midnight, Dublin Airport nearly deserted, REM playing on the PA system, and when I see the familiar shape of Conor's tall frame, his dark hair longer and curling at the nape of his neck, his shy delighted smile when he spots us, I feel a surge of relief and safety and love that floors me. I can't help but run toward him, my boots clattering on the floor, and when I hug him, he smells like rain and dog and soap and the wool of his overcoat and the gray scarf I gave him for Christmas.

"You're here," he whispers into my cheek.

We only kiss a little, since Lilly is looking on, then dash out through the rain to the short-term car park, arms around each other as we run. I can't help but look up at him every few minutes, taking in the details of his face, his chin and the broad sweep of his forehead, his dark eyes flicking over to mine, his shy smile appearing and reappearing. Driving back toward the city from the airport, I think of the first time I made this drive, twenty-four years ago, when I came looking for Erin. I arrived in the city in the back of a taxi, watching the gray skies through the rain-webbed windows, the old women in rain bonnets pushing trolleys outside, Conor not even a memory yet, Conor not anything to me yet.

Tonight, it's pouring rain, the windshield wipers on Conor's car barely keeping up with the deluge, the few headlights on the roads colorful through the fog. I take his left hand while he drives and talks to Lilly over his shoulder, and I love him for including her, trying hard to make sure she's not a third wheel.

"I thought we could have a lie-in tomorrow and then Adrien wants to show you around a little when he gets home from school."

"Can we take Mr. Bean on a walk?" Lilly asks him. She loved walking Conor and Adrien's corgi when we were here in the summer, and Adrien's been messaging her funny little pictures of the dog wearing hats and things around his neck.

"Of course," Conor says. "I think he's been missing you. Adrien told him you were coming to visit and he went and put on his little hat. He may be painting you a sign at this very moment."

Lilly laughs, and when I turn around she looks delighted. She looks gorgeous, too, her eyes big, all the angles of her face lit up in golden light from the streetlights, her glossy dark hair falling in a curtain across her cheek. It's the smile that does it, though, that makes her suddenly, luminously beautiful. I reach back and squeeze her knee and she doesn't glare at me.

"I may have to do a few interviews tomorrow," I tell Conor quietly as we cross over the Liffey. It's strange driving through a nearly empty city. "The victim's ex-girlfriend and boss both live in Dublin and I need to interview them and try to find out what he was doing in New York. But it should just be the morning and then I'm all yours. I promise." I know I'm downplaying it and I think he knows it, too, but he chooses to ignore the whole matter of my interviews for the moment.

He says, "I was thinking we could head to West Cork on Tuesday or Wednesday. The weather's supposed to be good the rest of the week. A colleague of mine has a place not far from Bantry and he said we could have it for a few days. And then we can just explore from there?" The question mark at the end of the sentence is accompanied by a nervous glance.

"Sounds great. My grandmother was from West Cork. Lilly, wouldn't you like to see the town my Nana Nellie was born in?"

"That would be fun," she says. "Which town was Grandma Nancy's family from?"

Grandma Nancy. Brian's mother. I force myself to breathe and say calmly, "Mayo, I think, in the west. Maybe we can go there too."

Conor glances over to see if I'm okay. I raise my eyebrows at him. Lilly hasn't seen Brian's parents in nearly a year.

"Here we are, then," Conor says, as he pulls up in front of his house. It's a semidetached white stucco house with a robin's-egg-blue door that he's owned since the early days of his marriage to his ex-wife, Bláithín, but as he says, the houses all around them have been "poshified" by wealthy international types moving in. He's had some offers on it, but he's reluctant to move Adrien, who's just coming out of a tough period after the divorce. I like the house; it feels like Conor, full of books, a little messy, lots of good details. We bring our bags in and I get Lilly settled in the newly painted guest bedroom. He's made it the same turquoise color as her room at home, and bought a new bedspread and pillowcases. The room is still full of his books, but now they're stacked neatly in a bookcase and he's cleared off a bedside table and desk for her.

"You can brush up on your Irish history before you fall asleep, Lil," I tell her, sitting on the side of the bed. "You can sleep in as late as you want. If I'm not here when you wake up, I'm off doing these interviews and I'll be back soon. You going to be all right hanging out here?" She nods, sleepy and compliant, and I remember how when she was little, she used to protest that she wasn't tired at all, really, not even the littlest bit, even while her eyelids sank and her speech slurred.

"Is there anything on the aid worker fella?" Conor asks when I come downstairs. He's making me tea and I watch him move around the kitchen with the practice of many years in the same space, stepping over Mr. Bean, who's sleeping on his back in the middle of the floor. It's how I am in my kitchen at home on Long Island. I don't even have to think about where the spatula is or where I'll find a Tupperware container. I just know.

"Nothing definite. Probably he was just in the wrong place at the wrong time, but I'm hoping I'll find out a bit more about him tomorrow. We need to get his phone records and whatever we can off his email accounts, too, to see if we can learn why he was at the beach, and I need to know what he was doing on Long Island. I'm so sorry, Conor. I know my job sucks sometimes. I really wanted to just completely turn it off these two weeks, but I think after tomorrow I can hand it all off to Dave and the team. I just want to make sure Marty and Pat know I'm giving it my all." I feel a little flash of guilt. Conor knows I've been worried about my job and my standing with the commissioner because of my issues with Cooney. I just used his sympathy to shift his annoyance about me having to work the first day of our vacation.

He comes over and puts his hands on my shoulders and kisses the top of my head. "We can handle it," he says. "I've missed you so much. I'm just glad you're here." I turn around and kiss him for real, standing up to press my body against his. We fit perfectly, my sternum sinking into the space below his chest, his arms tight around me and pulling me in.

I forget all about my tea, and later, he whispers in my ear, "I love you," and I whisper back, "I love you too," and his body is hot against mine, and outside the bedroom window the rain falls and I know that somewhere off to the east is the sea and to our southwest, the mountains where my cousin Erin lay at rest for so many years.

When I finally sleep, I dream of the mountains, the air smelling of pine and melting snow.

10

Roly's in front of Conor's at eight thirty the next morning. He leaps out of the driver's-side door just as I'm coming outside holding Adrien's umbrella over my head. It's a gray, wet day, the rain dripping down onto the leafing trees around the house. "Ah, good morning, you're very welcome to Dublin," he says, hugging me. "It's shite weather today. It'll clear later, though. Are you awfully jet-lagged?"

"Yeah, didn't get much sleep last night, either."

"Ah, I'd say you didn't, now," he says with a little lascivious sneer, which gets him a smack on the arm.

The first time I met Roly Byrne, he was running, and I always think of him in motion, a foot tapping or a finger drumming, even when he's driving, even when he's sitting still. I watch him beating a rhythm on the steering wheel with his thumbs. "Coffee?" he asks.

"Sure. I'd love an update on your end. There a good place nearby?"

"Ah, yeah, loads of them. This is the posh part of town, you know." He parks along Donnybrook Road in a legally questionable spot and we get lattes at a little Italian café with a black-and-white tile floor and photographs of Sicily on the walls. Roly gets a pain au chocolat and cuts it in half. It's good, sweet and buttery, and the double espresso focuses me. "Okay," I say. "First thing is, when can we get the phone records?"

"Working on it," he says. "Wednesday, I hope."

"How does it work here with email?"

"We'll get started with a warrant but we may be better off asking the girlfriend and the boss if they know his passwords. His work account should be available through the boss, I'd think. Lots of places would have saved passwords so they can recover company communications if someone dies or leaves unexpectedly."

"All right, maybe that will get us something." I chug the rest of my latte. "Let's get going."

"I thought we'd start with the flat and the girlfriend. Well, ex-girlfriend. That good for you?"

"Yeah, that's perfect. Flat first. I'd love to get a feel for him and maybe there'll be a list of passwords or something at his place."

We cross the river to the Northside. Gabriel Treacy's flat is on King Street, not far from the Jameson Distillery, in a neighborhood that feels old and new at the same time, shabby brick storefronts up against brand-new lofts and condos. Treacy's is a newly renovated building above a café, with contemporary metal siding on the front, and a minimalist metal door on the street. Roly has a key he got from the landlord, and even though it's not a crime scene, not as far as we know, anyway, we put on booties over our shoes and latex gloves before we go inside.

It's a nice place on the third floor, open and full of light, high enough that it has a bit of a view toward the river. "Where do you want to start?" he asks.

I spin around, looking at the black-and-white photographs on the walls, the sparse furnishings, just a black-linen-upholstered couch and a small dining table with blond wood chairs around it. A Moroccan carpet lies in front of the couch, but the rest of the shiny wood floor is uncovered. It doesn't feel lived in; I'm not getting a strong sense of Treacy. Not yet. I point to the bathroom. "There."

It's a typical single-man bathroom: toothpaste, toothbrushes, deodorant in the medicine cabinet, two-in-one shampoo and conditioner and an austere-looking bar of brown soap in the shower stall. There are a few folded towels in the cupboard, but they're cheap ones and he doesn't have any washcloths or hand towels. Strictly the necessities.

He doesn't have a lot of grooming products or shampoo bottles, which makes sense for someone who must have traveled with very little luggage and gone days or weeks without running water in the course of his job. There's only one prescription, chloroquine, for malaria, but it's three years out of date. In the back of the cupboard is a six-pack of Durex condoms and a small pink zippered case with some makeup, women's deodorant, and a couple of Tampax in it.

The girlfriend had been off and on, more off recently.

Roly follows me into the bedroom. It's like a monk's cell, just a queen-size bed with white sheets and a white-covered comforter and a small bedside lamp and table. The books stacked on the bedside table are a mix of nonfiction about global politics, history, and biography, and a couple of spy novels and short story collections. The bookcase against one wall has a similar mix. There's a framed photograph on top of a white-haired woman in a royal-blue wool cape, standing in front of what looks like a church, smiling broadly. There's something about her face that I like, a bravado, a twinkle, an irreverence. Another photograph shows Treacy sitting on a bench next to a woman whom I recognize as Abena Tekle. They're grinning and holding giant sandwiches. I study his face. I can see the resemblance to the woman in blue around his eyes. Despite the goofy pose, there's something sensitive and serious about his face.

"That's his mam, I'd say," Roly says, pointing to the picture of the woman in the blue cape. "The one who died. Stella Treacy."

The bedside-table drawer has tissues, over-the-counter sleeping pills, a bottle of melatonin prescribed to Gabriel Treacy, a ten-pack of earplugs, and a black sleep mask. "Frequent traveler," I say. "He's used to trying to fall asleep on planes. Or he had trouble sleeping."

"That's what I thought, too," Roly says. "That melatonin stuff's very good now. I got a prescription for it last year."

"You don't need a prescription in the States," I tell him. "You can get it at the supermarket."

"Well sure, you're all pill poppers over there, aren't you?" He raises his eyebrows judgmentally.

The other bedroom is a home office. There's a monitor on a simple desk, but its cord isn't attached to anything, and the drawers are filled with neatly packaged office supplies. There's a file of bills, which I take a look at, but Gabriel Treacy's financial life doesn't look terribly complicated. He had direct debit set up for his phone bill, rent, life insurance, credit card bill. I write down all the names. A marked file folder holds a couple of bank statements for accounts in his name and the name of Stella Treacy, and there's a box labeled "Mam. Estate" that contains documents, most on the letterhead of a lawyer named Noel Thomason in Sixmilebridge, related to settling his mother's estate last year.

I take a picture of the letterhead with my phone. We'll need to check in with the lawyer and see who Treacy named as the beneficiary of his will.

"That must be 'N,'" I say, explaining to Roly about the to-do list in the motel room. "Legal implications" must refer to something about the estate. "Gill" is probably the boss, and I still need to figure out what "H. T." refers to.

Roly and I look through it all but there's nothing that raises any alarms for me, no big debts that I can see, no sketchy corporations, no large deposits or withdrawals from any of the accounts over the last year.

And still no electronics. No laptop, no backup phone, no iPad linked to his accounts, no handy list of passwords. There's a turntable on a table in the corner, and a stack of vinyl records in the slots beneath. "Funny, isn't it, how the young ones are going back to records?" Roly says. "When Cecelia asked for a record player for her Christmas, I couldn't believe it. What's he got, then?"

I flip through. "Beatles, REM, Rolling Stones, classical, some trad groups, something called *The Best of Rabab*," with a description on the back describing the rabab as one of the national instruments of Afghanistan.

We finish up in the kitchen and living room. The kitchen is nearly empty, the fridge actually shut off and wiped clean inside, the cupboards containing only a few nonperishable staples.

"You think the fridge means he wasn't planning on coming back?" Roly asks.

I look around at the bare surfaces. "Nah. This guy almost never cooked. I'd say he ate all his meals out. I don't think he ever kept anything more than milk in his fridge and he was probably in the habit of just shutting it off whenever he traveled. Save the planet and so forth. The place is set up for someone who wanted to come and go without any trouble. He doesn't even have any plants."

Finally, I turn to the black-and-white photographs on the walls. They're all signed by the same photographer and I write down the name—Pietro Griselli—in my notebook. A few were obviously taken in the Middle East, minarets of mosques rising in the background, kids playing with a soccer ball in a bombed-out street, a mother smiling at her baby son, cradled in her arms. Another shows a lushly dense jungle landscape behind a small child with a bird perched on his shoulder.

But the largest of them is the one I can't stop staring at. I don't recognize the background immediately, but in the foreground, a woman bows over the body of a young man. From the look of utter anguish on her face, he can only be her son. The young man's face is frosted with soot or char and he's staring at the sky. A five-story apartment building in the background has been nearly destroyed, huge holes in the facade and smoke rising from the background. Like the others, it's signed *Pietro Griselli* at the bottom, and when I get close I can see that someone has written *Gori, 2008* along the bottom.

"Funny, isn't it, hanging something like that in your flat?" Roly says. "Horrible, that is."

I study every detail, drawn in and held by the mother's anguish over her lost child. "Yeah, but it's beautiful in its own way. The love and grief on her face, the composition of it." We stand there for a moment, taking in the photograph. The light shifts a little in the room. Outside, the rain has stopped. I can see a tiny sliver of blue over the river.

"Anything else you want to see?" Roly asks me.

"Nah, not right now." I use my iPhone to record all the rooms.

Roly locks the door again behind us and we go back down to the street.

As I get into his car, I look up at the building and think of the photograph on Gabriel Treacy's wall. For just a second, I imagine a bomb from the sky blowing a hole in this building. I shiver and duck in as Roly says, "Come on, D'arcy, time to go."

11

Abena Tekle lives in an older building in a neighborhood called Dolphin's Barn on the Southside. It's shabbier than Gabriel Treacy's neighborhood, but more vibrant, with a halal butcher and a little shop on the corner, and kids everywhere, walking home from school in their uniforms. Her flat is on the first floor of a redbrick house and she's clearly waiting for us because the door flies open before we can knock.

The woman who answers the door is grieving. Her eyes are red and swollen, and when she shakes my hand I can see that pain has pulled her mouth down, hollowed out her cheeks. She's wearing pajama bottoms and a sweatshirt and she doesn't even try to apologize for not dressing for our visit. The relationship may have been off and on, but Abena Tekle's feelings for Gabriel Treacy are raw and strong.

"My colleague has told me that you didn't know Gabriel was making a trip to the States," I say, once we're sitting on the couch in her flat's living room. It's a bright space, with new curtains in a shade of apple green that matches the cushions on the couch, but there's something about it that feels sparse and unlived in. She has a couch, but no coffee table, and one overfull bookcase next to stacks of books on the ground. It takes me a minute to realize that she only has half the furniture she needs for the space; Gabriel Treacy had the other half. They split their things up and neither one of them had filled in the holes. The realization makes me intensely sad for a moment. "Are you sure he didn't say anything about why he was traveling?"

"No, I just . . ." She looks at Roly. "As I said on the phone, we were no longer romantically involved, but we were friends and sometimes when he traveled for work I would pick up his mail for him. He'd usually at least let me know. But he didn't say a word about a trip to New York." Her accent is slightly English but mostly North American, and I remember that she went to Yale before beginning her career in humanitarian aid work.

"When was the last time you talked to him?"

"We spoke on the thirteenth. I was flying to Germany for a couple of days for work and I rang him while I was driving up to the airport, just to say hello. He'd had a bad head cold the last time we spoke and I just wanted to check on him because I knew that cold weather sometimes aggravated a chronic sinus condition he had. He was better and he said work was busy, they were launching a new anti-hunger project, and he told me to have a good trip. That was it. He didn't say he was going to the States."

"Do you think he would have told you?"

She hesitates. "Ninety percent yes, but I was . . . I was thinking, that if he was seeing someone, if he was going over there to see a woman, and that's why he was going, that would be the only circumstance under which he might not tell me. It was . . . difficult. We were finding our way, figuring out how to be friends and maybe, well, I guess what I mean is that *I* wouldn't have told *him* if I was seeing someone. Do you think that's what it was?"

I can feel Roly perk up. I do too. It's a good explanation. He would have met people from all over the place in his work. Maybe he met a woman from Bay Shore.

"We don't know yet," I say. "Can I ask you, why did you split? I sense you feel very strongly about him." I think of the photograph of her in Treacy's flat. "And that he felt the same."

Tears fill her eyes. "I did, I do . . ." She sobs and looks away to catch her breath. A tendril of dark hair falls in front of her face and she tucks it back up into the bun of curls held in place with a pencil. "But he couldn't . . . he didn't want a normal sort of relationship, he didn't want to stop traveling. I'll be forty next year. If I want to have babies, well, this has to be it, do you see? But he doesn't, didn't want that. It was heartbreaking, but we kept coming back to it, round and round in a loop, and finally I said I couldn't do it anymore." Tears stream down her cheeks for a second and she gets up abruptly and crosses the room to pull a tissue from a box on a table in the entryway.

I wait until she's blown her nose. When she goes to throw the tissue away, she stops in front of the window, holding on to the counter as though she's trying to draw strength from it. "Are you seeing someone new?" I ask her suddenly, taking advantage of her emotion.

She looks around, wide-eyed. This is the part where she realizes I'm not 100 percent on her side, that if there's something to find, I'm going to try to find it. "No, not really," she stammers. "A few dinners out, here and there, but nothing serious."

"Anyone who's serious about you? Maybe too serious?"

She looks at Roly. I've turned this conversation into something else and because he's not me, she sees him as her ally now, because he's the only other person in the room. That's not a bad dynamic for an interview. "You don't think someone from here . . . I thought you said it was a robbery?"

"We just don't know at this stage," Roly says soothingly. "It would just be to check. Why don't you make a list of the names of any fellas you've been out with, just to be sure, yeah?"

She nods and I figure I might as well keep asking the uncomfortable questions now that we're here. "Did Gabriel ever have a problem with substance abuse?" I ask.

Her eyes narrow a little. "No, I mean, when you're in that world, in crisis spots, there's a certain amount of self-medicating. Sometimes, people would use uppers to stay awake, the way soldiers do, you know, if there was something going on. But Gabriel wasn't one who did a lot of that and once he was home I don't think it was a regular thing. He liked his pints, and the odd bit of hash here and there." She gives Roly an apologetic shrug. "But . . . no, not so's it was a problem. As far as I know, anyway."

She's fading, but I have a lot more to ask her. So we need to switch things up a bit. "Would it be okay if I made some tea?" I ask her. "I flew in late last night and I'm starting to feel the lack of sleep."

"Yes," she says gratefully. "I can do it. I'll bring it in."

By the time she brings three mugs and a pitcher of milk into the small living room, she looks a little better. The tea revives me, too, and I wait until she's got a few sips of the hot liquid into her before I say, "I'm sorry, but I need to ask you about Gabriel's scars. How did he get them?"

She looks surprised for a moment, and then I see her realize how we know about them and the image of his naked body swims up before her and she remembers she'll never see him again. I want to hug her, to reach out and take her hands in mine, but I can't do that, so I just wait until she gets ahold of herself and says, "Afghanistan. He was working in Afghanistan and he was abducted for a bit, with some other aid workers, and he was . . . They cut him, as a sort of punishment, I guess. He always downplayed it, saying so many people had it so much worse and . . . well, he was released after a week or two. He felt lucky. He *was* lucky. Afterward, he didn't speak about it much."

I can feel Roly sit up behind me. "When was this?" he asks.

"I think it was 2011," Abena says. "He was working with an aid organization based here in Ireland. They were monitoring the medical situation and he was out in the field with some doctors and a translator, I think, and he was . . . taken. It was some local group who thought they could get some money for them. Not one of the big groups that you hear about. He wasn't held for long. He always brushed it off, said it was something that was happening a lot then. You might remember all of those reporters . . . He was lucky. He was saved . . . in time." We're all quiet for a moment, remembering.

"We looked him up, researched his background," I say. "It never came up in newspapers or anything. Wouldn't that have been quite a big story?"

"Well, they, the organization was negotiating and I think they tried to keep it quiet. That's generally how it's done. It's more common than most people know, for aid workers. I know he said once that they—his work—asked that his name and the names of the other people who were taken, that they be left out of it. I guess it worked, because they were released. Gillian, who he works with at Global Humanity, she could probably tell you some more. He didn't work with her then, but like me, she's been in this world for a long time."

"What did he tell you about it? Did he ever have any contact with the people who took him? Could they have come back to . . . hurt him? Anything like that?"

She looks incredulous. "No, they weren't . . . No. Those men, the group that took him. They're probably dead now. He . . . he didn't like to talk about it," she says. "But when we were first dating—this would have been a year or two after he was released—he did tell me that he'd been imprisoned for a couple of weeks with some other aid workers while he was in the field in Nangarhar Province. Later, I saw the scars and . . . well, of course he had to explain that they'd hurt him. I asked a few questions, but he really . . . It was like there was a wall that came down when you asked about it. I think he had some PTSD. There were things that . . . he didn't like darkness. He always wanted a light on, somewhere in the house. But in general, he didn't want people to know about it, you know? It was like he thought they would stop supporting humanitarian aid work if they thought of the places he'd been as dangerous. And he always said it had been such a short time before they were released, and that he didn't blame the men who had done it. Mostly they were just desperately poor men and boys, victims as much as he was. Most of the people who are abducted are Afghans and I think he somehow felt it diminished their experience, to make a big deal out of Westerners being taken, if you see what I mean."

I make some notes and then Roly says, "Did he have anyone who wished him harm, like, any enemies, people he didn't get along with? Anyone he was afraid of?"

Her eyes are wide. "No, nothing like that. He didn't . . ." She trails off, though, thinking, remembering. "This is . . . I just thought of something. We were in New York a few years back, and we came out of our hotel and there was . . . he must have seen something because he became visibly upset. I asked him what was wrong and he just said he thought he'd recognized someone he'd known once."

"Did you see who it was he was reacting to?"

"No, I tried to ask about it, but I had the sense he just didn't want to talk about it."

Roly and I glance at each other. That's the kind of detail from an interview that can drive you crazy trying to verify. It might mean something. It might not. The only person who knows for sure is dead. "Can you tell us more about him, where he was born, his family life?" I ask her.

"Sure, he . . . he was raised in a little town in County Clare. Six-milebridge. It's a small place. His mother was a lovely woman. She died of cancer a year ago. It was hard on Gabriel. I wondered if it might make him more . . . settled, you know. I still wonder if . . . given time, it might have. He was very good to her. He visited frequently when he was home, and when she was dying, we practically lived down there."

"His father wasn't on the scene?"

"Oh no. Never. Stella was a single mum. She had Gabriel without being married. She was quite proud of it."

"Did Gabriel know who his father was?" Roly asks.

She hesitates. "When we were first dating, he told me that he didn't know, that his mother refused to tell him. But later, when I knew him better, I had the sense that maybe he had his suspicions. I wondered if there was shame around it, that maybe his father was married or wasn't very nice or . . . Well, I wondered. We were very close, but Gabriel kept those two things—Afghanistan and his father—locked up tight."

I ask, "Do you know what kind of arrangements Gabriel had made in the event of his death? We found some papers from a lawyer . . . a solicitor, I mean, in Sixmilebridge, who seemed to have handled his mother's estate. Noel Thomason?"

She nods. "Noel was their solicitor and a family friend. He handled things when Stella died, selling the house and so forth, and he made Gabriel's will. He—Gabriel, that is—told me once that Noel had everything, in case something happened to him. I think Stella must have been the beneficiary, but I don't know if he changed his will after her death. I'm sorry. Noel will know." She's getting tired. The grief has receded a bit while she's been talking, but it's about to come roaring back.

"How about email accounts?" Roly asks her.

"Well, he had a work one," she says. "And then his personal account was a Gmail one. It was GabrielTreacy752. I don't think he had any other ones, though there may have been some old accounts."

"Do you know his password to that account?" I ask her. "It would save us a lot of time and help us find whoever did this."

"He changed it a lot," she says. "Because he traveled so much and it got hacked a few times. He was a little paranoid. He had me check it for him once, when we were traveling and his phone was stolen. At that point the password was *Sixmilebridge,* but I'm pretty sure he changed it after that."

"Gabriel grew up in Sixmilebridge, went to school there?" I ask. She nods. "What about college? University?"

"He went to the University of Bristol and studied international relations. I think he wanted to get out into the world for a bit but when he was finished and had started working abroad, he became more fond of Ireland, started coming back more and more. And then, in

2013, he got the job with Global Humanity and took on a role that had him in Dublin more. As it turned out, he still traveled quite a lot." She frowns. "But in 2015 he bought the apartment and we decided to live together. Stella got sick right around then."

"Where did you grow up?" I ask her. I'm wondering if she and Gabriel Treacy had a sense of dislocation in common.

"Between Addis Ababa and New York. My father was an economist who did work for the UN, and we left Ethiopia when I was five. We went back a few times to live, then came back to New York." She smiles as though she knows what I'm thinking. "Gabriel and I had such different childhoods, but we both felt like exiles in a certain way. It's hard to explain. It was a point of connection, I think."

"Where did you meet?" I can see her gathering her strength for the memory.

"In South Africa. This was 2014. I was working for UNICEF and we hired Global Humanity to run a project. We, I guess we were attracted to each other right away, but this life . . ." She holds her hands out at her sides. "It's hard, relationships, when you do what we do, they're hard. He's, he was so good at what he did. They needed him." She starts crying again. "That's what I keep thinking, how he won't be there for all the people who need him."

"I'm so sorry to have to ask," I say, "but when we release the body . . . it sounds like there isn't a next of kin. Would you . . . ?"

"Of course, of course I will."

We wait until she has hold of herself again to say goodbye.

12

"What do you think of that stuff about him being kidnapped in Afghanistan?" I ask Roly as we head back down to the street. "It seems so weird that it wasn't in the news at all, you know?"

"I'd say it's more common than you'd think. There was an Irish lad kidnapped in Iraq a few years ago and I remember they didn't give out his name right away," he says. He takes out his phone. "I've a good contact at the Department of Foreign Affairs. That's like your State Department. Let me see if I can get something from her."

We stop in the foyer of the block of flats and he dials and waits for voice mail. "Ah, Greta," he says after a few seconds. "Roly Byrne here. Myself and a colleague are looking into something and we have a question for you about a kidnapping in Afghanistan, 2011. Fella named Gabriel Treacy. Anyway, give me a ring, will ya, soon as you can?" He puts the phone back in his pocket.

"Now, that rain's cleared right out," Roly says once we're down on the street again. "It's going to be lovely tomorrow, I'd say." He's right. The rain clouds have been swept away and replaced by a blue-gray sky and even a little sun.

"That's good for our trip. I was worried about being stuck inside bed-and-breakfasts all over Ireland with two teenagers."

Roly grimaces. "I've been there," he says. "Majorca, 2015. Let's leave the car and walk along the canal over to Clanbrassil Street. We can get a takeaway before we stop to see her."

The canal is still, a mirror reflecting the swiftly changing sky. We walk in silence for a bit and then Roly says, "I'll get one of my lads to check out the dating sites, see if he was on any of 'em."

"Yeah, that's a good theory. We had witnesses say they saw a woman running away from the marina the night Treacy was killed. We wondered if someone set him up, if meeting him was a trap for a robbery, something like that. That's good, Roly. And that might explain the suddenness, too, right? He was chatting with a woman and she said, 'Hey, you should come to Long Island next week.'"

"It's awful tricky sometimes, those sites. If we can find his laptop, that's the best way. We'll have a look, though."

"Thanks, Roly. You going to get into trouble using resources for my case?"

"Not a chance. I'm 'liaising with an international law enforcement professional.' They love that kind of thing." He winks at me. "I've got a new lad on my team. He's a fuckin' wizard at the online stuff. Be good practice for him, looking for the dating sites. Ah, it really is lovely now, isn't it?" He sighs up at the blue sky, the improving day.

Clanbrassil Street is busy with cars and people darting in and out of takeaway places for lunch. We get doner kebab and eat it standing on the street. "Isn't Clanbrassil Street where Leopold Bloom was born?" I ask Roly.

"You mean your man from the book? Don't know, to be honest. We were supposed to read it in school, like, but I was a great one for pretending I'd read things I hadn't." He winks at me and makes a ball out of the foil from his kebab. "You'll have to ask your fella. I bet he did all his assignments."

The offices of Global Humanity are on the third floor of a brick building next to a butcher shop. Roly presses the buzzer and announces himself, and a woman's voice on the intercom says, "Come on up, Detective. Third floor."

Gillian Gleeson meets us on the landing, waving a file folder at us as though we might not see her otherwise. I recognize her from her picture on the organization's website. She's wearing jeans and a green velvet blazer and motorcycle boots, her reddish-brown glasses the same shade as her hair. Behind them, her eyes are pink-rimmed, but unlike Abena Tekle, she's making an effort to pretend she's not grieving. "Come in, come in," she says. "I'm still . . . I just can't believe it. I let most of the staff stay home. But I don't know what else to do with myself. Let's sit in the conference room. Do you want tea or anything?"

"Only if you do," I say. I'm still well caffeinated from the cup at Abena Tekle's flat, but Roly looks hopeful.

"Oh, I do. That's the thing about something like this, isn't it, you want tea, you want to make it. It's something to do with your hands. Hang on and I'll be in with it once it's reached the boil."

She does it right, a tray and china cups and real milk and a teapot. Roly looks delighted with his steaming cup, and I wait until Gillian Gleeson has had a long grateful sip and added a second spoonful of sugar before I say, "I'm so sorry for your loss, Ms. Gleeson. As you know, we're hoping to get some more information about why Mr. Treacy was in the States, and on Long Island in particular."

"Well, I'm not sure I can help you with that. He asked me for some holiday time. I had no problem with it. He never took leave or holidays. He had months and months accrued. He asked if he could take a week and I said of course. He didn't say where he was going, which was a bit odd I suppose, but I assumed he and Abena were going somewhere, that maybe they were going to try again, somewhere warm, I hoped, and maybe he didn't want to jinx it by telling me. He'd been a bit sad since his mother died last year."

"So he didn't say anything about going to the States?"

"No, not a word. I was shocked when I heard. The whole thing, I mean, his death, but also that he was . . . over there. It was so disorienting."

"Can you tell me a bit about his work life?" I ask her. "What kinds of things did he do here? What was his expertise?"

"I thought you might want his CV," she says, pushing a manila file folder across the table. "I found it in his personnel file and made a copy. You can read for yourself. It's current as of five years ago, when he came to work for us. But I'm happy to give you a sense of what he did for us. We're a nongovernmental organization, a nonprofit focused on humanitarian aid. We raise funds from a variety of sources and we do lobbying on humanitarian issues, but we also provide direct support in countries experiencing disaster and/or migration and refugee crises." Her little speech has a practiced feel. She's repeated these words many, many times.

"He worked in a variety of roles—his real talent was in logistics management. He was very good at figuring out how to move large quantities of food or water or medical supplies. He was very good at logistics within refugee camps, setting up the structures to deliver medical care. That's what he did for Irish Aid and the UN. This is terrible, but the first thing I thought was of how hard it will be to replace him. He's saved lives, too many to count, by figuring out how to get lifesaving things to the places they needed to be. Then I thought of us, of him, of how much I'll miss him myself. We were partners, but we were friends, too." She starts to get emotional, but hauls herself back, stopping for a moment and using her breathing to slow her emotional response. I know exactly what she's doing. I do it myself.

I open the folder to give her a moment and glance at the résumé. "We know from Abena about Gabriel's kidnapping in 2011. Was it something he talked about with you?"

The look that comes across her face is so complicated, so troubled, that I immediately lean forward, waiting for whatever she's going to say.

"Ah, Afghanistan. Gabriel didn't like people bringing it up. I'd heard some rumors about it, within the community, but . . . it's hard to explain. It sometimes goes with the territory and those of us who work in international humanitarian aid, well . . . we don't want to focus too much on it. For a lot of reasons. One is that you don't want to give the kidnappers publicity, the other is that it's better if the workers' names are kept out of it. If they think they have someone prominent, well . . . you remember what happened to some of the reporters who were taken, don't you? And we, well, you don't want to center Western experience, if that makes sense. Most of the people who are killed and abducted are local people working for our organizations, but it's the Westerners whose stories make the news. So, yeah, he didn't talk about it, I didn't really hear any details, but that was normal in our . . . in the aid community."

"We wondered why it wasn't in the newspapers," I say. "That explains it."

"Right, so, it's better to keep it quiet, let the organizations and the governments negotiate and pay sometimes if they need to. Most people are released quickly, as Gabriel was. You don't think it had anything to do with his death, though, do you?" She looks genuinely shocked at the possibility.

"No, but we're just trying to get a picture of him. Did he ever talk to you about being hurt while he was in captivity?"

She starts to speak, then stops and says, "I saw the scars once. We were in the field, and his shirt got . . . covered in grease, and he had to change it, and I saw the scars. I didn't say anything of course. He never talked about it. You couldn't go there with him. Really. If you went anywhere near it, he just shut down completely."

Roly and I glance at each other. "Can you think of anyone who might have wanted to harm him? I imagine that sometimes people in these places, where there's war or conflict, sometimes people don't like what you're doing. Was there anyone in particular who might have had a problem with Gabriel?"

She looks surprised but considers it. "Well, yes, you're right. They . . . there are people who don't like the work we're doing. But it's not personal, if you see what I mean. And these are mostly people who . . . well, they'll never leave the places where Gabriel met them, you know? We're mostly talking about local militias, made up of starving people, desperate people, sometimes very brutal people, but people without resources. The idea that someone might have followed him, to New York, well, it's . . . I suppose it's possible, but it doesn't really make any sense to me."

"He was working for CAREIreland in 2011. Do you know who his supervisor was there?"

"As far as I know the current CEO, Mary Gilroy, was there then. Here, I'll get her details for you." She goes over to a desktop computer, finds the information, and writes it down on a piece of paper.

"Okay, thanks," I say, taking it and tucking it into my pocket. "What about Abena? What was your sense of their relationship? You said you thought they might be trying to make the relationship work again. Did he say something to you to make you think that?"

"No, I was just assuming. Abena's brilliant and lovely. To be honest I thought he was a colossal eejit for not marrying her, since that's what she wanted, but I also understood. I'm not married. I don't have children. I probably never will. You need to be ready to leave when there's a place that needs you. That doesn't go with a normal sort of family life."

"But they were still close?"

"Seemed that way. He still talked about her all the time."

"She wondered if maybe he'd gone to the US to visit someone he was seeing. Did you have any inkling he had a romance going?"

"He didn't say anything to me." Her glance slides away, though. "Maybe . . ."

"What?"

"I don't know. I had the sense there was something. To be honest, I was worried he was applying for other jobs. I thought . . . There were phone calls, that he took downstairs rather than up here in the offices. It struck me as odd."

"On his cell phone?" I ask quickly.

"Yes."

"So why did you think he was applying for other jobs?" The phone calls don't explain the specificity with which she mentioned he was looking for another job.

She looks embarrassed, then says, "This was end of last year, November, maybe. I walked behind his desk and there was a page up on his computer. It was an organization that works in some of the same spaces we do. MVTW. Medical Volunteers for the World. It's in New York. Perhaps he was interviewing with them?" She tries but can't keep a little twist of shame from crossing her lips. I understand. She's mad at him; she sees it as a betrayal, and at the same time, she feels guilty for thinking that.

"Where's that computer?" I ask. "We'd like to see it."

"I assume he took it with him," she says. "It's a laptop and he usually traveled with it. Was it not with his luggage?"

I don't answer. "Did you have a backup system, anywhere we could see what he searched for, his emails?"

She rolls her eyes. "The backup system. We had so many issues with it. Gabriel thought our security wasn't strong enough, so he insisted we get a new system with some sort of . . ." She waves her hand. "Encryption. And it banjaxed the whole system and we had to start over. I was furious. I hate all this technology stuff in any case, and it slowed us down at a point that we really couldn't afford to be slowed down. Anyways, we had a new system. All organization emails are backed up on some server thingy," she says. "I'm sorry I don't really know the details. Because he traveled so much, he did a lot on the phone and his laptop." She writes down his email address on a piece of paper. "I believe he also had a personal Gmail account."

"When was this? That he was worried about security?"

"Ah, right around the first of the year, I'd say. He thought someone had attempted to hack into our server and he wanted to make sure we were all buttoned up. He had some fella in to look at everything and they got a new security yoke or added something onto it. I don't know. To be honest, I thought he was a bit mad about it all."

I study her face. She's nervous, embarrassed about something. "He said he thought someone had tried to hack in?"

"Well, yes, but you know . . . I think people are always trying to hack into email and get passwords. He was obsessed with it. I thought maybe it was the break-up with Abena. He hadn't been sleeping well, and I think he'd got a bit paranoid, to be honest."

"Paranoid?"

She looks away and waves her hand dismissively. "He must have read something or watched a film. He thought someone was following him, had me look out the window to see if anyone was on the street. Of course, there were loads of people on the street. It was the lunch hour on a weekday. He laughed about it later."

Roly's studying his phone. He pockets it and stands up. "I'll be sending someone around," he says. "To try to see what we can find on the server."

Gillian Gleeson swallows. "Are you certain that's necessary? I really don't think it was anything serious. Gabriel was always quite cautious about those things."

"We'll just have a look," he says. "I'll send someone. It won't be much of an inconvenience to youse."

She looks away. "Well . . . all right."

Suddenly, I remember the list next to Gabriel Treacy's bed in the motel room. *Gill account.* I can't think of a way to ask her about it now that won't put her on her guard. We'll have to see if there's anything in the backups and go from there.

"Is there anything else you can tell us about Gabriel that we should know?" I ask her.

There's a sound, somewhere in the building. She looks up at me with an expression of wariness. "I thought it was just a random crime," she says. "He wasn't . . . targeted, was he?"

"We think it probably was random, but it's our job to make sure.

Can you think of any reason he *might* have been targeted? Anyone who had a problem with him?"

The look that comes over her face is complicated. There's affection there, resentment, sorrow. "Not Gabriel," she says. "Gabriel was a saint."

13

....

"My contact messaged me while we were up there," Roly says once we're outside. "She can meet us in Iveagh Gardens in thirty minutes. That okay with you?"

I check my phone. It's three, just about when I said I'd be back to Conor's. "Yeah, let's do it. She might have something good. I'm just going to try his old boss now." I dial the number Gillian Gleeson gave me for CAREIreland and ask for Mary Gilroy. When she answers, I explain who I am and what I want. She's already heard about Gabriel's death, but she doesn't waste my time asking questions.

"I'm afraid I don't have much to add," she says. "We were notified that Gabriel and some other aid workers had failed to arrive at the camp when they were scheduled to arrive, and we notified Foreign Affairs, Foreign and Commonwealth, the State Department, all the agencies, the Defense Department. Negotiations, whatever that meant, were ongoing and then we heard that they'd been freed. I guess some American soldiers came upon the house where they were being held and rescued them. We were grateful. The outcome in these situations isn't always . . . a positive one."

I thank her. Roly hails a cab and it drops us on Harcourt Street.

"She said she'd meet us by the roses," Roly said. "All very hush-hush." But when we get there, the gray-haired woman sitting on a bench and scrolling through her phone catches sight of us and stands up, waving as though she doesn't care who sees us.

"Hiya, Roly," she says. "How are you?"

"Fine, Greta. Yourself? Good, yeah? This is Maggie D'arcy. She's over from the States investigating Treacy's death. Maggie, Greta here has been with Foreign Affairs for what, twenty years?" He doesn't give me her last name. Greta may officially work for Foreign Affairs, but I'm betting she's done a few turns for whatever the Irish version of the CIA is.

"Thanks for making me feel ancient." She smiles and shakes my hand. "It's nice to meet you. Mind if we walk? I like to get a little bit of exercise when I can." We fall in, three across on the wide path, and she says, "I was working in the political division in 2011. I can confirm that he was kidnapped in Nangarhar Province, Afghanistan. I can't tell you too much else."

"Did you know he was tortured during his time in captivity?"

She turns to look at me, her greenish eyes alert. "Not for certain, but there were rumors."

I say, "Both his ex-girlfriend and his boss said that the kidnappings of aid workers are something that happens fairly frequently, that abductees' names are kept out of the press. Is that true?"

"Yes, I suppose it is. These things are very delicate. There are times it's better to release the name, sometimes it's better not to. It depends on a number of factors. But yes, in this case, there were certain negotiations going on and they wanted to keep it quiet to see if they could arrange something."

We stop to look at a bank of unbloomed rosebushes and Roly says,

"Do you think that his experience could have had anything to do with his death?"

She looks at him a bit incredulously. "I don't know how."

"The people who . . . who took him wouldn't have come after him, right?"

"I wouldn't think so. There was . . ." She trails off, and I can see her thinking, deciding whether to tell us whatever it is that's occurred to her. "There were some strange things about that one, but . . . not that." A young guy with a baby strapped to his chest and a toddler in a stroller comes down the path, keeping up one end of a conversation with the toddler about whether they'll be buying more packets of crisps at the shop. We step out of the way to let him pass. "How old are yours now, Roly?" Greta asks. "They must be getting big."

Roly smiles, full of pride. "Yeah, the girls are seventeen and fifteen and the boys are ten and twelve."

"God, time passes, doesn't it?"

"What do you mean, there were strange things?" I ask her, once I've waited what feels like the appropriate number of seconds for us to think about children growing older and the passage of time. "About the kidnapping?"

She exchanges a glance with Roly that I can't quite read. "No, about how they were released. Look, this is confidential, okay?" She gets a nod from Roly before going on. "There was a lot of interest from a Clare TD. He was well-connected, and it got a lot of attention."

"TD's for Teachta Dála, like your congressmen," Roly explains to me.

"Gabriel Treacy was from Clare," I say. "I assume that's why?" She nods. "What's this TD's name?"

"Jonathan Murray," she says. Roly makes a little sound.

"What?" I ask him.

"Just, they're a big family down there, the Murrays. His father it was, I think, he was the TD for a long time, twenty years. Now it's the son, is that right, Greta?"

"That's right. The son was quite forceful about us negotiating for Treacy's release, but it was complicated. I'm not actually sure why. I'll see if I can find out anything else, given this development."

"Thanks for your help," I say. "I'd like to solve this one if I can. He seems like he did a lot of good for a lot of people around the world."

She hesitates, stopping to look at another bank of rosebushes. "I wondered," she starts. "Well, it might make sense for you to look to some of your own, well, institutions. I always thought there was something funny about the way they were released. It was sudden. There was some kind of involvement from the US military, someone told me it seemed irregular, but you know, we were just glad they were alive." Her face is hard to figure out. She's pressed her lips together in a disapproving way, but her eyes are wounded, hurt.

"You can't tell me who the other captives were?"

"I don't know, but I'm betting there was an American amongst them." She raises her eyes. "We . . . we were working on it, I believe. But one day, we heard they'd been freed, and well, it was all a bit unclear." A slight look of indignation comes across her face. Now I understand. The Americans had been working secretly to free them; no one had told the Irish diplomats.

She's done. "I'm sorry I don't have anything else for you."

"No, that's very helpful," I say. "Thank you so much."

"Yeah, thanks, Greta," Roly says.

"Ah, I forgot to tell you," she says, looking at Roly. "We got a press inquiry about this case. That's why I rang you back so fast. Reporter from the *Independent* is looking into this and he got the word somehow about the kidnapping."

My stomach drops. "Was it Stephen Hines?" Hines is a reporter whom I tangled with during the investigation into my cousin Erin's case last year.

She nods. "Yes, it was. Ah, well, I've got to get back. Roly, I'll be back to you if I hear anything." She gives him a little salute and peels off, heading for the Harcourt Street exit.

"What did you think about that?" I ask Roly. "Why is Stephen Hines so interested in this case?"

"I'm betting he's got a news alert set up with your name," he says. "When it came up you were the investigating officer over there in the States, he couldn't help himself."

"You're probably right. I was hoping she'd have something more definitive for us. Well, maybe she'll find something more."

We walk toward the exit, past a huge statue of a seated man.

"Who's Lord Ardilaun then?" I ask Roly, reading the carved words beneath.

"Ah, now *that* I can tell you," Roly says.

"So you did pay attention in school once in a while."

"No, but Lord Ardilaun was the Guinness fella." He taps the side of his head and I burst out laughing. We get a cab back to his car and drive through rush-hour traffic toward Conor's.

"I'm going to call the lawyer and see what he's got for me," I tell Roly. "You can have your people look at the server at Global Humanity? And see about the Gmail account?"

"Yeah," Roly says. "We'll let you know when we've got access to his emails."

"Okay, thanks. I'll write up my notes and send them to my team.

I'm going to have Berta and Dave see what they can find out about the kidnapping from our military contacts. We may need to have Abena Tekle and Gillian Gleeson do formal statements at some point. I guess we can leave tomorrow and I can always come back if I need to. What do you think, Roly?"

He takes a deep breath and glances over at me. "I think you're doing the right thing, doing your due diligence over here, D'arcy, but it seems to me like this fella was robbed while he was out there having a slash on the beach or whatever. The kidnapping thing sounds awful, yeah, and like you, I want to know why he went to Long Island." He runs a hand over his forehead. "We've got to clean up these loose ends, no question there, but the idea that someone followed him over there from here . . . I'm not feeling it. I think we're gonna find out that he had a girlfriend on Long Island, maybe they'd been chatting and decided to meet in person. He goes over there, things don't go as well as he'd hoped. He's out on the beach on his way home, after she tells him that she doesn't think it's going to work out, and your particular brand of local criminal sees him there, decides to rob him. He must have had his rucksack with him, so it would have looked good to your man with the gun."

When he says it like that, it sounds so plausible, I can't believe I was considering anything else. "You're right, Roly. That's probably it. I'll set a few things in motion tomorrow morning and then we'll just have to see. But you're right. Conor and the kids and I can leave tomorrow and I'll be reachable if anything comes up."

It's almost four-thirty by the time we pull up in front of Conor's. "Have fun. I can't wait to hear about the holiday. Hope it's good craic."

"Yeah," I say. "I'll get you a souvenir." I'm forcing myself to be enthusiastic. I can hear it and I know Roly can, too.

He winks at me. "I'd love one of them stuffed leprechauns. And a pair of socks from the Blarney Stone. See ya, D'arcy."

I stand in the driveway for a minute and watch him go. I'm about to turn and go inside when I get that feeling again of being under surveillance, the same feeling I had when I was on the beach with Dave. But when I look up and down the street, there's no one there, just the breeze ruffling the branches of the cherry trees, which I suddenly realize are in full, glorious bloom, each flowering tip reaching out to the wide blue sky above.

14

We drive out of Dublin the next morning, following the Grand Canal and then heading southwest, through big industrial estates and into the flatter middle of Ireland, down through Portlaoise to Kildare along the M7. It's just motorway, long stretches of road with towns off to the sides, and then suddenly we're in the wide plain of the Curragh, a flat expanse of vibrant green that seems to go on forever, reaching out to hills and lines of trees in the distance. It feels like Kansas to me, wide and smooth, but with a different color palette, all lime and grass greens rather than golden and brown and red.

The farther we get from Dublin, the more relaxed I feel. There's no Jay Cooney here. No Anthony Pugh. No school stress for Lilly. No house to tidy and refrigerator to fill and case paperwork to file. I cleaned up a few last details on Gabriel Treacy's case this morning, left messages for Treacy's former bosses, the lawyer in Sixmilebridge, and at Medical Volunteers for the World in New York to see if Treacy had been in touch with them. Then I typed up notes from my conversations with Abena Tekle and Gillian Gleeson, and called Dave just before we left, getting him out of bed at five a.m. his time.

"We won't have autopsy or firearms division results for a few days," he said once I told him about the interviews. "I can get Berta on to the kidnapping thing. Wow, that's kind of crazy, huh?" I remembered Dave telling me that one of his fears during his time in Afghanistan had been being taken.

"Yeah. Did you know any aid workers when you were there?"

"Not really. I was there early on, and it wasn't safe for the aid workers yet. My second tour there were a few. Most of them hired their own security, though." As he talks, I realize how little I know about what happened in Afghanistan for all those years, what's still happening. I couldn't tell you what the current state of the war is if my life depended on it.

"What was it like there? I have this image of a desert, sun beating down on you."

"It was fucking cold a lot of the time. That's what I remember. It was pretty, too, though. I didn't expect that. Up north? It was really green out in the country, like Ireland or something. Ha! That's funny."

"Well, we'll see what Berta finds. Any video surveillance at the motel?"

"Oh yeah. I was going to tell you. We have the white SUV that Mr. Ahmed thought he saw parked in the lot when Treacy was staying there. It pulled into a spot for about ten minutes on the sixteenth and then pulled out again. Probably just someone who needed to make a phone call, but we've got a plate so we can track it down."

"Great, thanks, Dave. We're heading off on our road trip. But I'll have my phone, so call if anything comes up."

"You have fun and try to unplug," he says. "It may be a couple days for the firearms evidence to come in. I don't think this thing is gonna move much."

"Alicia bugging you?"

"Not too much. Don't worry. I can handle her. Go."

The day is bright and calm, and now that the rain has stopped, I can see that while it's still winter at home, in Ireland the roots of the plants and trees have been busy under the soil. The grass is a vivid, alive sea green; daffodils and egg yolk–yellow gorse are blooming in the fields and along the roads.

In the distance, we can see the white forms of sheep at pasture. "It'll be lambing season soon," Conor tells us. "My da's expecting a big crop this year. Adrien, you'll be needed soon enough." He grins at his son in the rearview mirror. "Adrien's an old hand at putting his hand up a sheep's backside, aren't you?"

Adrien gives Conor a sarcastic face back in the mirror. "I'll never be as good as you," he says, with a bit of an edge. He's grown about four inches since I first met him last spring, and he reminds me of a puppy, his big feet and long legs not yet comfortably integrated with the rest of his body. His face doesn't quite make sense yet; you can see both the kid he was and the adult he'll become. Lilly's puberty growth spurt was a few years ago and she came through it with grace. Adrien's not having such an easy time of it and he swings between sweetness and sarcasm. His mother is dating a French guy he doesn't like, and Conor has told me Bláithín has asked if Adrien can live with him more than 50 percent of the time so she can spend more time in France.

I don't look over at Conor. We had talked about whether we should visit his parents on our trip and decided it was too soon, that it might be confusing for the kids, especially Lilly, who has an extremely complicated relationship with her only living grandparents now. We decided not to do it this trip, but I can't tell how he really feels about it.

Another hour and we're in Cashel, in County Tipperary. We get a pub lunch at a place someone tells us is one of the oldest pubs in Ireland. I've been craving fish and chips and even though Conor tells me it won't be good this far from the coast, I order it and devour every crispy bit. I give Conor a tiny taste and he revises his opinion. "Not bad, but when we get to Galway, you'll know what real fish and chips taste like."

When we're done, we decide to play tourists and hike up a steep hill to the collection of buildings that make up the Rock of Cashel. Conor's been, but not for a long time, and Adrien's never seen it. When Conor says, "I can't believe I've never brought you," Adrien replies, "No! It's not possible, the site of some kind of horrible battle you haven't brought me to?" and Lilly laughs, causing my heart to soar unreasonably. If making fun of Conor improves Lilly's mood, I'm willing to throw him under the bus.

"Adrien, my dad was a Civil War history buff," I tell him. "I've been to every battlefield there is, so I feel your pain."

There's a thirteenth-century round tower up on the site, along with the cavernous ruins of Cormac's Chapel, and a cemetery outside, with views all around the site, down into a valley stretching all the way to distant hills. Lilly and Adrien wander off to explore the cathedral and Conor and I walk outside to stand among the gravestones and look out across the broad green sweep of fields. I have the sense of being the lord of the castle; I can see for miles and miles in every direction, the land billowing around me. The sky is clear and blindingly bright blue, not a single cloud to obscure it. I turn my face to the sun, feeling its gathering strength, and realize I feel calmer and more peaceful than I have in months.

"This is pretty," I say.

"It's called the Golden Vale," Conor tells me. "There's a story that long ago, the devil and Saint Patrick were having a battle in those mountains there in the distance, and it was a great battle with the devil leaping around, waving his tail, and Saint Patrick trying to catch him, and the devil began to be afraid that he'd be caught."

"Patrick was an athlete, then?" I ask him. "Seems like it would be hard to catch the devil."

"Oh yeah. Patrick was really fit, did his lunges every day." He winks at me. "And the devil could see that, so he bit off a piece of the mountain, creating an escape route for himself, but he was furious about Saint Patrick chasing him off, so he spat out the piece of rock he'd bit off and it landed right here, in the Tipperary plains. That's where the Rock of Cashel came from."

"So we're basically sitting in the middle of a giant pool of the devil's saliva?"

He grins. "Yeah, lovely."

"Who lived in this castle, anyway?"

"The high kings of Munster. Then they gave it to the church and that's when the cathedral was built. I think it's got the oldest stairs in Ireland."

"Now *there's* a claim to fame."

"Mmmm. The high kings built it here so they could see armies approaching for miles. Do you want me to tell you about the Sack of Cashel? It's quite grim, really, one of the worst atrocities of Irish history." He raises his eyebrows and wiggles them just a little. Conor has a huge store of distant and especially grim historical facts. He knows I love them.

"Ooooh, you know I want to hear about it now."

"Well, in the 1640s, there were these wars going on called the Irish Confederate Wars. They were between Irish Catholics, aligned with English Catholics, and on the other side, English and Scottish settlers. They were fighting over who would rule Ireland, of course, but it was complicated by the English Civil Wars, and it's sorta hard to keep track of the alliances. Anyway, they'd been fighting and then in 1647 this fella named Murrough O'Brien, the baron of Inchiquin, who was aligned with the English Parliamentarians, stormed this place right here. People from the village had taken refuge up here after some earlier raids. It seemed defensible and the Irish Confederate forces had quite a few companies here to protect the rock. But in the end Inchiquin's forces made it through. They slaughtered everyone they could, including priests and civilians, and even when the remaining men surrendered by throwing their swords down, the invading army killed them all."

"Bastards."

"Yeah. Baron Inchiquin, he was a bastard, all right."

"How grim. It's hard to imagine it on a day like today," I say. We look up to see Lilly and Adrien coming toward us.

"Come see this cool sculpture we found," Lilly tells us. "Adrien saw it." We follow them back into the skeleton of the church and they point to a relief high up on the wall. It takes a minute to make it out: a dragon, with an arm sticking out of its mouth.

"Is that a dragon just snacking on a guy's arm?" I ask.

"Yes," Adrien says. "We asked someone and he said they don't quite know what it means."

"I think it was a warning," Conor says. "'Don't commit any sins, or you'll be eaten by a dragon!' Remember that, Lilly."

"I will." She grins, her eyes crackling with humor, her smile true and full.

"Lilly seems happy today," I say, once she's gone off to find the restroom and Adrien has gone outside to explore a bit more before we leave. "I'm so glad we got out of town."

"I know," Conor says. "She seems lighter, doesn't she?"

I look up at him and smile. "That's what Marty said about me. When he encouraged me to come on the trip, he said that I seemed lighter in November, when you were visiting, and that I needed to get some of that lightness back."

"Well, I'm glad he didn't say you seemed more depressed when I was around."

"Never." I lean into him and he puts his arm around me. "I'm really glad we're here."

"Me too. I'm happy you were able to leave the case alone for a bit." He must sense the little spark of defensiveness I feel. "I don't mean I don't want you to do your job, Maggie. You know that. I was just . . . I'm glad we're here too."

"I know what you meant," I say. I look up at him, meeting his eyes, feeling our history there between us, all the years I thought about him, thought I'd never see him again. And now the thing between us is so real, so concrete, and it fills me up with an intense joy that feels barely contained. The land rolls out in front of us toward distant hills, the green fields rippling and unfolding.

"I'm really happy," I say. "You make me happy."

Conor pulls me into his arms and whispers in my ear in a way that thrills me, makes me press myself against him as he kisses my ear. "I love you as much as that dragon loves gobbling down arms."

Back in the car, I keep an eye on Lilly in the rearview mirror, trying to gauge her mood. She's looking out the window as we drive, her eyes on the distant spires and rooftops of the towns we pass. Her cheeks are pink and she has a small, secret smile on her face that makes me think, *It's going to be okay. It's all going to be okay.*

My phone rings while we're driving, the sound shattering the happy silence in the car. I look down to see Berta's number and give Conor an apologetic look as I answer. "Berta? I'm here," I say, turning my body toward the window. "What's up?"

"His carrier came through," she says. "I can send you the list of numbers he called before the trip, but there's something strange. He arrived in New York on the fourteenth, in the afternoon, and made one phone call back to Ireland. It was to the Global Humanity main number, so he may have been checking his voice mail, or he may have spoken to someone there. He then called the motel in Bay Shore. Then a call from a blocked number came into his phone that night." She hesitates.

"Yeah," I say. "What else?"

"Well, that's the strange thing. There's nothing else. Not long after that phone call, the phone was either shut off or, you know, destroyed somehow. It doesn't ping any of the towers near Bay Shore that night, nor on the fifteenth or sixteenth. By the seventeenth, he's dead."

"What the hell?"

"I know. It's possible the phone wasn't working so he just shut it down and used email to communicate."

"Shit. Why would he shut off the phone?"

"Maybe he lost it and the battery ran out. Maybe he bought a cheapo one when he got here. Maybe something was wrong with it. I was thinking. My last iPhone? The touch screen stopped working, so I shut it down and left it in a drawer in my kitchen until I could get a new one. Maybe it was something like that."

"You're probably right, Berta. Thanks. We really need the email account now."

"Okay. I'm looking into the kidnapping thing, but there's nothing I can find in online news archives. I'll keep at it. Sorry to bother you. Dave said you'd want to know."

"Yeah, he's right. Thanks."

I put the phone back in my bag and reach out to rub Conor's shoulder. He smiles. "Everything okay?"

"Yeah. Berta got some phone records but they don't really give us any more information than we had."

"That's weird," Lilly says from the back seat.

"What?" Adrien asks.

"I got a weird text." In the rearview mirror I see her hand her phone over to him.

I turn around to look at them. "What do you mean, a weird text?" I ask.

Adrien holds up the phone. There's a text message from a number I don't recognize. All it says is *Hello, Lilly.*

"You sure it's not from one of your friends?" I ask her. "Some boy at school who likes you?"

"I don't think so. It's not a Long Island number." She's right. I don't recognize the area code, 720.

I take the phone from Adrien and look at it. There's something about the message that puts me on guard. It's the fact that it uses her name. If it just said "hello," I would think it was a wrong number, but her name is what has my heart beating just a little too fast. I type the number into a new text message on my phone and send it to Dave with a message saying, *Can you try to track this down? Lilly got a weird text message.*

"Let me know if you get another one, but it's probably just kids at your school playing a prank," I say. I hand it back to her and try to put on a reassuring smile for Conor. He knows a bit about Anthony Pugh, but I haven't told him about Pugh being near my house yet.

Twenty minutes driving brings us to Fermoy, a town just north of Cork City. We find a bed-and-breakfast and walk around the little town center, a few blocks of pretty shopfronts, offices, and pubs, and then across a wide bridge just off the main street. We stand in the middle of the bridge and look down at the dark, swirling waters of the river Blackwater.

"This is a nice town," I say. "I love stopping in towns like this, just regular little places where people are living their lives and you get a window into this whole other existence you might have lived, you know? Like, what if we were from Fermoy? And we'd just lived our whole lives in Fermoy?"

"Like Red Lodge, right, Mom?" Lilly says. Her hair is blowing around her face in the breeze coming off the water. She's wearing her denim jacket and a pink scarf and she looks like a magazine model, leaning out across the edge of the bridge. The little ridge of worry that had settled on her face from the weird text is gone. She looks relaxed and happy, the strangeness of the text message past.

"Yeah." I smile at her.

"What's Red Lodge?" Adrien asks.

Lilly says, "We went to Montana a couple years ago, me and Mom. And we stayed one night in this town called Red Lodge and we loved it. It was so cute, like an old western town. It was right in the mountains and there were like, real cowboys living there, and this amazing hotel that had these pancakes with fresh berries and whipped cream on them and they were sooo good."

I give her a squeeze. It's one of my favorite memories of traveling with Lilly. We'd stayed in Red Lodge for a night on our way to Yellowstone. We were both so taken with it, we'd had fun talking about moving there.

"Whenever we complain about something on Long Island," I say, "we always say, 'Okay, we should move to Red Lodge.'"

"Did you go to a rodeo?" Adrien asks Lilly. "I want to go to Wyoming and see a rodeo. Dad said maybe we can go sometime."

"We should go!" Lilly's saying. "We could all go. You would love Red Lodge. And we can go to Colorado, too. It's so pretty there."

I catch Conor's eye over their heads and we smile at each other. This is exactly what we were hoping for from the trip, a sense of the four of us as a unit, some projection into the future.

Below us, the river swirls and runs on. We're heading back toward the main drag when my phone buzzes and Roly's number shows up on the screen. I'm about to let it go to voice mail when something tells me to answer.

"Hey," I say. "We're in Fermoy. No stuffed leprechauns yet, but I'm looking. How are you?"

"D'arcy," Roly says, and something in his voice, in the sounds behind him, makes me stop walking and turn my body back toward the river, waving to Conor to go on ahead. "You're not going to fucking believe this."

"What? Where are you?"

"I'm just outside Sixmilebridge. Guards from Shannon responded to a call from a concerned family member this morning. Woman said that her father hadn't answered his phone last night and hadn't answered again early this morning when she rang. It was very unlike him and she was concerned, so the guards did a welfare check and found a deceased male, age sixty-nine, apparent homicide. Looks like a burglary. We got sent down, Griz and I, and we've got the techs working here. But this guy, D'arcy. You're not going to believe this."

I hear a car horn, something that sounds like crunching gravel.

I know before he says it.

"His name was Noel Thomason," Roly says. "Gabriel Treacy's solicitor."

The trees behind Gabriel's nan and granddad's house were his friends. He knew each one, its unique shape and the texture of its bark, so that when he ran his hands over its bumpy surface, he knew which tree it was, even if his eyes were closed. There was a rowan tree and a few oaks and a stand of hawthorn trees that sent puffs of scent out across the garden in the spring. His mother liked the smell, but he thought it was too strong, too sweet.

He was six when he discovered the heart.

After he got home from school, he liked to go out to the trees and sit quietly, talking to himself and to them about what had happened that day, or play a war game that he had seen boys playing in the yard at school.

It was a warm, late-spring day when he looked up to see a series of cuts and scratches in the bark of one of the trees. He had never seen them before, but it was clear they had been there for a while; he could tell from the way the edges of the cuts had curled over. It occurred to him that they were like the edges of the wound he'd gotten when he fell and cut his knee: They had healed. They had stopped stinging. It made him feel better somehow, that the tree didn't hurt anymore. His hand ran over the gouges in the bark, his fingers in the grooves.

The shape made by the cuts was a heart, like the ones the girls at school drew on their diaries during lessons. Inside the heart someone had carved the initials S. T., and below that had been another set of initials, but someone had scratched those out. He tried and tried to read them, but he couldn't, that day or any other.

He wasn't sure when he started thinking that maybe the other initials belonged to his father. Boys at school talked about their fathers. One said to him, "Where's your father, then?" but he didn't have an answer. His silence was all the boys needed and they tortured him about his father's identity for years.

He'd heard his nan talking to his mam once, saying, "You must tell him something. It's cruel, Stella. You know it is." He waited for his mam to tell him, understanding somehow that they had been talking about his father.

She never did, and so he found himself going more and more to the tree, trying to read it like one of his books. The missing letters felt important somehow, like the solution to a mystery he didn't know he was trying to solve.

15

Roly's already there, at the pretty house in a little village outside the town. Noel Thomason's daughter called the guards at eight a.m. after she failed to hear from her father last night. She'd been expecting him to drive to her house in Kilkenny this morning, but when she tried to call him a couple of times and he didn't answer, she'd called the local guards in Sixmilebridge to do a welfare check. They had someone from Shannon go out, and they found the lock on the front door of the house broken and the initial rooms in disarray.

The body was near the back door. He'd been running for the door, trying to escape, but his assailant had caught him there and beaten him to death.

"Jesus," I say. "What are you thinking?"

"It looks like a robbery. Been a few in the town recently, I've been told. Computer may have been taken, among other things. We just don't know yet. The daughter's too upset to look at photos and tell us what's missing, but hopefully she can do that later."

"I need to come," I tell Roly, trying to keep my voice down. "There may be evidence related to Gabriel Treacy's murder. There may be emails we can pull from Thomason's electronics. There may be something there that tells us why Treacy was in Bay Shore. Have your people secured the scene?" Back on the other side of the bridge, I can see Conor, Lilly, and Adrien looking in shop windows as they make their way toward our bed-and-breakfast.

"Of course they've fucking secured the scene. What do you think?"

"Sorry, sorry." Conor turns back to check on me and I wave reassuringly and force myself to smile.

"Aren't you supposed to be on your holiday? I rang to tell you, like. I didn't mean for you to come running out here."

"Come on, Roly. It may be connected to my case. It may be my break. I need to be there."

He hesitates. "I don't know. I'm going through scenarios, D'arcy. What are we looking at? What are you thinking? What's the connection?"

"I have no idea, Roly, but it's a hell of a coincidence if there's no connection, and it's a good opportunity for me to establish why he was on Long Island."

He sighs. "Yeah, okay then. We're setting up an incident room at the Sixmilebridge Garda Station, but we'll be at the house tomorrow starting early. You want to come in the morning?"

I tell him to text me directions and hang up.

Conor and the kids are waiting for me on the other side of the street, everyone smiling and laughing. The sun is low on the horizon; the air feels colder suddenly. As soon as Conor sees my face, he knows something's up. He looks away, his eyes shutting down and his body pivoting away from me. It almost makes me reconsider.

But I can't.

I watch him wave the kids ahead and turn back to look at me. His eyes are worried but remote.

"I'm so sorry, Conor," I say. "Gabriel Treacy's solicitor, in Sixmilebridge, was murdered last night." I'm conscious of what I'm not saying, of how I've already started protecting the case.

His eyes widen. "You're not serious?"

I don't say anything.

"Do they think it's connected?"

"I don't know." I look away. "I need to go. I don't know what to do about Lilly. Roly's already there so I'd have to take a bus or something. How long does it take to get there?"

He runs a hand through his hair. He's not looking at me. "It's nearly an hour and a half from here to my mam and dad's in Broadford. I'd say the Bridge is about the same. Maggie, there are no buses from Fermoy. You'd have to go to Cork and then catch at least two buses. I'll have to drive you."

"No," I say. "I can't let you do that. Maybe I could rent a car and drive myself. Except . . . Lilly." Being an hour and a half away from Lilly right now doesn't seem like the best idea.

"Are you sure you have to go?" he ventures, his eyes darting away from mine. "Couldn't someone else handle it?"

"Someone was shot on a beach. There's a . . . there's a killer out there. On Long Island. If there's any evidence at this scene that can help us find this person, I need to see it quickly. I need to be able to follow up . . . to coordinate with my team back home. I need to do my job."

He looks away.

"There's a killer in Sixmilebridge," I say. "If there *is* a connection between the cases, we can protect people there, too."

He looks out across the swirling ribbon of the river, then sighs and says, "Look, I'll drive you to Sixmilebridge first thing in the morning, then Adrien and Lilly and I can go and spend the night in Broadford with my parents. It's peaceful there. She'll like it. My mam will love fussing over her and she'll only be twenty minutes away, so if she needs you, if I think she needs to see you, I can let you know and I can come get you. Or I can bring her. Then you can come to us when you're finished. Will that be okay?" His face is cloudy, its hollows pronounced in the early evening light.

The flood of relief I feel floors me, brings tears to my eyes. "Thank you," I say. "Your parents won't mind?"

His eyes soften. "They'll be delighted."

"Oh God," I say. "It's not exactly the way I planned on meeting your parents for the first time."

He smiles a little. "They'll be all right. Nothing can be as bad as the first time they met my sister Janey's husband, Lars. He's this lovely Danish guy, right? Really quiet. She took him out to the pub and the next morning he was so sick he couldn't get out of bed. They thought he couldn't handle his drink, but it turned out he had food poisoning."

I'm so grateful for the smile, for the funny story, for him trying to make me feel better, I almost start crying. But I know I need to get ready for what's coming, need to toughen myself up for Lilly's reaction. So, I just say, "Thank you. I'll go tell her."

That night, I lie awake for hours in the narrow double bed, Conor's breath even and steady next to me. He's starting to smell familiar again, the sweet fluffy scent of his laundry detergent, the spicy green of his deodorant. I finally sleep as the sun starts to rise, but I'm awakened by a dream I think must be about Brian, a dream of water and murky clouds of mud and seaweed obscuring something I'm supposed to be finding, something that's always just out of reach.

16

We get to Sixmilebridge by nine the next morning, taking mostly narrow local roads. Lilly and Adrien are laughing at funny political memes on their phones in the back of the car, effectively shutting us out, and Conor is quiet, focusing on the road ahead of him. I've already shifted into work mode, my brain planning, making lists of what I want to know. *What did the neighbors see? Who was the last person Noel Thomason spoke to? When was the last time he spoke with Gabriel Treacy? What did they talk about?* The energy in the car is low, Lilly annoyed at me, Conor sad, Adrien just confused about what's happening and why.

I'm ashamed of it, but I can't wait to get there.

The road unspools in front of us, the green fields lining the roads. I see the sign for Sixmilebridge and then the pale shapes of a graveyard just before we get to the town.

We slow as we come to the heart of the business district: a square, a few streets of pharmacies and shops and takeaway places and real estate agents and pubs. Thomason's house is in a small village a few miles outside Sixmilebridge called Carraghmore. The road winds past fields and more fields, stone walls close to the road wound with ivy. An abandoned, ruined castle tower slumps by the road and when I point it out to Lilly, she says, "Cool" in a listless voice, then goes back to looking at her phone.

When we get there, it's hardly a village, just ten or so houses and farms, with fields stretching out in both directions. Conor easily finds Thomason's one-story beige cottage surrounded by neatly trimmed hedges, a sign at the road reading "Thomason and Feeney Solicitors." There are marked garda cars everywhere, Roly's BMW parked at an angle on the road. Conor pulls the Skoda up a bit before the driveway and shuts off the engine. I take off my seat belt and turn around. "Lil, I'll talk to you later. I'm really close if you need me. You can call me anytime. Conor can bring you or he can come get me. Okay?"

She nods and sits up so I can reach back and hug her. Conor gets my bag out of the car and hands it to me. I kiss him and lean in for a hug. "I'll call later," I say. "Thank you." Conor nods, his eyes troubled. He makes a tight turn and the Skoda disappears back toward Sixmilebridge and Broadford.

I take a deep breath, pushing the guilt away, and look around to get my bearings. Carraghmore is essentially a crossroads, with Noel Thomason's house up against the northeastern corner, a pretty, sprawling whitewashed cottage across the road, a bigger house catty-corner, and three newer-looking houses stretched out down the northwestern end. Two are close together; the third has a bit of space around it, farm buildings and a large garage. There are other houses beyond the crossroads and we passed a shop and school on the way in, but this feels like the heart of it, such as it is.

I walk up the driveway just as a man and a woman come around the side of the house. Detective Sergeant Katya Grzeskiewicz, wearing a navy blue blazer and velvety-looking trousers tucked into tall rain boots, grins and runs to hug me. She's cut her light brown hair shorter since I saw her in June and she has a new pair of blue-rimmed glasses that make her look like a hipster poet rather than a police detective. I give her a huge hug, feeling a surge of love for someone who's a little bit of a daughter to me, but mostly just a good friend.

"It's so lovely to see you," she says. "Though I'm sorry we dragged you off your holiday. Oh, this is Detective Sergeant Peter Mooney. He's the local investigator and he's got all the gossip. Grew up here in Sixmilebridge. So, he's an invaluable local resource, like." She winks at the short, dark-haired guy standing next to her and he blushes with pleasure, keeping his eyes on her even after she looks away.

"Great to meet you," he says, turning his attention to me. "I heard all about your work in Wicklow, of course." He looks up at Griz. "Katya's work, and Detective Byrne's and yours. Now, we've got a pretty messy crime scene here. Not sure what I think about it yet, but we'll find out, won't we?"

There's something about him that lifts my mood; he radiates cheer and positivity.

I could use some of it right now.

I turn to Griz. "Where's Roly?"

"He's inside. We can let you have a quick look at the crime scene. They've taken the body now. Our techs are working away in there and Peter's lads have everything under control out here."

"You got anything?" I ask.

Griz nods to Peter, who says, "Nothing really good yet. Clear signs of forced entry but no prints inside or outside. Some electronics gone, some jewelry that must have belonged to Mr. Thomason's late wife was spilled about in the bedroom, so some of that may be gone, too. We won't know until we get photos done and the daughter has a look. That should be tomorrow. Feels like a standard home burglary to me. We've had a fair number lately, mostly related to the drug trade in Limerick."

"Have you had any other burglaries where the homeowner was beaten to death?" I ask him.

"It's not the usual thing, no," he says good-naturedly. "But we did have a machete attack last month. That was a mad one. Romantic thing, you know."

Griz raises her eyebrows. "Machete attacks are romantic?"

"Ah, yeah," he says, grinning. "Better than Quality Street and flowers any day."

"Tire treads?" I ask.

Griz says, "Not a one. Thomason's car was in the drive. The ground was still a bit wet yesterday so we would have found something if the assailant had parked in the drive. Nothing."

"So he came on foot?"

"Yeah, or . . . he parked on the road." She doesn't sound convinced.

"That suggests he knew he'd leave tire treads," I say.

Peter shrugs. "Maybe. Or maybe it's some little bollix too skint to own a car. We'll be making visits to all our known criminals in Sixmilebridge and the surrounding towns. See what's what."

I hear Roly's voice as soon as we're inside the house, a booming Dublin accent saying, "Don't suppose anyone brought a packet of biccies, now? I'm fuckin' famished. Could you not find me a cup of tea, there's a good lad." He's handing some coins off to a young guy in a uniform. "D'arcy!" he says when he sees me. "Here, you, get the Yank a cup of tea, too. She'll have an awful thirst on her from the drive." He shoves more coins at the kid.

I can't help smiling, watching Roly throwing his buzzing energy around the house. The house is simple, frozen in 1982, with floral wallpaper on a lot of the walls and pink wall-to-wall carpet in the sitting room. The kitchen is from an even earlier era, with avocado-colored linoleum and tile and old-fashioned-looking appliances. But it feels prosperous, well cared for.

The techs give us boiler suits and gloves and booties and masks. I can see why they jumped to a robbery right away. The front door lock has been splintered and anyone could see there was a struggle here. A pottery vase is in pieces and a framed watercolor painting has been knocked off the wall, leaving broken glass on the floor. Books and cushions and papers lie on the carpet in the living room.

Every crime scene has an immediate atmosphere, visual details you take in unconsciously that your brain uses to create a theory of what happened. I stand there for a moment, and though my eyes are saying this scene is violent, chaotic, sudden, my brain is telling me it's more methodical than it looks. I need to figure out why.

The techs have laid tarps on the ground for us to walk on and we skirt the destruction and go into the main part of the house, following the trail of items knocked onto the floor through to the kitchen and the back door. I can see where Thomason died from the blood-stains on the ground. He retreated and then was beaten to death next to the back door. The amount of blood is shocking. I know what it means: Someone did a lot of damage to his head. Someone wanted to make sure he'll never raise his head again.

"He'd been dead eight or nine hours when the pathologist got here," Roly says. I start to construct a timeline in my head. If he was found at ten by the local gardaí, the pathologist likely got there an hour later, which means Thomason was killed sometime around three in the morning. Weird time for a burglary, though a great time for it if you want to make sure none of the neighbors see you. But that means someone with the wherewithal to wait around and plan, to stay awake until three, rather than a teenager with impulse-control issues and a drug addiction.

Before I can ask, Griz says, "He was in his pajamas and he'd turned on the hall light and the lights coming down those stairs. It looks like he woke up and heard someone breaking in, came down, and confronted his assailant. There was a struggle there and then in here." She points to the living room area and then to the blood on the floor.

"They won't know for sure until they get him on the table," Peter says. "But we think the weapon was a walking stick that was on the floor, covered in blood and hair. It was one o' those real wizardy ones, with a knobbly end. Weapon of convenience. The daughter said it usually resided in a stand by the front door. Thomason may even have grabbed it on his way down, thinking he could use it to defend himself."

"But no prints."

"None whatsoever from what we can tell. Our guy wore gloves."

"That shows planning."

"Yeah," Roly says. "Or someone who likes the old *CSI*."

"Something I noticed," Peter says. "That picture there." He points to the watercolor. "You bump into it, it's gonna go like this." He pantomimes hitting the spot on the wall where the painting was with his shoulder. "It's going to fall down there, with some momentum behind it." He points to a spot on the floor a few feet away. "But it's not. It's there, directly below, and it's leaning against the wall. That's not how it's going to fall. That's a heavy frame. It's going to topple over. But it didn't and I'm thinking that's because the intruder lifted it off the wall and placed it there."

"Good catch," I say. "When I first came in, I felt like the scene was better organized than it appeared to be. You put your finger on why."

I look through the glass of the back door. It's all fields behind the house, mostly open, but there's a stand of trees at the back of the second field, next to a narrow dirt road probably used by tractors and surrounded by thick growth. It would be a good spot to watch the house from, if you were casing it. And he could have parked on the road there and then come through the field to avoid leaving tire treads.

"Hey," I say, pointing to the trees. "Has anybody been back there? That looks like a good hide to me."

Peter nods. "I've got the lads searching. I'll make sure they do it. I don't think any of them would be afraid of the fairies now." I must look confused, because he says, "They're hawthorns. Some people think they're fairy trees. You can't cut them down or bad things will happen to you." Griz rolls her eyes.

"They found anything related to Gabriel Treacy?" I ask, watching the techs do their work, combing the house for evidence, looking for anything that wasn't Noel Thomason's. He lived alone, so it will be easier than a scene where a family of five or six lived, but his daughter and grandkids probably visited frequently, and he had a secretary and may have had a cleaning lady. Roly's techs will need to get samples from all of them to eliminate any biological evidence they find.

"No, but here's the office, where he has client files and so forth," Roly says. "It doesn't look like our fella came in here at all. But I thought you might like to see it."

They lead me through a connecting door to Noel Thomason's law office. It was decorated more recently than the house, but it's fairly utilitarian, simple wooden furniture from Ikea or similar and institutional beige paint on the walls. There are two rooms, one a sort of waiting room and reception area with a separate entrance and the other room serving as his actual office.

"You're sure he didn't come in here?" I ask.

"Doesn't look like it. No prints, nothing out of order, nothing obviously missing. We'll have the daughter and the secretary woman look to make sure," Roly says.

"The sign outside was Thomason and Feeney. Who's Feeney?" I ask Peter. "Do you know?"

"Ah, sure. Jim Feeney was married to my maths teacher from primary school. Mrs. Feeney. She was a lovely lady. Jim was a good man. He was the senior partner and retired in the nineties, and Thomason decided to go it alone and build onto the house out here. I gather his wife was ill and he wanted to be close by, but after she died, he liked having the office here so he kept it."

"What kind of law did he practice?" I ask. "He handled Stella Treacy's estate, but what else did he do?"

Peter takes a card out of a little basket on the desk. "There you are. He advertised himself as a family solicitor, and he did a bit of everything. Wills, trusts, divorces. He and Jim split up the work at first and then he sort of expanded. Margaret Morrell—she's the local woman who worked for him—can tell us more. She's going to come down to the garda station to give her statement as soon as she gets back from her daughter's."

"We're working on getting Thomason's electronics and phone records," Roly says.

"The big thing is, when was the last time he talked to Gabriel Treacy and what did they talk about?" I ask.

Roly looks annoyed for a second, but says, "We're looking at that, D'arcy. If there's anything there, we'll find it." He nods to Griz and then tells me, "My lad who's so good with the tech now, he's getting Gabriel Treacy's emails from Global Humanity for you and he'll be down tomorrow to show us what he's got. If there was any communication between Treacy and Thomason, it may be there, too."

He leads the way outside and we all stand in the driveway, blinking in the bright sun.

"This is a separate village, right?" I ask Peter. "Carraghmore? But it's part of Sixmilebridge?"

"Yeah, it's just the ten or twelve or so houses. There's the national school along there. I suppose at one point there would have been more houses and farms, but you can see. It's Mr. Thomason's, then Helen and Paddy Reid across the way there, then Stella Treacy's, though some woman from Sligo has bought it now, and then Millmans', they've got the farm there, and then the two new places are, uh, what's your man's name? Murphy, I think. And then John McCarthy's young one, who married the fella who works for An Post." He smiles as though I know who he's talking about. "And there are six or seven new houses up there." He's gesturing toward the fancy houses I saw on my way in, the ones with stone walls and gates. "Mostly people from Limerick, holiday houses."

But I'm staring at him. "Gabriel Treacy lived in that house right there? That was his mother's house?" I point to the long white cottage across the road.

"Ah, yeah. I thought you knew that. Yeah, that's where Stella was raised and then after she had Gabriel, they lived there with her parents until they passed."

"What were they like?" I ask him. "Did you know them?"

"Not well. Mr. Treacy would have been dead by the time I was born. I think he worked for Irish Rail. I'll check with my mam."

I'm studying the little cottage through the window now. "I know Noel Thomason was his lawyer, uh, solicitor, but were they close aside from that? I mean, they were neighbors all those years."

"I suppose so," Peter says. "You know how it is with people. I'd say they would have gone back and forth a bit. Helen Reid was a great pal of Noel's wife, Cynthia, before she passed away. I suppose they would have been friendly with Stella, too." But something in his face makes me wonder if that was true at all.

"I'd love to talk to the Reids about Gabriel. What about the, uh, the Millmans?"

"Ah, Theresa's a lovely woman. She's been a widow ten years or more. She's had a lot of health issues recently, though. We rang round yesterday and she's at the hospital."

"You'll be interviewing them to ask if they heard anything," I say. "Can I come along and ask about Gabriel Treacy?" I feel a little surge of excitement. These are the people who knew Gabriel Treacy the best, who knew his mother. There may be something here for me to find.

"I suppose," Peter says. "If it's okay with youse?" He looks inquiringly at Griz and Roly.

"Yeah," Roly says, winking at me. "She'd find a way to talk to 'em even if I say no, so bring her along. Griz, you go with Detective Mooney and our American friend here. Talk to all the neighbors. I'll stay here with the techs and see what they find outside. I'm hoping for a good shoeprint or tire tread. Nice layer of mud out there. We'll get him, lads."

Roly's all hyped up, still at the hopeful stage of the investigation, still thinking they're going to break this the normal way, by exploiting the carelessness of a less-than-brilliant criminal. And he may be right. Most murders get solved pretty quickly, when it comes right down to it.

I peel off my boiler suit in the driveway. Outside Noel Thomason's house, the fields are so bright I stop for a minute, overcome with the life of them, the figures of reddish-brown cows in the plot closest to us. I'd thought of this part of the country as flat, the Midwest of Ireland, but there's a low bank of hills in the near distance, beyond the stretching of flat browns and greens, and I remember Conor telling me about going out to look at the hills behind his house in Broadford. I think of him standing there, and I'm suddenly filled with love and apprehension, an odd mix of emotions that I can't figure out what to do with right now.

The light catches the nap of the grass, the breeze stirs up something fragrant in the hedgerow, and the cows turn their gleaming backs to the sun.

17

....

Peter Mooney and Griz and I walk across the road to Gabriel Treacy's childhood home. It's a whitewashed cottage, the outside neatly
kept, with deep flower beds wrapping around three sides and a new
coat of paint. It doesn't look lived in, though, and Peter Mooney explains that the new owner has been doing some work on the house
but hasn't moved in yet. We look through the windows and see construction materials lying around, buckets of paint and drop cloths
scattered on the floors. I'm not going to find any mementos of Gabriel Treacy's childhood here, but I still want to look around. The
house is bigger than it looks, with an extension out the back and a
separate entrance backing up to a pretty garden where fountains of
green are just starting to emerge from the soil. There's a thick hedgerow at the back and a stand of trees beyond it.

"I think Stella's da built the extension when she had Gabriel, so
they could have their own flat, like," Peter says. "Before I was born,
of course, but my ma knows all the gossip. We owned a shop in
town, so of course we had all the news."

"How would people in town have reacted to Stella being an unwed mother, in the early seventies?" I ask him.

"Ah, it trailed her, if you know what I mean. It was always like a little footnote when her name came up, 'Stella Treacy, who had the baby on her own.' There was always a bit of an eyebrow raise, you know? Even once she was an old woman. My ma's face would do something funny."

"What about Gabriel?"

"I don't know, to be honest with you. He was gone to college by the time I was aware of it. I'd see him around. I stopped him once when I was a new guard. We were doing a checkpoint or something like that. He was sober as a judge, but we had a chat and he told me he was home to see his mammy after being out of the country a few years. I liked him. He was a lovely fella, quiet, but intelligent, and he was interested in what I'd been up to, asked about my training and that."

"Thank you," I say. "That's really helpful." I study Peter Mooney for a minute. He's probably thirty, about Griz's age, though he looks younger. Gabriel Treacy would have been in his late thirties at that point, deep into his career, Afghanistan and Abena Tekle still ahead of him.

We cross again and make our way to the Reids' house. It was once a simple cottage like the Treacys' but it's been updated, with a coat of pinky-beige paint and new windows and a front door with an elaborate Celtic knot design in glass and metal. The landscaping is neat—severe, actually—with six bushes trimmed into perfect spheres and a closely cropped square of green lawn surrounded by a fence. Barking from inside tells me we've been spotted, and the door opens almost automatically when Peter knocks. "Peter!" says the small white-haired woman who answers. "What is going on out there? Poor Noel. It's terrible." A white terrier swirls around her feet and she scolds it and gently pushes it out of the way.

"I know it is, Helen. We're trying to figure out who might have done this, so we just wanted to ask a few questions. Is Paddy here?"

"Yes, where else would he be?" She leads us into the house and calls out, "Paddy, Peter Mooney's here to ask us about Noel. Would you not come out of the bedroom?" She turns to Peter. "He's been working on his computer in there. I don't even know what he gets up to. Reading the online newspapers all day."

An older man in slippers comes out of the back of the house. "Ah, Peter," he says with a delighted smile. "You caught the madman who killed Noel, have you?" Helen Reid tuts at her husband's joviality and gives him a little swat.

"Not yet, Paddy. But we're working away at it. This is Detective Sergeant Katya Grzeskiewicz from the National Bureau of Criminal Investigation in Dublin." He points to Griz, who looks surprised at how well he pronounced her name. He smiles at her, just a little turn of his mouth to say, *see then,* and then points to me. "And this is Detective Lieutenant Maggie D'arcy. She's over from the States now, looking into Gabriel Treacy's death."

"Do they, do they think they're connected?" Helen asks, her eyes wide. "I couldn't believe it when I heard the news about Gabriel and then . . . this." She shakes her head.

"We don't know yet. Can we sit down and ask you a few questions?" Peter asks her.

"Of course. I've just put the kettle on. I'll be back with the tea. You'd like a biscuit, wouldn't you, Peter. Girls, would you like a biscuit?"

Griz and I say we would, of course, and she goes, leaving us alone with Paddy Reid, who settles into an armchair and levels his gaze at Peter. "You looked at your man Gavin?" he asks him.

Peter looks surprised, but says, for our benefit, "Gavin Millman," then, to Paddy, "You have any reason to think Gavin had anything to do with this, Paddy?"

"Just that he's never been any good and well, sure, he's right there, isn't he? He'd probably been inside the house. And poor Theresa, she's a good woman, a saint. I don't know what she did to deserve that lad."

"I told him to be careful who he goes saying that to, didn't I?" Helen calls from the kitchen. "We don't know anything at all. But we can say it to you, Peter. You'll know what to do." She comes through with a beautiful tea tray, steaming teapot, nice cups, and a plate of chocolate and coconut cookies.

"Mr. and Mrs. Reid," Griz says once she's started on her tea and gotten a couple of chocolate cookies into herself. "Did you see anything Monday night that was out of the ordinary? Anyone parked on the road or in Mr. Thomason's drive who shouldn't have been? Hear any sounds in the night, especially towards the very early morning?"

Helen looks like she's tempted to make something up—I know the signs—but she gets the better of herself and says, "No, we were fast asleep. I was out in the morning to go to the shop, but everything seemed quiet then. The first we knew of it was the sirens screaming down the road the next day around noon. We were terrified last night, knowing there was a murderer running around." Paddy Reid rolls his eyes.

"Had Mr. Thomason ever expressed any concerns to you, about his security, or that he was afraid of someone?" Griz asks.

Helen shakes her head. "Oh, no. I don't think so."

"He told me that your man Gavin threatened him," Paddy cuts in. "A year or two ago now."

"Really?" Peter looks interested in that. "He actually threatened him?"

"That's what he said."

Helen looks surprised. "You never told me that," she says to Paddy.

"You didn't need to know." He nods and sits back in his chair.

"Why did Gavin threaten him?" Peter asks. "Do you know what it was about?"

"Noel didn't say specifically. We met in the pub, like, and I asked him how he'd been and he said that he'd been all right, but he'd had a bit of a scary moment the other day, that young Gavin had knocked on his door and threatened his life. He said they had some *personal business*. Said it just like that, *personal business*. But he said he just wanted me to know in case I came across him."

"Thanks, Paddy. We'll look into that," Peter says. "Was that the end of it?"

"I never heard anything more about it. Gavin moved to Limerick. It's only the last couple months he's been back with his mam."

I jump in. "Mr. and Mrs. Reid, how well did you know Stella and Gabriel Treacy?"

"I've known Stella all her life, haven't I?" Helen says. "She and I were at school together. She was . . . well, she was wild, as a girl. There's no other way to say it. People talked and then, well, with Gabriel coming along when she wasn't married, only . . . But time marches on and over the years I think people, well, it became more usual, didn't it? Having a baby without being married."

I can see Peter's right. For some people in town, Stella Treacy never got rid of that footnote.

"What was Gabriel like?" I ask her. "How would you describe him?"

"Gabriel, he was clever. That's what everyone said about him when he was a boy. He was a clever one, always at the top of his class, always a favorite of the teachers at the national school. Well, you know, that made people wonder about Gabriel's father, of course." She smiles a secret smile and Paddy murmurs something I don't catch. When I look at Peter, he seems confused.

"Sorry, Helen, you mean . . ."

"Oh, I don't mean anything," she says. "You know how people are. In any case, he was always a boy who you knew would do something, despite his disadvantages. He went off into the world and he helped so many people, such a good person, Stella was always boasting of him, and it's just terribly sad." She looks up at me with a bit of recrimination in her eyes. "After all those places he went, Africa and all, to think he'd be murdered in New York. Well, it's a terrible waste is what it is. And now this."

"Did you ever hear about something that happened to Gabriel when he was working in Afghanistan?" I ask her. "This would have been about six years ago. In 2011. He was kidnapped and held for a bit before he was released. Did Stella talk to you about it?"

"No . . . I do remember Stella seeming quite concerned around then—that was when you had your knee done, Paddy—and I wondered why Gerry Murray was at the house so much and . . . oh, Paddy, that must be why. And then Jonathan was there, too. Do you remember we wondered about that? He must have been helping her." They exchange a glance, and Helen smiles triumphantly, a mystery solved.

"Gerry Murray was our local TD," Peter explains to me and Griz. "His son, Jonathan, holds the seat now."

"Yes," I say, "I'd heard Mr. Murray was helpful during that time."

I think for a moment. "Mr. and Mrs. Reid, the reason I'm over here is that I'm trying to find out why Gabriel came to Long Island, why he was in Bay Shore, where he was killed. It doesn't seem to have been for work, and we can't find any connection he had to Long Island, to New York. Do you have any thoughts about that?"

"Would it not have been for his work?" Paddy asks. "That's what we all assumed when we heard."

"We just don't know," I say. "But do you ever remember Stella or Gabriel talking about Long Island, mentioning a friend there, anything like that?"

They both shake their heads. Nothing there.

"Would have been a robbery, I should think," Paddy says. "You have a lot of guns over there, don't ya?" he asks me. "People upset about this thing or that thing." Helen nods soberly.

"It's true. Well, thank you for your help," I tell them. "Please let us know if you think of anything." I nod at Peter to let him know I'm done.

"I'll say the same," Peter tells them. "Give me a ring if anything occurs to you. You know where to find me."

"Ah, we do. You find this fella now, Peter," Helen says at the door. "I imagine he's come up from Limerick to rob poor Noel." She smiles. "Take care of yourself, now." She looks at Griz. "Peter Mooney was always a good boy. He'll find this fella." When she shuts the door behind us, I can hear the deadbolt engage.

18

Outside, we cross the road again. "We need to talk to Theresa Millman, especially now Paddy's pointed the finger at Gavin, but she won't be back until later," Peter says, checking his phone. "I'll have the lads try to pin down Gavin. And here, I've a text that Margaret Morrell, Noel Thomason's secretary, is at the garda station in town. She's ready to talk to us."

"Sounds good," Griz says. "Maggie, why don't you ride with me? We'll see you there, Peter, yeah?"

He looks up at her and I can see him taking in the way the sun is hitting her hair and the line of her cheek. The hopeful look on his face is so raw, it makes me look away. "Sounds great, yeah, see you then," he says, a little too enthusiastically.

"How are you?" she asks me once we're in the car, heading back toward town on the same narrow road, the castle ruins on one side, the cows staring from a field across the way. "How are you doing then?"

I don't waste time on the usual things I say to people. "It's still pretty bad," I tell her. "I mean, I'm coping all right, but Lilly's still just . . . she's like a ghost, you know? It's like she's barely there. I have dreams sometimes, about the . . . the water, and the weight of him as I tried to tow him back. I know she has dreams, too."

"It takes time," Griz says quietly. "It's only been eight months, Maggie. Does Conor understand?"

"He's been great. I was hoping this vacation would be good for both of us, but of course I screwed that up. He took Lilly to his parents so she'd be nearby."

Griz doesn't say anything, so I keep going, saying things I haven't said to anyone yet. "The long-distance thing . . . I don't know what we're doing, Griz. He can't move, and it's not like I can just quit my job and get one here. So what are we doing? It seemed so clear, back in the summer, that we have to be together, you know? That whatever happened, we would be able to make it work. But with the kids, with the distance . . ." I don't want to talk about it anymore and we're almost to the garda station, so I say, "What about you? How is it going on Major Crimes? It's been, what, three months now?" Griz was promoted to Major Crimes not long after Roly was, the two of them riding the wave of the Niamh Horrigan case. It was a huge—and well-deserved—promotion for her and I've been wondering how it's going.

"Yeah, all right. We had a good solve a few weeks ago, gangland thing; we got the little bollix and probably stopped him killing someone else. I'm still getting used to things. You know how it is." Her voice cuts off the subject. There's something more there and I look over at her, trying to figure out if she wants me to push. I don't think she does. She pulls the car into a spot on the main street and we watch as Peter Mooney gets out of his car ahead of us and heads into the garda station.

"You know he has a huge crush on you, right?" I ask her. "He can't stop looking at you."

She turns the car off and releases her seat belt. When she turns to face me, she looks years older suddenly, and I make a note to ask Roly how she's really doing. "I don't know. Maybe. He's a nice guy, and a good detective." She sighs. "But he's not really my sort o' fella—too good-looking, too short—and honestly, that's the last thing I need right now."

I let it go.

The garda station is small, but they've brought a few computers up from Shannon and created a proper incident room, with everything Peter and Roly and Griz and their team will need to work this case. They've already got pictures of Noel Thomason and the house up on the wall and one of the younger guards who works for Peter is busy constructing a timeline of Noel Thomason's last days and hours.

I call Marty. I texted him last night about Noel Thomason but now I tell him what we know so far and say I'll keep him updated.

"You don't think it's connected to our case, do you?" he asks.

"Probably not, but he was Treacy's solicitor. It's a good chance to try to figure out why Treacy was on Long Island, anyway," I say.

"Okay," Marty says. He sounds tired, stressed.

"You doing all right?"

"Yeah, Pat just laid into me about letting you head off to Ireland with an active case."

"Shit, I'm sorry, Marty."

"No, I told you to go. I didn't mean that. It's just odd to me that Pat cares. I think Cooney got wind of it from Alicia and got in Pat's ear about it. You know, I think he hates you even more than I thought."

"Thanks for reminding me. Can you tell Dave I'm about to call him?"

"Yup. Take care now. Don't forget you're supposed to be on vacation."

When Dave answers, I say, "Marty will give you the update, but you get anything on that phone number, the one Lilly's text came from?"

"Yeah, it looks like a 719, but when I called it, it was out of service. Probably some scammy sales thing."

I feel relief trickle through my veins. Of course. If she had answered, the next text was probably going to be, *Let us show you how you can make a million dollars selling makeup on the internet.* I say thanks and tell him I'll check in later.

Then I call Conor to see how things are in Broadford. "We're all settled in," he says. "My da took Lilly and Adrien out to check on the ewes. He thinks we might have some early lambs so he's training her up as his assistant. She seems fine, Maggie. No need to worry."

"Thank you," I say. "Thank you so much, Conor." The words feel weak and fake in my mouth. I've been saying thank you much too much to someone I'm dating. "I'll call later. We're at the garda station now and I should know more in a bit. I may even be able to get to Broadford tonight. I'll have to find a car."

"Okay, I should go see how they're getting on," he says. "Speak to you later."

The incident room is busy, everyone pitching in to get this going. They find me a desk and I sit down and open my laptop. I'm curious now about what was going on in Sixmilebridge while Gabriel Treacy was being held in Afghanistan. Roly's friend Greta had suggested that Gerry and Jonathan Murray had been significantly involved in trying to get Gabriel Treacy released. I start out by searching for Gerry Murray and get a bunch of links to obituaries for him in Irish papers from five years ago. Most of them mention his twenty-seven years of service as Clare's representative to the Dáil, which, from what I can tell, is the Irish version of the US House of Representatives. I remember that Ireland has two legislative bodies, the Dáil Éireann and the Seanad Éireann, and the Dáil, to which the Murrays were elected, is the one that has the most power. They both seem to have been members of Fianna Fáil, which along with Fine Gael make up the two main political parties in Ireland. I have a vague memory that the two parties are somehow connected to which side of the civil war you were on, but I'll have to get Conor to explain it to me. Gerry Murray died of a sudden heart attack in 2012, when he was seventy-five. It looks like he was first elected in 1975 and served until 2002, when his son Jonathan was elected to the seat. Both Murrays seem to have served in a number of different ministerial roles—like our agency heads, I think—related to foreign relations and military affairs.

Jonathan Murray's website doesn't offer up an American-style dump of personal information, but there's one photo of him, a middle-aged guy, nearly bald, wearing thick glasses and a flashy suit. There's also an address for his local constituency office in Ennis, which I write down.

I'm remembering what Roly's friend Greta at Foreign Affairs had said: *Look at your own institutions.* If Murray had contacts in security or military circles, he might have been working back channels to get one of his constituents released.

"Look at that." I look up to find Griz standing over me, holding a copy of the *Independent*. She tosses the newspaper onto the desk. "You made the papers."

"What?" I scramble for the front section and find a headline proclaiming "Clare House Burglary and Murder Connected to American Case?"

"A death at a home in Carraghmore, County Clare, is being probed as the tragic consequence of a break-in early Tuesday morning, according to Garda sources," reads the first line. The story goes on to detail the basic facts of Noel Thomason's murder and then draws a connection with Gabriel Treacy:

"The dead man was solicitor for Gabriel Treacy, a partner at the Dublin-based humanitarian aid organization Global Humanity, who was shot to death on a beach in New York last week. Gardaí have not revealed a connection between the two men, but American homicide detective Maggie D'arcy, who readers may remember from the Niamh Horrigan case and who is investigating Gabriel Treacy's murder in the States, is rumored to be in Clare, assisting with the case."

"Shit." I don't even need to check the byline, but I do, and of course it's Stephen Hines. "He was asking Roly's contact about Treacy. How does he know I'm here?" I ask Griz. "Is he stalking me?"

"I don't know," she says. "But he's probably not the only one who's going to make the connection. We'll want to figure out what we'll say when they start asking."

"I think the answer is that I'm investigating Gabriel Treacy's murder. We don't know why he was in the States, and that because he was from Sixmilebridge, it's important that I interview some local people who knew him."

"I like it," Griz says. "Stephen Hines may not accept it, though."

"Stephen Hines can take a long walk off a short pier."

"See, that's how I know you're not Irish," Roly says with a grin. "If you were Irish, there would have been much more profanity in that sentence."

Peter gets a briefing going in their small conference room. The energy is good, familiar, a functional team jumping into the problem, everyone working at full capacity. As the local detective, he's technically in charge, so he presents the details of the case and starts giving out assignments. He's organized, articulate, full of energy, his wrap-up clear and concise. He describes our conversation with the Reids and says he wants to interview Gavin Millman and his mother as soon as possible.

Roly stands up. "Our priority is finding any physical evidence there might be at the scene so we can start to build a case. Chances are, you know who did this," he says to the local team. "Detective D'arcy is investigating the murder of Mr. Thomason's client Gabriel Treacy in the States last week. We don't know if there's a connection. There might not be, but uncovering the details of both men's lives may help solve these murders."

"Had Thomason and Treacy been in touch before Treacy's death?" someone asks.

"Detective D'arcy?" Peter says. "Can you answer that?"

I stand up. "We don't know. Treacy's phone was stolen or . . . lost. In any case, we didn't find it with the body. His phone records show that he stopped using his phone right after he arrived in the States, which seems odd. He had a laptop he used for work, but that's gone, too. Our working theory is that he had a backpack—a rucksack—or some other bag that had the laptop and maybe some papers and the phone in it, and that it was stolen by whoever killed him."

"You think he was carrying it when he was killed?" one of the local detectives asks. "That seems odd. If he was just going for a slash, like, or meeting someone for sex?"

"Yeah, it's odd, all right," I say. "Maybe there was something in the backpack that he was showing to whoever he was meeting. Maybe he just didn't want to leave it in the car. But yeah, it's odd. I want to know who he was emailing before the trip. We're working on getting the email records, right?" I look over at Griz and Roly.

"We'll have Thomason's phone records soon," says Griz. "And yeah, like Detective D'arcy said, our lads in Dublin are working with Global Humanity, where Treacy worked, to get his emails from their backup system. One of the techs is going to come out later today or in the morning with whatever they've got. Thomason's should be easier because he had an automated backup system, so we should be able to get all of his. He had a phone that was up in his bedroom, plugged in, no password. But the only person he really texted with was his daughter. Nothing unexpected there. A few texts about a trip she took to Sweden back in December and then a few messages from yesterday morning, when she couldn't get him on the phone. I'd say he used his landline for all his phone calls. Anyway, we'll keep working on it."

"Oh, one other thing," Peter Mooney says. "When we were interviewing the neighbors who told us about Gavin Millman, they said they remembered Stella Treacy seeming very worried about something back in 2011, around the time Gabriel Treacy was being held in Afghanistan. Obviously that would have been quite terrifying for his mother. I didn't know about it, but we need to find out if other people in town did, if it was something Stella ever talked about, okay?"

Peter starts making assignments, sending uniforms out to interview neighbors and visit any local who's ever been a suspect in a burglary. Then he says, "Margaret Morrell's ready to speak with us." He nods at me and Griz. "You two ready?"

Margaret Morrell is sitting in an empty room, at the head of a table, and my first impression is of her loneliness. She's a petite woman in her late sixties with green eyes and an unnatural shade of bright red hair that suits her skin, and she's wearing trendy jeans and a gray cotton sweater. The grief comes off her and fills the room.

She tells us she's lived in Sixmilebridge her entire life. She's worked for Noel Thomason for almost twenty years, "off and on," she says. "I took a few years off when I had breast cancer, but once I was well again, Noel had me come back. I just can't believe this has happened." Her eyes fill with tears and Peter Mooney signals for someone to get her a cup of tea. "Poor Noel. He was a very gentle man. It's just awful to think of him . . . of violence at the end of his life."

"I know this is hard, Margaret," Peter says reassuringly. "But we're trying to determine what was taken from the house. Can you look through these photographs and tell us what seems to be missing?"

"Of course." She takes her time, studying each one and making notes on the paper Peter's given her. When she looks up, she looks shaken. "It's so . . . violent. Like they really hated him." She takes a deep breath. "He had an old desktop and also a laptop computer. He usually brought it into the main house at the end of the day so he could finish things up. He also had a very pretty little wooden box on a table in the sitting room, an antique. French, I think. It was quite valuable. That's gone. I wouldn't know about the rest of the house."

"We don't think they went into the office," Griz says. "Can you tell us if there's anything obvious that's missing from these pictures?"

She looks at the photos. "Not really," she says. "It appears as normal. I'd have to have a real search through the files. And I've been working on transferring a lot of his files to digital, so I took quite a few of them home. I can see what's there and then I might be able to tell you if all the files are in place. But only, sometimes Noel created his own files or put things in them when I wasn't working."

"Would Gabriel Treacy's file be one of the ones you have at home?" Griz asks. "We didn't see anything for him in the office."

"Perhaps . . ." she says, but looks doubtful. "I can have a look."

She pushes the photos back toward us and I can't help but look down again at the damage done to the house. Again, I have the impression of more organization in the scene than seems immediately apparent. There's *too much disorganization.*

"Not to worry, Margaret," Peter says, causing me to look up from the pictures. "If you tell us where those files you took home might be, we'll send someone round to pick them up." She nods.

"Did Mr. Thomason ever express any concerns to you about his safety?" he asks her. "Was there anyone who might have wanted to harm him?"

She hesitates, then looks up at us with a fearful expression. "When I heard . . . when they told me about Noel, the first thing I thought was that Gavin Millman had done it. Noel represented Gavin's wife in their divorce. You know, that young one from Limerick he was with for a time. They had a darling little boy, Theresa adores him, but she was never any good, and of course, well, it should be said that Gavin himself, despite Theresa doing everything she could, well . . . Gavin was furious with Noel, because of the way it turned out, the wife getting custody and the house and all. He came to the office once when I was there and demanded to see Noel. He was fighting mad. I really thought he might harm Noel; I kept my phone in my hand, ready to call the guards, the whole time he was there."

Peter nods. "We'll be taking a look at him, all right, Margaret. This is Detective D'arcy. As you know, she's investigating Gabriel Treacy's death in the States. She'd like to know about Noel's relationship with Gabriel."

A hand flies to her cheek. "Oh, poor Gabriel. I was visiting my daughter and I found out on Facebook. Mary Faulkner linked to the story. And then just a few days later, the news about Noel."

I give her a second to collect herself. "When was the last time Mr. Thomason was in touch with Mr. Treacy?" I ask. "As far as you know?"

"Well, Stella died a year ago January so they were in touch quite frequently at that point. The house sold in May, so I don't think they would have been in touch much after that. But I've been . . . I haven't been working as much lately, since my daughter had her second baby. I've been going over as much as I can, and Noel has been winding down his business, I guess you'd say. He wants to retire." She realizes suddenly, gasps. "*Wanted* to. Oh, I'd have liked him to have his retirement." She takes a deep breath. "So, I suppose it's possible, but I don't think they'd been in touch since May, when they were wrapping up the house sale."

"This is a strange question," I say, "but in 2011, Mr. Treacy was in Afghanistan with his work and he was held captive for a few weeks. It wasn't much reported and I'm wondering if Stella talked to Mr. Thomason about it, if he knew."

Margaret Morrell's eyes widen and she nods. "I didn't know, but that explains something I've always wondered about. In 2011, my first granddaughter had just been born, and as you said, Stella came by the office one day and said she needed to speak to Noel. She looked awful, just shocked, and pale, like something terrible had happened. I thought that maybe Gabriel was dead; I knew he worked in all of these dangerous places, you know, but when she left, Noel said Gabriel wasn't dead, but that he *was* in trouble and Noel couldn't say anything. He drew up papers for her to get an equity release from the bank, and he had me do research on whether she could liquidate Gabriel's pension funds and sell his flat in Dublin. Clearly they were trying to raise money quickly. I wondered what was going on, but Noel wasn't saying a word. But then a week later it all died down and he filed all the papers away. And a few months after that I saw Gabriel at the pub when he was back visiting, and he was right as rain. The whole thing didn't make sense to me, but that would explain it, wouldn't it? If he'd been kidnapped and she thought she'd have to pay a ransom." Peter and I exchange a glance. He'll need to make contact with the bank.

"Someone else told us that Jonathan Murray was helpful during that time. Do you remember that?" I ask.

She stares at me for a second. There's something there that she's connecting with, some memory that's surfacing. "Jonathan Murray . . . ah, oh yes. That makes sense, doesn't it? That Gerry and Jonathan would have been there to help out with that . . . ah, poor Stella. Poor Gabriel. How awful. I always thought of him, you know, when I heard those terrible stories about the journalists or the translators, because I knew he was in these places. I suppose there would have been a lot of secrecy, wouldn't there? If they were trying to keep it out of the news?

"Poor Gabriel. I just keep thinking, thank God Stella isn't alive to see it. She would have been devastated to lose him. He was everything to her, you know. She gave up so much for him and she loved him so much. I think it was the second chance. She wasn't going to waste a minute of it."

It takes a minute for that to hit my brain. Griz's eyes widen. But it's Peter Mooney who asks her, "Sorry, second chance?"

She looks up with wide eyes, realizing she's made a mistake, that she's revealed something she didn't want to reveal.

"Oh . . . I, well, I was at school with her so I . . . well, I knew. Not many did. I suppose that she and Gabriel are both gone now, so sure, where's the harm? I . . ." She takes a deep breath. "Stella had another baby, before Gabriel. We were only sixteen. She went away in the winter of 1965, just disappeared one day, and then she was back in the spring. The stories that went around. You can't imagine. But I was walking with her one day that fall before she left and the wind blew her baggy jumper away from her body, so I could see her, her middle, under her blouse. It was unmistakable. She was going to have a baby."

Gabriel was twelve, reading in his nan's sitting room one late afternoon, when his mother came home from work and said she needed to talk to his nan about something and he should go through to their flat at the back of the house.

He had been reading about Alexander the Great and his horse Bucephalus for his history class, about how Alexander had tamed Bucephalus and ridden him to India. Later, it would be all mixed up in his head: his mother, the angry and hurt look on her face, the words on the page, "And they laid his body in a sarcophagus of gold and anointed him with honey . . ." In the other room, his mother's voice was urgent, too low to be understood. His nan's, louder, seemed to be trying to calm her. Carrying the book, he was on his way through to the flat when he heard his nan say, "And what if he's told about the baby?"

He stopped, waited, and his mother said something he couldn't hear. Carefully, quietly, he tiptoed to the edge of the hall, just before the spot where he could be seen by them in his nan's kitchen. Gabriel had become an expert at eavesdropping, at knowing where the acoustics favored him and where they did not.

"Stella, you know yourself," his nan said. "The way people are."

He would have heard his mother's response if his granddad had not come through the front door at that moment, calling out to his nan that he had the papers.

Gabriel kept walking through to the flat, his nan's voice in his ears for the rest of the evening. What if he's told about the baby?

19

....

The room is quiet. Peter Mooney's scribbling on his notepad. Margaret Morrell continues her story. "When she came back in the summer, there were rumors she'd gone to have a baby, but of course, no one knew for sure."

Peter looks shocked. "What happened to the baby?"

"I don't know," Margaret says. "Stella finished school and went away to Dublin. Her parents didn't talk about it. She had a good job, we heard. It seemed that was that. But five or six years later, she was back with Gabriel. She lived with them and they helped with Gabriel and she worked in an office in town. Stella was very clever. She read a lot and followed the news, always wanted to talk about what was going on in China or Japan or somewhere. She was a very good student. If she hadn't had Gabriel, she would have had her own career. She might have been a solicitor herself."

"Do you know who the first baby's father was? Or who Gabriel's father was?" I ask her.

She looks surprised for a moment. "I don't know. As for Gabriel, someone in Dublin, I assume. I think she once said something about how Gabriel's choice of a career wasn't a surprise, given what his father did, but then she sort of quieted, like she'd said too much. As for the first baby, there was the boy who was living with his cousins for a year, I can't even remember his name. They were the Prenders and they moved away soon after. But there were always stories about him. Stella told a number of the girls she'd been out with him. He'd be my best guess."

I write down *Boy living with cousins the Prenders in 1964 or 1965.* We'll have to try to track him down. "Do you have any idea if Gabriel ever asked her about the first baby? If he even knew there was one?"

She exchanges some sort of look with Peter, a look that I think is intended to ask him if he really wants her to do this. The almost imperceptible nod he gives her must be enough, because she says, "I overheard a conversation once. I wasn't eavesdropping. The office was . . . small, you see." She hesitates, starts to speak, then leans back in her chair again.

"Mrs. Morrell," I say, "Stella, Gabriel, and Noel are all gone now. If you overheard something that might have relevance here, telling us is the right thing to do."

She glances at Peter again, then says, "Around the time Stella died, I overheard Gabriel asking Noel if he could try to find out what happened to 'the baby.' It wouldn't have made sense to me, if I hadn't, well, if I hadn't seen what I'd seen, but I immediately knew what he was talking about and I assumed that Stella, ill as she was, might have said something. Noel said that he'd ring up William Devereaux. That's a solicitor in Ennis who Noel used sometimes for investigations that were, well, sensitive. Related to divorce and that. That's all I heard. Noel never mentioned it to me."

Griz nods. "As you know, we're trying to make sure there weren't any links between Gabriel's death and Noel's. Is there anything else you can think of that could be relevant?"

She takes a sip of her tea, which must be cold now. "I really can't," she says. "This is all so . . . strange. It seems like something that would happen in a movie, if you know what I mean. I just can't quite believe either of their deaths have anything to do with Sixmilebridge. We're such a quiet place."

Peter checks in with the rest of us with glances, then says, "Well, I think that's all for now, Mrs. Morrell. Thank you. We'll let you know if anything else comes up, all right?"

"I should send an email to all his clients to make sure they know what happened. His daughter will need help settling his estate. Please tell her I'd be glad to help in any way I can."

"Of course," Peter says.

"He was just such a lovely man," she says as he leads her out. "I wish he could have had his retirement."

"Well," Griz says when she's gone, "these small towns never fail to surprise me. It's all intrigue and secrets, isn't it?"

"Ah, that sort o' thing happens everywhere," Peter says. "It's just harder to keep it a secret in a small place."

"So Stella Treacy had another baby," I say. "I wonder what happened to it. We need to talk to William Devereaux."

"Yeah." Griz yawns. It's five now and the sun is starting to sink over the town.

"Are you staying in the Bridge for the night?" she asks me. She looks exhausted, her eyes sagging, her shoulders slumped.

"I don't know. It might be simpler. I still need to meet with your tech guy to look at Treacy's emails. I want to know a bit more about him. There must be someone who can tell us why he was on Long Island. And I want to know more about the baby." The truth is, I'm right in the middle of this case. If I go to Broadford tonight, I'll have to shift my attention to meeting Conor's parents, making conversation with them. I'll have to shift my attention to Lilly. And then I'll have to turn around in the morning and deal with everyone's disappointment when I announce that I'm going back to Sixmilebridge.

"Yeah, I think the techs are arriving later tonight or tomorrow," Griz says. "I can check with Roly. If you want to stay, there were extra rooms at our B-and-B."

I try to keep my voice from sounding too enthusiastic. "That probably makes sense. I'll call Conor and let him know. That way I can tie things up and head to Broadford tomorrow."

I can feel everyone's energy flagging, but given the new revelation about another baby, I have a strong feeling that I want to see Stella Treacy's home again. Griz and Roly look annoyed when I say it, but Peter says, "I can take you back to Carraghmore. I need to check in with the guards I have stationed up there overnight. Then I'll be ready for something to eat, I'd say." He looks hopefully in Griz's direction. "The Bridge Inn does a good meal. Shall we meet there in an hour or so?"

Griz and Roly agree and Peter and I get in his car and backtrack to Carraghmore. The village is pretty in the dying light, the houses glowing amid the saturated dark green of the fields. It's quiet now, many of the garda cars in front of Noel Thomason's house gone, the two uniformed officers guarding the scene standing discreetly in the driveway. I wander over to the Treacy house while Peter checks in with them.

I stand in the yard, trying to picture what Stella's childhood was like here. In some ways, it would have been a perfect place to grow up: safe, lots of grass and trees and places to explore. The house isn't fancy, but it has a solid, stable feel to it. If her father worked for Irish Rail, the family would have been fairly comfortable, or at least that's the sense I got from Peter.

Gabriel's childhood must have been different. Same idyllic spot, different circumstances. He must have felt different, all his life, not having a father, not even knowing who his father was. But Stella Treacy had given him a good life, a good education, grandparents close by. She had done the best she could. She had loved him, seen him successful in life. She had agonized for a few terrible weeks in 2011, thinking she'd lost him, and then had him miraculously returned to her. I feel my stomach pitch, thinking for an awful collection of seconds about what it would be like to hear that Lilly had been kidnapped.

Night is coming; colder air streams across the grass and I walk toward the back of the property and into the trees. Most of them are smaller, recent growth as the numbers of grazing animals must have decreased on these fields, but there are a couple of big old oak trees and a few other varieties I don't recognize, ash, maybe. I walk back into them and I'm standing there, just getting a feeling for the place, when I see a small pile of rocks at the back of the trees. They've been there for a long time; green and brown moss has covered most of them, cementing them into a permanent cairn. *Who built this little monument?* It feels like a tribute of sorts.

I'm walking back toward the house when I notice the scratched letters on the back side of the biggest oak tree. They're barely visible, the bark smooth beneath my fingers, but I can make out a faint "S.T." and a heart beneath it. The edges of the initials below are just barely visible, but I can't read them because long ago, maybe not long after they were written, they were scratched out with a sharp implement, the tree eventually healing around the wounds.

I shine my phone flashlight on the bark, trying to figure out what the letters are, but they're lost to time, the scratch marks soft and blank.

I find Peter in the garden of Noel Thomason's house, giving instructions to the techs who are still combing the grass for evidence. They're wrapping up since the light is disappearing, but they'll start again in the morning. Peter looks up when I come around the back of the house.

"Anything over there?" he asks.

"Not really." I tell him about the initials. "The more I learn about Gabriel Treacy, the more questions I have. There's the whole question of what happened in Afghanistan, and the question of what he was doing on Long Island, but it feels like there's something here, in the village, that led to both Gabriel and Noel getting killed. I don't know why I think that, but it just seems . . . logical, somehow. This is what they shared. This place is the common thread." I gesture around me at the darkening green blanket of pasture. "I just thought if—" I stop talking because I've seen something, movement at the back of the field behind Thomason's house. The light is so low that I'm not sure, but when I squint, I see him. There's a man in the trees at the back of the property. He's watching us. I grab Peter's arm.

"What?" He looks quizzically at me.

"Do you see someone back there in the trees?" I whisper.

Peter squints and peers into the dusky light. "I don't think so. Maybe . . . no, I think it's just a tree."

I concentrate on the spot where I thought I saw him. There's nothing there now. "I could swear there was a man there, watching us," I say.

"Might have been someone out walking or one of the farmers checking fences," Peter says easily. But when he sees my face, he looks again and says, "We'll send the techs out there in the morning to see if there's anything. Maybe we'll get some CCTV, too. If there was someone there, he must have come in a car, right?"

"I guess so," I say. But I'm unsettled now, seeing movement in the trees every time I turn around.

The first story was the one the men told them right after they'd been taken. "You be quiet, and you will go free," whispered the man who put the hood over Gabriel's head. "You be quiet, and you will go free."

He had believed it for a single, hopeful second before realizing how ridiculous it was. They had taken him for a reason. It had been meticulously planned. Why would they take him if they were just going to let him go free?

The lead-up to the story, the prelude, as it were, had been anticlimactic. Global Humanity's rented van had been stopped along the road. Gabriel had known right away what was happening; it had almost happened to him many times before, and he'd heard so many stories of it happening to others that it felt familiar when the men approached the van, guns up and out, and yelled at them in Pashto and then in English. He'd looked at their driver's face, to see if he'd known, and he couldn't tell. The man had looked scared, too, but of course he would be either way. When Gabriel had turned to look into the back, all he could see on the faces of his traveling companions was fear.

"Don't tell them your names. Do what they say," the driver had told them. They'd nodded. Tahir, their translator, had looked the most terrified of them all.

The men were hardly men—boys, really, just hoping this would all lead to a payout. That had made Gabriel feel better, as soon as he'd realized they weren't one of the groups he knew about. They weren't professionals. Their abductors seemed as nervous as Gabriel felt and he tried to smile at them as they forced him into the back of their truck, as if to say, I understand why you're doing this. Let's try to get through it together, okay?

But while they weren't professionals, they were scared, and that made them more cruel than they might have been otherwise. He never really saw the first two places they were held. It was all a blur of cold and terror and thirst. He was kept blindfolded while he relieved himself, into a bucket from the sounds and smell of it. There were voices in the distance and nearby as well; in the first place they were held, he had the sense of some kind of market just outside the windows, lots of voices and noise. They were only there for a few hours before they were moved again. This time there was a long drive, an hour or more, and from the temperature of the air as they were moved from the vehicle into a building, he assumed it was night.

Night, *he told himself, looking for an anchor.*

At that place, he was allowed to relieve himself into the bucket without the blindfold and he was given a small bowl of grains. He thought the others were there, too, felt their presence, but he knew not to say anything. It's what they told you in kidnap school: Don't say anything at first. Just survive. Look for opportunities for escape, but mostly you just want to be compliant, calm, and you don't want to give them your real name, unless they already have it. He slept for a few hours, but was awakened by voices sometime in the night. The voices were loud, angry. He sat up. The darkness of the blindfold was complete. His body was already alert to other signs. He didn't smell food, but he smelled gasoline, and he got his legs under him so he was ready when they lifted him and dragged him out to another van—he knew it was different from the way the floor felt under him.

Someone whispered, "Where are we going?" and he knew it was her from her accent.

"Shhh," he said. "Just wait."

The drive was much shorter this time, twenty minutes or so. There was the same routine: the car coming to a stop, doors slamming, the rough hands pulling and pushing him. They stopped for a minute and he felt a weak warmth on his face and thought, Morning. Then, more hustling and he was pushed down onto a carpet. The blindfold was ripped away from his face and he saw the others around him. They were on the floor of a large, square room. Through a doorway, he could see a room beyond.

It took a second to realize it, but as he looked around, Gabriel felt a sudden prick of a strange, incongruous delight: the walls of the room, and of the next room, were painted a gloriously alive turquoise blue, the color of bright Caribbean waters.

A blue house, he thought. It was like the beginning of a strange fairy tale: Once upon a time, there was a house with walls painted blue.

20

By the time we get to the pub, Roly and Griz are already there. I order and duck out to call Conor, and when I come back my food is waiting for me. I'm still feeling shaken and I take a long sip of my Guinness, earning me a look from Roly.

"Everything okay?" he asks.

"Yeah, everything's fine."

"Your fella happy you're spending the night in the Bridge with this sad shower of law enforcement professionals?" He's watching me too closely and I make a face at him.

"Delighted," I say. In fact, Conor sounded disappointed and a little cold when I called, but I don't want to think about that right now.

When my salmon and mashed potato and salad come, they're a good step or two up from your usual bar food, and I tuck into my plate, dragging the flaky fish through the lemon sauce that came with it.

"This is so good. Oh my God, this salmon. I was starving."

"Me too." Griz is eating a burger and I can't help but notice how Peter watches her, a delighted and awestruck expression on his face as she demolishes the whole thing, plus an overflowing plate of chips.

The bar starts to fill up around eight and I feel a little flash of joy at the familiar sounds and energy, the groups of men meeting up with friends, the tired parents dragging in a folded stroller, the teenage girls pretending they don't know that the teenage boys on the other side of the room are watching everything they do. We're done eating and Peter is telling us a story about the bartender's grandmother when he pauses and nods to the other end of the bar and says, "You've got an admirer over there, Maggie. That fella's been staring at you for twenty minutes." I turn to look and curse under my breath. "Not a fan?" Peter asks.

"No. And he's not an admirer. That's Stephen Hines, the reporter who screwed me over during the Niamh Horrigan case and wrote the story about me being here looking into Gabriel Treacy."

"So it is," Griz says. "He looks like he hasn't slept in weeks, doesn't he?"

"That's a bit judgmental, do you not think?" Roly says to her. "You're not looking too fresh yourself at the moment, Griz."

Griz makes a rude gesture.

"Why's he here?" I ask.

"I'd say he's covering the Thomason case. But some bonus Maggie D'arcy probably sealed the deal," Roly says.

"I want to see what he's got," I say. I drain my pint and get up.

"Don't give away any confidential intel, now," Roly calls after me, but he's only joking.

Hines is alone, just standing at one end of the bar, holding a glass of something pale yellow that I think is whiskey. He's a tall, broad-shouldered person with a barrel for a torso and a belly that strains the buttons of his blazer; his physical presence is intimidating when you're standing next to him, though I think he uses his bulk to cover his awkwardness. His face is all circles: round cheeks scarred by old acne, small nose, alert blue eyes. We got to know each other when I was in Ireland last year, investigating my cousin Erin's disappearance. He had worn his long hair in a small ponytail, but now it's cut into a modified pageboy that grazes his shoulders and gives him a bit of medieval flair. Hines had published leaked private information about me and made my life miserable for a bit, though it all blew over once we found Niamh Horrigan. I heard from him a couple of times last fall, looking for details about my ex-husband, Brian, but I never called him back.

"Mr. Hines," I say. "Of all the gin joints . . . I have to say you were not at the top of the list of people I expected to see in a pub in Sixmilebridge."

"Funny," he says. "You were right at the top of mine." He sticks out a hand, but I don't shake it.

"What are you doing here?"

He smiles in a way that annoys me, fake and smarmy. "It's lovely to see you again. Welcome back to Ireland."

"Come on, what are you doing here? Are you covering the Noel Thomason story? It seems a bit beneath your usual pay grade. A simple house robbery in Clare?"

"Mmm, well, I suspect I'm here for the same reason you are," he says.

"And what's that?"

"Gabriel Treacy."

I raise my eyebrows. "Why are you interested in Gabriel Treacy? As sad as it is, a tourist getting shot in America isn't really a story. We're a society plagued by gun violence, you know."

"Mmmm. I do. But when it came across my desktop and I saw you were the investigating officer, well, I became interested."

"That's not the whole reason you became interested," I say.

He smiles and shrugs. "Well, no. I knew he was a humanitarian aid worker and that he had been to some interesting places, like, for example, Afghanistan." He raises his eyebrows suggestively. "Then, when I was assigned to this terrible County Clare murder and I learned that Gabriel Treacy was a client of Mr. Thomason's, well, it just seemed like a promising story."

I think for a minute. Stephen Hines, I learned last year, approaches most things from a transactional point of view.

"What do you know about his time in Afghanistan?" I ask him. "I'm going to be completely honest with you. I don't have anything I can trade you for it, but I'd really like to know. It's been a bitch trying to get any good information about what happened to him over there. I can buy you a drink. How about that? I need another pint. Can I get you another whiskey?"

"It's ginger ale. I don't drink alcohol, Detective D'arcy. And I'm fine, thank you." Someone laughs loudly and we both look around at the bar.

"Look," I say. "I'm asking you for help. I've had trouble finding out about what happened to him when he was over there. It seems like it wasn't really covered by the Irish press, not to mention the rest of the world. But someone must have given you a heads-up, or else we wouldn't be here. I just want to know what you know about it."

"And?" He turns to survey the rest of the bar.

"And I can't speak to the Irish investigation. You of all people know that. But I'll give you what I can on Gabriel Treacy from my own investigation. Okay?"

He looks around casually again, then back at me, speaking in a low voice. "I have some sources in the defense forces and Foreign

Affairs. Gabriel Treacy was kidnapped in Afghanistan in 2011. Held with him were an American nurse, a doctor, an Afghan translator, and a reporter. I'm trying to find their names. My colleague who was covering the Taliban at that time said that he heard a rumor about it, but not until a few weeks after they'd been taken. The Americans told him not to report anything because they were trying to get them released and wanted to keep it quiet. That's standard operating procedure. A lot of times the captives' governments are negotiating, the family may even be paying, though of course no one ever admits that. Letting the captors know who their captives are is sometimes a bad idea."

"So you didn't report on it?"

"Not really. An Irish TD alerted Foreign Affairs and Trade and they were in touch with the Americans. Once the captives had been released, we published an item that didn't mention their names. Anyway, my colleague says the American nurse was named Anne something and the reporter was Pietro. What?"

I'm remembering the photographs hanging in Gabriel Treacy's apartment. *Pietro Griselli. It has to be the same one.* "Nothing," I say.

He doesn't believe me, but he says, "That's all I have, but it's a good story, the fact that he was an aid worker, the fact that he was kidnapped." He smiles. "The fact that hero detective Maggie D'arcy, who saved Niamh Horrigan's life, is involved in this one, too. Now, who do you think killed Mr. Treacy?"

"My colleagues back on Long Island are convinced he was shot by MS13 members, either as an initiation killing or as part of a robbery. The official line is that it was a random killing. It probably was a random killing. But I want to make sure. That's why I'm here."

He nods. "Thank you."

"Will you tell me if you find out anything else?" I ask him. I write down my email and cell number on the back of a coaster.

"Sure, of course," he says. "It's good to see you, Detective D'arcy. I'm very interested to see how this one turns out."

"Don't you mean you're anxious to see that justice is done?"

He just smiles.

"What'd he say?" Roly asks me when I get back to the table.

I share Hines's information about Afghanistan and my assumption that Pietro is a photographer named Pietro Griselli.

"We may be able to do something with that," Roly says. "I have an Interpol contact based in Milan. He could at least go talk to this Italian fella and see what he has to say."

"Would you? 'Anne' from America isn't going to get us anything. I'd just like to know more about what happened to him over there, you know? Even if it doesn't have a direct bearing on the investigation."

"You know what we call that? Writing a novel," Roly says. "Those little things about a person's life that didn't have anything to do with why they got killed, but are a thorn in your foot, like. You need to know. When one of the lads is following a thread like that, we say 'Ah now, he's writing a novel.'"

"That's my favorite part of this job," Peter Mooney says. "Usually, in this thing, people get killed for dead boring reasons. Sex and money, right? But that other stuff, the stuff that gets them there, the stuff that fills their days, that's the stuff that gets me back to the desk every morning."

"I know," Griz says. "The affairs, the mad hobbies. I heard an interview with a writer once and she said that the stuff that makes it into a novel is only a little bit of what you know about a person. But the rest of it tells you why they did the things they did, why they were in the place they were when they got murdered."

Peter says, "Yeah, I like the hobbies, too." He looks at Griz just a little too long, then takes a sip of his lager.

"Well, that's me ready for my bed," Griz says abruptly. "Can I give you a ride, Maggie?" We all get up to go, Roly amused and twinkling at Griz all the way out to the cars.

My room at the bed-and-breakfast is a symphony of purple: violets on the wallpaper, purple-striped sheets and duvet cover, purple tiles in the bathroom. I take a picture and send it to Lilly. I almost send it to Conor, too, but think better of it. I don't want to rub it in that I'm not in Broadford. I'm tired, but I want to see what's out there about Pietro Griselli, so I get into my pajamas and bring my laptop over to the bed.

Most of the hits I get are in Italian, and I limp through translations of captions under his photographs in *la Repubblica* and other Italian papers. He seems to have taken pictures all over the world, including in Afghanistan in 2011. He's not on Facebook or Twitter, from what I can tell, and I can't find anything on the kidnapping.

I dial Dave's number.

He picks up in the car on the way home from work. "Maggie! Just about to call you. What's happening?"

"You get anything on the gun?"

"Nah, not yet." I can hear the frustration in his voice.

"When do they think they'll have something?"

"Couple days."

"Let me know."

"Obviously. What's up with you?"

I give him the update and then say, "I want you to have Berta look into this guy Hines told me about, Pietro Griselli. Gabriel Treacy had a bunch of his photographs hanging in his apartment. So they're obviously connected in some way. If we can find out more about him, it may be our way into whatever it was that happened to them in Afghanistan."

"I'll get Berta on it," he says. He sounds tired.

"And listen," I hesitate. "Have Marty just check and make sure Anthony Pugh hasn't left the country."

"You okay?"

"Yeah. No. I don't know. There was something weird tonight. I could swear I saw someone watching me at the scene. The cop I was with didn't see him. I don't know. I probably imagined it, but combined with that text message to Lilly . . ."

"Got it. I'll let you know as soon as I can."

"Everything okay there?"

"Yeah, it's just . . . Cooney's still putting the pressure on. Alicia's been around a lot. It feels like Bill is . . . I feel like I can't just do my thing, you know?"

"What about Bill?"

"I don't know. Probably nothing. I don't want to bother Marty, but Alicia's making everyone nervous. Oh, we checked the plates on that white SUV at the motel, the one Uddin Ahmed saw there the day Treacy was killed. It had a commercial license plate, registered in DC. We think it was the painting company, like Sabbir Ahmed said, but we're confirming it."

We say good night. It's midnight now and I know I need to get to sleep. But I'm still feeling edgy and awake. I stand at the window, looking out across the moonlit fields around the bed-and-breakfast.

I'm about to turn away when I see movement in the driveway below.

But when I press my face to the glass, I can see the whole lawn and driveway clearly. There's no one there. I imagined it.

I open my laptop back up and start searching again for Pietro Griselli. But my computer feels somehow different, like someone's watching me, and I'm too anxious to talk myself out of it. I put it back in my bag and get into bed. It takes me a long time to fall asleep.

Pietro told the first story.

It was dark, the blue house quiet, cold air whipping through the spaces around the windows. The men who were guarding them sat at attention in the next room, but didn't interfere when they spoke a little. They whispered, telling each other that their organizations must know by now that they were gone, that their governments would already be starting to secure their release. They told each other lies and tried to believe them.

"Are you Catholic?" the reporter asked Gabriel. He was Italian. He spoke perfect English, but his accent was strong, and Gabriel had to listen hard to get it all. Pietro. If they were in Ireland, someone would have called him Peter already.

"I suppose. I mean, I was brought up in it and all."

"I was raised Catholic," Anne said. "I became a Buddhist in my twenties."

Pietro had an unblinking gaze and he turned it on her, wiggling his body around to face her, his tied hands useless as leverage. "Which God have you been praying to here?" he asked her.

She was silent for a moment. "There is no God in Buddhism. But I've been praying to my Catholic God." She looked almost ashamed.

"I have, too," Pietro told her. "I did not think I believed, but I do. I am surprised to discover that." He smiled and it transformed his whole face. "When I was only twenty, my mother became very sick. She had a blood cancer, it was very bad. The treatments made her sick. She was very religious, and she asked me to pray for her."

Like James Joyce, when *his* mother was dying, *Gabriel thought. He didn't say it, though. He found that he conserved his thoughts now. They had been in the blue house for two days and he found himself* boiled down *somehow. He only did what was necessary. Only said what was necessary.*

Pietro went on. "I told her that I would, but I didn't. I didn't believe. It didn't mean anything to me. I didn't do it."

They all waited. They knew where it was going. He was going to tell them that she died and he had always felt guilty about it.

"She recovered," Pietro said. "It was like a miracle. One day, she started to get better and the doctors didn't know why. Her blood counts, everything, it improved. The treatments they worked, but it was more than that. Her body . . . She got better. She is seventy-one this year and she is healthy. She walks each day to my sister's house for coffee."

They waited. "Once in the town where I grew up, there was a man," he said. "He was a very bad man, an uomo cattivo. *But he was very rich and he had a huge house and a car and my friends and I, we loved his car, and we would go and look at it. One of my friends, Giorgio, his mother worked at the house, and we would go with him and play on the grounds and look at the car. This man, when he went to town, he parked this car in front of the* farmacia *where my father* worked, while he conducted his business in town, and my friends and I would touch the car and look at it."

One of the guards coughed in the next room and they all looked up, waiting a long minute before turning back to Pietro. He was looking up at the wall. There was only a little light, from the next room. His face was mostly in shadow. "One day, we were playing by the car. We knew he was visiting the doctor and would be gone a long time so we were bold, pretending to get into the car, running our hands over the paintwork. It was a very light blue, like the shell of a bird's egg. Like the sky."

They all looked up at the blue walls, which had become a substitute for the sky. "Giorgio, he thought the man was not coming out for a long time and he decided he wanted to sit behind the wheel. He opened the door and he got in. He was smiling so big, his hands on the wheel, pretending to drive. The window was down and he was saying, 'Oh, I am a big man, this is my car,' that kind of thing, and we were all laughing and we didn't realize that the man had come back."

"What was his name, the man?" Gabriel asked. For some reason, he wanted to know.

Pietro smiled. "Ah. Signor Bianchi. He yelled at us and we ran away, but Giorgio was still in the car. When I got to the corner of the street, I turned around and I saw Signor Bianchi dragging Giorgio out and hitting him. It was broad daylight and there were people walking up and down the street and no one stopped him! He had a stick and he hit Giorgio with it and made his head bleed. He kicked him in the stomach! We were ten years old! I waited until the man got into his car and drove away and then I went back and got Giorgio. We knew it was wrong, what that man had done."

Another cough from the next room. One of the guards was sick, had been sick for three days, with a hacking, spasmy cough and a pallor to his face that made Gabriel think it was something more than a cold.

"The whole way home, we talked about how we wished that man would die," Pietro whispered. "We prayed. We said, 'God, make this man die. He is a very bad man. God, kill this man.' We knew that it was wrong, but we wanted that man to die."

He didn't say anything for a long moment and then he whispered, "The next day, Signor Bianchi was driving his car in the mountains and his brakes failed. The car was destroyed. He was burned terribly and died in pain, many weeks later, his skin peeling and infected. We thought we had done it, for years, until I was older and I no longer believed. But Giorgio, he became very religious. He is still very religious. I do not know what to make of this story."

There was something comforting about the sound of Pietro's voice, coming through the darkness. It wasn't until the next day that Gabriel realized what Pietro had been doing.

He'd been confessing. Because he didn't think he'd be walking out of the blue house alive.

21

I run first thing, trying to burn off the anxiety and worry from last night. It's a nice morning, the sun bursting up out of the fields, a little bit of warmth in the air. I push myself hard along the road between Sixmilebridge and Carraghmore, and by the time I'm dressed and ready to meet Roly and Griz in the dining room for our complimentary Irish breakfast, I feel considerably better than I did. We fill up for the day on crispy fried eggs and toast, melting broiled tomatoes, and plump Irish sausages, and then I drive with Griz into the garda station.

I call Marty's phone, knowing he'll be up. He gets up at four every morning, does some calisthenics, and drinks his coffee with a plate of Croatian pastries his cousin or niece or someone drops off at his house once a week. When he answers, I know he's been eating. I just barely hear him gulp down the last of his treat before he says, "Mags. What's up?"

"What kind of pastry did you get this week?" I ask him. I like when he says the names of the fancy pastries.

"*Pinca*. Now what's going on?"

I tell him about the interviews and Stella Treacy and the guy at the house. "I asked Dave to find out, but I gotta know, it's not Pugh, is it?" I ask him.

"Definitely not. My guys have been checking in every day, watching him go to the supermarket or wherever. He was safe at home last night."

"That's what I thought. Dave says you don't have the gun yet."

"Soon," Marty says. "You found out anything about Treacy's connection to the lawyer? They been in touch recently?"

"Doesn't seem like it, though I'm going to look at the emails today. The stuff about another baby, I don't know. I don't think it had anything to do with why he got killed, but we'll see if we can find out anything more today. I'll check in with Dave later. He doing okay?"

"Dave? He's doing great." I feel a little pang of jealousy. "Good luck."

I have an email from Uncle Danny, with a picture of him and Eileen at the bar, grinning and wearing top hats for some reason I can't figure out. I'm about to close it up when a message from Berta appears in my inbox and immediately, while I'm watching, goes from unread to read. I click on it, thinking I'm seeing things. It's a list of Gabriel Treacy's recent travel, with Berta's notes about the couple of New York trips he's taken, all more than a year ago.

When I click out of it, it appears as unread again in my inbox.

I stare at it. I'm about to show it to Griz when Peter Mooney comes in and says, "We've got a lead, and it's a good one. CCTV on a private home just out of the village caught a gray Renault heading into Carraghmore at eight p.m. Monday. The lads got it last night. They were immediately interested because there weren't many cars on the roads that time of night."

He's excited, his eyes bright and full of hope. "Didn't take long to track the registration down this morning because it was reported stolen from Shannon Airport. Car's owned by a family who live in Adare. They were on holiday in Germany and when they came back yesterday, the car wasn't where they'd left it in the car park. The CCTV shows the car exiting the car park at four p.m. Our suspect must have hot-wired it."

"Have you got it going back to the airport?" Griz asks immediately.

"Not yet, but we'll be checking more CCTV today."

Griz says, "Get the registration out to Roads Policing right now." Peter nods.

I stand up, excited now too. "If that was the car that brought Noel Thomason's murderer to Sixmilebridge, then whoever stole it from the airport must have flown into Shannon that day, right? Let's see if we can narrow down the flights that came in just before four."

"Maybe," Griz says. "Though there are probably local lads who'd know the car park at Shannon would have a lot of cars owned by people who might not know it's missing right away. On the other hand, that might be a lot of thinking for the local lads."

Roly's tech guy arrives from Dublin at ten. "I've got some files for you," he says. "We have all of Gabriel Treacy's backed-up work emails from the last six months or so. I'll help you go through them if you want."

He opens his laptop and shows me a file created by the IT team in Dublin. They've copied and pasted all the emails Gabriel Treacy received or sent from his GTreacy@GlobalHumanity.ie email address.

"It's all yours," he says. "We did a search for 'Thomason' and didn't find anything, but there may be something relevant to your investigation. One other thing, though."

"What's that?"

He sits down and opens up a folder on his laptop. "We couldn't find anything on the Irish dating sites, though without his laptop, we can't be sure he wasn't on them. But there's this: When we went to his office at Global Humanity to get the backups, we checked out his workspace. We took some papers and notebooks and so forth, and they finished going through them this morning. Nothing of note, except this." He clicks on a PDF and a photograph of a piece of note-paper comes up. I recognize the writing from the to-do list next to the bed at the motel. It's not a list, though, just a jotting, a reminder. It says *Heather,* and underneath that, *Odyssey.*

"It's probably a business thing, but I thought you'd want to see it," he says. "Maybe there's someone named Heather in his circle. I wouldn't know what 'Odyssey' refers to."

"Could be he was reading it," I say. "Going back to the classics. Thank you."

I start going through the emails. It's boring stuff, work emails about grants and funding and programs in India and Turkey and Guatemala. But reading them, I'm starting to get a sense of Gabriel Treacy, of his voice, his personality. He's a good writer. Describing a situation he encountered on his last trip to a refugee camp in Greece, he conveys the sense of desperation on the refugees' faces, the help-lessness of the workers in the camp.

An email he forwarded to Gillian Gleeson in September catches my eye. It's from an accountant, asking Gabriel some questions about a disbursement to a local organization on the ground in Turkey. "Gill, can you answer this?" he asks in the email. "It looks like one of yours." And then, a few weeks later: "Gill, see this again. Can you answer???"

The question must have been answered in person because there's nothing else. But I'm remembering the to-do list from the motel—*Gill account*—and it strikes me as important that he was still worried about it all these months later. We'll need to ask Gillian Gleeson about it. The three question marks look a bit desperate to me, like there had been some communication in between and he was losing patience.

September and October seem to have been pretty uneventful, if you can call a trip to Guatemala and then another one to Sri Lanka "uneventful." In November, there's an email that catches my attention, though. It reads: "Gabriel. I was trying to get through to you, but the number I had for you didn't seem to work. Wondering if we can chat. Here's my number. Hope all's well with you. Paul." A series of digits follows and I write them down on my notepad. At the bottom of the email is the sender's signature: *Paul Shouldice, Chief Medical Officer,* and the address of the organization in New York. The reason the email jumps out at me is the name of the organization: MVTW, Medical Volunteers for the World. It's the nonprofit Gillian Gleeson thought Gabriel Treacy was applying to. This email sounds like she may have been right. An old friend or business contact, reaching out to Treacy about a job opportunity. There's nothing else in the thread, so I'm assuming Gabriel called the number and they took the conversation there. "I'm going to call this guy Paul," I tell Griz.

I dial the number. It goes straight to voice mail, a man's voice, English accent: "Hello. It's Paul. You know what to do." I leave a message with my name and number, explaining who I am and why I'm calling, and asking Paul Shouldice, whoever he is, to call me back as soon as possible.

"That all clear to you?" the tech guy asks, poking his head in. He's young, perky, still eager. I wonder how long it will last.

"Yeah, thanks. Hey, any luck on his personal account?"

"Oh yeah. He had a Gmail account, like the ex-girlfriend said, but he deleted it a month or so ago."

"What?"

"Yeah, deleted the whole account."

"That's weird. And there's no way we can get those emails?"

"Nope, so they say. If you had a device he'd used to access the accounts, there might be some backups."

"Shit. Thanks. Can I ask you something?" I open my laptop up to my inbox and point to the message from Berta. "I could swear this was marked read and then switched back to unread," I say. "How would I know if someone else was reading my email?"

He looks surprised, but sits down next to me and slides the laptop over, typing and opening windows while I look on. "I don't see any obvious malware," he says after a minute. "But there are things that . . . My email has glitched like that too. I think it's just an error in the upload process, but you might want to change your passwords just in case, make sure you have two-factor authentication set up."

I take the laptop back. "That's a relief. You hear about all these things. Thanks."

He goes back to show Roly something and I sit there for a minute, just listening to the bustle of the station, everyone working their angle. Then I take out my notebook and write down *Gabriel Treacy* in the center of the page. I add in *Dublin* and *Abena Tekle, Gillian Gleeson,* and *Coworkers.* Then I write *Sixmilebridge* and everyone I know he interacted with here: *Stella Treacy, Noel Thomason, The Reids, Margaret Morrell, Gerry Murray, Jonathan Murray, other townspeople, Father?*

I write, *Afghanistan. Gabriel Treacy, Pietro Griselli, ??? (doctor), and ????? (American nurse. Anne).* I search for "Afghanistan. American nurse kidnapped," but I don't get anything useful.

And then, going back, I write in *Stella Treacy's first baby* and *father of first baby* and then *Gabriel Treacy's father.*

There are two people, I realize, who might have known about the first baby, who might know if Gabriel knew about the first baby.

Abena Tekle answers on the second ring.

I say, "It's Maggie D'arcy. How are you doing? I've been thinking about you." Roly told me that one of his sergeants had made a courtesy call to let her know about Thomason before it hit the news.

"I'm managing," she says. "I still haven't quite, accepted it, I guess you'd say. Is there anything new?"

"Well, not exactly," I say. "I'm in Sixmilebridge, at Noel Thomason's house."

"Yes. I couldn't believe it when they told me."

"How well did you know him?"

"Not very well. I guess the first time I met him was when we were coming down a lot when Stella was ill. He came to the house a few times, to talk to Gabriel and Stella about her will and selling the house and all, once it became clear that she wasn't going to recover. Then after she passed, we met with him once, Gabriel met with him a few more times. That was when we started to have troubles, so I think he started coming down here by himself after we . . . after we agreed to split. He had to pack up the house and everything all by himself. I offered to help, but he said no."

"Did Gabriel talk about Mr. Thomason?" I ask.

"Not really. I mean, not unless it was something related to Stella's estate."

"When do you think they spoke last?"

"Well . . ." She hesitates. "I don't know if this means anything, but when we spoke in January, he told me that Noel's daughter had just had twin girls. He was just passing it along, as we were having a chat, but I was thinking about it and I realized that they must have talked. The babies had just been born, so they must have been in touch."

I make a note. Once we get the phone records from Noel Thomason's office phone, we'll be able to confirm it.

"Thank you," I say. "Is there anything else you can tell us about Noel Thomason? Was Gabriel happy with his work, with how he represented him?"

"Oh, yeah. I think so. He was a lovely man. He was quite good to Stella. In fact, at one time, Gabriel wondered if they might not, well, get together. It sounds silly, but I think Gabriel hoped they might. I don't think they ever did. They looked out for each other, though."

"Thank you." I'm thinking about the email to Gillian Gleeson. "And how did he get on with his coworkers? Did he get along with them? What was his relationship with Ms. Gleeson like?"

"Oh, he and Gillian got along well. They were good partners, even if sometimes they bickered. They were like, siblings, you know?"

Something about her voice makes me want to dig deeper. "What do you mean? What kinds of things did they bicker over?"

"Well, she started the organization. It was her baby. But she brought Gabriel in because she wasn't as good at the business part of it. He tried to get her to hire more people, do things differently, but she had her ways and they sometimes bickered about that. But at the end of the day, they liked and respected each other."

"Did you have the feeling that things had been tense between them lately?" I ask her.

"Well. Maybe. The last time we spoke, I asked about her and he said, 'Oh, you know Gillian.' I had the sense that maybe they were in one of their spats."

"Abena, we spoke to someone who suggested that Stella may have had another baby, before Gabriel, that in fact she may have been so set on keeping Gabriel even though she wasn't married because something had happened to the first child or she had been forced to give it up. Did Gabriel ever say anything to you about that?"

She didn't know. I can tell from the way she stammers out, "Stella? Another baby? I . . . no, I had no idea. And I'm pretty certain Gabriel didn't know. I think he would have told me that."

Except he did know, according to Margaret Morrell's account of the overheard conversation. Gabriel didn't tell Abena about the baby or the details of what happened to him in Afghanistan. It makes me wonder what else he didn't tell her.

"Poor Stella," Abena says. "She must have been very young. Oh."

"Yes?"

"I just remembered something. When she was sick, I was sitting with her one day and she wasn't . . . well, lucid, I guess you'd say. She was talking about things from her childhood and she said something about a baby. She said, 'It's gone now. He told me it was gone.' I had no idea what she was talking about, but . . . do you think . . . ?"

I tell her we don't know and I'm about to let her go when I remember the piece of paper Roly's techs found in the office. "Oh, one more thing. Does the name Heather mean anything to you?" I ask her.

"I don't think so. Was she . . . was it someone he was seeing?"

"We just don't know. It was a name that came up and we just wondered. I'm so sorry to have to ask all these questions. Thank you so much. If you remember anything else, please get in touch."

"I will. But, only . . . Please don't tell Gillian that I said she and Gabriel were fighting."

"Of course not." I try to sound reassuring. "It's pretty much our job to keep everything confidential."

Gillian Gleeson doesn't answer her phone at Global Humanity, but I leave a message and she calls back a few minutes later.

When I ask her how she's doing, she adopts a brisk tone. "All right. I miss him, you know. And this . . . this other death. I didn't know Mr. Thomason at all, but somehow it affected me. I don't know why."

"It's not a predictable thing," I tell her. "Grief has its own time-line. I'm so sorry to bother you, but Mr. Thomason's death has made it necessary to ask some more questions. Did you know him?"

"Not personally. But Gabriel did mention him to me, during the time he was settling his mother's estate. He seemed grateful to him, and happy with his work."

"Nothing more than that?"

"No."

"Did Gabriel ever say anything to you about his mother having another baby, before he was born?"

"What? No. I knew he didn't have a father growing up, of course. He talked about how hard it had been for Stella. But no, he never mentioned anything about that. Did she?"

I ignore the question. "Thank you. You said that you saw Mr. Treacy's computer screen at some point and that he was looking at the website for an organization called MVTW. Well, we think he may have corresponded with someone named Paul Shouldice who worked at that organization. He doesn't say specifically that he had a job for Gabriel but that could have been why he was in touch."

"Ah." I can hear the relief in her voice. "Now I can see it. Maybe they had an opening and he contacted Gabriel. I don't know why, but that makes me feel better, that Gabriel didn't reach out to them, that it was someone he knew."

"Did you know Paul Shouldice?" I ask her.

"No, but I've heard of him. I think his name came up once with Gabriel. I forget why, maybe we were talking about a medical project with Médecins Sans Frontières or something and he said he knew him or had worked with him. He'd been quite high up there, Paul."

I make a note to look into it some more, but it makes sense. If Paul Shouldice was working for MVTW and he was looking to hire someone, he might have thought of someone with whom he'd worked.

"Oh, and did Gabriel know anyone named Heather?" I ask her. "A friend or girlfriend or work associate?"

"Heather? No, I don't think so, not for work, anyway."

"Thank you," I say. "I just have one more question. Did you and Gabriel ever have disagreements? Your work was pretty intense. You must have sometimes had different views about things. When you had differences of opinion, what did they tend to be about?"

She actually gulps. I can hear it over the phone. "Gabriel and I got along well. You know . . it's normal for partners to have different styles, like, around managing people. Gabriel was probably more . . . generous, to our employees. I tend to be a bit bossy. People don't like me as much, I suppose. They liked Gabriel. He was the kindly dad and I was the mean mammy. We used to joke about that."

"So, there was nothing specific you were fighting about before he went to New York?"

She hesitates again. "No, nothing specific. I . . . we got along well."

I calculate, trying to decide whether to ask her about the email referencing the accountant. Something tells me to get more information first so I say goodbye and that we'll be in touch.

What next? I'm still thinking about Stephen Hines's information about Afghanistan so I find Jonathan Murray's website again and dial the number for his local office in Ennis. "Constituency office for TD Jonathan Murray," says the woman who answers.

"Yes, I'm a police detective from New York and I'm in Ireland investigating the death of one of Mr. Murray's constituents in the US. I wonder if I could speak with Mr. Murray."

"Oh, it's terrible, isn't it? Such a sad thing to happen. I'll just see if he's available now."

It takes him a few minutes to pick up and say, "Jonathan Murray here."

"Yes, Mr. Murray, my name is Maggie D'arcy. I'm a police detective from the States and I'm investigating the death of your former constituent Gabriel Treacy. I was wondering if I could just ask you a few questions about your relationship with him, in particular your advocacy for his release when he was kidnapped in Afghanistan."

There's a long silence. Finally he says, "I don't have anything to say about that. I made a few calls, that's all."

"Well, but I'm wondering if you can give me some more information about him. I know that—"

"I'm sorry, I have a meeting starting. I really don't have anything to share with you."

The line goes dead.

I'm still sitting there holding my phone when Roly comes in and says, "Okay, D'arcy. Tell me the news. What's worrying you?" He pushes a pile of papers off the desk and sits down on the edge, his thumbs tapping out a drumbeat on the wood.

"Well, Jonathan Murray just hung up on me, so I want to know what he's so touchy about. And I feel like there was something there with Gillian Gleeson," I say. "I don't know . . . when I asked Abena about whether he and Gillian got along, she hesitated, said that of course coworkers had differences of opinion, but it sounded like more than that. He wrote her an email about an account, something their accountant thought didn't quite add up. I'd love to know more about that. You should interview the rest of the employees at Global Humanity."

"Okay. I'll send someone over. Good thought. What else?"

"I don't know. Stella Treacy, the first baby, I want to know more about that. Margaret Morrell thought that maybe Gabriel had asked Thomason to look into it and that maybe Thomason went to, I think his name was Devereaux."

"I want to know more as well," Roly says. "What's your plan?"

"Well, right now, I should probably get to Broadford to see how Lilly's doing and whether I can salvage my relationship."

"I'll give you a lift," Roly says. "But are you sure you're able for meeting the parents?" He casts a disapproving eye on my jeans, boots, and simple black sweater. "Would you not make a bit more of an effort?"

I give him the finger, then say, "You can drive me over there at five."

"Hey, I've got a few other things for you," Roly's tech guy tells me, poking his head into the office. He's holding a stack of paper. "The emails from Noel Thomason's backup system. It's all client stuff that you can look through. Nothing that raises any alarms. He and Gabriel Treacy were in touch by email as recently as January. Then Treacy deletes his account. But before that, on the fourth of January, Treacy sends Thomason an email from the deleted Gmail address saying, 'Noel, I've been thinking more and more about the matter we spoke about last month. Would it be convenient if I drove out for the day on Saturday?

I won't take much of your time. I just have a few more questions about the legal issues we discussed. Thanks.'"

"Probably related to his mother's will," Roly says.

"Yeah." I search some more through the emails. There's a return one from Noel Thomason, but it just says that Saturday will work well and he'll see Gabriel then. I put them in my bag to look through later.

"We should show it to Margaret Morrell," I say. "But she said she wasn't around as much then. Thanks."

I'm packing up my things when Roly's phone rings and we all look down to see Peter's name on the screen. Roly says, "Yeah, what's up?"

Peter says something that makes Roly sit up in his chair as though he's been electrocuted. "Okay, we'll be right there, Peter."

He looks up at Griz and me and says, "They found the items that were stolen from Noel Thomason's house. Peter says there's something we need to see."

22

It's five now, the sky pale orange and blue above the fields and stone walls. We park Roly's car in the driveway of Noel Thomason's house and follow one of the uniformed guards through the fields. Griz and I have ankle-height leather boots on but, true to form, Roly's wearing a pair of expensive-looking dress shoes and he steps gingerly around the circles of cow manure dotting the fields here and there. We walk along a track between two fields and step over a barbed-wire fence, then follow the guard around the back of a thick clot of hedges and trees. As we approach, we can see a crowd of techs and guards with lights. Peter waves us over.

"It's getting dark, but I think you can still see what we've got here," he says. He's excited, a delighted grin on his face, and I find it touching, how much he wants to impress the big city cops, how much he wants to get a win for them. We all gather around the lights.

"It was buried under those branches," Peter says, pointing to a large pile of tree limbs lying on the ground. "Garda Delaney only found it because she kicked one of the branches out of place." He smiles at a young woman in uniform standing off to the side. "We left some of them so you could see, but the techs are taking loads of pictures."

Roly and Griz and I step carefully over to the site. The techs stand aside for a minute so we can take a look, but I can feel their impatience. The light is dying fast.

There's a desktop computer monitor and a large laptop and an external hard drive. All are shattered, and I can see holes in the laptop and drive, as though someone's drilled through it. There's a small wooden box that looks like an antique, some jewelry—costume mostly, from the look of it—and some other small electronics: radios, what looks like an old CD player. That's it.

Griz looks up at us. "Whoever killed Noel Thomason didn't care about the things he or she took from the house," she says. "And the computer . . ."

"There was something on the computer the killer didn't want anyone else to see," I say. We step back and watch the techs do their work. The air is cool and smells faintly sweet, like new grass and gin and honey. The trees and hedgerow melt into darkness, but the circle of lights reveals a competence that strikes me as chilling. I think of my first impression of the scene of Noel Thomason's murder: It seemed more organized than we were meant to believe. I think that's true here, too. There's something about the thought that went into it, the carefully arranged branches, the methodical destruction of the computers.

It feels professional.

"This lot also went to talk to Gavin Millman," Peter says, nodding to the uniformed gardaí. "He was belligerent with 'em, but he did say that he noticed a gray car at the back of the road there. Yesterday, he said, so it's likely our killer was watching us, like you thought, Detective D'arcy."

"We need the car," Griz says. "Peter, check with Roads Policing and see if there's anything else. Get 'em out looking for it."

We're all silent and finally Roly says, "Well, we'll leave you to it. Good work, all. I expect we'll know more in the morning," and we make our way back to the driveway.

"I need to get up to Broadford," I tell them. "I promised Conor. I'm already late." I feel guilt wash over me. I forgot for a moment, where I'm supposed to be, in the excitement over the find.

"We'll take you," Roly says. "It's not far." We get into the car. Roly rolls the windows down and I can feel the shift in my brain as we head back through Sixmilebridge and east along the narrow main roads to Broadford, the cool air moving through the car.

"What do you make of that?" Roly says finally.

"Our killer really wanted it to look like a robbery," Griz says. "That's the first thing."

Roly nods. "But why hide the stolen stuff like that? Why not dump it somewhere far away so we would never find it?"

I think for a moment. "There was some reason our killer couldn't do that. Time was a factor maybe, or transportation."

"Yeah, the branches were meant to delay the discovery but he had to know we'd eventually find it, right?"

"It's got me thinking," I tell them. "Gabriel Treacy's laptop was stolen, his phone, too. We've been assuming it was because he was robbed, but maybe it was the same thing. Maybe he was killed not because of the electronics, but because of something *on* the electronics."

Griz says, "Our suspect is still driving around in the stolen car, so we might have a chance of finding him. We've got an alert out on the registration and we'll get travel lists for today and tomorrow. Maybe we'll get something there."

We drive in silence for a while, all of us tired, thinking. Finally Roly says, "Well, we ought to get some good evidence off it. He would have touched all those things. We may be able to figure out what he used to smash the computer."

"It's hard to really destroy a hard drive," Griz says. "He may not have made a complete job of it, you know?"

"I don't think we're going to get much," I say. "I hope I'm wrong, but this feels pretty methodical to me. I'm betting he wore gloves, I'm betting he was careful about trace evidence."

"We'll see," Roly says hopefully.

The road curves close to a long stretch of water, shimmering through the darkness, and Roly says, "That's Doon Lough there. Pretty around here. Nice place to be from. Your fella's lucky."

"It's going to be weird meeting his parents under these circumstances," I say. "We'd planned to wait a bit longer, but . . ."

"Ah, they'll love you. Might as well do it now, right. I suspect soon you'll be moving over here anyway, amn't I right?"

The lake goes on, a stream of silver to our left. I don't say anything for a minute and Griz jumps in with, "Roly, she's got a job. She's really good at it. Why would you assume she would just move here?"

He turns to look at me. "I thought he couldn't move because of his son, like."

"He can't," I say. "I don't know what we'll do. But Griz is right. What would I do if I moved over here? Would you give me a job, Roly? I know enough about the Garda to know you can't just hire whoever you want."

I thought I was kidding when I said it but it comes out semiserious and he says, "Well, you'd have to do the training at Templemore. I had a detective who applied a few years back. He was a German fella married to an Irish woman and they made him go through the course and everything. Even had to do the Irish, though they've changed that now. But if you did that, we might be able to get you on one of the specialty teams, as a buckshee, like. You ever heard that term, Griz?"

"No," she says, making a funny face at me. "But you're going to tell me what it means. I can feel it."

"They used to call them that. It was often a golden boy, like, someone well-connected or especially good at his job. Sometimes they'd get brought up from other departments or it might be a young fella from somewhere who showed some promise as an investigator and they'd bring him right up to the detectives, rather than making him go through all the years most of us had to. You'd likely have to do a year in uniform somewhere but then I might be able to bring you in as my buckshee." He grins. "What do you say, D'arcy?"

He's just thinking out loud, but my mind starts to go there and then I realize: Uncle Danny, my house, my job, Lilly's school, her friends. It's impossible, and it brings me down all over again.

"I think I'd better make sure Conor wants to even talk to me before I start calling the movers," I say, trying to make it breezy. "I think that's it up there. Conor said there's a bridge just before the drive." The house is a two-story white stucco and gray stone farmhouse, set up on a hill a bit, with an extension on one side and a long complex of barns out the back and around the sides and fields stretching out in all directions. It glows in the headlights of the car.

"Ah, very nice," Roly says. "Lovely here."

They drop me in the driveway. "We'll give you an update tomorrow," Roly says. "You try to enjoy yourself, now. It's all going to be all right." I wave goodbye and watch them head back toward the motorway. The air is chilled, smelling of rain. It's dark now. The sky is black and lit with stars. A light on the side of the house barely illuminates a walkway up to a door on the extension.

I watch the car until it's gone, then take a deep breath and head for the house.

23

I walk up to the door, trying to push down my nervousness by focusing on the details, the flower beds just starting all around the side of the house, the strong smell of animals that hits me. No one comes when I knock, so after a minute, I push the door open and walk into a tiled mudroom and then a big kitchen with white walls and exposed timbers and a hearth, the mantel cluttered with photographs of Conor and his sisters and brother when they were little, a photograph of a baby I recognize as Adrien, and a few of Conor's nieces and nephews in Australia and Denmark. There's a huge round wooden table and a looming cookstove with a loaf of bread on a cutting board. A cat is up on the counter, licking a plate of butter, and it barely looks up when I say, "Hey, you shouldn't be doing that."

"Hello?" I call out, but the house has a feeling of emptiness: an appliance humming somewhere, the cold, hollow feel of unoccupied air. I poke my head through a doorway to my right. It's a living room or den, a television in the corner with a well-loved couch and chair in front of it, and a bookcase against one wall. I run a hand over the titles: lots of poetry, Conor's mom's probably. Pinned to the wall above a little table is a handwritten haiku: "Yellow flowers burst/They are here so suddenly/The scent around me."

Conor's house.

More framed photos crowd a bookshelf, wedding pictures, more pictures of babies. There's one of Conor and Bláithín holding baby Adrien, smiling and looking young, closer to the Conor I knew twenty-four years ago. I feel a pang of something—not jealousy, exactly, but regret. If things had been different, if Conor and I had gotten together then, there might have been no baby Adrien. And no Lilly either.

"Hello?" I call again, just to be sure. Then I look down the narrow hallway to what I assume are the bedrooms at the other end of the house. Lilly's blue Alexandria High sweatshirt is draped over a chair in a small den/library. I press it against my face and smell her shampoo.

Outside, I walk around to the back of the house, guided by the light from the flashlight on my phone. A small cold breeze rises and stirs the grass around me. The band of cold air races along the ground. I can feel it move around my legs and suddenly I feel a sense of panic. Where are they?

I think about the man at Noel Thomason's house. What if he knows about Conor? Have I put Conor and his family in danger? Lilly? *Lilly.*

A couple of times now, I'd been sure someone was watching me. I'm still fairly sure. What if he followed me here?

Anthony Pugh? No. The man watching me at Noel Thomason's yesterday?

"Conor?" I call out. "Where are you?"

Silence.

The night suddenly feels dangerous, the darkness closing in around me.

A dog's bark startles me and I drop my phone, scrambling for it on the ground, my heart pounding. When I find it I look up to see a border collie coming around the side of the barn. I stop and lean down to let it know I'm friendly. "Ellie?" a woman's voice calls. The dog sniffs my hand and then heads back to the barn complex. I'm about to call out for Conor again when I hear Lilly's voice say, "Mom?" My body floods with relief. I make my way around to the open side of a large barn lit inside and filled with white and black forms pressing against each other and *baa*-ing. Lilly and Conor are standing against a gate at one end, watching something.

"Hi," I call out. Conor smiles when he sees me and waves me over, but his attention is elsewhere.

"Hiya," he says in a low voice. "Good timing. We had a ewe go into early labor. She was in trouble for a bit but Da finally got everything sorted. She's just delivering the second one now." He gestures toward the gate and I can see a big white sheep lying on the ground, straining, arching her neck toward the sky, an older man kneeling next to her in the sawdust, and by the sheep's head, a small white spider-legged lamb, soaking wet and bloody and struggling to stand. The sheep licks it a few times before she's seized by another contraction and strains again. As I watch, something emerges from her rear end—the head and hooves of another lamb, I realize. The sheep strains hard. There's blood and what must be an amniotic sac hanging from her.

"Oh my God, is she . . . ? It's coming right now? Lilly, this is amazing."

"I know!" She comes and stands next to me and lets me hug her and kiss her cheek.

Conor's father pulls gently on the legs when they emerge again. The sheep strains once more, and a long white-and-yellow shape slides out onto the hay, wrapped in a whitish membrane. It's absolutely still, unmoving, sprawled unnaturally. Conor's father peels the membrane away, then moves it up to its mother's head and she sniffs it half-heartedly. The other lamb stands, then falls, then gets up on its legs, stumbling across its sibling, and the ewe, who seems relieved, is nosing the first lamb, licking it and making low chuckling, grumbling sounds.

"Come on, little thing," Conor mutters. He pulls me in and presses his lips to my head, and I know he's thinking of Lilly, hoping against hope that she doesn't have to see a wet, dead baby lamb tonight.

"Come on," Conor's father says. "Breathe, ya little bugger." He puts his hand on the second lamb's narrow chest and presses gently a few times. Then he bends down and puts his mouth over its own mouth and blows.

We all hold our breath.

The lamb kicks, faintly. I can see it breathe, see air fill its lungs, see the moment it comes to life. Time stops. I feel like I've run a marathon, like I'm flying. The lamb raises its head, looking for its mother.

"Ah, very good," a woman—Conor's mother, surely—says. "She's going to be all right."

"She's okay!" Lilly says, rushing forward to see, and I feel tears spilling from my eyes. Conor hugs me. His dad stands up, grinning, and pushes the lamb toward its mother, who begins to lick and nudge it as it raises its head weakly and strains toward her sounds. The lamb bleats and the mother makes the low chuckling sound again.

Conor's father stands up and grins at us. "What a welcome," he says.

Conor's mother comes forward first. She doesn't hug me, but she takes my hand and smiles warmly up at me. "Oh, Maggie. It's so lovely to finally meet you. Ciaran, come say hello to Maggie. I'm Breda. We're so happy you're here." I barely have hold of myself; there are tears in my eyes and I feel raw, too open.

"Oh, he's got his hands full," I say. "That was very dramatic. I'm sorry, I . . ." Tears are running down my face. I wipe them away.

But she smiles. "No, it's quite something, to see a lamb born, especially when it's a bit touch-and-go like that. Seeing life come into this world, well, who would we be if it didn't make us a bit emotional?" She's a small, compact woman, with silver hair cut in a pixie cut and a heart-shaped face with elfin angles. She's wearing a chunky knit blue sweater. I always thought Adrien looked exactly like his mother, but I can see him in his grandmother's face now, too. I can't stop looking at her. *Conor's mother.*

"It's so nice to be here," I say. "I'm so sorry that we sort of descended on you, but thank you for making Lilly so welcome."

"We love having her here." She studies me for a minute and then nods at Lilly and smiles.

Ciaran Kearney is a grayer, thinner version of Conor, his shoulders stooped under his blue sweater, so alike in gesture that it throws me for a minute. He smiles again and I can see Conor all over his face. "I won't shake your hand now," he says. "Won't kiss you, either." We all laugh and Lilly comes over and hugs me again.

"Wasn't that amazing?" She's beaming, her face softer than I've seen it in months.

"Oh, Lil." I hug her again. "It's good to see you. I missed you."

Adrien is watching, too, and I give him a hug before awkwardly going to stand beside Conor. He puts an arm around me and whispers, "I missed you too."

"The lamb was stuck," Lilly tells me. "Mr. Kearney had to turn it around, right?" She looks at him and he nods.

"Lilly, what's her name, then?" he asks. "When you help save a lamb, you get to name her."

"Really?" She grins, thinking, then says, "Rosie."

Ciaran scratches the lamb's head. "Rosie it is then. I've got to dip their cords and make sure they're eating all right, but you can all head back to the house if you want."

"Let me take you in and show you around," Conor tells me. "You must be exhausted."

We stop to hug and kiss quickly by the back door of the house and I say, "She looks happier than I've seen her in months. Thank you."

"She's been really cheerful. My mam adores her and my da's ready for her to move in and help out on the farm. How did things go for you?" There's something hesitant in his voice, as though he doesn't really want to hear, so I just say quickly, "Oh, good, I guess. We had a bit of a breakthrough tonight, but we'll see."

"That's positive, right?" The look of relief on his face turns into a twisted little knot in my stomach.

"Yeah, it is." I don't want to say anything more. "Now, show me around. Can I see your childhood bedroom, all your posters of your teen celebrity crushes?"

"You can, but my mam's turned it into her studio. She's taken down my posters. Sadly." He takes me up the narrow staircase. There are three rooms at the top of the stairs. He opens the door to one; it's been painted a cheery yellow and there are photographs and bits of paper pinned to the wall. "That was my room. I shared with one of my sisters until I was ten and then I had it to myself." He drops my bag in a room across the hallway.

We go back downstairs and Breda comes in, holding a basket of eggs. "Can I make you some tea?" she asks. "I have a meal going but I'd love a cup now."

"I'd love a cup of tea, too," I say.

"Sit right here by the cooker. It's nice and warm there." I can feel the heat radiating from the cookstove and when she brings me my tea, I wrap my hands around the mug and feel warmth seep through into my bones. The kitchen is cluttered and alive, stacks of mail and magazines and books on every surface, knitting abandoned on a chair, a framed watercolor painting and painted blue and purple pottery displayed in a hutch are bright spots of color on the white walls.

"Lilly is a lovely girl," Mrs. Kearney says. "You should be very proud."

"Thank you," I say. "It's been such a rough time and it's been so hard on her. I wouldn't have planned it this way, but I think it's been good for her to be here with you."

Mrs. Kearney looks pleased. "She's very welcome, of course."

I ask her what I can do to help with dinner and she gives me a bowl of potatoes and a potato peeler. Conor is making something complicated for dessert, sifting flour and melting chocolate, and when I ask him what he's up to, he just wiggles his eyebrows.

"You don't mind peeling?" Mrs. Kearney asks me.

"Are you kidding? I grew up peeling potatoes at the bar. My uncle used to pay us a dime a pound. I should have asked for more, when I think about it."

When Lilly comes in, her cheeks are pink. She's wearing a big handknit sweater in a rusty-pinky-orange color that brings out the richness of her eyes. "I like that sweater on you," I say. "Where'd you get it?"

"It was one of the girls'," Conor says. "Hanging on a hook in the press. She can have it if she wants. It's just an old jumper."

"Are you serious?" Lilly asks. "I love how it's, like, vintage."

"Oh, it's vintage, all right. That jumper's seen things that would make you shudder." Conor smiles at her and she smiles back. There's a new bond between them that I can see and feel.

"I made that for Janey," Mrs. Kearney says. "I remember knitting that jumper like it was yesterday. It was for her eighteenth. Makes me happy to think of you wearing it, Lilly."

Lilly smiles, delighted with the sweater.

"So, you were down to the Bridge, were you?" Mr. Kearney asks once we're sitting around the table, eating lamb stew and potatoes. "This thing with Noel Thomason?"

"Yes."

Conor looks up. "Da, you didn't know the fella, did you?"

"Noel Thomason? Sure I knew him. I bought a horse off him years ago. He was the solicitor for that fella, what was his name, the one who bought the farm from Andy. My sister Kathleen lived in the Bridge for years. Taught at the national school. She lives in Ennis now, but she still chats to everyone out that way. Maybe we'll stop in and see her for a cup of tea and she can give you the gossip. It's interesting now, you know, the robberies seem to be increasing in Limerick. Drug trade, I suppose, but it's usually someone known to the victim, isn't it now?"

"Da's always wanted to be a guard," Conor says. "He's a bit of a detective. He'll have to tell you sometime about the Case of the Missing Tractor."

"Really? Did you solve it?" I ask Ciaran.

Breda snorts with laughter. "Quiet, you," Ciaran tells her. He turns to me and says mysteriously, "Let's just say the tractor wasn't really missing."

"I'd love to talk to your sister," I say. "I'm trying to learn all I can about Gabriel Treacy. We still don't know why he was over in the States. It wasn't for work, so I'm wondering if it's something related to his upbringing in Sixmilebridge."

"I'll ring her up," he says.

"Breda, Conor tells me you're a poet," I say, to change the subject.

She looks bashful and delighted. "Well, I love it. We have a little writers' group here in Broadford and we hold readings and publish collections of poems and stories."

"She just put out her fourth collection," Conor says proudly. His dad grunts but doesn't say anything and Conor looks down at his plate. He's told me that his father resents his mother's literary activities and friends, that it's a source of tension between them.

"They're just little chapbooks," Breda says, but she's flushed and smiling.

"I'll get one for you," Lilly tells me. She jumps up from the table before I can tell her we're still eating, and goes into the living room. "Come see, Mom."

I push my chair back and follow. "I showed her earlier," Breda says, following too and looking delighted.

"See." Lilly hands me a pile of thin paperback books. The cover of the one on top is a photograph of fields and sheep.

I hold it up. "I love this cover. Congratulations."

"Thank you. This is the newest one." She hands me a book with a painting of a woman on the cover. "This is by a friend of mine. She was sent to a mother and baby home when she was a girl, and her baby was taken from her. She's been painting portraits of other women who also were at the homes. That painting inspired one of my poems. I was thinking about my own babies and what it would have been like to have them taken from me. It seemed perfect for the cover."

I want to ask her more, to read the poem, to tell her about Stella Treacy's baby, but I know it's not the time so I smile at her, put the books down, and we go back to the table and finish eating. Conor and his dad are talking about road construction and something about the county council and when we're almost done eating, I say, "Are you represented by Jonathan Murray here in Broadford? His name came up in our investigation."

"Ah, sure, he's our TD," Mr. Kearney says, with something complicated on his face. "He lives not far from here. He came up in your investigation, you say?"

"Well, not as a suspect or anything like that. We were just trying to get in touch with him to find out a bit more about Gabriel Treacy's life. It seems like Mr. Murray may have advocated for him when he got into trouble overseas with his job once." Conor glances at me.

"That right? I wonder what his angle was. Jonathan Murray's always got an angle. Not like his father. His father was a good man. I never voted for him, mind you. With this one, you never know what he's thinking when he does something." Ciaran scowls and takes a bite of stew. "Sure, Kathleen can tell you about him. She's very involved in the local politics, with the county council now. Goes to all their meetings."

Later, in bed, snuggled up next to Conor, I'm conscious of his parents downstairs, of Lilly in the room next door. I whisper, "I like your parents."

"Even my da?" he whispers back, his arms around me, his chest pressed into my back.

"Yeah, he's a softie. You can tell."

"I don't know about that, now." He kisses the top of my head. "I thought we'd leave day after tomorrow. That okay for you? Maybe get a really early start. We can pick up where we left off and head to West Cork."

"Yeah," I say. "That sounds great. I need to go to Ennis to talk to this guy Noel Thomason worked with, I think, and there may be a few other details to clean up, but I think I can do it all tomorrow. Tell me about the house in West Cork again."

"Well, it's on a little peninsula called Ross Head that juts out into the Atlantic. It's lovely. You can see the sea in all directions. And it's not far from Crookhaven. There's a pub where you can get the most southerly pint in Ireland and sit by the fire. It's great for walking out there, but the house has a little patio with chairs and the best thing is to sit out there with your tea in the morning and watch the ocean."

"Mmmm. It sounds perfect," I whisper back. I can see it, the sun rising over the ocean, the sound of the waves, Conor and I huddled together under a blanket on the patio, pints in the local pub, Lilly and Adrien walking on the headlands, their hair blowing in the wind.

"The best thing about it," Conor whispers in my ear, "is the master suite. It's far away from all the other rooms so you can make as much noise as you like without worrying about teenagers on the other side of the wall."

"That's my favorite part," I say, and snuggle up against the warmth of him to go to sleep.

24

Ciaran is outside when we come down for breakfast and Breda pours us tea and says that he's been up since three keeping an eye on the second lamb born last night. "She wasn't eating well so he thought he might need to get some colostrum into her. After you've had your tea, you might go out and see if he needs a hand, Conor. Oh, and I was just chatting with Kathleen. She can't drive out here, but she said if you want to show Maggie what Ennis is like, she'll meet you for a cup of tea."

"That would be great," I say. "I need to talk to the solicitor in Ennis anyway, and see if Jonathan Murray will talk to me in person." I look up at Conor. "Do you mind?"

"No. I always like a wander around town. Maybe we can convince the young farmhands to come along, too."

We bundle up and take our cups out into the morning, steam rising as we walk out to the barn.

Ciaran and Lilly and Adrien are leaning over the gate, watching the mother with her two lambs. They're cuteness personified, their little bodies mostly dry and fuzzy now, their legs spindly, their huge eyes staring up at us as we get close. The bigger one butts up underneath its mother and starts drinking vigorously, but when the smaller lamb tries, the mother knocks it away. Without being asked, Conor goes to the wall and fills a bucket with water.

"Why's the mother doing that?" I ask.

"It happens sometimes when it's been a hard birth," Ciaran says. "If the lamb doesn't start drinking early enough, the ewe doesn't realize it's hers and she rejects it. She needs to get the smell of her and if she doesn't . . . well, I'll keep trying with her, but we might have an orphan. Little Rosie really hasn't had a good drink yet. I tried through the night but the ewe is determined not to let her in and she only got a few sips. We need to get some colostrum into her. Lilly, do you want to give her her first bottle?" He picks up the little lamb and hands Lilly a giant bottle only a quarter filled with white liquid. "Get her in your lap and hold her head up. That's right. You've to just get it in her mouth and she'll know what to do." Sure enough, the lamb starts to suck greedily and Lilly looks up at me with a huge grin on her face, her gifted sweater bringing out the pink in her cheeks and the golden brown in her eyes. I take a picture with my phone to send to Uncle Danny.

The lamb drinks all the liquid in the bottle and when she's done, Ciaran lifts her and places her back into the pen.

"There, that should do it, Lilly," Ciaran says in a quiet voice. "She'll be just fine now. Her mother might even start feeding her, but if not we can keep her alive on the bottle. Can you two keep an eye on them?" he asks Lilly and Adrien. "I've got to get some tea and toast into me or I'll fuckin' collapse." They settle in outside the pen, watching the little family. The lamb gets pushed away again, but she has a full belly now and snuggles in next to her sister. As long as she doesn't try to nurse, the mother seems happy to let her be there. Lilly and

Adrien are content and smiling, leaning over the fence to look into the pen, chatting about something on Lilly's phone. Conor and I try to convince them to come to Ennis with us but they say they'd rather stay at the farm and keep an eye on the lambs. "When you get back, I could use some help moving hay," Ciaran says, with a wink. "So don't get distracted by the temptations of the big town now."

It's nice to be alone and we hold hands as we drive through mile after mile of gentle agricultural land, marked by little clusters of houses and farms here and there, hills rippling softly into the distance. It's a soft part of the country, very different in feel from Wicklow or Dublin, and I find myself relaxing in this landscape. Conor has the radio on and we listen to the news, something about Brexit and then about politics back home, immigration and Russian connections and protests.

"You've got a bit of a mess on your hands, haven't you?" Conor says with a wink and a grin.

"Do I detect a bit of schadenfreude? It's not funny, you know."

"Ah, it's just . . . America, like. *America*. We're used to looking up to you, even when we think of you as warmongering imperialists. But now . . ."

"Now you feel sorry for us," I say.

He rubs the top of my hand with his thumb and grins. "A bit."

I check my phone but there's no update from Dave or from Roly and Griz. "So what do you know about Murray?" I ask Conor. "I'm trying to figure out how to get him to tell me about Gabriel Treacy and Afghanistan."

"His father was a legend around here," Conor says. "Murray the younger doesn't have anywhere near his charisma. Gerry Murray was a big good-looking fella, with a booming voice and a sort of warmth to him. He was kind of an old-style politician. He had that ability to make you feel like you were the only one in the room. His son seems hardworking, but he's a cold fish, and I think he trades on the name to win elections. I've never actually met him but he seems a bit stiff."

"If he was intervening with your state department to get Gabriel Treacy freed, he must have had some clout, right?"

"Not necessarily. Didn't you say Treacy was freed outside of his efforts."

"Yeah, that's true. What time are we meeting your aunt? And what do you want to do while I'm interviewing the solicitor?"

"Oh, I'll find a bookshop. There's a good one I remember." As we get closer to Ennis, the houses become more suburban looking and closer together. The town itself is picturesque, with a long main drag called O'Connell Street and a monument at one end. Conor parks in a lot off O'Connell and we walk around, looking in shop windows and at pubs. It's quiet now, midday on a Friday in February, which Conor says is rock bottom of the tourist season, but it feels lively anyway, with the brightly painted cafés and shopfronts lining the streets. "There's loads of good music here," Conor tells me. "Festivals and that. We'll have to come back in the summer."

I leave him in front of a bookshop and find William Devereaux's office on Abbey Street. When I called this morning, he said he could only give me twenty minutes or so, and he does seem like he's pressed for time, ushering me quickly into his simple office on the second floor of the building, over a women's clothing shop.

"You worked with Noel Thomason fairly frequently, didn't you?" I ask him, taking in his longish gray hair and leather jacket. He looks more like an aging rock star than a lawyer.

"I wouldn't say frequently. A handful of times over the past seven or eight years, he came to me for certain kinds of research he needed done."

"What kinds of research?"

He takes a deep breath. I can see him carefully considering his words. "I specialize in investigations into more delicate family matters— divorce cases, paternity cases, things in that arena."

"Margaret Morrell, who worked for Mr. Thomason, thought that he might have been helping his client Gabriel Treacy look for information on a baby his mother gave birth to in 1965. I know that you're bound by confidentiality, but both Gabriel Treacy and Noel Thomason are dead and I'm trying to find out why. Is there anything you can tell me that might help with my investigation?"

A phone rings in the outer office and William Devereaux looks up and waits for it to stop before saying, "Terrible news about Noel. He was a lovely man, the sort of country solicitor you don't see much anymore. He cared about his clients, I think, since they were his neighbors and friends. I can tell you that he did ask me to see if there were any records of a birth to a mother named Stella Treacy in 1965. I did not find any such record." His speech is careful, almost robotic. He's being very, very careful about what he's saying.

"Is it possible the baby was adopted?" I ask.

He hesitates, then says, "I asked Noel if he wanted me to search for adoption records. He said he did. You have to understand that the tracing of adoption records in Ireland is significantly different from what you may be used to in the States. Adoptions from the fifties and sixties were most frequently achieved with the participation of the Catholic Church. Many of the records were housed with various Catholic orders and organizations, others with the state adoption authority. Recently, there have been discoveries of what we call incorrect registrations, where a name other than the birth mother's name was placed on the registration of the birth."

"So they were fraudulent?"

"Technically, though the intent was to provide happy lives for the babies who were adopted. As I'm sure you know, there was a lot of shame around unwed mothers at that point. These births were kept secret in many cases, or people tried to keep them secret. It was part of a system. We're learning now about some of the horrors of that system, but I suppose in defense of the orders that did it, there were good reasons to create new narratives for the children born to unwed mothers, given the stigma."

"So, Stella Treacy's baby may have had one of these incorrect registrations? Is that what you're telling me?"

"Not necessarily. I did some preliminary searching for Noel but he said his client couldn't afford a proper search. I gave him some tips and he said he'd continue to work on it himself."

I can feel the disappointment sink in. "So you don't have anything you can point me to? You didn't find out anything about Stella Treacy's baby?"

He hesitates, looks away. "No. I didn't. I'm sorry." His eyes flick over to the door. My twenty minutes are up. But I have the feeling he's hiding something. "I'm afraid I have an appointment now, Mrs. D'arcy. I'm sorry I couldn't help you."

Conor has a bag of books when I find him, a novel set in France for Adrien, an Edna O'Brien novel for Lilly, and a thick Irish history for me. We meet his aunt Kathleen in a little bistro on O'Connell Street. She's on her way to a meeting, but she's only too delighted to stop for a cup of tea with her favorite nephew, she tells us with an intense twinkle. She's a tall, extremely elegant dark-haired woman in her late sixties or early seventies, dressed in black, a red silk scarf tied expertly around her neck. Conor introduces me and she studies me for a minute before saying, "I hear you're investigating Gabriel Treacy's death. I was very sorry to hear of it."

"You knew him quite well, didn't you, Aunt Kathleen?" Conor asks her.

"I did. He was truly a special child. Right from the beginning." She looks at me. "My late husband was the head of school at the national school in Carraghmore. So we knew all the children. Gabriel was truly exceptional. He was shy. Principled. That's the word I'd use to describe him. He stood up for what was right. He had a deep moral compass. I think he learned early on that he needed to prove himself with his actions, if you know what I mean. He was always the top student in his class and the other students liked him, even if he didn't have any really close friends. I knew he would do great things with his life."

"Tea?" Conor asks her as the waitress comes around. He orders some scones to go with it and when the waitress is gone, Kathleen says, "It's so nice to meet you, Maggie. We've all been curious about you, you know. And of course, you're a bit of a celebrity here in Ireland."

"Well, I don't know about that, but it's really nice to be here. Thank you for talking to me about Gabriel. We still don't know what he was doing on Long Island and it's really helpful to get a better sense of him, of Stella, of their relationship."

"I didn't know Stella that well, but she was very proud of him," Kathleen says. "After he left home, she often spoke about where he was, which country he was working in, the projects he'd started. Gabriel came and spoke to the pupils at the national school about his career once, talked about how he got into humanitarian aid work and showed slides of the places he'd been. It was so interesting." She checks her watch.

"How did he get involved in it?" I ask. "I've been wondering about that."

"I think he said that he had planned to study law at university and one night he went to a talk, given by an aid worker, about what was happening in Bosnia. He signed up to volunteer at a refugee camp in Croatia on his summer holidays and that was it. He showed the children at school pictures of children from the camp, just their ages, and talked about how he'd seen what a difference he could make. After that, he said, once he knew how much he could do to help, he couldn't do anything but continue the work. I'll always remember that. He told the children that if you have something to give, something the world needs, it's your duty as a human being to give it."

"Kathleen, what did you know about Stella's situation? Did she ever talk to you about Gabriel's father?" I don't know how much she knows, so I don't want to reveal too much.

"Of course, I didn't grow up in the Bridge, so I wouldn't have remembered when she came home with a baby, but I've heard enough gossip to know that people weren't happy. Her parents were very well respected. Maybe that helped." She raises her eyebrows. "Maybe it didn't. There were a few times when we had to intervene at school because other boys were being cruel about Gabriel not having a father. I always wondered why Stella didn't make up a story about him being dead. That was the usual thing then. But she was proud and she must have had her reasons."

The tea comes and once she's poured out for all of us, I say, "I heard a rumor about Stella having had another baby, before Gabriel.

I wouldn't ask if it wasn't important for my investigation, but did you ever hear that rumor, in town?"

Kathleen looks up at me with amused navy eyes exactly like Conor's dad's. She says, "You hear lots of gossip, in a town like that. My friend Yvette, who also worked at the school, once made a comment about how you'd never know it to look at her, but Stella Treacy was quite the, well, I won't use the word Yvette Coughlan used." She grins. "Yvette's very wicked. She never said anything about another baby, but her implication was that Stella had a *past*. Though that's what they said about any girl unlucky enough to find herself expecting then. It was a terrible double standard, the way boys and men could do as they liked and it was the girls and women who paid the price. There was a young one who worked in the shop when Ciaran and I were children. She disappeared and later I heard she'd had to work in one of the Magdalene laundries. I'll ring up Yvette and see if she knows anything else, and you can interview her if she's got something to tell you. She'll be only thrilled. It'll be the most exciting thing that's happened to her in ages."

"Thank you," I say. "Here's my card to pass on, with all my numbers. That's so helpful."

"No worries. It was nice to have an excuse to meet you." She winks. "Conor, how's my brother?"

"Oh, he's just the same. Had some early lambs last night, so he'll be busy next few weeks." She and Conor talk about Adrien, and Conor's sisters' kids, and Kathleen's sons, who both live in Dublin.

"Has your mam heard from Aidan?" she asks him nervously. "I haven't wanted to ask lately."

Aidan is Conor's younger brother. He lives in London, or did the last they heard. For most of his adult life, he's struggled with addiction and homelessness and while they tried for years to get him into treatment and stable housing, Conor's family has finally accepted that there's not much they can do. Once a year or so, though, Conor goes to London to try to track Aidan down. The last time he went, he saw Aidan on the street, but Aidan wouldn't talk to him. Conor's told me his mother goes through periods where she can't get out of bed, thinking about Aidan and worrying about him.

"Nothing new," Conor said. "Mam's okay for the moment, though. She's loving having Adrien and Lilly at the house."

"I bet." Kathleen smiles at me. "I can't wait to meet Lilly, Maggie. Now, I've to be going."

"Thank you again," I say. "I really appreciate the help."

"It's sad, isn't it?" Conor says, once she's gone. "Stella Treacy. That it had to be a secret. Thank God times have changed. It must have been a lonely life for her, after Gabriel left home."

He looks wistful and I reach out and touch his hand. "You thinking about your own impending empty nest?"

"Ha! Maybe." He smiles. "There's something attractive about it too, though, isn't there? Tidy the kitchen and it stays tidied. We could go on holiday anytime we want, no thinking about school calendars."

"We could," I say, smiling back. But I'm thinking about the cottage in Carraghmore, the loneliness of it, the heart carved on the tree, Stella's initials left solitary.

"What do you think happened to the baby?" Conor asks me. "You don't think it . . . died, do you?"

"I don't know. Roly and Griz can try to see if there are adoption records, but it sounds like a lot of them were falsified."

"Maybe it was adopted by a family in London or Manchester. Or

Chicago," Conor says. "It happened, you know. Children who never knew they were Irish and didn't find out until they were older. It was very sad."

I look up at Conor, my mind alert now. "Maybe that's why Gabriel Treacy was on Long Island," I say. "Maybe he was looking for the baby."

"Seems like he would have told someone, but people are funny." He takes my hand and says, "You ready to get home? Mam probably has dinner started and my da will be wanting our help with the hay."

On the drive home, I call Roly and give him an account of my conversation with Devereaux. "Do you want to come down for the case meeting in the morning?" he asked. "Before you go?"

"We're leaving around lunchtime, but if I can convince Conor to let me drive his car, I could come down for the morning," I say.

"All right so, we'll see you then."

Back in Broadford, we find Lilly and Adrien out in the barn, watching the little lamb jumping around with her sister. Ciaran asks if we can help him move some hay up into the top of the barn before dinner. "They've caught me flat-footed," he says. "These early lambs. I need to clear out the barn to get ready and I've got to move all those square bales of hay up so I can set up the pens."

I go up to the loft with him. Conor, Adrien, and Lilly carry bales up a narrow flight of stairs and drop them at the top so we can lift and stack them.

I take a bale and throw it up on the pile, then straighten it out. I do another one. It feels good to work my biceps and shoulder muscles. I get the whole row done and when I turn around, Ciaran is looking at me with an expression of admiration.

"That lad ever give you any trouble," he says with a huge grin, "you tell him I said I'd take you over him as farmhand any day."

I laugh and we work away in companionable silence for a bit. Then I say, "Kathleen was really helpful. I'm grateful to her."

He tosses a bale to me and winks. "I'm sure she was only delighted to share the gossip." Then he says, "Ah, now. She's just interested in people, what they do and why they do it." I take the bale from him and stack it on top of the row.

"You've pretty much described my job right there," I say.

He thinks for a minute and says, "I think when you're a teacher in a small town, like she was, and you see children grow up and turn into whoever they're going to turn into, you have a sense of, well, essential character, I guess you'd say. Sometimes you say, 'That one's going places,' or 'That one'll turn up bad,' and usually you're right, but sure, sometimes you're not. It's interesting to see how things turn out for people."

I toss a bale to him and say, "There was a guy in my town who killed someone in a dispute over lobstering rights. He and this other lobsterman got into a fight over their lobster pots or something and this guy had a gun and he killed the other guy. I don't think he meant to, but his temper got the better of him and he had the gun . . . Anyway, he had a kid who was in my class at school. The guy was in prison for most of the kid's childhood and the kid—his name was Derek—he was just angry, mean, a real troublemaker. You just knew he was going to get into trouble. He started in high school, some drug dealing, that kind of thing. When I started working as a detective, I responded to a murder scene. There'd been a fight in a bar downtown and someone had been shot in the parking lot. It didn't take us long to sort it out. The dead guy was the son of the lobsterman who had been killed, and

Derek had killed him. They got into an argument about their fathers and . . . one thing led to another."

Ciaran has stopped working. His eyes are wide and delighted. He reminds me of my father suddenly, something about the intense humor in his eyes, his delight at human nature. I feel a pang of sadness, of something undefined, homesickness, I guess, though my father isn't even there anymore. "Ah, fuckin' Shakespeare that is," Ciaran says. "That's a good story, now. I'll be telling that story. Kathleen will love that one."

I call Dave just before dinner to give him the update. He sounds tired and discouraged, and when I ask him why, he says that everyone's on edge back home. "The press is going crazy. Why haven't we caught Treacy's killer, can people feel safe in their own homes, is MS13 murdering people in cold blood, et cetera, et cetera. FYI, Mags, Cooney freaked out when he heard you were over in Ireland. He's gunning for you now and Marty got caught in the middle."

"Marty told me. Well, I have my phone. I'm going to a case meeting tomorrow and I'll let you know if I hear of anything you should follow up on. Hope you get something on the gun soon. Bye, Dave."

Conor's mom serves us fish pie and salad, one of Conor's favorite suppers, and I let her pour me a full glass of red wine, enjoying the taste of it, the warm room, Conor next to me at the table, his arm stretched behind me on my chair.

"How was Ennis?" Breda asks us. "Did you get what you needed from Kathleen?"

"She was great," I say. "Really helpful. Last night, you told me about your friend who was forced to have her baby at one of the mother and baby homes. Did she ever find any information about her baby? Was she ever able to find him or her?"

Breda shakes her head. "No, she wasn't. She had a little boy and she never found him. She had other children but she says she still remembers his little face, remembers how much he weighed. Some of the women whose portraits she painted were able to find their babies, though."

"What were mother and baby homes?" Lilly asks.

"Oh, it's shameful part of Ireland's history, Lilly," Breda says. "They were places run by religious orders. They were supposed to be for 'fallen women,' but all kinds of girls got sent to them, if they became pregnant, sometimes if they had mental illness, if they'd been abused. If you could pay, you had your baby there and went home. If you couldn't, you had to stay and work or you were sent to one of the Magdalene laundries to work. Some girls spent their lives in them."

"It's shameful," Ciaran says. "We knew it was happening. Our parents did. We all knew girls who disappeared into those places. And the babies . . . I was just reading about the home up in Galway. They think that babies died there . . . Well, it was a terrible thing."

"A colleague of mine is writing a book about them," Conor says. "There's an investigation going on right now. The number of recorded deaths at some of these homes was quite high. There may have been death records falsified and then the babies were adopted out or sent to America. Or they may have died of malnutrition or . . . other causes."

The meaning of his words is heavy in the air and we all sit in sad silence for a minute before Conor and Adrien clear the table and come back with vanilla ice cream and an apple pie they made earlier. Adrien serves wedges to all of us and we eat appreciatively.

"Granddad, will you play something?" Adrien asks when we've brought the plates into the kitchen. He turns to Lilly. "He's really good on the guitar. He used to play in a band."

"You did? What was it called?" I'm delighted, thinking of Ciaran Kearney as a rock star. "Did you know about this, Conor?"

"Of course. What were you called, Da? The Rovers or something?"

"No. We were The Shepherds. Because we were all off sheep farms." He goes and gets an acoustic guitar from the other room and sits down by the fire to start strumming.

He's just playing around, but when he plays the opening chords of The Beatles' "In My Life," Lilly joins in, singing the first lines in her sweet alto, so quietly we all have to lean forward to hear her.

"Lilly, you've a lovely voice," Breda exclaims. "We'd no idea."

"Let's do it properly, Lilly," Ciaran says. "You know all the words?"

"I don't know." She blushes. She loves to sing, but not in front of people she doesn't know.

"We'll figure it out," he says, then sings, *"There are places I remember."* Lilly harmonizes with him and it's perfect, her voice achingly pure, Ciaran's guitar floating up and around us. I think of my mom and her voice when she sang and how my dad loved to watch her. Conor looks on proudly, holding my hand and stroking the top of my thumb with his own.

They do the whole thing and we're all clapping when a text comes in from Conor's aunt.

"Kathleen sent me the number of her friend in Sixmilebridge," I tell them all. "She says I can call—I mean, ring her, tonight. Do you mind if I go in the other room?"

"No, of course not, Maggie. Here, I'll turn the light on in the sitting room for you," Breda says, leading me into the next room.

Yvette Coughlan has been waiting for my call. I know from the way she picks up and breathlessly says, "Hello?"

I explain what I'm looking for and she says she was good friends with Stella. "I worked at the school and I'd bring Gabriel home sometimes. We became friendly. I knew her for many years, and when she was dying, I went and sat with her sometimes. Her mind was affected, not that she was making things up, but her defenses were down, now. She'd never talked to me about Gabriel's father, but one day, it was like she wanted to confess. She told me she'd had another baby, before Gabriel."

"Did she say what happened to the baby?" I ask. From the living room, I can hear Ciaran playing a trad tune I think I recognize. I hear Conor's laugh and then Adrien's.

"No, but she said she went to give birth at a private nursing home in Tipperary and when it was all over she came back without the baby. But it was what she said about how she got to the home that I remembered when Kathleen asked me if I knew anything about Stella's first baby. I never said, because of Gabriel, you see. But now that he's gone, now that they're all gone. Well, it wasn't right."

She waits a second, building up drama. "Stella told me about the baby. She said, 'Gerry Murray arranged it. He paid for it. He arranged the whole thing.' She said he was the father."

"Gerry Murray, the TD?" I ask.

"That's right. He was Gabriel's father, too. Stella said they were in love, but sure, she was only a girl and he was a married man and a well-known one, too. It was terrible how we blamed girls for the things that happened to them then. I told Kathleen I'd like to help find out who killed Gabriel if I can."

It was a few days before they were allowed to talk again. There was a visitor to the blue house, a man dressed in Western clothes who came in and looked at the five of them, sitting on the floor, and asked questions of the guards. He seemed to make everyone nervous, but after he left, the atmosphere in the house changed, became lighter. Whatever news he had delivered made the other men happy. Gabriel wondered if that should make them happy, or whether it should scare them.

That night, they asked the American nurse, Anne, about where she'd grown up, how she'd gotten involved in international aid work. He'd met her for the first time the morning they'd gotten in the van together and she'd struck him as serious, introverted. There was something fragile about her, something that hid behind her pale blue eyes. She had a flat accent he associated more with Canadians, though she told him she'd been raised in Idaho. "Everyone thinks we talk funny," she said, smiling for a second before it melted away. She was terrified, barely able to function, and Gabriel asked her about her work to try to put her at ease, but as soon as she started talking, he regretted it. She told them she'd been treating shrapnel wounds in children and began describing the wounds she'd seen, obsessively recounting the children's ages and genders and what names she could remember. They all exchanged glances and finally someone said, "It's okay, Anne."

"Did you always want to be a nurse?" Gabriel asked her. "From the time you were a girl?" That seemed like safer ground, but she blanched and said she supposed so, then went silent. One of the guards brought in rice and bread, with a tiny bit of rancid-tasting sauce. At first, they had been guarded closely, but everyone seemed to have relaxed in the days since they'd been taken, when it became clear they weren't going to try to escape.

Later, Pietro asked her the same question, and she said, "Oh no. In fact, it was the last thing I wanted to be. I don't like blood, don't even like bodies, really." She was very blond, very fair, and her face, when she looked up at him, was childlike. "But I had to. I owed it."

They were interrupted once more, by a guard coming in and taking their bowls, and it wasn't until much later that Gabriel asked her what she'd meant.

It was late now, the guards were sleepy. Gabriel had the sense they had time.

Anne sighed. "Oh, well," she said. "It's quite a story."

No one said anything. She sighed again. "Well," she said. "I grew up in Idaho, western Idaho. My family had a ranch. I learned to drive when I was ten. My sisters and I, we knew tractors, trucks, combines, inside out. We could drive anything." She took a deep breath. "My oldest sister and I, we were shy, not as social as Claire, my middle sister. Claire loved people, parties; she was always sneaking out and getting into trouble. But she didn't mean any harm. She was just . . . so social. She loved conversation, and we lived in the middle of nowhere and worked all the time with my parents and she wasn't really allowed to date or anything like that."

The twang of her accent got stronger as she settled into her story. Gabriel remembered attending a conference once in Denver, remembered accents like hers.

"She wanted to go to a party. I was a sophomore in high school. I'd just gotten my license. Claire was a junior, Sissy a senior. We were packed in tight, like sardines, my mother always said. Claire wanted to drink and she knew she shouldn't drive home so she asked me to drive her. I didn't want to go. I argued with her. But she pleaded, said there was a boy she liked, she had to see him. So I did it."

It was cold in the blue house that night, the wind whistling through the crevices. Anne stopped speaking, and in the silence, they heard a dog—or something else—howling in the distance.

Anne smiled. "We had wolves in Idaho. We used to go out and bang pots and pans to scare them away when we heard them too close." They all waited, knowing she would finish. Gabriel pulled his thin shirt more tightly around himself. The room was always cold. "We went to the party. It was boring for me, but Claire loved it. As we drove home, she told me all about it. She said the guy she liked had asked if he could take her out sometime. She was so happy." She sighed again. Gabriel thought he would never, ever forget the sound of her sighs. She sighed as though all the sadness of the world were in her.

"I don't know what happened. I didn't fall asleep. I know that. I just, I swerved, I guess. Maybe there was something in the road. I swerved and there was a van coming in the other lane. We hadn't seen another car for twenty minutes and then . . . I swerved and there was a van and I knew . . . there was a moment where I knew we were going to collide and I knew I was going to die."

They all held their breath. Gabriel could feel everyone, even the guards, listening to the story. Pain radiated from her body, soaked her voice. He didn't want to know, didn't want to hear it. If he could have run out of the house, he would have.

"There was a family in the van," she whispered. "Four of them. Plus Claire. That's five. I've counted over the years, all the lives I've saved, or helped to save. It's more than two hundred and sixty. But it isn't enough."

25

We wake up the next morning to the smell of bacon from downstairs and a chill in the air outside. The morning is bright, and once I've got a cup of strong tea in me, I get Lilly started packing up her stuff and then take Conor's keys, telling him I'll be back by noon so we can get on the road.

It takes half the trip to get comfortable driving on the other side of the road, and by the time I walk into the Sixmilebridge Garda Station, my eyes and brain are burning with the effort. I need to tell Roly, Griz, and Peter about Yvette Coughlan's revelations. My mind's been turning it over and over. Did Gabriel Treacy know? According to everyone who knew him, no.

As soon as I walk in, I know something's happened. Peter is huddled with a group of uniformed gardaí, organizing a canvass of petrol stations and motorway service stations, and Roly's on the phone. Griz looks up and waves me over.

"Guess what? We found the car," she says, grinning. "There's a business park next to Shannon Airport, yeah? It's all farms, though, cows right up against the offices. One of the farmers was out fixing a fence last night and found a vehicle in a ditch. The guards didn't get around to checking it out until this morning, but it's the stolen Renault. We're going to go out to see it now, before the techs come to tow it. Want to come?"

"Of course."

The airport's only a twenty-minute drive. I ride with Roly and Griz, green fields unfolding outside the windows of Roly's car. As soon as we're on the road, I say, "I have some news, too. I talked to an old friend of Stella Treacy's last night. She worked with Conor's aunt for a long time and she told me that Gerry Murray was the father of Stella's first baby, and of Gabriel as well."

"You're serious?" Roly takes his eyes off the road and turns to look at me quickly. "Gerry Murray?"

"Yeah. That's what she said."

"What do you think it means?" Griz asks. "You don't think it's connected with Treacy's death, do you?"

"I don't know. I was thinking that maybe the baby was adopted and I was wondering if maybe Treacy came to Long Island to meet him or her. But then why didn't the sibling get in touch after he was killed?"

"Maybe the sibling had something to do with it," Griz says.

"Maybe. Shit." When I reach into my coat pocket for my phone, it's not there, and I suddenly remember plugging it into the bathroom outlet at Conor's parents' this morning while I was taking a shower. In the rush to get out of the house, I left it there. "Ah, I guess I can live without my phone for a couple hours. Conor knows where I am."

The techs who I've come to recognize from the Noel Thomason scene are already there when we reach the business park. It's like Griz said, a commercial development off a narrow country road in the middle of farmland, a few brown and black cows watching the scene on the side of the road. The Renault has been ditched in a low drainage field, almost completely hidden from passing traffic. The techs stand aside and we all look into the car. Even from a few feet away, I can smell bleach.

"You got anything?" Roly asks the techs.

A young woman in a boiler suit shakes her head. "It's been wiped clean. You can smell it, but when we dusted we couldn't find a single print." She looks a bit shaken, weighing the implications of it. "Just like the house. Just like the . . well, we'll tell you about the stolen goods when we get back to the station. Let's just say this isn't your usual skanger robbery."

"I've already got the lads out looking for the shop where he bought the bleach," Peter says.

I stand up and look into the distance. "How far are we from the airport here?"

"Not far, but it's all fenced and without a car it'd take you a fair bit o' time to walk it," Peter says.

"I'm betting he's already gone," I say. "Let's see if we can get a list of the flights that went out today."

Roly nods and says, "Let's head back," then, to the techs, "Thanks, lads. Good work."

Back at the station, I'm pouring a cup of warm, sludgy coffee into a paper cup for myself when Peter Mooney comes into the staff room.

I take a sip of the coffee and grimace and he says, "Sorry. It's shite coffee. Never drink it myself."

"I should have stuck with the tea. Griz warned me."

He smiles and flips the switch on the electric kettle. "Sound plan." Then he asks, a little awkwardly, "How long have you known Katya?"

"Just since last year, when she was working on my cousin's case," I say casually.

"She's an excellent detective," he says. "Do you know if, uh, if she's seeing anyone right now?"

I smile. "I don't think so. I think she's, well, focusing on her career right now."

"She really is a great detective," he says earnestly. "I've liked working with her."

"She is a great detective," I say. There's nothing else I can say. *Too good-looking, too short,* she'd said. But I have the sense that the really relevant part was what came after: *That's the last thing I need right now.*

As if she felt her ears burning, Griz pokes her head in and says, "Maggie. I've got the flights."

Close to fifty flights came into Shannon Airport on the twentieth: eight from the United States, two from New York, and two from Newark. Then on February 24, and today, February 25, there are about equal numbers of flights going back to New York.

"What are we going to do with that?" she asks. "It will take a while to get the airlines to just give us passenger lists. We're going to need more than we've got right now for a warrant."

"What about gas stations—petrol stations?" I ask her. "Credit card records?"

"Credit card records. That's good. If he stopped for petrol. Peter has his lads out looking for CCTV footage, and if we find the car we can get those records. Then we can try to get names from the airlines."

A tech sets up for a presentation on the stolen items and Griz and I find a place to stand at the back of the room.

"Let's see those prints," Roly calls out. "You got some nice, clear prints for us?"

The tech gives him a withering look. "Actually, no," he says. "We didn't get a single print off any of it. Whoever did this wore gloves and wiped everything down, just to be sure."

We all take that in.

"Just like the car," someone says.

"Yeah, and this thing with the branches," the tech continues. "It's not like anything I've ever seen. The branches were cut with an extremely sharp knife, something most people don't just have hanging around, you know? Our perpetrator cut all these branches, arranged them carefully—it was a pretty professional job."

Someone shuts off the lights and a photograph of the pile of branches comes up on the screen. The tech clicks to the next slide and we all see a close-up of the cut on one of the branches. There are faint saw marks, but the wood looks remarkably smooth. Whatever separated these boughs from the rest of their branches was sharp.

"These were from nearby trees," the tech says. "Oak mostly, and a few boughs from a hawthorn. We found the cut marks on the trees. No forensic evidence anywhere."

"Whoever I saw back in the trees must have been hiding the stolen goods," I say. "Maybe he left after the murder and then came back to hide the things later."

Griz asks the tech, "You think it was planned in advance?"

He considers that. "I don't know. If you were planning this in advance, wouldn't you have a car waiting, wouldn't you have an accomplice? Wouldn't you dump the items as far away from the house as you could? This strikes me as something different."

"What about the computer and backup drive?" I ask.

"No luck there. He did a thorough job destroying them, knew what he was doing. It looks like a screwdriver was hammered through the center of both hard drives, and both devices were submerged in water. The screwdriver and hammer were taken from a shed on Mr. Thomason's property and the water seems to have been a standing pool of rainwater at the back of the property."

Peter and his team ask a few more questions and make a plan for more door-to-doors in the area, asking specifically about the Renault and whether anyone saw the driver who ditched it.

"What do you think?" Roly asks everyone once the tech has left. "What's the psychological profile of someone who would do that?"

"He wanted to be pretty fucking thorough," Peter offers. Everyone laughs, but we know he's right.

The room is silent for a minute and then I say, "He was inventive. He made use of what he had to hand. He . . ." I search for the word. "He innovated."

Something about the word chills me. It must show on my face because Roly gives me a funny look.

Griz says, "He didn't have a place nearby to go to. Yeah, he innovated, but it feels like he didn't have a choice, you know?"

Roly nods. "I agree. But that makes it feel like maybe it wasn't planned, like maybe he wasn't planning on killing Noel Thomason but something happened and he had to, or felt he had to."

Everyone considers that. Finally, I say, "I don't know. I think he went in there intending to kill him. Detective Mooney said that it looked to him like the pictures on the walls had been placed on the ground, and I had the same feeling, that things had been knocked off surfaces on purpose to make it look like a robbery."

"But if it was planned, why not take the stuff with him? Why create a second crime scene?" Roly asks.

Peter Mooney nods toward the close-up of the shoeprint on the screen. "Detective Grzeskiewicz said it. He didn't have a place to go. That pile of stuff out there was the best he could do under the circumstances. He didn't have a lot of time."

Griz sees where he's going. "He wasn't from here. He flew into Shannon Airport to kill Noel Thomason."

Everyone's looking at me. "That's what I'm thinking, too," I say. "It's looking more and more likely that there's a connection with Gabriel Treacy's murder."

There are nods and Peter says, "All right then, everyone back to work. Our best bet now may be the car on CCTV and tracking his movements more closely. I want someone out checking every house between here and Shannon. Don't take anyone's word for it that they don't have anything. Fucking verify it. Right?"

I say goodbye to everyone, reminding them I'll have my phone and they can call anytime. Roly and Griz walk me out to Conor's car. "We'll keep working all our angles," Griz says. "Hopefully we'll catch the car on video and we can narrow down the flights. Don't worry. If there's a connection, we'll find it. And we'll interview Jonathan Murray and Gillian Gleeson and let you know."

I leave reluctantly. I can feel the remaining questions like solid things, dangling threads of this mystery just hanging out there, but I need to get back.

I drive the narrow roads east, back toward Broadford, and realize I've started to recognize the landmarks, a yellow house a mile from the Kearneys', the first white flash of Doon Lough, the bridge before the house. Ellie comes out to meet me, barking frantically, when I pull into the drive. I get out of the car and I'm heading into the house when I look up to see Conor coming out of the front door, a worried look on his face. He's holding his parents' cordless phone.

"What?" I'm on alert anyway and the look on his face ratchets the adrenaline. I think, *Lilly?*

Conor hands me the phone. "Dave called and Marty Cascic has been trying to get in touch with you. He said you weren't picking up and then we heard your phone ringing in the bathroom. I gave him the number for the garda station in the Bridge but he probably missed you. He says it's urgent."

I take the phone from him and dial the country code and Marty's number. He answers on the first ring. "What is it?" I ask him.

"We've had a big development, Maggie," he says. I can hear the busyness behind him, people talking, phones ringing. "We got a hit on the gun used to kill Gabriel Treacy."

"Oh my God, Marty. Really?" I put a finger in my other ear so I can hear him over Ellie's barking. A hit means that the gun used to kill Gabriel Treacy was used in another crime logged in the system. When someone loads a bullet into the chamber of a firearm and then fires it, the bullet casing gets marked with a unique set of tiny ridges and scratches as it passes through the barrel. Casings from suspicious firearm deaths are logged in a centralized system and can be matched with other casings fired from the same weapon. What Marty's telling me is that the gun used to kill Gabriel Treacy was used in another homicide somewhere in the US. "What was it?"

"First of all, he was killed with a 92FS."

The Beretta 92FS is the civilian version of the gunmaker's M9 semiautomatic pistol, used widely by the military and law enforcement. Suffolk County PD's service weapon is a Glock 9mm, but many police departments use the Beretta. Basically, the M9 and 92FS are pretty standard handguns for anyone who wants to carry a handgun. You can buy one for $500 at almost any gun store or online. My uncle Danny used to keep one behind the bar. Criminals kill people with 9 millimeters; so do cops.

"And the cartridge casing was a Speer 147gr JHP"—a 147-grain jacketed hollow point, made by Speer, an American ammo manufacturer. "But get this," Marty says. "It's from the same 92FS that was used to kill Juan Bollina last year."

"Holy shit. Seriously?"

My brain is stopping and starting. I'm not sure what to do with this, not sure where to put it.

"Yeah," Marty says. "There's a lot of excitement around here." He lowers his voice. "Alicia looks like she won the fucking lottery. We're going to pull in Miguel Aguillar. Remember him?"

"He was a possible witness from the Bollina case. I interviewed him." Miguel Aguillar was seventeen when Juan Bollina was killed. They were classmates and casual friends and a few people had seen them together earlier the night Bollina was murdered. It was clear to Bill and me that he knew who had pulled the trigger, but was terrified for his life. Bill had gone in hard and I'd tried the "understanding mother figure" approach, but neither of us had been able to get the story of the murder out of him.

"Yeah. Hopefully he'll feel like talking if we can tie Bollina's killer to this thing, too." I'm trying to remember his face. He'd looked a lot younger than seventeen, just a kid.

Something in his voice makes me say, "You think this is it, Marty?"

He hesitates. "It's the same gun," he says. "I don't know what else to think." The silence is heavy across the line.

"What?" I ask him.

"Listen, Maggie. I hate to do this, but you gotta come back here. This case is breaking and Pat wants you back. Like I said, he didn't know you were going to Ireland. When I told him about the gun match, he said he wants you back on the next plane to work this back here."

"What? We just got here. We're supposed to be leaving on our trip today." Conor's listening to me. I meet his eyes. His face is grim.

"Look, I know. I tried to talk to him, but . . . I think Cooney was in his office this morning. For some reason, it really pissed him off that I let you go on vacation in the middle of the case. I don't know what . . . This is coming down from the top. They want you home right now. We've got to bring that kid in and I want you to talk to him. I'm sorry, Mags. Maybe you can go back next week once we get someone in custody."

I'm about to keep arguing when I hear a voice on the other end and Marty says, "Mags, I need you."

So I just say, "All right, Marty. We'll get the first plane we can."

26

I hand the cordless phone back to Conor. Ellie has stopped barking. She's come over to sit by my legs and I scratch her head and stroke her silky ears.

"Conor," I say. "I'm really so, so sorry. Please don't be mad. I just . . . this case is breaking. We got a match on the gun. It looks like there's a connection with a murder last year. I need to go back. I'm so sorry."

"When?"

"As soon as possible," I say. "I'll have to go see what I can find for tickets." I look up at his face. "Please don't be mad. I know this completely screws up our holiday. I just . . . Marty doesn't order me to do anything very often. He really meant it. I think my job is on the line."

"I'm not mad, Maggie." He doesn't meet my eyes. "I'm just disappointed."

"I am too. I'm so sorry."

A bird rises from a tree at the back of the field. The sky is huge and gray. He opens his arms. I step into them and press my face into his chest and Conor hugs me, though I can feel his body resisting. Finally he says, "I'll go pack up our things."

Lilly and Adrien are listening to music in the kitchen, sitting at the kitchen table and sharing out Smarties from a tube, talking about a movie they both saw before the holidays. When I say, "Lil, I need to talk to you," she looks up and narrows her eyes.

"What?"

Breda is at the stove, stirring a pot of soup for lunch. "Let's go in the other room and talk," I say. Breda glances at Conor. Something passes between them and I know she knows now.

"What?" Lilly searches my face. She knows me so well, she finds the regret and apprehension in a matter of seconds. Lilly's had plans blown up by my job more times than I care to think about. "You have to go home for your job? We have to go?" Anger sweeps across her features. I can't tell if she's going to cry or scream at me.

"Lil, let's go talk. Marty called and there's been a development." I reach out to touch her shoulder, but she jerks out of the way, knocking against Adrien's arm and sending the Smarties cascading across the table and onto the floor. Breda's eyes widen. Lilly's face crumples, her hair swinging across her cheek as she scrambles to get up from the table. She doesn't want Adrien and Breda to see her cry. She slams the chair back under the table and runs upstairs.

"I'm so sorry," I say to Breda. "I'll just . . ."

"Of course." Breda looks like she's going to cry, too, and as I climb the stairs, I can feel tears pushing up into my eyes.

"Lilly," I whisper, knocking on the door. "Can you let me in so we can talk? I'm so sorry our plans got changed." Silence. I can hear her sniffling. I try the door, but she's locked it. "Lil?" I turn around and press my back against the door. I can't stop the tears from coming, so I stand there for a moment, in the hallway of Conor's childhood home, across from a photograph of his sister in her communion dress, letting them fall. There's a stillness from inside that makes me think Lilly's listening to me.

I hear her moving around. I knock, wait, and then finally she opens the door and drops her packed duffel bag at my feet.

"There," she says, her face obscured behind her hair, her shoulders hunched protectively, her voice filled with hurt and anger. "Are you happy?"

"She'll be okay," Conor says later as we're packing the car. Lilly is alone in the barn, cuddling Rosie and her sister, saying goodbye.

"I don't know. She may never talk to me again," I say.

"She's just having a tough time," Conor says. "I think she's been happy here." It feels like a rebuke and I try not to react. He's right. She has been happy here. Conor looks out across the fields. A bank of gray clouds has moved in over the farm and the temperature has dropped a few degrees since this morning.

"Before we leave for the airport," I say, thinking of a way to make amends, "I want to see your special standing spot. Will you take me up?"

Conor nods. Wind sweeps along the grass behind the outbuildings. He opens a gate and we start walking up through the gently sloping field at the back of the house. We climb a little, and when I turn around, there's a view of the lake and the fields all around.

The air is cold, but it smells of growing, living things, the grass and a sweet spicy smell from the trees.

Conor squeezes my hand. "You know, it's not like a *magical* special standing spot or anything. I just want to adjust expectations here."

But then we get there and it *is* magical, a little dip in the field that makes it feel private and offers more views of the low hills in the distance and the faraway glittering of the lakes. I lean into his chest, breathing in the smell of him. He's wearing an old blue oxford shirt and jeans and he hasn't shaved in a couple of days now.

"It's oddly attractive, you being a sheep farmer," I say, raising my face for a kiss.

His lips are warm. "Ah, now you know there's a fella the next farm over who would be very glad to hear you say that," he says. "His name is Paddy Geering. Would you like me to introduce you? He's been looking for a wife for about forty years now. Nice farm. He'd be impressed with how fit you are."

"It *is* beautiful here . . ." I say. He laughs. "No, I'm not looking for a new boyfriend. I like the one I have. Even if I've completely screwed up our vacation."

"I'm glad to hear that, though Paddy, poor man, will be desolate," he says, not acknowledging my apology.

We look at the view together. "Gabriel Treacy," I say, wanting him to understand. "I told you he was kidnapped when he was in Afghanistan. I didn't tell you they cut his back, tortured him, and his girlfriend said he never talked about it, that he didn't want to go anywhere near it. I keep thinking about all that trauma, about how it must have built up in him. But he used it, to help people, to turn it into something else." I hardly know what I'm trying to say. I want him to understand why I'm so focused on solving this case. "I keep thinking about what happens to trauma, about where it goes." I look up at him. Conor knows about trauma. He understands how it sits sleeping, for years, and then comes back, in ways you never would have expected. "I'm so sorry about this, Conor. My job's on the line here. I need to get home and do this right. I feel like I know him now,

Gabriel Treacy. I need to see this through. I don't want you to think that it's . . . that I don't love you. I love you. You've been incredible with Lilly. You're right, she's . . . happier than I've seen her in a while. Until just now." He smiles. "Not just her. Me too. I love you. I just have to do this."

Conor starts to talk, then stops, then starts again. "I'm struggling not to get attached to her," he says. "I don't want to presume. I don't want to . . well, provide something I'm going to take away." He looks at me. "My mam feels the same way. I can feel it. She's been careful with Lilly, though I can tell she wants to . . . to . . . love her. She's a nan, you know, she loves kids, especially older ones, once they're interesting. She and Lilly were talking poetry. She fucking loved it. But we're holding back. It's the right thing to do, and yet I know Lilly just needs us, needs the love. Maggie, I'm afraid to ask you about the future, about what we're going to do. I thought we might know, by the end of the trip. But now I . . . I wonder if you'll ever be ready to leave your job, to move here. I . . . I shouldn't even say that. I know it's too soon to even think about it, but I can't help but look ahead. We're not twenty-three."

Panic starts to overwhelm me. "Conor, I . . . there's Uncle Danny, Lilly's friends, not just my job. Roly said for me to get a job as a detective, I'd have to do the training all over again, have to live at the training college while I'm there. That's a year, another year in uniform." I feel him start to pull away and I force myself to breathe, to turn toward him and reach up to hold his face. "But I love you and I want to make this work. I do. All the rest of it is . . . Well, it seems small when I just focus on that. I love you. I need to go back and work this case and then . . . the rest of it, we'll figure out."

We lean against each other, just sitting with the uncertainty in the middle part of the afternoon, the swirling, damp air like the air of another dimension, showing us otherwise invisible motes of dust when they pass into the rays of the sun.

Most of the guards were men in their twenties or thirties, malnourished and terrified. They'd been terrified their entire lives and it had made them angry and the anger made them cruel. One of the guards liked to kick Anne whenever he passed her. Gabriel tried to show them kindness, a smile, a thank you for the food they brought, but it only made them desperate to show they were not handing out special treatment.

But then, one day, there was a kid.

He may have been eighteen or nineteen, but he looked like a kid, with ears that stuck out and uneven teeth that made his smile, which he seemed unable to contain, charming and infectious.

His was the only name they knew. The other men greeted him, called him in a way they didn't call each other. So they knew his name. Ibrahim.

Ibrahim started arriving with the guards on the day shift after they'd been at the blue house a week or so. Gabriel found himself wondering where he had been, what he had been doing. Was he someone's brother? Son? He was always in a good mood. He seemed to put the others in a good mood, too. If Ibrahim was there, everything *seemed more manageable. They all felt it. One morning Gabriel said to Anne, "I hope Ibrahim comes today," and she said that she did, too, and a thought came to him, he wasn't sure from where:* Maybe Ibrahim's here to save us.

27

After I've got a large coffee in me, I take a shower, get dressed, and knock on Lilly's door. She was furious with me after we got home yesterday, moody and silent while Uncle Danny drove us back from the airport, the tension in the house thick and dangerous. I tell her I'm turning on the alarm and not to go outside. "Uncle Danny's coming down to be with you, okay?" I say through the door, antsy and ready to get going. "Don't just play on your phone all day. Call me if anything comes up."

Silence.

The LIE isn't too bad and I'm in Yaphank by nine. If I'm honest, it's a relief to be back in the squad room, with its familiar smell of old coffee and microwaved meat, the clattering of shoes on the horrible linoleum in the hall, the wobbly desks and old phones and equipment. The energy's good, Monday morning, everyone excited about a break in the case. Bill looks up and nods when I come in, something wary in his eyes. Everyone else seems happy to see me, and I wonder how many people know about Pat and Marty ordering me home.

"Hey," Marty says when I poke my head into his office. He raises his head from whatever he's looking at on his desk and his reading glasses slide down on his nose. "You're back. Shut the door." He gestures for me to sit down. "What you got? You find anything over there?" He seems nervous, looking around the room, flipping a pen back and forth in his right hand.

I say, "Nothing definite on why Gabriel Treacy was over here, though I got some intriguing stuff about his mother. Roly and Griz are looking into that. I told you the stuff on Afghanistan. We need more on that. And Dave and I are working on establishing contact with Paul Shouldice, Treacy's friend who lives in the city. On Noel Thomason, it's looking like someone stole a car at Shannon Airport, killed Thomason, and tried to make it look like a robbery." I tell Marty about the stolen items, the car, the branches, the hard drives.

Marty looks up at that. "What the fuck?"

"I know." I take a deep breath. "They're looking for more CCTV footage of the car. Maybe if they get that, they can get a warrant for the flight manifests. If you weren't so definite about the gun, I'd be sure Thomason's murder is connected to Gabriel Treacy."

"Why?"

"The destroyed computers. Both cases, Marty. Thomason was his lawyer."

Marty rubs the bridge of his nose. "Yeah, yeah. Okay, anyway, listen, we got this case meeting now. I want to hear the whole update. Okay?"

I nod.

"You sure? Everything okay with the boyfriend?"

"Would *you* have been happy with me?"

"Look, I'm sorry about making you come back. I don't know what got into Pat." He looks away.

"I know. It's a big case. Marty?" He looks back at me, wary. "Anything on Anthony Pugh?"

He slaps his forehead. "I meant to tell you. They were watching him, not as much since you were gone, but a couple days ago they followed him to the airport. He's in Florida. They confirmed with the airline and we alerted Fort Lauderdale police. The airline will tell us if he comes back, but you can relax a bit, kiddo." He smiles. "I can too."

I feel relief wash over me. Lilly's strange text. I don't have to worry about it now.

The case room's full already when Marty and I get there. Alicia Piehler comes in, sits at the back of the room, and mouths *Welcome back* at me. She's wearing a hot pink blazer and black pants and there's something triumphant on her face that keeps drawing my eyes. She's won; in some unknown way, she feels she's won a round. A case like this, a seemingly simple murder, if we get a hard gang connection, offers all kinds of possibilities for plea deals that can lead the task force to higher-ups in MS13. If we can get Miguel Aguillar to talk about what happened the night Juan Bollina was killed, then they've got leverage they can use to get to gang members.

I can feel the case slipping out of our hands. I should be happy about it, but I'm not. In some undefinable way, I feel like Gabriel Treacy is mine. I want to know what he was doing here. I want to know why he died. And this, the match on the gun . . . this means no one cares about the why anymore. They only care about the how and the who.

Bill Trillio stands up and gives us the basics. "So, as most of you know, the bullet that killed Gabriel Treacy was fired from the same weapon that was used in the homicide of Juan Bollina last year. We were pretty sure, based on information from confidential informants, that Bollina was killed by MS13 members from Islip who had some connection to MS13 in the DC area, but we couldn't prove it and we don't know for sure who shot Bollina. You probably all remember, but we had a possible witness, Miguel Aguillar. He was seventeen, and he was with Bollina the night he was killed. He didn't do it, he's a nice kid, scared shitless, but he knows more than he told us last year. I think he knows exactly who pulled the trigger, and I want to get it out of him."

"What's the operating theory?" Marty asks from the back of the room.

"Crime of opportunity," Bill says. "Treacy was standing on the beach and his killer or killers were driving around, saw him, and decided to rob him. Either they planned to shoot him from the beginning—maybe it was a gang initiation, something like that—or he fought back and they killed him spur of the moment."

Everyone lets that sit for a moment. "Okay," Marty says. "I want D'arcy and Milich to interview Aguillar. We're gonna do it after we're done here."

"But—" Bill starts.

Marty waves a hand and says, "D'arcy took statements from him before."

Bill looks pissed. It's clear he thought he was going to be doing the interview, and I catch him glance toward Alicia, whose lips are pressed together in disapproval.

"Okay," Marty goes on. "Assuming D'arcy and Milich don't get anything from Aguillar—I know, I know, vote of confidence, right?—we'll stay on the evidence. Press conference will be tomorrow or the next day. It's going to focus on getting the public to spill if they know something. Alicia? You want to say anything about that?"

She looks up. "Yeah, the task force is offering a reward and we're going to really put pressure on anyone who might have heard something. As you all know, other than the gun, the evidence didn't really come through from this scene, so someone's going to have to talk."

Marty nods. "Okay, sounds good. In the meantime, though, I want you all to continue following up on the loose ends. If this is it, we want a clean case. So I want all our questions answered about what Gabriel Treacy was doing on that beach and whether there's any chance he knew the person who killed him. Maggie, why don't you update us on what you got over in Ireland."

I step to the front of the room. I can feel myself assuming my usual style of presenting, feet planted, my eyes roaming around the room. It took me a long time to learn how to command the attention of a room full of men twice my size. The key is silence. Stop talking, stare at them. Eventually all the attention in the room comes to you. I wait. When everyone's focused, I say, "It's good to see you all. It sounds like you've been doing amazing work while I was gone. So, as you know, I was looking into Gabriel Treacy's life while I was over there. Of course the big question is why he came to Bay Shore, why he was staying here, why he was on that beach. I didn't find an answer to that question, which of course is interesting in and of itself. His ex-girlfriend, with whom he was still close, and his boss both said they had no idea why he was here. We found a slip of paper with the name Heather on it. It didn't mean anything to those who know him so it's possible he was over here to see someone named Heather. We'll continue to follow up on that. The other thing I found out was that Gabriel Treacy was very likely the biological son of an Irish politician named Gerry Murray. His mother seems to have had another baby with Murray prior to Gabriel, and either something happened to it or she gave it up for adoption. Police in Ireland are looking into that." There's a little buzz in the room at that.

"What about his electronics?" Alicia jumps in. "Why don't we have the emails?"

"Personal emails are weird. He had a Gmail account. But he shut it down in January."

"He shut off his phone, he shut down his email. Any chance he was suicidal?" Bill asks.

"No one said so and there's no way he shot himself, but yeah, it's weird, isn't it? Maybe he was tired of technology? Wanted to simplify," I say. "Work emails weren't very exciting. Just what you'd expect. There was an email from someone named Paul Shouldice at a nonprofit in New York. From November. Wanted to chat with Treacy about something. It's possible that's why Treacy was in New York, so I want to talk to Shouldice. I've left him a message. Dave, you have too, right?" Dave nods. "If we don't hear back soon, I think he needs a visit."

"What about the Afghanistan thing?" Bill asks.

"It was barely reported at the time. Because they were negotiating for his release. Apparently that's standard practice with these things. They don't release names if they can help it. In this case, they were set free after a few weeks, so I guess it wasn't a huge story. He was apparently held with an American nurse, a doctor, an Afghan translator, and, we think, an Italian photojournalist named Pietro Griselli. I have a bunch of calls out to try to find out more about all of this. Berta, you've been working your contacts too, right?"

Berta stands up. "Nobody knows anything about it. But my army contact said that kind of thing was happening a lot at that point. It was pretty confusing, and sometimes the aid organizations don't want anyone to know."

"Thanks," Marty says. "Everyone keep working their angles. Maggie and Dave, you ready?"

I grin at him and repeat the words I said outside Cooney's office what seems like a lifetime ago.

"As I'll ever be."

When I met Miguel Aguillar last year, he was seventeen but looked like he was twelve. He's eighteen now, but he's not quite formed yet, awkwardly straddling the line between boy and man. He's tall, thin, his ears and feet too big for his body, but he has a pleasant face. I remember a shy smile that came out occasionally, but now he's terrified. When he sees Dave, takes in Dave's hair and skin and eyes, the look of relief on his face almost breaks my heart.

"Miguel," I say, "I'm Detective D'arcy. You may remember me from last year. I interviewed you right after Juan was killed?" He doesn't say anything. "This is Detective Milich. We want to ask you a few questions to help us with an investigation we're conducting. You're not under arrest and you do not have to answer our questions, but we would appreciate any help you can give us. Okay?"

He nods and I look to Dave to get us going. The kid is going to trust Dave before he trusts me. "So, Miguel," Dave starts, "we talked to you last year after a boy named Juan Bollina was murdered. He was a friend of yours from school. At the time, you said you didn't know anything about that, even though a few of your friends said they saw you with Juan earlier the night he was killed. You told Detective D'arcy that you walked home and left Juan alone outside the pizza place. He said he was waiting for a ride. Correct?"

He nods slowly, doesn't say anything.

"Can you confirm that?" I ask him.

"Yes," he says quietly.

"You sure?" Dave says. "Because the way this works is that if you help us with our case, we can help you, we can protect you. You lie to us, we can't help you."

"I'm not lying," he mutters.

Dave goes on. "Miguel, you knew Juan, you were family friends, right?"

He shrugs.

"You must have been sad when he died. If you didn't have anything to do with it, why don't you help us get justice for Juan's family?"

Something about that gets him. His eyes cloud for a second and he looks away. "I don't know anything," he says finally. "I told you everything." He's buttoned up tight. I don't think he's going to talk.

"Where were you on Thursday night of the week before last, the sixteenth?" I ask him suddenly.

"What?" He looks genuinely surprised.

"You heard me. Not last week, but the week before. Thursday. What were you doing?"

He hasn't heard anything about Gabriel Treacy. I know right away, from the way he actually takes a minute to think about it, to go over the calendar in his mind. He looks up at us and says, "My girlfriend's sister had a baby shower. I was there till one in the morning."

"Thank you." I smile. "I know how hard it is, Miguel, worrying that you're getting someone in trouble, worrying that you're putting yourself or your family in danger. But sometimes, telling the truth helps everyone, in ways you can't even imagine. Give us a name, just give us the name of the person who killed Juan. Who pulled the trigger? We can protect you, Miguel. We can protect your family."

I try to remember what I know about Miguel Aguillar. He came to the US from El Salvador when he was two. His father works at a restaurant in East Islip. His mother cleans houses. He's had a stable childhood, parents with some emotional and financial resources to spread around. Like Juan, he was a good student, though we heard that he stopped going to school after the murder, never graduated.

As the MS13 stuff was ramping up last year, I called up a professor at Stonybrook, wanting to learn more about where it had all come from. I got an education. While we drank coffee in her office, she told me about how American foreign policy in Central America created the conditions driving immigration to the US. But when the immigrants got here, they were denied asylum, driving them to remain in the US undocumented, which leaves them vulnerable to exploitation by gang members.

"When they get here, these kids can't go to school—everyone is afraid of them—so they get sucked into the gangs. It never ends. And you only sit up and take notice when someone who looks like you is affected." Anger and frustration poured off her.

"That's why I'm here," I told her. "That's why I'm here. For Juan Bollina." But we'd never solved his case. MS13 had closed ranks and spread so much fear around that even a good kid like Miguel wasn't willing to tell us what he'd seen.

For the second time, I try to figure out how to make Miguel tell me something that could get him killed.

"Last year, you said you didn't want to tell us the name of the person who killed Juan." I'm manipulating him. In fact, he never even admitted he had seen anything. I go on. "I get that. I do. We have a pretty good idea who it is now. We think the same person may have killed a man last Thursday at the marina in Bay Shore. We just need you to confirm some things."

He looks up at me, surprised, then goes back to staring at a spot on the wall behind me.

"You were there just before Juan was killed, maybe you saw who did it, am I right?"

Nothing.

"We know you didn't do it," Dave says. "We know."

He keeps staring. Same spot.

"Come on, Miguel," Dave says. "You were there, right?"

Nothing.

"We can't help you if you don't help us," I say.

Slowly, imperceptibly, a single tear squeezing out of his right eye, he shakes his head.

The room is too cold. I can feel my hands getting numb and I pull them up into my blazer. "We're going to take a break," I say. "Can I get you something? A Coke?"

"Okay." He keeps his head down, doesn't look at me.

Marty and Bill step out of the observation room and meet us in the hallway. Bill has a cup of coffee and the smell is driving me crazy. I'm starting to feel the jet lag, the stress gathering behind my forehead, my stomach empty and growling. Dave sees me looking at Bill's cup and says, "I'll get the Coke. Want some coffee, Mags?"

"Yes, thank you. What do you think, Marty?"

"I think he's scared shitless of someone."

"This is ridiculous," Bill says. "He knows who killed Bollina. You need to get it out of him." He's got a coffee stain in the shape of an apple on his white button-down shirt and his hair, which he usually keeps on the short side, is flopping over his forehead. Maybe he's going to try for a combover.

"He's not going to tell us. He gives us the name of an MS13 member and that's his life. But I have an idea of something I want to try," I explain. Marty nods, but Bill scowls at me and doesn't say anything.

Dave comes back, hands me a hot coffee, and I down it before we go back in, burning my tongue a little. I can feel it as I sit down at the table again, a fuzzy numbness that's there every time I say a word.

The Coke can is wet with condensation, and when Dave hands it to Miguel, I can feel Miguel's relief as he pops it open and takes a long drink.

I wait for him to put it down before I say, "We're desperate, Miguel. We want to find whoever it is that killed Juan. For his family, and to make sure no one else gets killed. I understand, though, that whoever killed him, well, he's dangerous, isn't he?"

He's clutching the Coke can, silent, a muscle next to his left eye twitching.

"When my son was little," I say, "he sometimes broke things or did things I didn't want him to do." It's a common thing, for cops, inventing family members. If you have to give a personal detail to a suspect, you switch it up, change the gender, say you're married if you're not, say you're single if you are. "Did you ever break something? When you were little?"

He lifts his eyes to mine, to see if I'm kidding. When he realizes I'm not, he nods very slightly.

"I used to say to him, 'I don't care who broke the vase, I just want to know what happened to it.' I think there was someone who you may have seen before or after he killed Juan. I think he said he'd kill you if you told anyone his name."

His eyes are wet. He's struggling. He shakes his head.

"I'm not going to ask you his name, Miguel. I know you won't tell me. I don't need a name. All I want to know about is the gun. What is the story of the gun?" I stand up and lean over the table, looking him right in the eyes.

Dave whispers, "What happened to the gun, Miguel?"

He's crying now, tears streaming down his face. "I don't know," he says. He looks up, about to say something else, then decides not to. I can see it, can see the unspoken words sliding away like drops of water on glass.

"Come on, Miguel," I say. "Please, I'm begging you."

"I don't know."

Bill is furious. "Maggie, why'd you let him go? He had something on Bollina. I know he did. We gotta go back in and make him give it up. You were too easy on him. '*Oh, I don't want the name.*'—I want the name. Juan Bollina was a good kid. Of all the vicious things we've seen, this had to be one of the worst. They *executed* him, Maggie. You know that."

"I do know that, Bill. I was there with you when we saw the body."

There's a bit too much of an edge to my voice. Bill doesn't like it; he scowls and walks over to his desk.

"Okay, go back over all the known associates," Marty says. "Bill, look at all the interviews and see if anyone jumps out at you."

We all settle down to work. But I catch Bill looking back toward my desk a few times and I can feel his resentment coming at me all afternoon.

Roly calls me just as I'm getting ready to leave. "You got this all solved, D'arcy? All wrapped up for us?"

"I wish."

"Well, I'm back in Dublin. We wanted to talk to Jonathan Murray, see if he knew anything about his father and Stella Treacy. He wasn't too happy when we showed up at his Dáil offices asking about his da's sex life, but he told us he hadn't known for sure, but he'd always suspected something like this. In 2011, Gerry Murray rang him up, said one of his constituents was in trouble and he needed Jonathan to step in and help in any way he could. He implied that the constituent's mother was *important* to him. Jonathan made a few calls, but Treacy was released before he could do much. He says he didn't know anything about the first baby. I'd say there was no love lost between him and his father. That's the sense I got."

"You think he was telling you the truth? About not knowing about the baby?"

"I don't know, to be honest with you. Might have been a little hesitation. He wasn't enjoying the experience of talking to me anyway. I'll do a bit more digging."

"Thanks. Is it good to be back in Dublin?"

"Ah, yeah. I get twitchy in the countryside, like. Griz is tying up loose ends in the Bridge and following up on the CCTV footage, seeing if they can find the Renault, see where he went."

"Okay, thanks, Roly. Let me know."

After we hang up, I stop at the grocery store, then swing by Lilly's favorite restaurant to pick up burritos for dinner. When I get home, she's lying on the couch watching cooking shows. She looks up at the sound of me entering the alarm code, but doesn't acknowledge me. Uncle Danny's fast asleep in the recliner and I shake him gently and give him a hug before he heads back up to his house. I put the burritos on plates and pour myself a glass of wine; Lilly sits at the kitchen table and eats with me but won't engage in conversation except to say she took a nap and is still really tired.

"You want to go to school tomorrow?" I ask her. "Might be nice to see your friends." I got out my mom's favorite napkins, bright '70s-yellow linen with little chickens embroidered at the edges. They've always been Lilly's favorites, too, but she doesn't even bother to put hers in her lap.

"I don't know. I'm still kind of jet-lagged. I'll see in the morning," she says, throwing her burrito wrapper away as soon as she's done eating.

"Lil, I know you're mad we had to leave. I'm so sorry my job got in the way of our vacation, but I'm going to make it up to you, and to Adrien and Conor, when this case is over. Maybe we could go out to Montana this summer, like we talked about."

Her face is frozen. She doesn't want to give me an inch. "Whatever," she says finally. "I'm going to bed."

I put the groceries away and start a load of laundry out of our luggage, stopping for a minute to sniff my pajama top, which still has the scent of Conor's parents' house on it, a soapy smokiness that suddenly erases the distance. I check the time and dial his number.

"How are you still awake?" he answers. "I'm exhausted. You must be exhausted."

"I'm okay," I say. "I miss you. I just took my pajama top out to wash it and it smelled like your parents' house."

"Your pajama top smelled like sheep?"

I laugh. "No, like the kitchen, but sort of like sheep, I guess." I'm walking through the living room while I talk, turning off lights. I stop for a moment at a black-and-white photograph of Erin that I hung up a few months ago. I wondered if I should, because of Lilly, but I like having it there, like being able to see Erin when I want to, and I've seen Lilly stop in front of it, touch her fingers to the glass.

"Hmmm. How does it feel to be back?"

"Fine, but we miss you. I'm so sorry, Conor. I'm so sorry my job screwed everything up. Lilly hates me. She's barely talking to me."

He hesitates, then says, "We'll try again. It's okay, Maggie." But he sounds tired. "It's late—"

"Yeah, I'll talk to you tomorrow?"

"Yeah. Love you."

I pour another glass of wine and take it outside, feeling a little bit of relief accompany the alcohol through my bloodstream. I hadn't realized how much the Anthony Pugh thing has been bugging me. Knowing he's a plane ride away is like a weight I've been carrying has lifted. I walk down to the beach, stand on the sand, and look out across the dark water, sipping my wine. Something about the air and the patterns of reflected light on the water makes me remember how Erin and I would come here in the dark after bedtime sometimes, our nightgowns swirling around our feet, my mom pretending she hadn't seen us sneak past the living room. We had a game we liked to play that we called Darkfall. We would close our eyes and hold hands, twirling around and around and around until we fell back on the sand, and then we'd open our eyes and look up at the stars and they would blur and shift and sparkle . . .

A text comes in. Conor. *Sorry so sleepy. Love you.* I send back a red heart.

Another text shows up immediately. It's only six words, from a number I don't recognize. I freeze.

Hi Maggie, it says. *Lovely evening. Take care.*

I force myself not to run back to the house but my heart is thumping and the darkness has become ominous and threatening by the time I stumble through the front door and call out to Lilly. I race up the stairs and knock on her door, feeling relief at her annoyed, "What?" My phone buzzes again—panicked, I look down to see Griz's number.

"Griz," I say. "Sorry, I was just—"

"Maggie," she cuts in, "I'm about to send you a photo. It's something we found in a file folder we got from Margaret Morrell's house. Remember she said she had some of Noel Thomason's files at home? It's . . . well, you'll see. I recognized the name from when you were telling me about your job. Well, take a look."

I touch the message icon and a text from Griz appears. I open it and a photograph of a sheet of paper comes up. It's hard to see so I enlarge it enough that I can read the neat, handwritten words. My brain is slow and it takes a few seconds to realize what I'm reading.

Stella. Baby boy. Born 1965. Healthy at birth, it says. *Sent to America?*

And then below that: *J. Cooney, Bay Shore, Long Island, NY.*

28

Dave doesn't argue with me or ask questions when I tell him to come over as soon as he can.

I check on Lilly, then put on a fleece jacket and running shoes and set the security system before I meet him outside. I point to the beach and we start walking. It's cold, overcast, the kind of day that gets into your bones. I take a deep breath. But I'm not ready to start yet. I keep walking.

"You okay, Mags?" he asks finally. "What's going on?"

I stop and pick up a piece of green beach glass for the collection Lilly has on the windowsill above our kitchen sink. "Look, I gotta tell you something, Dave. You're not going to like it. I don't like it."

He just waits.

"This guy who got murdered in Ireland, Noel Thomason, Gabriel Treacy's lawyer? I told you we went through his files, didn't find anything related to Gabriel Treacy. We found some stuff for his mother, related to her will."

"Yeah?"

"But Thomason had a secretary, who was slowly typing up all of his notes in the paper files and getting them into a computer. She had some files at home she was working on, ones she hadn't read yet, and Griz, one of the detectives, finally went to her house to get them yesterday and there was one for Stella Treacy, one that was related to the adoption. The secretary admitted she eavesdropped and overheard Stella Treacy asking Noel Thomason to try to track down the first baby she gave up. Look what Griz found in the file." I take out my phone and show him the photo.

It takes him a minute. "What the fuck? Cooney? It can't be the same one."

"Bay Shore? How many Cooneys are there in Bay Shore, Long Island?"

He stares at me. "Cooney?"

"Yeah."

"So, what are you saying here, Mags?"

"I'm saying that Gabriel Treacy asked this lawyer to try to find his brother and he came back to him with 'J. Cooney in Bay Shore.'"

He stares at me for a moment. "You think Cooney was Gabriel Treacy's brother and that's why Treacy came over here, to meet him?"

The water is choppy, white-capped. We watch a gull surfing the wind along the waterline.

"There was an email from Gabriel Treacy to Noel Thomason in early January. Treacy said he wanted to discuss something they'd been talking about. What if he found out about the baby when his mother was dying and asked Thomason for the information about where the baby had been sent?

"I looked it up, Dave. Cooney was born in 1965—*1965*. That's when Stella Treacy's baby was born, too. He's an only child. Jack Cooney and his wife never had any other children. I did a little research last night. There were a lot of babies from Ireland, from those mother and baby homes, who were adopted by Americans in the fifties and sixties. There was an article in *Newsday* about how some of the adoptees are only now learning they were born Irish, only now learning about how they came into the world. They're mad. There's a woman from Manhasset who's trying to learn about all the Irish adoptees on Long Island, Dave. Trying to help them connect with their heritage."

"Shit." He stops walking and stands there staring at me with a shocked expression on his face. "What are you saying?"

"Look, Dave. Gabriel Treacy was in Bay Shore, at a marina really, really close to Jay Cooney's house, right? Bay Shore plus Cooney's name in his lawyer's files, in freaking Ireland, narrows it down so much I think we can assume that's why Gabriel Treacy was there."

Dave just stares at me. He knows I'm right. Then he says, "But the guy was killed by MS13. We have a match on the gun. So, does it matter why he was there? When it comes down to it?"

I nod and start walking "You're right, but . . . I don't know, Dave. It's weird, though, right?"

Dave's speed walking trying to keep up with me. From behind me, he says, "What? I can't hear you."

I stop and turn to look at him. A guy is walking past us and I wait until he's out of range before continuing. "The guards found a car. It was stolen from Shannon Airport and it showed up on a video camera not far from where Thomason was killed. To me that points to someone who flew over there to kill Noel Thomason, someone who stole a car to avoid having his name on a rental car agreement."

Dave's looking at me like I'm insane. "What are you thinking?"

"I don't know. I don't know what I'm thinking. You said that

Cooney was pissed I went to Ireland. What if he was pissed because he was worried I was going to find out about Stella Treacy? What if the reason I had to come back was so I couldn't learn about Stella's baby?"

Dave takes that in. Finally he says, "All I know is Alicia was asking about where you were. Marty just said you were on vacation but I guess someone told her you were in Ireland and she must have told Cooney because he and Pat called Marty after that and chewed him out. Then, Marty said you were coming back."

The wind blows a plastic bag down the beach and I sprint to catch it before it hits the water. Once I catch it, I stuff it into my coat pocket and look at Dave.

Dave runs his hands through his hair. "I never heard anything about Cooney being adopted. And I always notice that stuff, when a public person talks about it, on account a being adopted myself, you know? Did you ever hear anything?"

"No," I say. "All I got when I searched were unrelated stories from old newspapers about Jack Cooney when he was a family court judge and a bunch of Suffolk County Family and Child Services adoption events that Jay Cooney promoted a couple years ago. But it doesn't seem like he ever talked openly about being adopted."

"I just don't see it. I don't get why it would be a big deal," Dave says. "I mean, I hardly think about it—it's like, I'm adopted, so what? My parents were always trying to get me to talk about it when I was little and it just never affected me that much, you know?"

I pick up a rock and skip it into the ocean. "Cooney's an elected official, he's running for reelection. We know he's worried about Lizza. Maybe there's something off about the adoption. I don't know, Dave.

Maybe it has absolutely nothing to do with why Gabriel Treacy and Noel Thomason got killed. But . . . it was there in the file. And . . . all these weird things have been happening?"

"What weird things?"

"I swear to God someone was watching me at the crime scene when I was over there. There have been a few other times, too. Lilly got that weird text message. I got one last night. And there was something odd with my email." Now that I say it, it sounds crazy.

Dave seems to think so, too. "I thought you were worried about Anthony Pugh. Isn't that why you asked me to check and make sure he hadn't left the country?"

"Yeah. I was. I know. Pugh's in Florida now."

"Have you told any of this to Marty?"

I look away. "You're the only person who knows, other than Griz. She'll want to know if we uncover anything that indicates Cooney was involved, but they're working the car angle the next couple days, seeing if they can trace the movements of the stolen car after Thomason was killed."

"Don't tell Marty," Dave says. "You need more than you've got. We can look around for stuff on Cooney, see if we can find out some more stuff on the adoption angle. His father was already a big deal in 1965, right? Maybe there's a picture of Marion Cooney pregnant or something. We've got this Paul Shouldice guy to work on, the email, right? He hasn't called you back so we need to talk to him, see if Gabriel Treacy contacted him here. Maybe he said something about Cooney to him. And Berta might find something more on the Afghanistan stuff. That's a lot to work on. And there's a press conference tomorrow, I meant to tell you."

"That's good," I say. "We'll just keep working on all that stuff. We can look into Cooney's background a bit more. That's good, Dave."

He thinks for a minute and then says, "Let's say that Cooney *is* the reason Treacy was here." He stops.

"Yeah?"

"I mean, let's say he is. You're not saying you think he *killed* Treacy, are you?"

I just stare at him. "He lied, Dave. He's the fucking district attorney. He didn't have to kill him for this to be bad. If he knew the victim but didn't tell anyone? I mean, that's . . ." I mime a bomb exploding, bringing my fingertips together and then opening them up. "He doesn't have to have pulled the trigger himself for this to be really bad."

"I know, I know, Mags. But, we have to be careful here. He doesn't trust you. He knows you hate him. It's . . ."

"You think I'm making this up because I'm still mad at Cooney?"

"No, of course not, Mags. Look, we'll see what we find, and if we get anything, we'll go to Marty. Yeah?"

"Yeah," I say. "Remember, though, that if Cooney decides to make life miserable for us, he can do it. Marty's on our side, but Pat is Cooney's buddy. At some point, Marty won't be able to protect us." I look up at him.

"Okay. What do you want to do now?"

"I'm going to try Paul Shouldice again and then let's go back to Bay Shore." I hesitate. "Dave, thanks. I know what I'm doing, telling you about this. If you want to pretend I never told you, I would understand."

Dave grins at me and picks up a rock, arcing it into the water in a long, left-handed throw that makes me remember he played baseball in college in Florida.

"Fuck off," Dave says, smiling a tight little smile. "Let's see what we can find."

29

Paul Shouldice doesn't answer his cell, so I leave a voice mail that I hope sounds stern: "Please call me back as soon as possible, Mr. Shouldice. I'm going to try your office as well."

When I call the main number for Medical Volunteers for the World, I get stuck in a voice menu maze before finally connecting with a receptionist who tells me that Mr. Shouldice doesn't seem to be at his desk but that she'll make sure to tell him I called.

Dave drives us down to the South Shore and we park on Garner Lane and walk into the neighborhood. It's a much warmer day than it was when we were here last time and I get a vision of what it must be like in the summer, the gardens in bloom, the lawns green and lush, teenagers walking home from the beach on hot asphalt. We skirt Cooney's house, taking a right before his section of the street and walking the square to the beach and then around the little streets next to the canal.

"It'd be nice to have a boat, you know?" Dave says, as we pass a couple of slips in the canal. "I think I'd like that, take it out on the weekend?"

"Brian had a sailboat for a while. It took so much work. It was like having a horse or something. Better to have a *friend* with a boat. That's what I do."

"Right," he says. "Yeah." There's something a little sad in his voice and I remember a comment he made a year or so ago about how he's been living on the island for ten years but he doesn't really feel like he belongs here. He told me a few months ago that all his online dating has only made him lonelier. I make a mental note to invite him over for a barbecue with some of my neighbors and Uncle Danny and Eileen.

We come around to Cooney's by way of one of the side streets and I put my head down, keep walking without looking at the house. I'm thinking about what Peter Mooney said to his team the last day I was in Sixmilebridge. *Don't take anyone's word for it that they don't have anything. Fucking verify it. Right?* "There really wasn't anything on the beach association video?" I ask.

"Nope. It was pointed in exactly the wrong direction."

"They asked at every house?" I ask Dave. "About security cameras?"

"Yeah, I think so." But he doesn't sound convinced. "Everywhere the security company said they had cameras, anyway."

I'm already walking toward the house across from Cooney's. "Come on, Dave," I say. "Let's do this job right." I try the first house and get a young woman, dressed in exercise clothes and holding a baby. When I ask her if she has any security cameras on the house she says that her husband was thinking about it, but they hadn't pulled the trigger yet. "This neighborhood is pretty safe," she says. "But now, with what happened at the marina, we might just decide to do it." We thank her and move on to the next house. No one's home, so we try the next one. This time, we get a middle-aged guy in his bathrobe. He says not to get too close because he's home from work with a bad cold. I explain what we're looking for and he says that he doesn't have security but the family next door does. "The Friels next door, Trevor? He's a bit of a security nut," he says. "He's got a gun and everything. I never quite understood it, but his wife told me he grew up in the Bronx in the eighties and he's kind of paranoid."

Dave and I glance at each other.

"Thanks," I say. "We'll go talk to them. Hope you feel better."

Trevor, as it turns out, is at work in the city. But his wife is home and when we introduce ourselves, she says, "Oh, have you caught someone? We've been so worried. You would think in a neighborhood like this, well, you wouldn't expect it."

"We're working hard on the case," I tell her. "In fact, we think you might be able to help us. Your next-door neighbor says that your husband has a great video security system that he set up himself? That he knows a lot about technology? Is that right?"

She starts to roll her eyes and then catches herself and says, "Well, yes, he set something up because there were some burglaries in the neighborhood."

"Could we look at his footage?" I ask. "Just to see if there's anything that might be helpful."

She looks annoyed for a second. She's trying to figure out a way to say no. But we're standing there and we're the cops and she doesn't really have a choice. "I guess. Come in. It's on a motion sensor, I think, and the clips stream to the family computer in the kitchen. It's as good as useless, though, because it takes video every time a raccoon or a bird crosses the street. There are like a thousand of them." She stares pointedly at our feet and we take the hint and slip our shoes off by the door. "I don't even know if he checks it anymore," she says. "He's been so busy at work lately." The house is an explosion of French farmhouse style, yellow roosters and yellow-and-red-painted pottery everywhere you look. It smells so good I have to resist the urge to ask her what kind of lemony spray or candles or whatever she uses.

She boots up the Mac desktop. The desktop photo is of her with a dorky-looking guy and three blond kids at Disney World, standing with a bunch of Disney characters in front of Cinderella's palace. "Okay, here it is," she says. "It's some app he got that saves the videos for you. You can click on the different days."

"Thank you," I say. "I'll take a look." I click through the folders and find the one for Monday night, the sixteenth. I click on a file inside it, but it won't open.

"He has some other program on his laptop he uses to look at them," she says. "Sorry. Otherwise they'd be too big. I don't really understand."

"Our tech people can figure it out," I say. "Could we copy these files?"

"I guess so," she says, coming back into the kitchen with a cup of coffee that smells so good I want to grab it out of her hands.

The files are too big to email, so I have to upload them to one of my online file storage accounts. It takes a while, and Dave and I stand around awkwardly while she gets food out of the refrigerator for lunch. When the upload is finally done, we thank her and head back outside.

The day's warming up, and Dave and I walk down to the end of the street to see if there are any security cameras on the house along the water.

The big house that's under construction, which I've come to think of as Tara because of the columns in front and the faux plantation look they seem to be going for, looms in the late afternoon light. No one's working out front, and we stand there and look across at the marina. The vantage point offers a perfect view of the spot where Gabriel Treacy died.

"Can I help you?"

Dave and I spin around and find a middle-aged guy standing in the open garage, holding a bucket. He's wearing sunglasses and a baseball hat with the Boston Red Sox logo on it.

"Sorry, we're police detectives," I say. "We're investigating the incident over at the marina last week. Are you working here at the site?"

He gives us a wry look and says, "I'm not supposed to be. It's my house that's being built, but they're so far behind schedule I had to clean up after them to keep them on track. I live in Boston so it's not terribly convenient. I didn't hear about the incident. What happened?"

Dave clears his throat. "Well, there was a shooting at the marina on February sixteenth."

"Oh my God. This . . . We're building in this neighborhood because we thought it was safe. What happened?"

"Well, we don't know yet. That's why we're here investigating."

He thinks for a couple of seconds. "The sixteenth? Wait . . . I was here that night. I had business in New York and I was flying to London on the seventeenth so I came out to check up on things. It was such a mess that I decided to stay and clean up and make a list of all the details they were getting wrong. You should have seen what they put up for molding. It was horrible."

"What time would you say you were here?" I feel a little prick of excitement. This guy might be a new witness.

"I must have left around nine. I could have stayed many more hours but I had to get back to the city."

"Did you see or hear anything that might be relevant to our investigation?" I ask him. "Anything at all?"

He starts to shake his head, but then says, "This is bizarre. I honestly had completely forgotten until this minute. I . . . I was hauling bags of trash out of the house to the dumpster and there were two guys having it out. At least I think it was two men. One of them could have been a woman but I don't think so, for some reason. I looked down the street and I saw them standing in the street, yelling at each other. It was some kind of domestic argument, I thought, brothers or father and son. I don't know why I thought that." He smiles wryly. "I have a brother I get into it with sometimes. Anyway, one of them walked away after a bit. I guess that's why I didn't think much about it, because it seemed like he was heading off to cool down."

"Could you describe them?"

"No, it was pretty dark. One of them was tall, about my height. Not sure about the other person—smaller, I guess, which is why it could have been a woman, but I couldn't really say either way. That's it. Sorry."

"No, that's very helpful." I scan the street, looking back toward Cooney's house. "When you say 'down the street' what do you mean exactly? Where were they standing?"

He points. "In the street, out front of that house right there."

He's pointing to Cooney's house.

30

"What the hell are we going to do now?" Dave asks after we've gotten the guy's contact information in Boston and walked back to the car. The skies are moving fast overhead, stringy clouds snaking out across the Great South Bay toward the Atlantic.

I put my seat belt on and lean against the window for a second. "I don't know. Let's get something to eat, okay? Some coffee? I gotta think about this."

There's a strip mall deli on the way out of town, a dingy place that looks promising as soon as we're inside. There's a good range of sandwiches and a cooler full of salads that look like they were made today and not last week. Everything's clean and I know the coffee will be good as soon as the kid pours it and I smell dark roasted beans. We order chicken cutlet sandwiches to go and hot, sweet, milky coffee and I say, "Dave, let's go out across the causeway. I haven't been out there in a while. We gotta think about this and I need to get my head clear."

We climb back in the car. It's been a long time since I drove out to Robert Moses State Park and the barrier beaches of Jones Beach and Fire Island. "You ever been out here?" I ask Dave.

"Oh yeah. Not for a while, though. I gotta get out for a day this summer." We're out over the water now, sailing along the nearly empty causeway. We pass over Gilgo Beach, the first barrier beach, and then we're out over the bay again, heading toward the water tower at the entrance to the park. It does something to me, seeing the familiar approach; it's a place I associate with Erin, with the hot summer sun and the smell of salt water and Popsicles from the ice cream trucks that used to park along the beach. I must sigh, because Dave looks over and asks, "You okay, Mags?" and I nod.

Most of the parking lots are blocked off since it's out of season, but the one down near the boardwalk to the Fire Island Lighthouse is open and we park there and take our sandwiches and coffee down to the beach. Dave had an old blanket in his trunk and we spread it out and sit on the beach. The sandwiches are perfect, the tomato somehow juicy in February, the chicken cutlet freshly breaded and fried, more than enough mayo, flecked with fresh ground pepper, to squish out the sides. I chug my coffee and by the time I'm done eating I feel one hundred percent better. "Walk?" I ask. Dave nods and we wrap our trash up in the blanket and leave it next to the boardwalk to pick up later.

The sand is clean and wet, pocked here and there with shells and rocks.

"What are we gonna do?" Dave asks finally. "About *that*?" I know exactly what he means. *That* is the guy who told us about witnessing the fight, but it's everything else, too.

I start by playing devil's advocate. "He didn't say it was Cooney. He said they were in front of Cooney's house, but he didn't see anyone go into the house. It could have been Cooney's neighbor, it could have been anybody. Two guys having a fight? Maybe a woman? Could be a couple, right? Or a fight that started at one of the bars?"

"Yeah, sure." He bends down and picks up a little white rock, rubbing sand off it with his thumb and then tucking it into his pocket. "Let's say it was Treacy and Cooney fighting in the street, though. Why?"

"Here's what I'm thinking. I'm just playing what-if. Think through this with me, okay? Cooney is Stella Treacy's son. He was adopted by his parents and either he knew or he didn't know, but either way, Gabriel Treacy comes to Long Island to meet him, to say, 'Hey, you're my long-lost brother. Let's get to know each other.'"

"Okay," Dave says. "What happens next?"

"They get together at Cooney's house and . . . what? This is the part I don't see. Treacy says, I don't know . . . 'I want to tell everyone we're brothers! I'm going to go public.' But Cooney doesn't want that?"

"Okay," Dave says. "But why would Cooney care so much? If it happened that way, why didn't he tell us as soon as Treacy was found? Why didn't he say, 'Hey, strange coincidence. That guy is my brother.' These days, that kinda stuff happens all the time. All these DNA testing sites. I mean, like I told you, I don't care about being adopted. I talk to my birth mother every once in a while and it's fine." I'd forgotten that Dave connected with his birth mother a few years ago. She found him, as I remember, and they had a nice reunion, but they're not in touch a lot and the whole thing was fairly low drama.

"That's what I can't figure out. It's gotta be related to the fact that he's up for reelection, right? Maybe he didn't want it as a distraction during the campaign and he tried to put Treacy off and Treacy didn't like it. Something like that. But it makes me think something happened that night. Otherwise, why didn't he tell us?"

Dave looks freaked out, but he says, "Maybe Cooney says, 'I don't want my family to hear about this. Let's meet up later over at the marina.' They get together on the beach and . . . Cooney's brought a gun and something goes wrong, or if Treacy brought it with him . . ."

As soon as he says it, I know it doesn't quite fit. There's the match on the gun. There's no way Cooney could have faked that. I keep going. "There's the weapon . . . But Cooney might have been able to get someone to give it to him. He knows people who have questioned those gang members, right?" I meet Dave's eyes, see them widen as he realizes what I'm thinking. *Alicia. The members of the task force. Bill.*

Silence. "Shit, yeah," Dave says finally. "Or he hired someone to do it. Told them he'd get them off if they did it. Now we've got this whole task force going and he and the US attorney are in control of who gets charged and who doesn't . . . I was thinking about that DA upstate, the one who got that drug dealer to kill his girlfriend?" The details of the case are sketchy in my mind, but I think Dave's right. The girlfriend of a district attorney in Buffalo or Schenectady or somewhere was threatening to go public about their relationship and the fact that she was pregnant, so he hired a guy his office was investigating to kill her.

There are more of those than you'd think: cases where prosecutors feel backed into a corner by someone threatening to tell their story, where they abuse their power over suspects to get them to commit crimes.

I don't say anything. We know this is the one that might make sense.

He's quiet and then he says, "But we're just playing what-if, right?"

"Yeah. But . . . it's possible."

"But why? It's possible, but why? That's the part I don't get. You're right, the idea of his adoption being found out isn't enough. At least, I don't think it is. There's something we're not seeing."

The wind dies down for a minute and we both stand and look at the water. The waves are angry today, their edges white with foam, the sand darkening toward our feet.

We turn around and start heading back to the parking lot.

Dave shakes out the blanket, and I stuff the trash from our lunch in my pocket and take the corners to help him fold it. I say, "If Mr. Disney World got the fight on tape, then we gotta go to Marty, right? We'll have to go to the commissioner."

"Yeah, but we might get something from your friends in Ireland. Or you and me might be able to get something from this Paul Shouldice guy."

"You and I."

"Thanks, Mom."

"Treacy might have told Paul Shouldice what he was doing here," I say. "If they were old friends. You're right. That might be it."

As we drive back toward the causeway, I'm looking at my phone when Dave suddenly slams on the brakes. I hit my seat belt and his arm comes up to keep me in my seat. When I look up, a deer is stopped in the middle of the road, its eyes huge and scared. For a long moment, it stares at us, frozen in place, and then, when Dave taps the horn, it runs off into the scrubby trees next to the road. "Sorry," Dave says, easing his foot off the brake. "It came out of nowhere. You okay?"

"Yeah." But I'm not. I'm shaking, and something about the deer's eyes on me has me spooked.

"You sure?"

I take a deep breath. "This thing, Dave, it feels like there's someone out there, keeping an eye on me, you know what I mean? A couple times I've had the feeling someone's watching me. There's someone who's moving this thing, behind the scenes." I come back to the word I used before to describe the crime scene. "Someone *professional*."

Dave doesn't say anything. I can't tell if he agrees or if he thinks I've lost my grip on reality.

On the LIE, I find Paul Shouldice's number on my phone. "This would all be a lot easier if Treacy told Shouldice all about why he was coming here," I tell Dave and I dial the number. It goes straight to voice mail, and this time I try to put even more menace into my message: "Mr. Shouldice, this is Detective Lieutenant Maggie D'arcy and I'm really hoping to speak with you in the next twenty-four hours. Please call me at your earliest convenience. Otherwise, we'll need to pay you a visit."

"That should get something moving," I say to Dave, and he makes a funny face, pretending to be scared of me, but I can't help feeling a little nudge of caution. *Why hasn't Paul Shouldice called me back?*

Back at headquarters, I stop in Berta's office. Everyone's busy and I think I can get a conversation in with her without Bill getting suspicious. "Hey, Berta," I say. I shut the door behind me, which makes her look up and narrow her eyes. She knows something's up. I sit down and slide a piece of paper across the desk. On it I've written *NY to Ireland Feb. 19th or 20th AND Ireland to NY anytime on after Feb. 24th.*

She reads it and then says, "What's this?"

"I'm wondering if you can get travel records, anyone who traveled between here and Ireland on these dates."

"You're looking for someone who killed Gabriel Treacy, then flew to Ireland and killed Noel Thomason, then flew back here. No way the airlines are going to give me anything that broad. You know that, Maggie."

"Can you try?" I ask her, making puppy-dog eyes. She pulls the note over, sighs, and nods. "And Berta, can you keep it quiet, just for a couple days?" I look right at her, serious, showing her how important it is. I haven't asked Berta for a lot of favors. She nods again.

"Thanks. Let me know if you get anything? Maybe call me?"

"Yup. How about the Afghanistan stuff you have me looking at? Is that a call, too?"

"No. That's okay for everyone," I say. "Thanks, Berta."

"In my father's village, there was a man who was very learned, very smart. He told the children in the village that he had read every book there was to read in the entire world, that there was no book anyone could name that he had not read."

That was how Tahir's story had started. They could tell, from his tone, that it was a comic one, that it was different from the others. Gabriel had known Tahir for a few months now. He was funny, and he was fascinated by comedy, by why it worked when it worked and why it didn't work when it didn't. He was a student of it, had memorized famous jokes in English and would sometimes ask Gabriel or Gillian, when she was in country, to explain them. He had asked them to explain Henny Youngman's "Take my wife" jokes and they had tried their best, realizing in the process that they did not actually understand some of the jokes themselves.

Tahir went on with his story. "This man, people would come to him and say, 'What about Jane Austen? Have you read the books of Jane Austen?' and he would recite all the titles and he would tell you what each was about. One day, a man said to him, 'Have you read The Sparrow in the Window?' He had never read this book, but he *decided that he would try to find it. He had to travel very far to a library, but he found this book and he read it and when he returned to the town, he said that he had read this book and it was not a good book, but that he had now read every single book in the world." Ta-hir smiled, full of the knowledge of what was to come, anticipating their reactions. That was what a joke was, Gabriel thought, knowing something your audience does not know.*

Then, Tahir waited, to make sure they were ready. "He said that what he had learned was that not all the books in the world were worth reading, and after that he never bragged again about having read every book in the world."

31

We clean some stuff up at headquarters and I head for home at six. I'm getting off the LIE when I spot the headlights. There's someone driving behind me, nothing strange there, but my hypervigilance causes me to keep track of the blue-tinged lights in my rearview mirror. They drop back a few cars at one point and then they're there again as the traffic eases.

I'm listening to the radio and trying not to obsess, but when I get off in Dix Hills, the headlights follow. I'm alert now, constantly checking the rearview mirror; when I turn onto New York Avenue, they're gone, and I start to relax, but five minutes later, there's someone behind me again.

I'm trying to catch the license plate but the angles are wrong, so I just keep driving at a steady pace. When I stop for a red light on Park Avenue, I check and see a light-colored SUV behind me. I'm not sure if it's the same one, though. The driver is hidden in the darkness, in the blur of lights.

Park Avenue isn't too busy and I'm at the turnoff out to the Bay in another five minutes. I'm not sure what to do. If someone's following me, I want to know. But on the other hand, the winding roads of Alexandria Bay are quiet and dark for long stretches.

I don't signal, swinging off onto Bay Avenue and keeping an eye on the rearview mirror. I pull over as soon as I can and just sit there, waiting. No one's followed me. My hands shaking, I dial Dave's number.

"Hey, Mags," he answers. "What's up?"

"Someone just tailed me into the Bay," I say. "I didn't go home and I lost them, but they were definitely following me."

"Did you get the plate?" he asks.

"No. Too dark. But it was a light-colored SUV. I was just thinking about the one parked at the motel in Bay Shore. It was white, right? Did you ever confirm it was the painting company?"

"Yeah. I can check but I think we talked to them. What do you want me to do? You want me to come meet you?"

"No, I'll be okay. But check on the SUV, right?"

Lilly's finishing dinner when I get home, sitting at the table and flipping through her phone while listlessly eating a bowl of chicken soup from a can in the pantry. I'm still shaken, but she doesn't seem to notice, and she just shrugs when I ask how her day was and then goes right up to her room after dutifully putting her dishes in the dishwasher as an extra *fuck you* to me.

I make some scrambled eggs and salad for myself while I listen to the news—more stories about the new administration hiring agency heads and directors, more stories about protests for and against the new president's statements on immigration. There's an edge to all of it that makes me nervous. It's been a long time since I was in uniform, patrolling parades and concerts and protests, but I remember the feeling of being in a large crowd just before things start to go bad, the way muttered words join together into a chorus, the way agitated people feed off each other, spreading their energy through the throng. The whole country feels like that now.

I find myself wondering about Miguel Aguillar, imagining his journey here, imagining how many times someone's told him he doesn't belong, that he's not American. I clean up the kitchen to calm my jangling nerves, then drink a glass of wine too fast and go upstairs to check on Lilly. I find her door closed, the light off. I knock softly, but there's no answer. "Lil?" I whisper. "You asleep?" Either that or she's ignoring me. I have to resist the urge to go in and check to make sure she's breathing, the way I did when she was a baby.

"'Night, Lil," I say to the door, then go put on my pajamas and get into bed. I fall asleep almost immediately, wrecked from jet lag and everything else, but at one a.m. my eyes fly open, my brain certain I've heard something. My service weapon is locked in the safe, so I pad down the stairs without my gun and carefully check the front and back doors, all the windows, the alarm system, which is still armed. I get my Glock out of the safe and step out into the backyard, listening to the ocean below me, the silence of the neighborhood. Our backyard is empty, the fence ghostly white in the little bit of moonlight, the flower beds at the back in shadow.

Everything's fine. It's just my anxiety.

But now I'm awake and I know from experience that I'm not going to be able to fall asleep anytime soon.

I make myself a cup of tea and sit down at the dining-room table with my laptop. I search for "Afghanistan 2011" and do some reading on what was happening there when Gabriel Treacy was abducted in Nangarhar Province.

I feel like an idiot, flying over decades of history in seconds, realizing how much of it I wasn't even aware of. Lilly was born in 2001 and I remember sitting on the couch, nursing her at night and watching cable news reports about us bombing Afghanistan after 9/11 and then Tora Bora and bin Laden escaping. As I scroll through the timelines, the pieces start to come back. It wasn't until they'd defeated the Taliban and started rebuilding that aid organizations could even get into the country. By 2011, things had been more stable for a while but then had gotten worse again with the resurgence of the Taliban and al-Qaeda. We sent more troops to the area, along with huge numbers of private contractors. In May of that year, bin Laden was killed.

The stories about the deaths of US troops are terrible, as are the stories about the much larger numbers of Afghan troops killed. One of the articles I read says that more civilian contractors have been killed in Afghanistan than US troops, and I read accounts of private security personnel, translators, technology contractors, and the like killed by suicide bombers and in mortar attacks.

Aid workers, too. There were quite a few kidnappings of aid workers in Afghanistan in 2011 and in the years after Gabriel Treacy was released. Many of the accounts are vague, without names or details, and others reveal that the victims' governments were negotiating to get them released, often successfully. I make a note to check back in with Roly to see if his friend Greta found anything more for us.

When he was released, Gabriel Treacy must have felt relieved, but forever changed. I think about what I said to Conor, that somehow the trauma Treacy experienced in Afghanistan had come back and led to his death.

I'm tired of war but not sleepy yet so I decide to see if I can get into the security footage from Garner Lane. I have to download a converter to my laptop but I finally get it to work. I start with the file from February 9, the week before Gabriel Treacy was killed, just so I can get the hang of skipping ahead, and start watching. I go methodically through the videos and eventually I get through one whole twenty-four-hour period. It takes forever, but it's something to do and there's something about the tedium of it that's a relief. When I'm looking at the clips, I can't think about Conor or Lilly or Cooney or anything else. I'm just focused on the empty street and yard, on watching for something or someone to show up. I do the whole week and get a couple of cars.

On February 13, three days before Gabriel Treacy was killed, a small sports car drives slowly through the neighborhood at 3:04 a.m. It comes down Garner, just past the Friels' house, turns around at the end of the road near the beach gazebo, and goes back up the road. Then, a couple of hours later, at 5:07 a.m., the same car comes back down the road. I pause the video and write down what I can see of the license plate. We'll be able to trace it and see who our driver was.

I keep going. Most of the clips are cars or animals. Only a few pedestrians, which makes me take note of the name of the system Trevor picked and vow never to buy it myself.

I'm getting lulled by the monotony of the video again when all of a sudden, on February 15, the night before Gabriel Treacy was killed, the car is back. This time it goes quickly past the Friels' camera and doesn't come back again. I check the time stamp. Four thirty a.m. Unless someone in the neighborhood works at a bar, the timing is suspicious.

I get another glass of wine and start looking at the sixteenth. The images are blurring together and I almost miss the slight darkness at the top of the frame as I skip forward. I stop, go back, and watch as a figure in dark clothes walks across the road from the Friels' side and hesitates for a minute in front of Cooney's house. The time stamp says 8:23 p.m. The man walks up to the front door, knocks on the door, and a few seconds later the door is opened. I can't see who opens it. I stop and watch it again. The quality of the video is good enough that I can make out that the man is wearing a blazer. When he turns his head to the right, I see his beard and I know immediately who it is. The clip stops and I click on the next one, then the next. A couple of cars pass the house. A woman walks by the camera with a small dog on a leash. Thirty-one minutes after the man went into the house, he comes out again, stands in the road briefly, and then walks out of the frame.

I sit there for a minute, just taking it in.

On the night he died, Gabriel Treacy went to Jay Cooney's house and stayed for thirty-one minutes. He came out just before nine and only a few hours later, he was dead.

32

Lilly begs off school again and I'm in such a rush to get out of the house, I don't fight her, even though I don't love the idea of her home alone. She's still pissed at me, still silent, her negative energy drifting down from upstairs in a cloud. But I don't have time for it this morning, and I leave her a note on the kitchen table, telling her I've locked the house up and set the alarm and asking her to unload the dishwasher and check in with me later.

I meet Dave at the deli. He knows as soon as he sees me that I have something to tell him. "Get your breakfast," I say. "I'll tell you outside."

We take our egg-and-cheese bagel sandwiches and coffees out to my car. I'm anxious, nervy, suspicious of the full parking lot, so I drive down Yaphank Avenue a bit and pull over into a residential neighborhood. I shut the car off, open up my laptop, and play the video clip I've saved on the desktop.

"That's Treacy," he says. "Holy shit. He visited Cooney."

"This is on the sixteenth," I say. "On the fourteenth, he flew into JFK, came out to Bay Shore. He stayed at the motel for two days, and on the sixteenth he goes to visit Jay Cooney at his house, stays for thirty minutes, and a few hours later, he's dead."

Dave sips his coffee. I take a bite of my bagel and can hardly taste it.

"What the fuck do we do?" I ask him. "Do we talk to Marty?"

"Not yet. We still need more. We need something showing that they knew each other. That video? He could make up anything. He could get his wife to say she was home and a tourist stopped by to ask directions and she gave him a cup of tea. He can come up with something, especially if he gets a heads-up. We need more."

"Well, he didn't call him on the cell phone," I say. "But somehow he got in touch with Cooney and made an appointment to meet him. There must be an email or . . . somehow they got in touch, right? Shit, I wish he hadn't deleted his email account."

I finish my bagel, not because it tastes good, but because I just need to get some calories into me. I watch a car pull out of a drive-way across from where we're parked. The driver eyes us suspiciously. At the end of the street, there's an old pay phone, the phone itself long gone, but the booth apparently used for graffiti practice. "Dave, there weren't any working pay phones near the marina, were there, or near the motel?"

"Nah, they checked. And he didn't make any calls from his room."

"That place is too small to have a business center, right?"

"I'd say so." He pops the last chunk of bagel into his mouth and licks his fingers.

"Hang on. There must have been a phone at the main desk. We didn't check that, did we?"

Dave looks up. "Shit. It wasn't obviously for guests' use so I guess we didn't think of it, but yeah, you do that sometimes, right? Ask to use the phone at the desk if your phone is dead or whatever?"

I dial the number for the motel. Uddin Ahmed answers and when I identify myself, he says, "One minute please," and his grandson comes on the phone. "Yes, Detective?"

"I'm so sorry to bother you again, Mr. Ahmed, but I was just wondering. This phone, the one you're talking on, it's on the desk in the lobby, right?"

"That's right."

"Is there any possibility that Mr. Treacy used this phone? Instead of the one in his room? Any of the days he was staying there?"

There's a short silence. "I'm trying to remember what was going on that week," Sabbir Ahmed says. "I don't have any memory of it, but of course it's possible that he used it when we weren't here. It was so quiet then, there would have been periods where my grandfather was in the back. I'm often at Stonybrook during the days. We have a bell on the counter so guests can call for service, but perhaps he didn't want to bother us and just . . . made a call. The phone sits right out on the counter."

"Okay, thank you," I say. "We'll have to get the records from the phone company. If you don't object, it might go faster if you tell them it's okay . . . I'm so sorry for the continued inconvenience to you and your business."

There's a moment of hesitation and then he says, "We have access to a call log through our online billing account. We have this kind of account because we need to be able to itemize calls for our business records. Would you like me to just see if I can find a record of it?"

I say a silent thank-you to whatever cop god is looking down on me today.

"Yes, that would be fantastic," I say. "I can't tell you how much I appreciate it."

"I'll go sign in and call you back," he says.

I tell Dave what he said. "Why all the hush-hush stuff?" I ask him. "If his cell phone wasn't working, why didn't he just use the phone in his room?"

"I don't know, but Mags, we gotta think about what we're gonna do if it comes back Treacy called Cooney."

"I know." I ball up the foil from my bagel. "First, though, we better go smile for the cameras."

Headquarters is busy with everyone getting ready for the press conference. We get to work on the stuff we said we'd do: compiling witness statements. I try not to check my phone too often, and I try not to notice Dave looking over at me every couple of minutes to see if I've checked it, but I'm not sure I'm doing a good job.

Finally he comes over and drops a paper on my desk. "Here's the reg on the SUV," he says. I look down. He's scrawled out *Dynasty Logistics, Washington, DC*.

According to its website, Dynasty Logistics is a "full-service trucking and logistics company with offices across the country." It makes sense that a painting company might have rented the SUV, but I want to confirm that. I call the main number and get a general inquiry voice mailbox. I leave a message saying that I want to confirm who was using the vehicle on February 16.

I'm in the hallway outside our one semidecent press room, trying to comb my hair and put on some lipstick, when Cooney arrives. He catches me with my compact and mirror in my hand, which I don't like, and he comes right over, trailed by Alicia and another ADA, and shakes my hand, forcing me to shift the compact to my other hand. "Good to see you, Detective D'arcy. Welcome back from your trip. I understand you're working hard on this case. So glad we all got a break."

"Yes," I say. "We are working hard. And I know you all are, too." I'm searching his face, trying to find Gabriel Treacy in it, trying to find Gerry Murray, who I've only seen in pictures, there, too.

"You can say that again," he says, with a smile that starts strong and then slides away. "Ah, I guess we're ready to begin." He tries for another smile but he seems stressed and, I think, a little pale. His normal color is ruddy, like he's been out on his sailboat all day, but this morning, his cheeks are waxy and his eyes bruised with lack of sleep.

Alicia doesn't look great, either. Her makeup is expertly applied, but her eyes are red and irritated looking, the way mine are when I haven't slept well, and her usually relaxed smile seems strained. She's been working her ass off, though, and I'm sure she was up all night with the gang task force, so I tell myself not to read too much into it.

The reporters get set up and then Pat and Marty come in, along with Shawn Hopke, chief of detectives, and Frank Guglio, chief of department, plus the US attorney and the FBI field office chief, and by the time they wave me and Dave up there next to Alicia, we're challenging the limits of their wide-angle lenses.

"Thank you for coming," Pat says. He's not looking good today; his skin has a grayish tinge. He coughs and says, "I'm now going to turn things over to the commanding officer of the homicide squad, Martin Cascic."

Marty steps up, all business, his suit pressed for the occasion. "Just to review, late on the night of February sixteenth, a forty-five-year-old Irish national named Gabriel Treacy was shot and killed as he stood on the Bay Shore Manor beach in Bay Shore. This is a recent picture of Mr. Treacy." We all look up at Gabriel Treacy's passport photo on the screen. "Over the weekend, we received confirmation from the Suffolk County Crime Lab that the firearm used to kill Mr. Treacy was also used to kill Juan Bollina last year." Gabriel Treacy is replaced by a picture of Juan Bollina. In it, he's grinning and has an arm draped around his elderly grandmother. "Mr. Bollina's death was a senseless tragedy for our community. We believe Mr. Bollina and Mr. Treacy were both innocent victims of a vicious gang. It is all of our responsibilities to put a stop to their terrorizing of the citizens of Long Island."

There's a buzz among the reporters. MS13 stories get lots of clicks and views. They all know it. "Hold on, hold on," Marty says. "We'll take questions in a moment. But right now, we want to say that Suffolk County Police would like to speak with anyone who may have seen Mr. Treacy in the days before his death or on the night of February sixteenth. We would also like to talk to any local residents or visitors to the area who may have seen anything that might be helpful. We are offering a reward for any information. Someone out there knows exactly what happened and we hope that person will come forward." Marty steps back, the picture of Juan Bollina still on the screen, and Pat says we'll take a few questions.

The press starts right out with the alarmism. "Do residents of Bay Shore have reason to think this is going to happen again?" someone shouts out. "What precautions should residents be taking?"

Pat wobbles a bit, then catches himself, and says, "We do not have reason to believe that the public is in any danger at this time, but residents should take the same precautions they would take at any time."

"But if MS13 is randomly killing tourists on beaches, what's to say it won't happen again?"

Pat looks at a loss for words and Shawn Hopke steps in neatly. "We believe this was a crime of opportunity. We have no reason to believe it will happen again," Hopke says. "But again, use precautions."

There are a few more questions along those lines, one about whether Treacy was buying drugs, and then Eric Coombs, the reporter from *Newsday,* says, "We know that Detective Lieutenant D'arcy recently traveled to Ireland to look into the victim's life and that Gabriel Treacy's lawyer was murdered there during a house robbery. Was that just a coincidence? Did the trip yield any information relevant to Treacy's murder?"

I get ready to answer but Marty says, "That's all part of an ongoing investigation. We don't have anything to share at this time."

They save the best for last. "District Attorney Cooney, you're up for reelection and you have a serious challenger," says one of the reporters. "Are you concerned that a murder that took place only steps from your own home in Bay Shore is still unsolved? Will it affect your reelection?"

Cooney steps forward, glaring at the reporter. "I am very concerned, but not because of my reelection. I am concerned because a human being, a visitor to our country, has lost his life and we do not yet have his killer in custody. I am concerned that MS13 continues to terrorize communities in Suffolk County. I am concerned that Juan Bollina's family has not seen their son's killer come to justice. That's what I'm concerned about. We have made a major break in the case today and we will continue to aggressively pursue whoever is responsible for this crime. Members of the public with information to share about MS13 members must come forward."

That about does it. I watch Cooney walk away from the podium. He smiles at someone, shakes hands with one of the FBI guys, then stands there for a moment, waiting for Alicia to finish chatting. He's stoic, and then, suddenly, he looks utterly terrified, his eyes widening as though he's just remembered something awful. He looks up to see me watching him. Our eyes meet and he looks away. Alicia turns to him with a smile, and it's like a switch flips. He stands up straighter, nods solemnly, and lets her lead the way out of the room.

33

We're walking back over to our desks when a call comes in from a Bay Shore exchange that I assume is Sabbir Ahmed. I don't want anyone to overhear us, so I catch Dave's eye and motion toward the door, mouthing, *Five minutes.*

"Hello?" I say, crouching down in a corner in the hallway.

"Detective D'arcy, this is Sabbir Ahmed. I'm sorry that took so long. I couldn't remember the password because my sister usually does the books and has all of that. Anyway, there's one number associated with an outgoing call during those days that wasn't one of our usual contacts. It was from February fifteenth at one p.m. Of course, I can't be sure that someone else didn't make the call, but Mr. Treacy was the only guest—the others had checked out that morning—so it seems like it might be a call he made."

"Who was it to?" I ask him. "It doesn't give a name, does it?" I'm holding my breath, my body frozen as I lean against the wall. If it's Jay Cooney, I have to tell Marty.

"No, just the number. It's uh, 631-532-0061."

"Hang on." I type that into my notes app and then say, "Okay, thank you so much, Mr. Ahmed. You've saved us a lot of time.

We'll need to get the whole statement at some point, but this is very helpful."

I stare at the number for a few minutes. It used to be that a phone number could tell you a lot about where someone lived, but now that people take their cell phone numbers with them when they move, it doesn't tell me as much as it used to.

So I dial it. It goes straight to voice mail: "This is Heather Thornton. Please leave me a message and I'll get back to you as soon as I can." Her accent is mild Long Island.

Heather. We've got her. Then I remember the list at the motel: *H. T.*—Heather Thornton.

"Ms. Thornton," I say after the beep, trying to keep my voice even. "My name is Maggie D'arcy. I'm a police detective with the Suffolk County Police Department and I'm wondering if I could talk to you. It's very important. Please call as soon as you can." I leave my number and hang up.

I go out to my car and get my laptop out of my bag. Using my phone as a hotspot, I start searching for "Heather Thornton" and "Long Island" and get a number of hits for a Heather G. Thornton.

I figure out immediately why she uses her middle initial: She's a reporter with a semi-common name.

Heather G. Thornton has a profile on a site for freelance journalists and I find lots of links to her articles on various other sites, some high profile, some not, but across the board respectable: the *Chicago Sun-Times*, the *Baltimore Sun*, *Newsweek*. From 2003 to 2012, she was a staff reporter for *Newsday*. Her profile says she's based in Farmingdale, where she covers local politics. That's half an hour from here, forty minutes with traffic; Dave and I can go talk to her. We *have* to go talk to her. I text him and tell him to meet me in the parking lot.

As he walks out, he keeps checking behind him to make sure he isn't being followed. He's like a parody of a spy. I can't help laughing when he looks in both directions then quickly gets in my car and slides down in the passenger seat.

"Who are you, James Bond? I don't think anyone followed you," I say.

"You never know. What you got?"

"He made a call from the motel. On the fifteenth."

"Yeah? Who'd he call? Do I want to know?" Dave thinks it's Cooney.

"Someone named Heather G. Thornton. Heather. He scrawled *Heather* on a piece of paper in his office in Dublin. Get this. She's a reporter. Used to work for *Newsday*. But lately, she's been writing a lot of freelance stories about politics."

"Seriously?"

"Yeah. We need to talk to her. I left a message, but she hasn't called back. She lives in Farmingdale. We can probably find her house, you know. Maybe if—" My phone buzzes and I look down to find Conor's name on the screen. I hold a finger up for Dave and say "Hang on" while I accept the call.

"Hey," I say. "I'm right in the—"

He cuts me off. "Maggie, is Lilly home alone right now?"

There's something urgent in his voice that sends cold ripping through my veins. "Yeah, why?"

"Look, Adrien was texting with her and he said she sounded really down. She said some things that, well, that concerned him enough that he came and told me. I'm not certain what . . . he didn't want to show me the messages, but I think she said it might be better if she weren't around, things like that, and then he tried to call her and she didn't pick up. I thought I should ring you and let you know.

I'm sorry, Maggie, I know things are busy." His voice—concerned, nervous—cuts right through me.

"Oh God. Thank you, Conor. I'm going right now. I'm driving straight home. I'll call Danny and have him go down to the house. Oh God, Conor, thank you. Thank you. I'll call as soon as I'm home." I start the car, slam it into reverse as I pull my seat belt across my body.

"Oh my God, Dave. I gotta go. Conor's worried that Lilly . . . might hurt herself. Something she texted to Adrien." The terror is rushing through me, focusing me on the next thing I need to do to get home.

Dave has the passenger door open already. He's out. "Go," he says. "I'll explain things to Marty. Go, do what you need to do. I'll handle things here. You go. I'm praying for you, Mags." His face almost breaks my heart. "I'm praying for you."

I get on the LIE and swerve into the left lane, frantically dialing Lilly's phone on the car system. I'm thinking of where I left the key to the gun safe, whether I have any pills in my medicine cabinet, razors— terrible thoughts. She doesn't pick up, so I try Uncle Danny, but it goes to voice mail. I don't know what to do so I try the bar and when one of the new bartenders answers, I say, "This is Maggie, Danny's niece. Is he there? It's an emergency." There's an SUV in front of me in the left lane and I lay on my horn to try to move him over. He ignores me and slows down and the rage I feel at him burns through my chest.

"No, I'm sorry, Maggie. He and Eileen were maybe gonna go to a movie. He probably shut his phone off. Can I do anything?"

"No, no, that's okay. If you talk to him, just tell him to get to my house and call me, okay? It's really important." I hang up before he can say anything.

I'm driving too fast and I'm almost to Dix Hills now. I've got a few neighbors' numbers in my phone and I'm trying to scroll while I drive but I'm already on Park Avenue by the time I get through to the Yaktitises' answering machine. I hang up. I think about calling 911, but I'll be home by the time they get there. I have lights I can put up and I'll use them if I need to, but the truth is they can make people slow down and can actually make traffic worse.

"Please, please, please, God," I mutter out loud. It's been a long time since I prayed, but I think of Dave praying for me and for Lilly and I go ahead and pray right along with him. "Please let her be okay. Please let her be okay. Please, please, please. Anything. I'll do anything if she can just be okay." By the time I screech into my driveway, I'm crying, still praying, and I leap out of the car, running up to the door just in time to see Uncle Danny practically sprinting down the street. "Whatsamatter, Mags? Is it Lilly? Is she okay?"

I can't even answer him. I stab my key into the lock to open the front door and start screaming, "Lilly? Lil? Where are you?" and I'm at the bottom of the stairs when she emerges sleepily from her bedroom, standing at the top of the landing in her pink unicorn sweatshirt, confused and scared. I take the stairs two at a time and I grab her and hug her so hard she yells out in pain. The alarm starts sounding. The tears are pouring out of my eyes and Lilly keeps saying, "What? What's going on?" and I say, "Thank you, God, thank you," and call down the stairs to Uncle Danny, "She's okay, Uncle Danny, she's okay."

After Uncle Danny goes home and I've talked to the alarm company, I text Dave and Conor and then I make Lilly rice pudding with raisins, which is the only thing she says she wants for dinner. Stirring it gives me something to do with my hands; the repetitive motion is soothing, and by the time it's done, I'm calmer, spent. It's five now, the evening coming on outside, pinkish clouds settling in over the bay. I sit next to Lilly at the kitchen table and say, "What did you text to Adrien, Lil? He was really worried."

"I didn't tell him I was going to, like, kill myself or anything," she says, but she's not making eye contact with me. "I swear. We were just talking about stuff and I said I was in a bad mood because we had to leave Ireland and I was just . . . I said I was really bummed out. I didn't say I was freaking *suicidal.*" Something flashes across her face and I know she's thinking of Brian.

It took Lilly a long time to be able to talk about Brian's suicide. At first, she acted as though he'd been killed by some outside force, a thug whose name we couldn't say. Then she acted as though I was the outside force. Finally, she seemed to accept that he had chosen it himself. Her therapist told me to be on the lookout for suicidal ideation, for any sense that she might be glorifying her father's final actions.

I'm furious with myself. I can't believe I let my guard down.

"Why didn't you answer your phone? I was so worried, Lil. Adrien and Conor were so worried."

"Seriously, Mom, I was so tired from jet lag and everything. I turned it off and fell asleep. And then you woke me up screaming and crying."

"I'm sorry, Lil. I was so worried about you. I couldn't get Uncle Danny on the phone, you weren't picking up."

"You really think I'd do that, you really think I'd do something like that?" It's too cold in the house. The temperature's dropped in the last couple of hours and the furnace hasn't kept up. Lilly's shivering. I'm shivering. I get up and raise the thermostat. When I sit down again, she says, "I can't believe you really think I'm, like, suicidal."

I have to push down the annoyance that's rising in my blood. "Lil, I don't know what's going on with you. You don't tell me. It's been a hell of a year and you are completely within your rights to feel however it is you feel. But Conor was worried. I was worried. I'm just glad you're okay."

She looks up at me and I can see the vulnerability again. "I just felt really lonely when I was chatting with Adrien. I was here all day and it was just like . . . you know how your mind does weird things when you're alone."

Her voice has gotten quieter and quieter. I feel the guilt like a knife. "Lil, honey, I'm sorry I've been working so much. This case completely screwed up our vacation, I know that."

She doesn't say anything, but she eats her rice pudding and when she says she's tired and wants to go up and lie down, something on my face makes her add, "Don't worry, I'm not going to do anything."

"Lil, I love you so much. Let me know if you're feeling down, okay? We can be down together." I reach out to touch her arms as she leaves the kitchen, but gracefully, elegantly, like a ballet dancer, she steps out of my reach.

I call Dave, give him the short version. "I think she's okay now, but I need to stick around tonight."

"Listen, right after you left, Paul Shouldice finally returned my call. I explained that we wanted to talk to him in person and he said that would be okay, so I said we could drive in early tomorrow morning and meet with him. He suggested a coffee place in Midtown. You think that would work? I can go by myself if you need to stay home." He's hesitant, not sure if he should say it.

"Let me see how she is later. I don't want to leave her alone but maybe I can get Danny to stay with her."

"Okay, good. You get some sleep and we'll go see him in the morning."

After Lilly falls asleep, I call Heather Thornton again. It goes to voice mail and this time I say, "Ms. Thornton, I really need to talk with you. If I don't hear from you by tomorrow, we're going to make a visit to the address I have on file for you. Please call me."

And then, since I've been doing so much praying, I say another little prayer. *Please call back. Please call back.* And for good measure: *Thank you for letting Lilly be okay. Thank you, God, more than anything, for that.*

I call Conor, even though it's late. I know he'll be waiting.

He is. He answers on the first ring and I say, "Hi. It's me. She's okay. She was just really depressed. We're both exhausted—and it's definitely a lot my fault for working so much and not being here and . . ." My voice breaks and then I'm crying. "I'm just so glad she's okay. When I was, when I was driving home, I thought she might have—I couldn't stop thinking terrible things. I thought . . ." I try to get control, breathing in a raggedy gulp of air.

"I know," he says. His voice is so soft, so full of gentleness, it breaks me. "I know, Maggie. I'm so glad she's okay."

"I'm just . . . I guess I shouldn't have let her stay alone. There's so much going on with this case. I've been so preoccupied and I thought she was okay, I thought we were safe." I'm looking for reassurance. I'd relaxed after hearing the news that Anthony Pugh had gone to Florida. I forgot, for a moment, about the danger in Lilly's own head.

Conor says, "It seems like she just really needs someone there right now."

I feel it like a slap. "Well, I am here. I'm working really hard right now, Conor. I'm doing my best."

There's a quick silence and then, "I know you are. I didn't mean it like that. Hopefully Marty will let you take a break. It's so much for you to be dealing with."

Anger flashes through my veins. "It's not about him *letting* me. This case is breaking. I'm trying to . . . figure it out." *Trying to work on it without Cooney knowing what I'm up to,* I'd been about to say. But of course I can't tell Conor that.

"I know, Maggie. I didn't mean to . . . I know you're working really hard."

My eyes are leaking tears again. I feel like I can't stop the fear and emotion from bubbling up and out. It's going to swamp me if I let it. I wipe my eyes with the blanket hanging over the back of the couch. I'm so tired I can barely think.

"I need to get some sleep," I say. "And I really am doing the best I can." I hang up before he can apologize again. The anger is back. It rises up and I feel it settle in my stomach.

You just have to get through the next couple days, I say to myself. *That's all you have to do.*

Gabriel tried to think of a story while they were cutting him, while the important man drew the knife through the skin of Gabriel's back. He thought if he could remember a story, it might help his mind separate from his body.

But the pain blocked out any thought but itself. The pain was its own story. It had a beginning and a middle. For a long, long time, it didn't end.

34

I sleep fitfully, dreams about water and drowning waking me up every hour or so through the night. I check on Lilly each time, find her sleeping peacefully, and try to get back to sleep. There are a few texts from Conor when I wake up, apologizing, but I don't have the bandwidth to respond, so I leave them. Uncle Danny comes at seven so Dave and I can get an early start. He arrives with Dunkin' Donuts for Lilly and a big coffee for himself. I've already called the school and explained to Lilly's therapist about last night.

"I feel terrible leaving her today," I say to Danny. "But I've got to talk to this guy. I'm going to get back as soon as I can. You sure you're okay to stay with her for the day, keep an eye on her?"

"Of course, baby. It's so cold. They say it might snow. I'm gonna suggest a movie marathon. I'll make her some popcorn. We'll have fun." The happy, goofy smile he's got on lifts my mood a little and I kiss his cheek and tell him he's the best.

I finish my coffee and drop the mug onto the top rack of the dishwasher. "I just checked on her and she's sleeping. If anything worries you, don't be afraid to call, okay? I put her therapist's number on the refrigerator in case you think Lilly needs to talk to her. She said she's available most of the day."

"Yeah, 'course. You gonna be okay?"

"Yeah. I'm just . . . Last night, Lilly, that was rough. And this case is nutty. It'll be okay, though." I don't say anything about Conor. "I owe you big time, Uncle Danny. Thanks. I just gotta talk to this guy and then I can come home and work from here, I think. I'm okay." I give him a hug and he brushes the hair off my face in a way that makes my throat catch with gratitude.

But I'm really not okay. My stomach is buzzing with acid and coffee and adrenaline. A night of little sleep has me distrustful of myself. I feel like there's danger somewhere, but I can't see it and I don't know where it's coming from and a big part of my brain is convinced I've made it up. I think about what I said to Dave out by the beach. It feels like someone's manipulating me, behind the scenes. But who?

The morning rush-hour traffic is bad, stop and start on the LIE, stop and start through Queens. Dave wants to know how Lilly is and I get annoyed talking about it, second-guessing myself for leaving her with Danny. So I call him and he says she's up and eating breakfast and seems good, but I can't help kicking myself for leaving. Dave's got one of the morning talk shows on the satellite radio and they're talking about the new administration, about how everyone's upset about who they want to hire for some job in the Defense Department, and a protest outside the White House, and a court case over some guy who worked on the campaign. "Geez," Dave says. "You ever see anything like this?" He wants to talk the whole way into the city, and finally I say, "Dave, I gotta take a little nap. Do you mind if I close my eyes?"

"No, of course not." I lean against the cold window and try to tune out the cars and Dave's intermittent humming and muttered comments to other drivers, but I can't, and by the time we're in the Midtown Tunnel, I've given up completely.

Despite my crappy mood, it feels good to be in the city, to soak in the energy of eight million people, the white-gray skies above Midtown, the air tasting of salt and car exhaust and snow.

The diner where Paul Shouldice said to meet him is an old-style Midtown twenty-four-hour job, with cracked vinyl seats and huge plates of food that seem to come out only seconds after we tell the waitress what we want. It's full of people having breakfast meetings, messengers grabbing eggs between jobs, night-shift workers having dinner before going to bed. Shouldice said he'd meet us at nine and it's ten past when I look up from my coffee and ask Dave, "Where's he coming from?"

Dave pulls out his phone. "When we did the address search, the phone listing was on, uh, West Seventy-Third."

"Hmm." I pick up a piece of bacon and fold it in quarters, like a stick of gum, before popping it into my mouth.

"Why do you fold it like that?" Dave asks.

"I like a quadruple layer of bacon."

"That's weird."

I pick up another piece and fold it and stick it in my mouth. Dave shakes his head.

"What do you think he's going to tell us?"

"I honestly have no idea. If Cooney is somehow wrapped up in this, then I guess he might tell us that his old friend was in town and told him he was here to meet his long-lost brother who's a district attorney or . . . I don't know, Dave. There's something we're missing. I just keep coming back to what you said. Why would the adoption be a big deal? There must be something else Gabriel Treacy knew."

"About Cooney?" Dave is only humoring me. I can see it on his face.

"Maybe. I don't know."

We finish eating. It's 9:40 now. I say it before Dave can. "He's not coming. He stood us up."

"No shit." Dave pulls out his phone and dials. He listens and mouths *voice mail* at me and then he says, "Mr. Shouldice, this is Detective Dave Milich with Suffolk County P.D. My partner and I are at the diner and we're wondering if we can expect you soon. Please let me know. We really need to speak with you."

I pay the bill and say, "What was the address?"

"You want to go up there?"

"This guy is avoiding us," I say. "We need to talk to him."

"Okay. Drive? Cab?"

"Ah, let's walk." Dave raises his eyebrows. It's freezing outside, the sky gray and threatening now.

"Come on, your Florida blood can take it. We'll walk fast, get our blood pumping."

"You're like some kind of nightmare gym teacher," Dave says, but today, he's actually brought gloves and worn a scarf with his leather jacket, and he wraps it around his neck and pulls it up over his nose, covering the moustache completely.

"Ah good, your little friend is all cozy in there, huh?" I say.

"You're just jealous of how irresistible the moustache makes me," Dave says, and we grin at each other. It feels good to settle into our old joking. Everything's been so serious lately.

"You ever wanted to live in a city?" I ask. Dave grew up in suburban Miami-Dade County and went to college in Florida, then joined the army. He did his training and got his first cop job on Long Island after he was out.

"Not really, though I like being in 'em, you know? The people, the way you're never really alone. But not really. I wouldn't want to raise kids in the city. How about you?"

I try not to smile. Dave's thirty-four. He has this unwavering belief that he *will* have kids, even though he's never maintained a relationship for more than six months. The charitable view is that his job gets in the way. The uncharitable view is that he's afraid of commitment.

"I thought I'd live in the city at some point, when I was younger. But then . . . you know, shit happened. After Lilly, well, we weren't going to move, and I really like the job. Other than my asshole partner, of course." I grin at him and bump into him on purpose as we cross Seventh Avenue.

"I guess when you're over there, it's the city," he says hesitantly, once we've started up Forty-Seventh Street.

"Yeah. I actually like Dublin. As cities go, it's a good one. So, I don't know, maybe I could live in a city."

He glances over at me, just barely, and says casually, "What do you think is going to happen with Conor? You think you'll move over there?"

We stop on the east side of Eighth Avenue and wait to cross with the clot of people, everyone ready for the day, nervously eyeing the sky.

I take a deep breath. This is the first time Dave has even acknowledged that that might be a possibility. "At this point, I don't know, Dave. It's hard when you have kids. He can't move. Working as a cop over there, it would be . . . complicated. I can't just get hired and start work the next day, you know? And Lilly . . . she's been through so much. I don't know. Maybe after the kids are in college. Maybe he could move over here or something. I don't know."

"That's a few years off, though," Dave says. "The way you described how it happened with him, and that week in Dublin, that doesn't happen a lot, you know. Life's short."

I can't remember now what I told Dave about the week I spent with Conor in September. It had been perfect, a week of rediscovering each other, of falling in love. Uncle Danny had stayed with Lilly in Alexandria and Adrien had been in France with Bláithín and we had gone out for long dinners and walks. But last night, as I lay alone in bed, I started thinking that maybe that had been the cap to years of longing and wondering. Maybe it had been the conclusion, rather than the beginning of something. I sigh.

We walk up Eighth Avenue into the wind, just trying to stay warm.

Paul Shouldice's apartment is in a nondescript building without a doorman on West Seventy-Third, and when we identify ourselves to the woman who answers the buzzer, she says, "I'll come down. I don't want . . . the children."

Dave and I look at each other. The stress in her voice comes down and out through the intercom.

When she arrives, she's dark-haired, with delicate features and a terrified expression. The too-big down coat she's wrapped herself in to come down to the street makes her look like a child playing dress-up; she shivers and looks around her as though she can't believe she's landed in this freezing place. The door clicks shut behind her; she's holding her phone out like a warning, ready to dial 911 in case we're not who we say we are, which tells me a lot.

"I'm Francesca Shouldice," she says after we show her our IDs. She has a slight accent, Italian, I think. "I didn't want the kids to hear."

"Do you know where your husband is?" I ask her. "It's very, very important that we know. For his safety as well as others'. We were supposed to meet him this morning to talk about a case we're investigating, but he didn't show up."

"Can you tell me what's going on? I don't know where he is," she says. "I woke up this morning and he was gone. I knew there was something bad happening. He told me he thought he was being followed, but he didn't want me to know anything because he didn't want me to be in danger, too, that's what he said—*in danger, too*. But that means *he's* in danger and I don't know where he is. I don't understand this. He's a doctor. He's not . . . What could be happening? Do you know?"

"We're investigating the murder of a man named Gabriel Treacy. Does that name mean anything to you?"

Her eyes go wide. "Gabriel . . . There was a man named Gabriel who Paul talked about sometimes, an aid worker, I think, an old friend. They were in Afghanistan at the same time. They went through an intense experience together and became close during that time. He said once that they knew things about each other nobody else knew."

"Gabriel Treacy was held captive in Afghanistan," I tell her. "Was that what your husband was talking about?"

Her eyes are wide. "Yes. He didn't talk about it much, but . . . yes." I look at Dave.

"Did they stay in touch over the years, your husband and Gabriel?" he asks her.

"A bit, maybe an email here and there."

"We think whatever he's afraid of could be related to his friendship with Gabriel, Mrs. Shouldice," I say. "This is very important. I know you said you don't know where your husband is, but do you have any idea about what's going on?"

She hesitates and then says, "A couple months ago, he seemed more secretive than usual about his phone. It would ring and he'd go in the other room to take it, that kind of thing." She looks up at me, looking for someone to understand where she's going. "The move has been tough on us. I don't like New York. I miss my family in Rome. He's traveling a lot and we have twin boys who are three. We'd been fighting and I thought he was having an affair or . . . something like that. Over the holidays, things were bad. He was short-tempered, accusing the kids of messing with his computer. One night I was crying and I asked him if he was having an affair and he . . . his reaction told me he wasn't. He said that wasn't it, but he couldn't tell me what was going on. He said he was going to figure out a way to keep us safe, there was someone he was going to talk to. I thought things were better, but then this morning, he was gone. That's all I know. I've been so worried. Is he okay? Can you find him? I didn't know if I should call the police."

"Do you have *any* idea where he might have gone?" I ask again. "Can you see where his phone is? Do you have that set up?"

"He didn't take his phone. He had stopped using it the last couple days." She looks up with a terrified expression on her face. She's shivering now, her whole body vibrating, her breath clouding in front of her. "I think he thought someone was tracking him."

Before we leave, I give Francesca Shouldice a piece of paper with every conceivable way to get in touch with me—cell number, my home address, landline, headquarters address and number—listed on it. She takes it and raises her huge dark eyes to mine. "Is my husband in danger?" she asks.

"We think he might be," I tell her. "Please let me know if he gets in touch or if anything seems off to you. If you're worried don't hesitate to call 911." I don't know if it's true he's in danger. I don't know anything. I keep running through scenarios in my head, trying to figure out what Paul Shouldice could know that has put his life in danger. Something about Gabriel Treacy? The truth about Jay Cooney's birth?

I call Griz as we're walking back to the car. She needs to know about Paul Shouldice. They need to start talking to his known associates in London. There's something very wrong here.

I explain and she says she'll follow up over there but that she has something for me, too. "We caught the Renault on CCTV," she says. "He stopped at a petrol station in Clonmoney on the evening of February twenty-fourth. I can email you the clip. It's not much to go on. You can see the car pull up and then someone gets out. You can only see him from the back. It's definitely a man. We're trying to figure out if he used a credit card to pay for the petrol."

"Thanks," I say. "I'm betting he's too smart to leave a trail."

"Maybe, but Maggie, I can't hang on to the information we found in the file any longer. I wouldn't be doing my job if I didn't ring Jay Cooney up to ask him about it."

"I know, I know, Griz. Look, I think we're going to get something today. Can you hold off until tomorrow? Then you can call him."

I can hear her hesitating. "Tomorrow," she says.

"Thanks. And let me know if you find anything on Paul Should-ice, okay? Whatever he's afraid of, I think it's the key to this whole thing."

35

It starts snowing on our way back out to the island.

"We gotta talk to Marty," I tell Dave as the skyline appears in his rearview mirror. "This has gone beyond anything we can keep to ourselves. What she said about Shouldice thinking he was being tracked? Lilly's phone, my phone? Remember when we were in Bay Shore, that day, right after we responded to the scene, and I said I'd felt someone's eyes on me? I don't think I was imagining it. And whoever it is followed me home the other night."

Dave glances over. "But who is it? Cooney?"

"I don't know . . . Maybe. It was like . . . someone I was never going to see."

Dave signals and changes lanes. "What do you mean?"

I try to think how to say it. "Roly said the car Thomason's killer stole was wiped completely clean. That's kind of what I mean, I guess. Someone who's a . . . professional. I know that sounds weird, but I think that's what I mean, someone who understands how investigations work, someone who understands what we do."

"Like a cop?" Dave asks. "What if that's how the gun got from Bollina's killer to Treacy's killer?"

I meet his eyes. We both know what that would mean.

"When I asked Miguel Aguillar about the gun, I felt like he knew more than he told us," I say finally.

"I did too."

I already have my phone out. "Where does he work? Do you remember?"

"Car wash, auto detailer, right? Somewhere in Babylon?"

I find it on my phone and call to make sure Miguel is working today. He is, and Dave parks in a spot by the door. As soon as he turns off the engine, snowflakes start to stick to the windows. The waiting area is empty and smells strongly of chemicals and soap and the television mounted on the wall is blaring a game show. Dave hits the bell on the counter and Miguel comes out from the back, saying, "Hi, how can I help—" until he sees who it is and fear overtakes his face.

"It's okay, Miguel," I say. "It's okay. We know you aren't responsible for Juan's death. We still know that. But we're desperate to find out what happened to the gun." We hear voices coming from the back and Miguel glances in their direction. He doesn't want his co-workers to know we're here. "Can you tell us? The sooner you tell us, the sooner we'll be gone."

He closes his eyes and then says, "All I know is something I heard. I swear I wasn't there."

"We know that. We know you're a good kid," Dave says. "And your name won't come into it. We just need to know who might have ended up with the gun."

The voices again. He glances back nervously and says, "I heard someone ask him . . . ask someone . . . what he did with the gun. He said he gave it to a guy to take down south."

"What did he mean by that?"

"I think he meant DC."

"Remember what the guys on the task force said?" Dave asks me as we're driving east again. "There's a lot of MS13 activity in the DC suburbs—drugs, guns trafficking. Right? You think that's what he was talking about?"

"I don't know. Maybe. We'll have to get those guys looking into it, Dave. You gonna call Marty?"

He nods. I rest my head against the window and this time I doze off, waking with a start when Dave comes to a sudden stop on the expressway.

We're back in Alexandria by four and the snow comes faster as Dave drives me back out toward the bay. I've always loved watching the water when it's snowing, and suddenly I remember how Erin and I would run down to the beach the first time it snowed each winter and try to catch snowflakes on our tongues. *Catch one, Maggie, see if you can catch one.*

Without being asked, Dave takes the route down by the beach club and stops in front of the pavilion for a minute so we can watch the snow swirl into the line of mist hanging over the shoreline, then pulls out and takes me up to the house. Out front I say, "Tell Marty we need to talk to him. I gotta stay home with Lilly tonight, but if you guys want to come over, I'll make you a late dinner. Tell him I'll make Italian." Dave says he'll be in touch.

Uncle Danny's in a cheery mood. He says he and Lilly had a great day watching movies, and she smiles when he tells me he got her to watch all of *Saving Private Ryan,* which is his favorite movie of all time. "Did he cry?" I ask her.

"He totally cried." She's wearing one of my old sweatshirts and her pajama pants, but her hair is clean and Danny says they had turkey clubs for lunch.

"How can you not cry at that movie? It's a great movie, right, Lil?" He gives her a bear hug. "Ah, I love this kid so much. She's a good kid. I'll see ya later, Lil, okay?" Lilly rolls her eyes but she's glowing and I have a sudden revulsion at the thought of taking her away from Uncle Danny. Of course we can't move. Of course we can't.

Apparently she's forgiven me because we cuddle up and watch a few episodes of her cooking show. She goes up to bed at eight thirty to read and talk to her friends, I assume, and I breathe a sigh of relief at her improvement in mood. I should call Conor and tell him, but my brain is fuzzy with exhaustion and I want to focus on telling Marty about Cooney, which isn't going to be easy.

Dave texted that they'd be at the house by nine, so I've had homemade Bolognese simmering since five. I put the pasta on at ten to, and when they come in, snow on their hair and shoulders, Marty sniffs the air and says, "Not a lot of cooks would get me out on a night like tonight."

I hand them each a soup bowl full of radiatore with Bolognese and a handful of Parm on top, and let Dave pour wine.

After Marty's had a few bites and properly shown his enthusiasm, he says, "Okay, which one of you is going to tell me this big secret?"

I go first, explaining about the file Margaret Morrell had at home and Griz finding Cooney's name in it.

Marty's face is granite. I talk too fast, explaining. "I didn't tell you right away because well, it didn't seem like a sure thing. And if I'd told you, it would have put you in a tough position, without a lot to go on. I thought we could do a little digging around and see if there was anything there. If the dates were wrong, if there was a picture of Cooney's mom pregnant or something, well. Then it's a mistake, it's nothing."

"But the dates weren't wrong," he says.

"No. Stella Treacy's baby was born in 1965. So was Cooney. And there's more." I tell him about Paul Shouldice. I tell him about the security footage. I tell him about someone following me, about the texts. "Shouldice's wife said he was scared, that he thought he was being followed. I think he's afraid of someone, that he knows something that someone doesn't want him to talk about."

I nod at Dave and he says, "Here's the other thing, Marty. On February fifteenth, Treacy used the phone in the motel to call a Long Island number. It's a reporter named Heather Thornton."

Dave tells him about Heather G. Thornton, how she covers politics. Marty listens, really quiet, and eats his supper, and when Dave's done, he says, "So Gabriel Treacy comes to Long Island to meet his brother and goes to Cooney's house. Cooney doesn't like it, he doesn't want Treacy to tell anyone. They fight?"

"The security footage showed Treacy coming out of the house alone after thirty minutes," Dave says. "But then the guy down the road saw two men fighting in the street. Camera wasn't angled right to catch it, so we don't know how it started."

Marty looks incredulous. "So, what are you saying? Jay Cooney fights with him and then says to Treacy, 'Hey, I can't talk now, but let's meet up at the marina in a bit?' And he kills him?"

"Cooney knows people," I say. "Dave and I were wondering about whoever killed Juan Bollina. Maybe that explains the gun. Miguel Aguillar said something about the gun going down south, to DC he thought. Maybe Cooney had contacts from his work and he had them bring someone up from DC to do it. Someone MS13."

Marty's eyes widen in disbelief. "So he tells Treacy to meet him later and then he sends an MS13 gang member to shoot him with the same gun used to shoot Juan Bollina?" He's telling us the story, trying to find the holes. This is what we do: telling stories, making them up, testing them out to see which ones are true. You tell and retell them, change the details, compare them to what you know, until one day you say, "That's it. That's the one that's true."

And then you try to get a confession and you wait to see if you got it right.

"I don't know, Marty. I don't know. It all sounds nuts. I know that. But Treacy was in touch with Shouldice. He visited Cooney the night he died and they had a big fight. A witness saw them fighting. A few hours later, Treacy was dead. Cooney's name was in that file and something made Paul Shouldice terrified for his life and the safety of his family. Either that or he has something to hide. And Noel Thomason, who was Treacy's lawyer and knew about his connection to Cooney, was killed by someone who stole a car at Shannon Airport and then ditched it. That's what I know. That's all I know." I wait a minute. "Marty, Dave said Cooney was mad when he found out I was in Ireland. Maybe this is why."

Marty gets up and paces around the kitchen, then pours himself another glass of wine.

Finally he sits down and sighs and says, "I don't have to tell you, Maggie. Cooney doesn't like you. He thinks you pushed the thing with your brother-in-law too hard. He knows you don't respect him. He didn't know you were going to Ireland. That's on me. Alicia must have told him and he called me up, raging, asking why I let you go there, in the middle of a huge case. It was . . . overkill, you know? I wondered. Why was he so set against you being there? All he had to say was I should have thought about it. It's not even his chain of command. Anyway, it seemed off, like it was Ireland that bugged him, you know? Pat said I should get you back and to be honest, I could have said no, but I was curious why he wanted you back. It felt like there was something up with him and I figured maybe you coming back would shake it loose. I didn't think it was this." His eyes meet my own and I feel a surge of affection for him, for his ugly tan shirt and the galoshes he wears over his good shoes and for how much he loves my Bolognese.

"What are we going to do, Marty?"

He gets up and goes over to the stove with his bowl, puts some more pasta in, and eats it standing up. "Pat's not doing very well, but he's a stubborn son of a bitch and he's gonna hang on until he can't anymore. As long as he's commissioner, Cooney can get you fired if he wants. This goes wrong in any way, it's going to be hard to protect you. I've been fighting your corner—" He puts up a hand. "For me, 'cause you're a good detective, not for you. But you gotta know that." He drops his empty bowl in the sink. "We gotta be careful here. I've known Cooney a long time and I don't know what he's capable of. I really don't.

"You find that doctor and that reporter. See if there's anybody who went to Ireland who's connected to Cooney. I'm going to just keep an eye on this. I'll cover for you, but you gotta find Shouldice. If he confirms that Gabriel Treacy told him he was here to see his long-lost brother, then I'm going to have to go to Pat, but I don't know what's going to happen. We gotta do this quiet, we gotta get some more information. I've got your backs, but we've gotta do this right."

Dave nods and says, "I think Bill might be telling Cooney what we're up to. There's been some weird stuff."

Marty turns up the collar of his jacket against the snow as he and Dave walk to the door. "I'll take care of Bill. Do what you have to do. Keep looking around. If you get something definite, we'll have to go to Pat." He looks at me sternly. "And this time, keep me in the loop."

I lock the doors, set the alarm, and take the Glock up with me. I'm almost asleep when there's a quiet knock on my door and I hear Lilly's voice say, "Mom? Are you awake?"

"Yeah, what's wrong, sweetie?"

I hear her pad into the room and come over to my bed. When Lilly was little, she used to sneak into my room during the night and cuddle up to me. I'd find her nestled against my back in the morning. "I thought I heard something downstairs," she whispers.

I sit up and turn on the light and she sits down on the edge of the bed. "Stay here," I tell her, sliding my gun off the bedside table. "I'll be right back."

I check the alarm and all the doors. Switching on the deck lights, I look though the kitchen windows at the falling snow. The backyard is empty.

"Must have been the wind," I tell Lilly as I slide back into bed. She's under the covers now, her head on the pillow, her hair making an S on the pale pillowcase. "Want to sleep here, though?"

She doesn't say anything, but she doesn't go anywhere and when I've turned the light off again, she whispers, "I'm sorry I scared everyone."

I turn around so I'm facing her. I know enough not to hug her, but I reach up and brush her hair away from her forehead. "Oh, Lil, I don't care about that. No one does. You can scare me a thousand times and I'll love you to the moon and back. All I care about is that you're okay, you know? And I'm glad you could tell Adrien how you felt."

She moves and I smell her shampoo. "It's weird. I don't really know him, but because he knows everything about Dad, I don't have to explain. He just gets it. Everyone else, I have to start at the beginning. And then I feel like shit."

"That makes me happy," I tell her. "I'm so glad you have such a good friend in him. Whatever happens with me and Conor, you and Adrien go on being good friends. It's hard to find a friend like that." My voice catches.

"Is Conor mad at you?" she asks.

"No, he's just . . . disappointed. I need to figure out this case and then I'll make it up to both of you, okay?"

"Okay." Her voice is sleepy and she snuggles into me the way she did when she was little, her hand on my arm. I lie there feeling lucky, so lucky it makes me breathless, until I fall asleep.

36

FRIDAY, MARCH 3, 2017

I wake up to a thin layer of icy snow on everything, the skies threatening more of it. Lilly sleeps until seven and comes down while I'm making coffee and says, "Ugh. It's so cold out."

I smile at her. "You feel up to going to school? Uncle Danny can pick you up and bring you back and give you dinner, okay? I might have to do something around dinnertime, but I'm going to get home as early as I can, okay?" I study her face, trying to read the particular arrangement of muscles that might indicate whether she's feeling better today.

She smiles, a little. Her eyes are still puffy and full of sleep. "Okay. I'm actually kind of excited to get back."

I drop her at school, sitting in my car for a minute at the curb to watch her walk across the pavement and blend with all the other kids crowding toward the front door. The news on the radio is full of tension: more protests, the new president threatening people, reporters saying they've never seen anything like this. I shut it off and ignore my phone, which is buzzing steadily the whole drive.

When I finally check it, I see Griz's name in my email inbox and I open the message to find she's attached a video clip and a PDF of a credit card receipt. The signature is unreadable, but the printed name is clear: *Marcus Weller*. Griz's message says, "I think this is it. The young one in the shop said she remembered him because he wanted to use the cash machine and he was upset it was out of order. We'll see what we can find on our end, maybe through the airlines, but I thought your people might be able to do something with the name."

And then, "She remembered because he was so cross and because he had an American accent."

I try some searching. There are a surprising number of Marcus Wellers, especially in the Midwest. I find old ones and younger ones, but not enough information to get a sense of which one our Marcus Weller might be.

I need Berta. She knows how to access databases I don't. I poke my head in her office and close the door.

"Berta," I say. "I've got a name. He bought gas not far from where Noel Thomason was killed in Ireland. CCTV footage places the stolen car at that station at the right time." I hand over a Post-it with Marcus Weller's name on it. "Can you see what you can do with that? Let's keep it at an age range of say, twenty-five to fifty-five. If this is our guy, he's pretty competent." I think of him walking an hour to the airport after ditching the car. "Pretty fit."

"When?"

I smile. "Uh, now?"

Berta just rolls her eyes. "Okay," she says. "But I need some breakfast. And a coffee."

I run to the deli and come back to deliver an egg sandwich and coffee to her. "Thanks, Maggie."

I wave it away. "How's everything with you anyway? How are all the grandkids?"

"Good. Oldest one is graduating from high school in June."

"Seriously? How does that happen? Lilly's heading in that direction too and it seems so strange."

Berta looks up. "How's she doing?"

"Okay. You know. She went to school today and I'll have to pick her up, so I'll let you get to it. We have a case meeting in a half hour."

I'm walking out when I think of something. "Hey, Berta? Lilly and I both got weird texts from someone not in either of our contacts. Dave said it was a Denver number. Can you take a look and see what you think?" I hand over my phone and Berta looks through it and then does a quick reverse search for the two numbers.

"I don't see anything on those numbers but there's all kinds of technology that makes it look like a call or text is coming from somewhere it's not. And there's nothing obvious on your phone, but you could get the tech division to look. There's malware now that's almost undetectable. You don't even know it's on your device and it's tracking every keystroke."

"Okay, thanks. Maybe I will."

The case meeting isn't long. Marty asks for an update and I tell everyone what we have and haven't found. Alicia is in the back of the room for the second half of it and when we're done, she waves Marty over and gestures toward his office. He nods and they go in and close the door.

Dave and I glance at each other and I go back to my desk. I'm sitting there reading emails when Berta comes over and pulls up a chair. She has a handwritten bulleted list and she passes it over. There are three bullets, three Marcus Wellers. One of them is thirty-two and lives in Kansas City. "He's a middle school teacher," she says and shrugs. "Maybe. I don't know. This one"—she points to the second one—"has a real estate business in New Orleans. I don't think it's him. He's on Facebook with a bunch of kids and grandkids, church fundraisers. I mean, maybe, but . . ." Then she points her yellow highlighter mark under *Marcus Weller, dob 4/12/75.* "I'm betting this one is your guy. There's something odd about him. I found a military record for him. He enlisted in the army in 1993, was discharged in 2003. Then he doesn't really show up anywhere for a long time. The only thing I could find was a phone number registered in his name in 2007 in Vandenburgh, Maryland. That's it. Like that's all. Now that I have a name, I can try the airlines and I can try to get something from the State Department—if he went to Ireland, he must have had a passport."

I thank her and start looking for more. In a local newspaper archive, I find a reference to a Marcus Weller appearing before a local zoning board to request approval for a building project in Vandenburgh, Maryland. Must be the same guy.

At lunchtime, we get some more evidence from the lab, but there's nothing we don't already know and I'm feeling antsy and aimless. I want more on Marcus Weller, but he's like a ghost, surprisingly absent from the internet for someone his age and barely in any of the databases where we normally find people.

I know Berta is still trying to get the passenger lists I asked for, but airlines don't like to give that out unless you have a really good reason, so it may take some time.

But I have Griz's list of flights that came into Shannon on February twentieth, I remind myself. I might be able to do something with that.

Looking at the list, I try to find the most likely flights. If the Renault was caught on CCTV leaving the parking garage at four, I'm going to assume the flight came in sometime between one and three. I check the list, looking just at LaGuardia, Kennedy, and Newark airports to start with. There was a United flight that arrived at nine a.m., and an Aer Lingus flight that got in at eight. A Delta flight from Chicago got in at ten, but otherwise nothing in the right time frame. He could have flown from New York to London and then over, I tell myself, or just about anywhere else in Europe. When I call up the list of arrivals at Shannon Airport, there aren't as many at Shannon as there would be at Dublin Airport, but there are five or six it could be. I dial the customer service number for Lufthansa at Shannon Airport and when a man answers, I say, "Yes, my employer flew into Shannon on February twentieth and thinks he left a small computer bag on the plane. I'm wondering if you could check and see if it was turned in."

"Hold, please," the man says. He's back only a few seconds later and he says, "I don't see a computer bag in the bin, sorry" and he's gone before I can ask for anything else. I decide to skip Lufthansa for the moment and try British Airways. Same routine. The customer service agent clearly goes off to check the Lost and Found and doesn't see anything. I start thinking about the flights from New York. If Noel Thomason's killer was planning on stealing a car to avoid showing up on rental car documents, he would have needed to make sure that the car wasn't going to be reported right away. So what would he have done? He would have waited for someone with a fair bit of luggage to park their car and go to departures. He could have watched the parking garage until he saw someone who fit the bill.

I try Delta first. "Yes, hello," I say, when a woman with an Irish accent answers the phone. "I'm wondering if you can help me. My boss flew through Shannon on February twentieth and lost a computer bag. He told me which flight but I lost the piece of paper and I'm really worried he's going to be mad at me. Could you check his name and just see if anything was turned in? His name is Marcus Weller."

I hold my breath, waiting for her to tell me she'll check to see if it was turned in.

But instead I hear tapping and then she says, "Yes, it looks like he was on flight three-oh-four that day, but I don't see any notes here about a lost item. It would be here. I'm so sorry."

"That's okay. Thanks for your help."

Marcus Weller. I've got him, whoever he is. He flew into Shannon early on February 20 and waited in the car park until he found the perfect car to take.

Now I need to figure out who he is and whether there's any connection to Cooney.

I yawn, feeling every minute I haven't slept over the past couple of days. Dave catches it and says, "Hey, let's get some lunch."

"Yeah," I say. "Good idea. And I have something to tell you." My phone buzzes in my lap. I pick it up.

"Maggie D'arcy."

I hear traffic, then a woman's voice. "This is, um, Heather Thornton," she says. "You've been trying to reach me. I'm calling from a friend's phone. I think we should talk."

Heather Thornton says she'll meet us at a diner in Alexandria.

"We'll be there," I tell her. "My partner and I. I'm wearing a blue winter coat. He has a ridiculous moustache." Dave gives me the finger. "Let's say an hour. That'll give you enough time. But we'll get there early just in case."

She hangs up and Dave and I head back to Alexandria to wait. We get to the diner at one, and at one ten, a slight young woman with long brown hair wearing a brown tweed overcoat and orange scarf comes into the diner and searches the room. She sees us before I have a chance to raise a hand and she comes over, sliding into the booth as though she knows us. When she looks up, she's older than I thought, maybe mid-thirties, but with a thin, childlike frame and delicate features and huge brown eyes that seek me out. She's nervous. Scared even. I can see that now. I wave the waitress over and tell Heather to get whatever she wants. She orders coffee and a bowl of chicken soup.

"I'm Maggie. That's Dave," I say. "Thanks for meeting us."

"Heather," she says. "Can I see your ID?"

We take them out and she inspects them carefully, then says, "I checked you both out, verified you were who you said you were, printed off your photos from a couple *Newsday* stories." She pushes the stories across to us. But she doesn't say anything else.

I start. "Why don't I tell you why we're interested in talking to you. That okay?"

She nods gratefully. While I'm the one talking she can pretend she hasn't done anything, she can pretend she hasn't said anything she can't take back. "We're investigating the death of a man named Gabriel Treacy on February sixteenth. As part of our investigations, we discovered that he made a call to your number on February fifteenth, the day before he died. We need to know how you knew him and why he was calling you. Can you tell us?" I like to ask people if they can tell us what they know, rather than ordering them to, to make them feel like they have some choice in the matter, even when they don't.

She hesitates for a minute and then says, "I don't know him, but I'll tell you what happened. I'm a journalist. I was with the AP and then I was on staff at *Newsday* for a long time. I did a lot of different kinds of reporting. But then I was diagnosed with MS a couple of years ago. I started freelancing, so I'd have more control over my schedule. I've been doing longer pieces I can research and work on on my own schedule, and with minimal travel." She drops a cube of sugar into her coffee and stirs it. When she looks up at me, I can see how scared she is. "A source, someone I'd worked with, whose name I can't tell you, well, he told me he wanted me to speak to someone named Gabriel, that he might have a story for me.

"Gabriel Treacy called me, from Ireland, I think, back in November. He asked me a lot of questions about how I work, how I interview people, how many sources I need for a story, if I can arrange protection for sources. He asked me if I would be able to keep what he wanted to tell me completely confidential, until I was ready to publish, of course. He said a friend had pointed him to me, that he had read my work and some of the stories I had written were relevant to what he wanted to tell me, to the story he wanted to tell me."

She stops to drink her coffee, cupping her hands around the white diner mug to warm them. "I asked him if he could give me any details. You can imagine how many nuts I get calling me and telling me they have the story of the century, and then when I actually talk to them, the story is that their ex-wife is one of the lizard people or something."

"Seriously?" Dave asks, his eyes wide. "You get guys telling you that?"

She smiles at Dave, her face transformed by humor. "Oh, that's one of the least crazy ones. Gabriel Treacy told me he couldn't give me any details, but that he would be in touch. He was planning a trip to the States and he said he would let me know when he had his dates pinned down."

The waitress comes to check on us and Heather Thornton asks for a refill on her coffee. "I'll be jittery later but it's really good coffee," she says, smiling. "I'll have to remember this place."

"Did he get back in touch?" I ask her.

"Yeah, he emailed me in early February and said he was going to be on the island in a week or so. I told him to call me when he got here and we'd make a plan to meet. Honestly, I still wasn't sure I was actually going to meet him. I thought maybe I'd see how busy I was, whether I wanted to see what he had. I was hoping he might give me some more information about what we were going to talk about.

"He called me on the fifteenth, in the morning, and suggested we meet the next night at this marina in Bay Shore and then we could drive somewhere to talk."

"Did that strike you as odd? That he didn't just say, 'Meet me at so-and-so restaurant'?"

"Yeah. It did. But he seemed nervous talking about it, and I get it—some of my sources, well, they like to be sure no one's followed them."

"What time were you supposed to meet him?"

"Nine thirty. I had a county legislature committee meeting I had to go to for a story I'm working on. I figured I'd stay in my car until I got a sense of him. I had done some research on him and he seemed non-insane, you know. And my . . . my source had vouched for him, so I was pretty sure he wasn't a psychopath. He definitely seemed like he was trying to make sure no one tailed him to our meeting place."

"Did that strike you as odd?"

She hesitates, has a bit of her soup, then looks up at me. "No, because, well, I'll explain in a minute."

"So what happened? Did you meet him?"

"No." She looks away. There's something she's ashamed about, something that's making her not want to meet my eyes. "There was . . . something strange happened. I guess, well, I think someone followed me. From a meeting I had in Mineola, at a law office, to my apartment in Farmingdale."

"When was this?" Dave asks her.

He has a notebook out and I can tell it's making her nervous, that he's writing everything down. "Earlier that day. I was at the meeting and someone was driving behind me the whole way home, and when I got back to my apartment, I looked out the window, and I'm pretty sure I saw him in the street. I didn't know what to do. I was scared."

"Was it a white SUV?" I ask. She nods. "So you didn't meet Gabriel Treacy?"

"I didn't have a number for him. I had no way of contacting him. He'd called me from his hotel and told me he didn't have a cell phone and not to call back there or email him. I figured he'd wait for a bit and then try me and I could explain that I needed to postpone meeting him in person. But he never called."

"You were afraid for your safety." I can see it on her face.

"There was . . . something else odd had happened. A couple months before that. I may be going crazy, but . . . I went out to buy coffee. When I got back to my apartment, the door was unlocked. I swear I had locked it when I left. And my laptop was still on the desk, but it was in a slightly different position."

"Do you have a password on it?"

"Of course."

"Did you notice anything else?"

"No, just . . . a feeling maybe. That someone had been there. But I could have just been imagining it. After that night, feeling like I was followed, though, I was freaked out enough that I asked a friend to stay with me. And then the next day . . . I saw the news, that he'd been killed."

"Why didn't you get in touch when you saw the news about his death?"

"I know I should have, but I was . . . I was scared. That's my only excuse. It's not a good one. But I'd had some weird things happen to my phone—strange glitches, a bunch of spam, messages I hadn't read yet disappearing. I had a colleague whose phone was hacked while she was working in Russia and it made me paranoid."

Messages I hadn't read yet disappearing. Dave raises his eyebrows at me. "So why did you get in touch with us now?" he asks her.

"Honestly?" She looks up and she looks very young all of a sudden. "You wouldn't stop calling. I didn't want you to come to my house. In case . . ." She trails off.

"In case someone's watching?" Dave asks. A dish clatters somewhere in the kitchen. We all start. "Heather, do you have any idea what Gabriel Treacy was going to tell you?"

She looks up at Dave. "Not for sure." I think she does, though. She's keeping something from us. Her eyes dart away. She reaches up to rearrange her hair. I can see her going back and forth. Journalist. Scared civilian.

Journalist wins. She stands up abruptly and fumbles in her coat pocket, pulling out a twenty and leaving it on the table.

"I can't talk anymore right now," she says. "I'm sorry. I have to go. I have to protect my sources."

I ask Uncle Danny to pick Lilly up at school, then we pay our bill and walk back to Dave's car, blasting the heat to warm it up. "What are we going to do, Dave?" I ask, while we're waiting for the thin layer of ice on the windshield to clear. "We can't arrest her. But we need to know what she knows."

"She seemed scared," Dave says. "And that stuff about her computer. You think those weird texts you've been getting, that thing with your email, you think any of that is related?"

Now the dashboard window is fogging up from our breath but it's warmer at least. "I don't know, Dave. I think we have to assume it is."

I tell him about Marcus Weller and my call to Delta and then say, "Look, I've got to get home. Danny's at the bar tonight. Okay? I'll try to call Heather Thornton again later and see if I can get her to talk some more."

"You don't think we should offer her protection, do you?"

"I don't think we're there yet. How did Alicia seem to you today?" I ask him.

"Nervous," he says. "But that may just be because the papers are going crazy. I'm sure Cooney's giving her a hard time about why we haven't made an arrest."

"What do you think she and Marty were talking about?"

"I don't know. He'll tell us. I'll call him right now and tell him this." He turns to look at me. "You look wrecked, Maggie. Go home. This will all be there in the morning."

I do a few errands and I'm on Park Avenue when I see a light-colored SUV behind me. It's only six, but it's dark and the air is cold and feels like snow again. I slow a bit, testing him. He slows too. The brake lights of the cars ahead of me pulse on and off, blurry through the condensation. My heart speeds. Suddenly alert, I wait a few minutes before making a decision. I have half a tank of gas still, but I pull over at a busy gas station, fill up my tank, and watch the entrance.

He's gone. No SUV waiting for me on Park Avenue. I turn onto Bay Avenue and head for the water, checking every few seconds.

There's no one behind me. Sleety snow is falling fast now and my windshield wipers are working to keep up with it. I'm almost to Shore Drive when suddenly, a pair of headlights appears in my mirror.

It's a big car, light-colored. It's the same SUV. I'm sure of it. I don't know where he came from. He must have been waiting for me in a turnoff or a driveway along my route home. He knows where I live.

I can't let him follow me home to Lilly.

I radio in, identify myself, and tell the dispatcher what's happening. "Can you send a car?" I ask her. "I'm going to find a safe place to pull over and maybe we can get him. At least I can get a plate number."

I'm thinking ahead, trying to choose a spot, when he speeds up and the headlights get so close I think he must be almost touching my rear bumper.

He's trying to force me off the road.

I speed up to get a little distance, but he speeds up too, and suddenly I realize what he's planning. Up ahead, there's a concrete retaining wall against a steep embankment off Sandy Cove Drive.

He's going to force me into it.

His lights are right behind me.

I've only done one evasive driving course during my career. Most cops get some training in safe pursuits and basic defensive driving, but I have to struggle to remember what I learned about getting out of dangerous confrontations once it's clear defensive driving won't prevent them. The key thing, I think, is leaving yourself some room and keeping your speed down. Speed is lethal unless it's your only way to escape.

I slow down a bit and I feel him ram my bumper. There's a car coming in the opposite lane, and I think about hitting it or stopping so maybe it will stop, too, but I'm a police officer. My duty is to protect the public, not cause accidents. I need to get him somewhere where I can see who he is and try to detain him until the patrol car arrives.

I feel him behind me again, nudging me, urging me ahead. He wants me to speed up so he can get me into the wall at a high rate of speed. Instead, I press the brakes, causing him to brake, too. I speed up again, so he does too, and then I brake again. I'm waiting for a spot up ahead where I know the road curves and widens just before the embankment.

Through the dark space behind me, I try to get a glimpse of his face in the mirror, but he's just a blur of unlit features.

I wait until I'm almost there, then slam on my brakes and make a wide left turn, crossing the median and yanking the wheel as I wobble onto the shoulder. I look up then, and I get just a glimpse of him:

thin, outraged, his hair light-colored, I think, but nothing about his face really emerges from the darkness. And yet even in that fleeting instant, there's something familiar about him. I've seen him before. I know him. I'm not sure how.

I hear sirens in the distance and I pull over, my hazards on, throw my car into park and fling my door open. I'm sure he was about to turn and pursue me but instead he speeds up and disappears in the other direction. By the time I'm back in my car and waving the Alexandria Bay patrol officer over, I know he's long gone.

37

I give my statement to the officer, then tell him I need to get home.

I don't say anything to Uncle Danny, just kiss him thanks so he won't worry. I get Lilly dinner and help her with a science project and I'm loading the dishwasher when the landline rings. We hardly use it anymore; even Uncle Danny calls my cell now.

"Hello?"

"This is Stephen Hines." His voice is cool, cast low. "Did you happen to get the email I sent you?"

"I didn't get an email from you," I say. "How did you get this number?"

"It wasn't difficult," he says. "Your mobile is probably okay, but I didn't want to risk it."

"What? What do you mean?" I put down the glass I was holding and scramble to open my laptop on the kitchen table.

"Don't open your email," Hines says softly. "I think you want to assume that someone is watching everything you're doing online, that someone at the very least has read all your emails. That may not be the case, but I think it's what you want to assume. I only realized tonight. I'm still not quite sure how whoever it is got into mine."

Suddenly, the laptop feels like a bomb in my hands.

Hines says calmly, "The gist of the email was that I finally got in touch with a colleague who worked in Italy for many years. He said the photographer who was with Gabriel Treacy was named Pietro Griselli."

"I know," I tell him. "I've got that already."

"Ah, well, my colleague knew the *La Stampa* reporter Pietro Griselli was working with in Afghanistan. The reporter wasn't with Griselli the day he was abducted, but he learned many of the details. Griselli met Gabriel Treacy in Kabul. Treacy and Griselli were kidnapped with an American nurse who also worked for MSF. Her name was Anne Smith. With them were an English doctor named Paul Shouldice, as well as an Afghan translator, Tahir Dirani.

"They were held for a couple of weeks and then they were released. But the circumstances of their release were very odd. This source said that there were rumors that one of the captives was CIA, something like that. He said it just didn't feel the way it usually did when those things happened, and that Pietro Griselli was very secretive about it afterward. They didn't really talk about it, and then they were gone. They left Afghanistan within a week, all of them. My source said that it was one of those strange things that happened that everyone put down to some sort of CIA involvement or a secret American military operation."

I don't say anything for a minute. I don't know whether to trust him or not, but I'm at sea and I need help. "Okay," I say. "I had some of that, but not all of it. We were supposed to meet Shouldice yesterday. He stood us up and he seems to be on the run. His wife is concerned about his safety."

Stephen Hines is quiet for a moment and then he says, "Shouldice knows something. Whatever it is seems like it might be dangerous to his health. I should say you'd want to find him as quickly as you can. Anne Smith and Pietro Griselli as well."

Lilly is fast asleep when I check on her, her face in shadow on her pillow. I get my Glock from the gun safe and go downstairs to make sure the doors are all locked.

I remember that night at the bed-and-breakfast in Sixmilebridge, the way I'd felt that somehow my laptop was watching me.

It was. I go to the jumble of electronics and cords and old remotes in the cabinet under our television. One of my old computers is under there, a MacBook I'd let Lilly use for a few months before I got her a new one, and I boot it up and search for Heather G. Thornton's stories in the *Newsday* archives. Just as she told us, she's been working on stories about Suffolk County politics, including stories about the DA's office. A month or so ago, she wrote a story about Cooney's race, about how he could be vulnerable in the face of his challenger's claim of ethics violations in the DA's office. I have to go back and read some of the other stories to understand what the claims are, but it looks like Cooney's office is being accused of declining to charge a Smithtown businessman charged with embezzlement because he had an unspecified business relationship with Cooney's brother-in-law.

A sound outside the living room window makes me start, and when I cup my hands around my eyes to look through the window, I can see that the wind's up and has blown an ice-encrusted branch of my azalea bush against the glass. But I'm on edge and paranoid now and I move the Glock to the edge of the coffee table. Then I pour myself another glass of wine and settle back down on the couch.

Who's watching me?

And what does Paul Shouldice know that's put him in danger?

The only way I'm going to find out is to talk to him.

I search for him again on the old laptop and find mostly what I found before, stories about his work at Médecins Sans Frontières and at Medical Volunteers for the World. I think about dialing his number again, then remember his wife said he didn't take his phone with him.

It's midnight now and the darkness outside the house is nearly complete, only a tiny bit of moonlight reaching the yard. When I get up to look out the front windows, I can just barely see the open sky above the bay; the murkiness feels claustrophobic.

Paul Shouldice, out there somewhere, has the answers I need, I'm sure of it.

What did Francesca say about her husband and Gabriel Treacy? *He said that they knew things about each other no one else knew.*

What if Treacy told Shouldice something about his father, about Gerry Murray?

I search for Gerry Murray again. It's mostly the stuff I saw before. He represented Clare for a long time and seemed to have an expertise in foreign affairs. In fact, after he retired in 2002 he spent a year in Boston, as a visiting fellow at Boston College, and he acted as an advisor to various entities, including the US military.

I stand up and pace around the room.

When I search for Jonathan Murray, I get similar hits; he served as minister for foreign affairs and trade at one point, visited the US as part of government delegations.

I let him go and microwave some leftover pasta for a midnight snack. When I'm done, I search for "Anne Smith nurse kidnapped Afghanistan."

It gets me nothing—the name's too common. When I search for Pietro Griselli again, I come up with the stories I found in my initial research. I use the translation option and read through a few recent articles for which he provided photographs, a piece about an exhibit of his work in Milan, and, finally, with a growing sense of dread, a story from *Corriere della Sera* about a hit-and-run accident at an intersection in a Milan suburb on February 3, a month ago.

A 41-year-old photojournalist was killed instantly early Friday morning when he was struck by an unknown vehicle at an intersection in Lambrate. There were no witnesses and CCTV cameras did not capture the accident. The victim was identified as Pietro Griselli, who had been a photographer for La Stampa, *among other publications, and was well-known for his photojournalism. Anyone with information about the incident is asked to call police.*

Gabriel's story was the one he'd been carrying around with him most of his life.

It was the story that was inside him, the story he had kept a secret from everyone who loved him. It was the secret no one else knew. Until now.

"You haven't told us a story, Gabriel," Paul said one night. Gabriel knew he was doing it to cheer him up. Gabriel's back still screamed with pain, the open edges of the wounds laying his nerves bare to the frigid air. He couldn't bear wearing a shirt. He couldn't bear not wearing a shirt. He lay there shivering. He had never felt so sure he was going to die, that they were going to kill him, and he realized that if he was going to die, he wanted someone to know his story, so that maybe they could tell his mother.

"Come on," Pietro said softly. "Only you and Paul are left."

"Right, then," Gabriel told them. "How about this? You'll like this story."

He tried to readjust his body, to ease the pain while he talked, but there was no position where his back didn't scream at him, so he curled up on his side and started talking, trying to ignore his body.

"My mother had me outside of marriage," he began. "She never told me who my father was."

"What was that like?" Anne asked. "In the 1970s?"

"It wasn't much fun," Gabriel said. "In Ireland. And she didn't like to talk about it. Whenever I asked her about him, she would pretend she hadn't heard me."

"I had a friend growing up who didn't know his father," Paul said. "Then he met him and wished he hadn't. Did you really have no idea who he was?"

It was a sign of how hopeless he felt that he thought, What does it matter? None of us is getting out of here. "There was a man who used to stop sometimes to see my mother and me, if we were outside or if we were shopping. He was a well-known man, the government representative for our part of the county, and he had an office in my hometown, Sixmilebridge. When I was with my mother, he would just ask what I was doing in school. She would tell him about my marks and make me recite a poem or something. I never thought much about it. But once, when I was a bit older, fourteen, maybe, I was walking home and I saw this car that had gone off the road. I recognized the car. It was his, so I ran over and I found him in the car, passed out behind the wheel. He'd had a heart attack. I ran home, got my nan, had her call the ambulance service. They brought him to hospital and saved him. They told me later that if I hadn't found him and gotten help, he would have died."

Paul made a little murmuring noise and Gabriel knew what he was thinking, that this was where the roots of his career lay, that he had gotten addicted then and there to the feeling of saving a life.

"A couple of months later, he stopped in his big car—a new one— and offered me a ride. He told me he was grateful to me, described *how he'd been driving along and suddenly he'd felt like a load of bricks was on his chest. He didn't remember anything after that.*

"'Think of it,' he said. 'Just think of it.' I had the sense he was try-ing to tell me something and I must have had a sense what it was, but it wasn't until he said that he'd heard good reports about my school-work that I saw it. He was going on about how Dessie Folger said I was a good student, and it was that he seemed proud, talking about how he had been top of his class himself and so forth, that made me see it. I was old enough at that point that I had an idea about things, you know? He took a Saint Christopher's medal off the rearview mir-ror. He handed it to me and said, 'That's yours now. I've told your mother, but if you ever need anything, don't be afraid to ask. You and I, well, we share blood. Do you know what I'm saying, Gabriel?'"

Gabriel stopped talking, remembering Gerry Murray's eyes, the way he'd suddenly realized they were like his own. He shifted a bit, trying to make the pain go away.

"That was your father," Anne said. "Did you ever tell your mother that you knew?"

"No. He made me promise. He said she wouldn't like it, that she didn't want me to know."

"So that was it? You must have seen him around. Was it strange?"

"A bit. It was like we always had this little secret. To tell the truth, I liked it. I liked not telling anyone."

"Was that it?" Tahir asked. Gabriel understood. It wasn't a very good story, like that. There was no satisfying conclusion. No tragic wrap-up, as with Anne's. No punchline, as with Tahir's. He knew the actual ending wasn't any better, but he told them anyway.

"I'd see him from time to time. I was home from university, and I ran into him at the pub. He'd had a few, but he had hold of himself,

like, and he came over and told me he was proud of me, I was doing well."

"How did it feel?" Anne asked. "It must have felt good, to get that from your father, after growing up without him?"

"Maybe," Gabriel said. "It was what he said next, though, that stayed with me. The pub was noisy, it was one of those really busy nights, everyone packed in, good craic. And he leaned in and he said to me, 'You have a brother, you know. We sent him to America.'"

38

I'm shaking now and I stand up, go to the window, look outside into the darkness while I take in what I've learned.

Whoever killed Gabriel Treacy killed Pietro Griselli, too.

And wants to kill Paul Shouldice.

And me too. Tonight wasn't just a warning. It was an attempt on my life.

I tuck the Glock into the pocket of my fleece jacket and double-check the alarms and all the doors.

Pietro Griselli and Paul Shouldice were both in Afghanistan with Gabriel Treacy. Afghanistan is the link between all three of them. Something makes me remember the first time I searched for Heather Thornton. I have a vague memory that she'd written some stories about Afghanistan, and when I search the *Newsday* archives again, there it is. Until 2013, she was covering the wars in Iraq and Afghanistan. She only seems to have gone over once or twice—*Newsday* relies on wire stories for a lot of international and national security stories—but she wrote a number of stories about Long Island angles to those wars, local servicemen and -women and a three-part series about private military contractors, including something called the Odyssey Group.

Something about the name rings a bell and I have to search hard to remember why.

Gabriel Treacy's office. There had been a piece of paper on the desk on which he'd written *Odyssey*.

Another hour or so of research and I've put together a history of the Odyssey Group. It was founded in 1995 by a former Navy SEAL named Darrell Peterson to provide specialized security training to military personnel and later to law enforcement. During the early years of the wars in Iraq and Afghanistan, Odyssey seemed to have been busy providing private security services to the military and construction and engineering companies. In 2006, Odyssey began construction of a huge new training complex and headquarters in western Maryland.

I'm reading an account of an Odyssey employee's training when I come across a sentence that makes me sit up: "The training grounds in Vandenburgh, Maryland, comprised nearly three thousand acres. Many of them were fenced in and inaccessible to local hunters and hikers."

Vandenburgh, Maryland.

Marcus Weller.

I search for "Odyssey" and "Marcus Weller." Nothing comes up. But when I search for "Marcus Weller" and "Vandenburgh," I get a few more references to his appearance before the zoning board and to him working for a company called Dynasty Logistics.

The white SUV in the parking lot of the Bay Shore motel was registered to Dynasty Logistics.

I keep reading, and after twenty minutes I'm pretty sure that Dynasty Logistics is a shell company created to allow Odyssey to get the initial permits for the Vandenburgh campus without having its name attached to it. Dynasty has no other digital footprint, other than an office in Washington, DC.

Then I search for "Marcus Weller" and "District Attorney Cooney." Nothing. But when I pair Cooney's name with Darrell Peterson's, I get a bunch of hits on the New York State Board of Elections website. Darrell Peterson has given money to Cooney's campaigns. A lot of it, thousands of dollars over the years, in amounts I suspect are right up to the contribution limits for a district attorney campaign.

Marcus Weller is connected to Cooney through Darrell Peterson.

The possible sequence of events unspools in my mind as I pace around the house. Marcus Weller drove up from DC in the white SUV sometime before February 16, when he seems to have pulled into the parking lot of the motel in Bay Shore, likely to do reconnaissance on Gabriel Treacy, and then driven to Farmingdale, to keep an eye on Heather Thornton. That evening, Gabriel Treacy had an appointment to meet Heather Thornton at the marina. First, though, he went to Jay Cooney's house nearby and stayed for thirty minutes. He left Cooney's around nine p.m. and then, for some reason, Cooney came out of the house and had a verbal altercation with Treacy in the street, witnessed by the neighbor.

At that point, Treacy drove or walked back to the marina to meet Heather Thornton, and while he waited for her, someone who I'm assuming is Marcus Weller approached him and shot him dead. Weller then stole his phone, wallet, and laptop.

Then, probably on February 20, Marcus Weller flew into Shannon Airport. He stole the car, which he used to drive to Sixmilebridge. And in the early morning hours of February 21, he broke into Noel Thomason's house and killed him, taking a few small items to make the burglary look real as well as Thomason's electronics, which he destroyed so that some piece of information couldn't be extracted from them. On February 25, Marcus Weller flew back to New York.

On February 28, he followed me home, and tonight, I think he tried to run me off the road.

Why?

I grab a piece of paper from Lilly's backpack and draw the timeline. Underneath it I write, *What is it that Gabriel Treacy and Noel Thomason knew that Jay Cooney and Marcus Weller (and perhaps persons unknown) want to keep quiet? What is Weller's involvement?* Then I add, Why *did he kill Thomason?* And then I get to the heart of it, writing down a question that gives me chills. *If Treacy is Cooney's brother, did Cooney hire Weller to kill Treacy and Thomason?*

I pace around the living room, trying out different possibilities. Marcus Weller works for Darrell Peterson. He was hired by Cooney to kill Gabriel Treacy because Treacy was going to reveal something Cooney didn't want revealed, most likely that he was Treacy's brother. Cooney knew about Odyssey because he knew Peterson. Peterson probably recommended Weller to Cooney. Weller killed Treacy, then somehow realized that Noel Thomason knew the truth, too—maybe because he stole Treacy's laptop and found emails from Thomason, or documents with Thomason's name on them—so he flew to Ireland and killed Thomason and made it look like a robbery. He destroyed the computer and the external hard drive. That day on the beach, when Dave and I were at the scene, it was Marcus Weller who I felt watching us. It was Marcus Weller who hacked Gabriel Treacy's email, Paul Shouldice's, Noel Thomason's, Heather Thornton's, mine, who knows who else's?

I think for a minute.

But the gun. What about the gun?

That's the part that doesn't make sense.

Just to be safe, I use the landline instead of my cell. Dave answers on the second ring. "What?" He knows it's me.

I tell him about Pietro Griselli and Marcus Weller, about everything I've figured out. "That's the guy? That's the guy who followed you, who killed Gabriel Treacy? Marcus Weller?"

"I think so. Maybe Cooney hired him or something." I can hear Dave's disbelief come across the phone line. "No, listen. Maybe Treacy came over and he was going to let everyone know that Cooney was his brother, whatever—I know it's not a big deal, but for some reason it was to him."

"Okay," Dave says. "What next?"

"Something happens. Maybe Weller was just supposed to talk to him, but he kills him and he takes his phone and his laptop and he realizes that Treacy has told Noel Thomason about Cooney, too. So he goes to Ireland and he makes it look like a robbery but really he's getting rid of the evidence in Thomason's house."

Dave's eating. I can hear him crunching on the other end. "How did he know to do all that stuff, Mags?" he asks. I don't have an answer. "What do you know about Marcus Weller? What's everything you know about him?"

"Well, he was Army and then he's been working for this military contractor, Odyssey Group, which has some sort of relationship with Dynasty Logistics."

"Contractors," Dave says. "I knew some of those guys. There are a lot of them over there, even more now than when I was active duty. Some of 'em are really hard core. Like, spy hard core." He crunches some more. "Maggie, I don't see Cooney being involved in this. I just don't."

"I know," I say. "And there's the gun. Hang on. Didn't Aguillar tell us that he heard the gun went down to DC? Well, Odyssey's in Maryland."

Dave stops crunching. There's a long silence.

"You know what, Mags? I'm going to come over." I picture him, up and out of bed, checking his service weapon, dressing quickly, his military training still with him.

"Okay, make sure you're not followed."

I pad upstairs and open Lilly's bedroom door just a little. She's fast asleep, so I shut her door again. On the landing, I look out the window to the side yard and catch movement out there, someone moving slowly along the street and then around to the little strip of yard I share with the Yaktitises.

There's a man in the backyard.

He disappears around the side, back toward the street, and when I tiptoe down the front stairs and let myself out the side door and into the yard, I can see a small dark-colored car idling fifty yards down the road, toward the water. I can't tell, but it looks like there's someone in the driver's seat. Keeping the Glock against my body, I keep my back to the siding and ease around the side of the house to watch.

The man is walking quickly toward the car and I see him look both ways on the street and then slide into the passenger seat. I've already got the make, color, and plates memorized—black Toyota, NY DER-3824—and I wait for the car to pull out.

It doesn't. It just sits there. The windshield is steamed over a bit, but I can make out two forms. They're sitting there talking and looking back toward my house.

They're planning.

I take stock. I have the Glock. I didn't reset the alarm when I left the house but I did lock the door, and it's probably better that if one of them makes a break for the house, Lilly isn't awakened anyway. I'm wearing pajama bottoms, but they're close-fitting and I have on a fleece jacket and my running shoes. I'm feeling awake, energized, now that I know I wasn't imagining it.

They're here. They're here to hurt me and Lilly.

I can do it.

The wet pavement muffles the sound of my feet. I get down low and cross the fifty yards quickly, all my senses on high alert. I keep the Glock close to my leg and come up on the passenger side, my hand opening the door and my body pivoting to get inside the open door as quickly as possible. I have my gun up and I use my left leg to jab at the area where a weapon would be if he has one, then get my gun out in front of me. "Hands on the dash," I say in a low voice. "Now."

The man looks terrified, his eyes wide, his hands up in front of him.

"Get them on the dash!" I say again and it isn't until he complies that I look over at the other person in the car.

It's Heather Thornton.

"Who are you?" I ask the man, my mind racing to figure it out. He's thin, slight, barely taller than Lilly.

"I was just—I want to talk to you," he stammers. His accent is English. "We . . . I wanted to make sure he wasn't watching the house. My wife gave me your address."

"You're Paul Shouldice," I say.

He nods. Heather Thornton says, "I'm sorry, Detective D'arcy. We wanted to make sure your house wasn't being watched by . . . well, by him."

Fear crosses Paul Shouldice's face. "We need to talk to you," he says quietly. "I think I know why Gabriel Treacy was killed."

39

Dave arrives fifteen minutes later. I check on Lilly again and then we all sit down in the living room.

"Thank you," Paul Shouldice says gratefully, taking a long sip of the strong, hot tea I hand him. "Englishmen and their tea, you know. I've been sleeping in the car the last couple days. I went to Heather's earlier today and we weren't sure what to do. Then I rang Francesca and she gave me your numbers and address. We drove by this afternoon and there was a guy standing on the corner, pretending to be on his phone, but there was something off."

I feel cold all of a sudden, then remember Lilly was at school.

He looks up at me, his eyes wide and terrified. "I recognized him, you see. Heather and I drove around some more and then came back to make sure he was gone."

We wait.

Paul sighs and slumps in his chair. He glances at Heather, who nods, and then he says, "I'd better start from the beginning."

The house is quiet as he starts his story.

"I met Gabriel Treacy in South Africa," he says. "I was working for a medical aid organization mostly doing HIV prevention, and he was working for Irish Aid, and we became friends. He was a wonderful person, kind, funny, brilliant, totally dedicated to his work. In 2011, we found ourselves in Afghanistan at the same time, with different organizations, but in the same spaces a lot of the time. He was operating under a grant that included a lot of public health projects, so we worked and traveled together quite often. We were in a van, driving to a refugee camp on the border, in Pakistan, when we were taken. With me was one of the nurse managers who worked for me, Anne. And this Italian photographer had asked if he could get a ride with us. He was doing a story on one of the camps, a big one that we were monitoring for cholera. And Gabriel had a young Afghan translator he'd been working with, Tahir. Five of us. We were all taken."

He spreads his hands out at his sides. "We'd heard stories. They make you do training. We'd all been in situations that could have gone that way. Pietro had actually been taken once before and released immediately. At first it was like a dream, a bad one, like being in a movie. The shock. It was just that shock of everything changing in an instant, of not quite being able to believe that this had happened to us. We were sure we'd be killed. The reporters . . . we knew what had happened to them." He glances up at us with a haunted look, his eyes wide, his mouth drawn down.

"We all knew we shouldn't let them know too much about us at first. They tell you that, when you do these trainings they make you do. If they know who you are, then they ask for money, and they ask for more if they think your family's rich, if they think you're American, all different things.

"We were moved . . . a few times, I think. After the first couple of days, they moved us to a house somewhere in the mountains. That house, it was so small and it was so cold, but the walls . . ." He looks up at us in wonder. "The walls were painted blue. And there was something about it that was so magical. Like we were in a fairy story. I don't know. The nights . . . you couldn't sleep. It was too cold. So we talked. About ourselves."

"Who was guarding you?" Dave asks. "How did they treat you?"

"They were . . . they were just kids, local boys and men with nothing to look forward to, skinny, poor, barely educated. They kept us alive. Some of them were merely . . . authoritarian." He smiles grimly. "Others were sadistic. They thought they could get some money out of us."

We wait. I have the sense he's getting to the heart of his story.

"There was a boy," he says finally. "He brought food, he watched us. He seemed to be sort of a younger sibling to some of the guards. Everyone liked him. That was clear."

He takes a long sip of his tea. "His name was Ibrahim. He was always smiling. That was the thing you noticed about him. He was just a happy, good-natured boy, and yet he was doing this thing that . . . He liked jokes and his English was quite good, and he started listening to us as we told stories to each other and one night, he told us his own story.

"He told us a story about how when he was small, he had liked to look up at the stars above his family's home. He looked up at them and they were his friends, because wherever he went, the same stars were there. There was something delightful about him. You know how there are people who . . . who have a humanity that shines through, even in utter darkness and despair? I've seen it in refugee camps. That was Ibrahim. The men who took us, I don't know what they thought was going to happen. I've thought about this so many times. I think they believed that they would get some money, they would let us go, and that would be it.

"But after we'd been there a week, a new guy came. He was Taliban, obviously. He must have heard these men had taken some Westerners and he came to see what they had.

"He was different from the other guards. He spoke excellent English and he seemed to have a sense of who we were. That was when we realized that our organizations must have known we'd been abducted. It made us feel better that they knew, that maybe someone was coming. That maybe the Americans . . . We knew the military, US Special Forces, rescued aid workers who had been abducted sometimes. Sometimes, if the captors thought they were going to be caught, they would just let the aid workers go, just say . . . 'You're free to go.' We knew that's what happened to Pietro the first time he was abducted."

Dave and Heather have been listening closely, nodding here and there, and it strikes me that they both know what Shouldice is talking about. They can see the mountains and the buildings and the trees, can hear the voices of children and the men guarding Paul Shouldice and Gabriel Treacy.

Dave asks, "How long had you been captive at that point?"

"Two weeks." Paul looks up at us and smiles. "Nothing. A lifetime. We heard them talking one night. Gabriel and I didn't have very good Pashto. We'd always gotten along with interpreters, but Tahir could understand of course, and Anne had been over there longer and she'd gotten quite fluent. They overheard them talking about how Pietro, as a journalist, was a high-profile captive, how he was probably CIA, how they were going to make an example of him.

"We didn't know what to do. I was paralyzed. The fear, it just . . .

stopped you. Stopped you from planning, from being human. Gabriel had noticed that one of the windows was loose and he told us that if we could create a diversion, then Pietro might be able to climb out and . . . run, if we did it at night. I was terrified. I think Anne and Tahir were, too. We were against it, but Gabriel, to his credit, said that he would do it. We would stay in view of the guards and he would try to keep them occupied while Pietro escaped. He told them that his leg hurt, made a big show of moaning and everything. Pietro went for it. He even made it, but of course they knew that Gabriel had helped him."

He looks up at us, his blue eyes troubled. Unconsciously, he hunches his back, a hand going up to his shoulder, and I know what's coming.

"Pietro was brought back by someone in the town; he barely made it a mile from where the blue house was, and they took him and Gabriel into a room and we heard them screaming. It was . . . I can't describe to you how awful it was. We knew they were being tortured. Anne and Tahir and I, at some point we covered our ears, we couldn't listen. But when they came out, Pietro told us they'd made him watch while they cut Gabriel's back. He said he'd tried to close his eyes and they wouldn't let him, they'd forced him to watch, to see what he'd done, he said.

"The guards were different after that. Even Ibrahim was sad, downcast. We could tell he felt guilty. He gave Gabriel extra food. One night it was so cold and he took off one of his own shirts and gave it to Gabriel. It was so kind. He was just . . . he was a kind, young boy who was wrapped up in this awful thing that wasn't his fault. He . . . you could see, he'd aged because of what he'd seen.

"We were talking one night and Gabriel, while he was telling a story, said that once upon a time there was a boy who carried a message to some men, some Americans, and he was a hero. He just threw it into the story. He waited until Ibrahim was the only guard awake who understood some English. And he threw it in. I knew what he was doing. And Ibrahim looked up, he understood what Gabriel was saying. He understood what Gabriel was asking him to do."

He takes a long sip of his tea. "I'm sorry," he says. "I'm tired. Heather's heard this already tonight. You're very good to go through it again, Heather." She offers a sad smile, shivers.

Dave takes a blanket off the back of my couch and hands it to her. "It's chilly," he says. "Here." She takes it gratefully and wraps it around her shoulders.

Shouldice keeps going. "A couple of days later, we woke up in the middle of the night to an explosion. Not a big one, like we were being bombed, but a stun grenade, flash grenade, something like that. The front door was bashed in, and these men, all of them in green or tan, with vests and helmets and weapons, they stormed in and they rounded up the guards and Ibrahim." He looks up. "It was the Americans. We were being rescued. It was what we'd been hoping for. There were men in helmets, with guns. *It was what we'd been hoping for.* But all I remember is being terrified."

His voice catches. "Tahir, he was . . . he was terrified. I didn't understand why. He kept saying, 'Thank you, thank you.' I didn't understand.

"Gabriel was still weak. They brought us all into the same room and they had all the men, the guards, lined up." He repeats it. "Lined up."

He looks at Heather, starts, stops, starts again. He's babbling now, speaking so fast we have to concentrate to understand each word. "There was this man. An American. At first, it made me so happy, his accent. I knew we were saved, you see. He was clearly in charge. He was tall, with this gray hair, in a brush cut, like a silver brush, even though he wasn't very old, and he had a big gun, an assault rifle, strapped across his chest. They were all wearing vests, boots. They didn't have names on their fatigues, the way soldiers do.

"It was early morning. The sun started coming up. That's the part I remember, the sun just barely there, just peeking above the horizon through a window, and when it was all over, it was barely higher in the sky. It felt like a fucking year, but it was barely higher in the sky.

"It was . . . there was so much confusion. So much noise. The blue walls . . . But he was calm. They'd lined the guards up, Ibrahim and the other men, and he shot each of the guards in the head, at point-blank range, just executed them right here in front of us, against the blue wall. It was like he wanted us to see. They weren't fighting back. They weren't doing anything." He takes a deep breath.

"Ibrahim was last. He looked . . . he was terrified. And Gabriel was shouting, 'Don't kill him. Don't shoot him. He saved us. He's the one who told you we were here. Don't kill him.'

"Tahir joined in. He said, 'Please don't do it. He saved us. He found you!' But the guy just smiled and he turned around and he put the gun to Tahir's head. He said, 'You want to give your life for his? Is that what you want? Say the word. I'll shoot you instead!'

"He was very excited, the man with the gray hair. He enjoyed it, enjoyed putting Tahir in that position. He said again, 'Is that what you want? Because he'd kill you if he had the chance.' Tahir was crying. He said no, and he was pleading with him. And the man just turned around and shot Ibrahim."

Paul Shouldice looks up at us with an expression of disbelief. "There was no reason for it. It was . . . I still can't. To this day." He's shaking his head, reliving the trauma again and again. When I look over at Dave, he has tears in his eyes.

"It's not your fault," he says quietly.

"He saved us," Paul Shouldice whispers. "He saved our lives and that man killed him anyway. He killed him for fun."

40

We're all silent. It's nearly three now, the darkest part of the night, and outside the house, I can hear the ocean, faintly, and the low moan of the wind.

Paul Shouldice goes on. "They brought us back to the base, to Connelly, which is the forward operating base outside of Jalalabad, and that was when we realized they weren't Army at all. The guy who was in charge, the guy with the gray hair, he told the soldiers at Connelly that they'd rescued us from some local men and the men had been killed in the raid. No one seemed to want to ask too many questions. They were something else, these guys, something in between. They were contractors. We found out later that they were in Nangarhar providing security to engineering teams building road infrastructure. There was no one to go to, no one to tell about what they did, because, as the guy told us as they drove us back, they had saved our lives. He said the army never would have come in and saved us. It was too risky. He was the only one who had the balls to do it. That's what he said. He said we'd better feel lucky we were free and never tell anyone about what had happened that day. 'There's so much fucking BS with these things,' he said. 'Better to handle it yourself. You'd better keep your fucking mouths shut, okay?'

"I was just so . . . we were all, we were grateful to be alive. We were. And we all went home, and for a while I tried to forget about it, and I did, you know. There are so many moral calculations that we make in my line of work, all the time. You're saving lives but you're taking them, too. You use the last dose of a lifesaving antibiotic on this man, not that one. You get to the twelfth child in line, but not the one hundred twelfth. All the protocols, all the plans we make, so much of it is so that when we make those decisions, there's a structure for it. Because there's so much death, so many choices. I rationalized it for years. I think Gabriel must have, too."

He's quiet. His story isn't finished, but he needs to rest.

"The guy. I'm almost positive his name is Marcus Weller," I say. "He works for a private security company that provides contract services to the US military in, among other places, Afghanistan, from what I can tell, and I think he killed Gabriel Treacy and Pietro Griselli so they couldn't tell their story and he killed Noel Thomason because Gabriel had asked him for legal advice and must have told him about what happened."

"I didn't know his name," Shouldice says. "But I figured out who he works for."

Heather fiddles with her phone and then holds it up, showing us a *New York Times* story from November with the headline "Odyssey Group CEO to Join Department of Defense."

"I saw this right after the election," he says. "And I never would have put it together except there was a link to another story about that CEO, Darrell Peterson, from three years ago, when he testified before Congress about an incident where some of his employees massacred a group of protesters in Iraq." Heather fiddles with the phone and shows us another story. There's a picture of Peterson, and behind him are a couple of other men who seem to be bodyguards or security. "Him," Paul says, pointing. "He's not identified in the caption, but it's him." I squint at the picture. The man is tall, with a gray crew cut and a hard, broad-nosed face. His attention is on whatever is just beyond the photographer's lens. *Marcus Weller,* I think. I'm pretty sure he was driving the SUV that tried to force me off the road.

Paul takes a long sip of his tea. "I saw that picture and I just . . . I was filled with rage about what he'd done. And I just knew that if this Peterson became the first deputy director or whatever at the Department of Defense, that he'd put this . . . this psychopath in a position of power. I know how these things work.

"Pietro and I had been in the same places a few times over the years since . . . since Afghanistan, and I told him I was thinking about telling my story. Our story. He told me he knew a reporter who had done some good work on private military contractors. He gave me her name and I read a really good three-part story she'd written about private military contractors."

"Heather," I say.

"Yeah." He smiles at her. "She had done her work and she seemed to be trying to unmask them for what they really are—a private mercenary army." He's so angry I can see it on him.

"How did you know Pietro?" I ask Heather.

She pulls the blanket more tightly around her shoulders and says, "I met him when I was over there. We dated a little, but mostly we were friends, and we stayed in touch. He visited me a few years ago." She looks back to Paul.

"I sent Gabriel a message in November and he rang me back and we talked a few times," he says. "It was . . . it was good to speak to him. He said that he thought he had seen the guy, Marcus Weller, I guess, on a street in New York and ever since then, he hadn't been able to stop thinking about the blue house. He said he'd thought about coming forward with what we knew, but he wasn't sure how to do it and now, here I was telling him how to do it. I said we'd do it together. I said we'd tell Heather what had happened. I got in touch with her, though I didn't tell her what it was about. I thought she'd be able to find out this man's name."

He runs a hand through his hair. "Gabriel said he was thinking about coming to New York in February. He had a personal thing, a reason to come to Long Island, he said, but wouldn't tell me what it was. And as it got closer, I became concerned. Some strange things started happening."

Dave leans forward. He knows. We all know. "You felt like you were being followed? You were worried someone hacked into your email, your phone?"

"That's right. It was . . . it was very strange. Just a sense really, that someone was there. I would have recognized him if I'd seen him. It was never that . . . Sometimes, I'd be walking and I'd feel someone behind me. I got all these strange texts on my phone, phishing things. I ignored them, but I'd clicked on one by mistake . . . At first I was sure it was paranoia. But I kept remembering him, how cold he was, how clinical. I started to worry that I might be putting my family in jeopardy. So I told Gabriel I'd changed my mind. I assumed he'd give up on the idea, too, but he said, 'That's all right. I understand. You have a family. I'm going to do it and I won't bring you into it.'"

"He contacted you himself?" I ask Heather. She nods.

"Were you telling us the truth?" Dave asks her. "About how he contacted you, about the meeting?"

"Yes," she says. "I just couldn't tell you what I thought it was about without revealing Paul as my source."

Paul says, "Gabriel stuck to his word. He didn't tell me when he did it. He didn't even tell me he was here."

"How did you find out about his death?"

"From the paper. There was just a small item in the *New York Times*. I went and looked at *Newsday* and saw the stories and I knew, I knew who had killed him. The number I had for Pietro, when I rang it I didn't get any answer, so I searched for him and, well, because of Francesca, I speak good Italian and I saw he'd been killed a month or so ago. I panicked. I knew I needed to get away from Francesca and the kids. If he was watching, I wanted him to see I wasn't there. I just . . . drove, slept in the car. I wanted to put as much distance between me and my family as I could. I called Heather last night and she said I could come to her house and we'd figure out what to do. And then, when I talked to Francesca, well . . . here we are." He meets my eyes. "I knew I needed to go to the police. I read about you. I saw what you've done . . . It seemed like . . . it made sense."

He sits back in his chair, exhausted from his story. "Gabriel saved my life. It's my fault he was killed. I couldn't live with myself if I didn't do something."

For a long time, I just sit there, taking it all in. And then I say, "Did he ever tell you about his mother? That she'd had a baby before him, that he had a brother?"

Paul Shouldice smiles. "Yeah, his father was a local politician, a muckety-muck was my sense, and he and Gabriel spent some time together, over the years, and his father told him about his brother, that he'd arranged for Gabriel's mother to have the baby and have the baby adopted in America. He knew some people connected with a church who were facilitating adoptions. Gabriel said that he'd promised his father he wouldn't say anything to his mother but that if he survived, he thought maybe he was going to talk to her, going to see if he might find the other baby, just to make sure his brother was okay."

I see it then, see the whole thing, how it happened. I'm not quite ready to explain it, though. The one thing I still don't understand is what Jay Cooney and Gabriel Treacy were fighting about in the street.

And I still don't know how we're going to get Marcus Weller.

Paul Shouldice looks hopeless. "People like that, the ones who work for these private security outfits, they're like spies. They have training that . . . You can't even imagine some of the stuff I've heard. I don't think it would have happened if it weren't for Weller. He was some kind of psychopath, I'd swear it. The way he looked at me when he killed Ibrahim. He was controlling me and he was getting off on that control."

Dave rubs his face. "We need to bring him in. Maggie, we've got to get onto the Odyssey Group as soon as possible. It'll be the feds. They'll have to go to Maryland and raid that place, see if he's there."

"He's not there," I say. "He's here. He's been watching us. He's waiting for something to happen." I think for a minute. "But he might not know Heather and Paul are here. Dave, can you go move Heather's car up to one of the side streets? They're going to need to stay at my house until we get on top of this and if he's watching, I don't want him to see it." He nods.

I'm exhausted all of a sudden, but it will be a while before I can rest. "We need to talk to Marty," I say. "And probably Cooney, too."

41

We tell Marty the whole thing in the morning, in my car, sitting at the marina in Bay Shore, explaining how Gabriel Treacy came to die here on a frigid winter night.

After sleeping for a few hours, we left Heather and Paul at my house, with the alarm set and instructions to call 911 if anything seems off. I took Lilly up to Danny's and told them in no uncertain terms that they're to keep the alarm armed all day, too, and not to leave the house unless I tell them they can.

Uncle Danny didn't ask any questions; he just nodded and asked if he should bring his old Beretta up from the basement, the one he used to keep under the bar. I thought about it for a second, then said, "Nah. You're out of practice. It hasn't been cleaned. Just keep the alarm on and call me if you need to."

When I hugged Lilly, she hung on for an extra second and I whispered, "It's okay, Lil. It's going to be okay." Her face was warm against mine and I remembered the way she used to hang on at bedtime, nuzzling my neck until I had to peel her off.

Marty sighs a long sigh, like he's done with all of this, though I know that it's just that he knows what's ahead. I feel a surge of affection for him—love, really—and I reach out and touch his shoulder. He looks up and smiles at me. "We gotta sort this thing out," he says. "Let's go see Cooney. Dave, give him a call and tell him we're here and we're walking over. Let's do it now."

Cooney answers the door, but he doesn't say anything, just leads the way to a closed-in porch at the back of the house. Alicia's waiting there. He's wearing "The DA at Home" clothes: khakis, a blue shirt open at the collar, leather docksiders. There's wicker furniture with blue-and-white-striped cushions and nautical art on the walls. I was right about the whales. They're everywhere: on coasters, on the walls, on the picture frames arranged artfully on a side table. There's a copy of the family photograph from Cooney's office, and as I look at it, I know that I'm right. I know I've figured it out. The windows look out onto the backyard and the snow is coming down fast now, small flakes collecting in a thin layer on the ground. We all watch as a cardinal alights on a birdfeeder and scatters seed onto the ground below. A squirrel darts out of the holly bushes along the side of the yard and feasts on the overspill.

I can feel that the house is empty; the blond wife, the three blond kids, the elderly parents, none of them are here. Alicia nods at us and goes to sit in a chair near the door. There's a big coffee table book called *For the Love of Long Island* on the table. Cooney looks at us and I think I see a muscle twitch next to his eye.

"Okay," he says. "What is it? What's going on?"

I catch it again. The twitch. He's nervous.

Marty just sits there. We agreed I would say it.

"We think maybe you knew Gabriel Treacy," I say quietly. "We wanted to give you a chance to explain."

There's a huge silence in the room, a silence that fills up all the space between us. I can see the gears going, see him calculating. As a prosecutor, he's known for keeping his cards close to his vest; he isn't going to give us anything until he sees what we have.

"Marty, what the fuck is this?" Cooney says. A piece of hair flops over his forehead, ruining his perfect hairline.

"We're not accusing you of anything, Jay," Marty says in a soothing voice. "We're all investigators here. Maggie's just asking you, giving you a chance to offer some additional information, if you want to."

"Where is this coming from, Marty?" Cooney asks. "You owe me that. What's the information you have that makes you think you can accuse me of . . . I'm not even sure what you're accusing me of here."

"We think he came to your house on the sixteenth," I say. "Just before he was killed."

He takes a sip of his drink. "As it happens, Jenn was home when he stopped by. I was out. When I got home, she told me that an Irish guy had knocked on the door and said he wanted to talk to me. He thought he might know me."

He's lying and we all know it. Gabriel Treacy was inside this house for thirty minutes. There's no way it took Jenn Cooney thirty minutes to tell Treacy to take a hike.

The snow falling outside makes it feel like we're underwater. The house is silent, still. I look Cooney right in the eyes. I can feel my anger at him rising. I'm remembering his words to me in his office. *It was twenty-seven years ago! I'm not going to risk the good reputation of this office in order to satisfy some personal grudge.*

"Why didn't you tell us he'd been to your house?" I ask.

I can see how much he hates me. His eyes narrow, and he presses his lips together like I just let my dog shit on his lawn. But he's afraid, too.

"If you want to know, I didn't know about it. Jenn and I have . . . we've been separated, just to work some things out, and I had been staying at a, at a friend's house." He glances involuntarily toward Alicia. "It wasn't until a few days later that she mentioned it."

We all wait. He can't think that's going to do it.

His eyes dart away from us. He picks up a dog toy shaped like a bone off the floor and holds it, twisting the ends. His body is in motion. He can't stop. It's one of the sure signs someone's lying. Alicia puts out a hand, like she's trying to tell him to calm down, but he ignores her and keeps fidgeting. "She said that she thought the man who had been killed was the same guy who stopped by the house to ask after me." He looks away. "It was a few days after. I knew it would just . . . muddy the waters. We needed to investigate without distractions. Jenn and I will of course make a statement, once we have a confession in hand from a gang member. I fully expect that's going to happen in the next day or two, right, Marty?"

The only sound in the room is the *scratch scratch* of Cooney's hands on the stiff cloth of the dog toy.

"You're lying," I say, staring him down.

He's pale. His face is a mess. I can see the signs; he hasn't slept in days.

"Excuse me? Marty, what is this? Are you accusing me of something, Maggie? I know we've had our differences of opinion, but this is beyond anything I ever thought even you were capable of."

"Jay," Marty says sternly.

Cooney looks outraged. "What are you claiming?" Alicia gets up and comes to stand next to him.

"At first I thought you and Gabriel Treacy were brothers," I say. "Gabriel Treacy's mother gave up a baby for adoption in 1965. Noel Thomason was her lawyer, too, and when the Irish police were looking at his files, they found your name." I gesture to the picture of his father. "Or what I thought was your name. But you know all of that. I think you *were* here and I think you know why Gabriel Treacy came to see you. He thought you were his brother. He thought you were the baby his mother gave up in 1965."

Cooney stands by the window. He's defeated, all the fight gone out of him for now. I don't know exactly why, but it seems to have something to do with Alicia, with the way she's standing next to him, with the way she touches his shoulder. "I should have told you right away that I'd seen him that night. But I knew how it would look, I knew what a mess it would be. I assumed he'd been shot by some druggie or gang banger and that we'd find the guy in a couple days, arrest him, and it'd be done."

"At first, I couldn't understand why you didn't tell the truth, why you didn't think that we'd keep trying to figure out why Treacy was here," I say. "But then I realized: You knew he was here to meet someone else. He must have said something to you, about how he had an appointment, and you figured we'd find that person and the whole thing would be wrapped up like a Christmas present and you'd never have to be a part of it. Then we got the match on the gun and, well, that was even better, wasn't it. MS13? That would suck up any oxygen in the room. No one would care about anything else."

He doesn't say anything, just looks at me, and I can feel his anger. His weakness.

"You're not Gabriel Treacy's brother. Looking at you and that picture of your father, there's no question you're related." I study the photograph, seeing the resemblance between all of them, but especially between District Attorney John J. Cooney Sr. and District Attorney John J. Cooney Jr.

"You weren't the baby. You were never the baby. It was all those other babies, though, wasn't it? Those poor babies. They were brought over here, but it was all kept quiet. It wasn't legal, what they were doing, sending the babies out of Ireland without permission from their mothers. So they needed to create new birth certificates for them. They needed to falsify new ones. And for that they needed someone with access to the courts, to a seal. Someone like a judge. Your father. Jack Cooney."

He looks terrified now. This is why he wanted to keep it quiet, why he didn't want anyone to know.

I go on. "Most of the babies—Gabriel Treacy's brother and the rest—I suppose most of them were given to good homes, though I don't really know. I couldn't find any evidence of abuse. But I read an article about a woman who only found out in her forties that she was Irish, that she'd been born an Irish citizen. And she was angry that she'd been denied that knowledge. I think she wondered why your father's name was on her birth certificate, too, and I think she may have contacted you, and I think you were afraid that during a campaign, going into your father's fraud many years ago would be a distraction you just couldn't afford. So when Gabriel Treacy contacted you, when he showed up at your house, you were scared he'd make it public."

He's watching me, but he's terrified. Alicia is looking on, an expression of horror on her face. She didn't know. Whatever he told her, he didn't tell her this part.

"You told Gabriel Treacy that you weren't his brother. I don't know if you told him the truth about why your father's name was in that file, about why his was the name Noel Thomason found when he went looking for the records related to Stella Treacy's baby, but he was happy enough to let it go. He was curious but wasn't going to badger you. He must have sensed he'd come to the end of the trail. Besides, it wasn't actually why he was here. I still don't understand why you followed him out to the street though, why you argued. Did he say anything, about where he was going?"

Cooney looks confused for a moment, then sighs. "Just that he had an appointment. You have to understand, my father. He thought— they thought—they were doing a good thing," Cooney says lamely. "My mother, she was . . . she was very involved in the church, and they knew . . . they had friends in Ireland and they said there were babies, but they needed birth certificates for them, so they could be adopted by good Catholic families. She had my father do it. He had the best of intentions."

"But they never knew," I say. "They never even knew they had come from Ireland. They were denied ever contacting their birth parents if they wanted to. They didn't know the truth."

Cooney's eyes flash at me. "She said their mothers were girls who weren't fit to be parents. It was the best thing for everyone."

"It wasn't their choice to make," I say. "This all needs to come out. The people who were adopted by American families need to be told. You need to come clean about the fact that he was here the night he was killed."

There's a long silence. Cooney's staring at me. "I've done nothing wrong," he says. "Gabriel Treacy was killed by a vicious gang assassin. *That's* who you need to focus on."

Marty steps forward. "It's not that simple, Jay," he says. "You need to tell Pat. You need to tell county officials. You need to make a statement."

I say, "After he left here, Gabriel Treacy drove over to the marina. We think we know who killed him there. His name is Marcus Weller. He works for a military contractor called the Odyssey Group. You know the guy who owns it, Darrell Peterson. He donated to your campaigns." Cooney looks panicked.

"What are you saying? You think I had something to do with his death?"

"Not directly, but if you had told us he was at your house that night, we might have found Weller sooner. Now, we need to act fast. We need to locate him."

Cooney turns on me. "I don't *need* to do anything. I'd like you out of my house. Maggie, I'll be speaking to the commissioner about your conduct. You've withheld information that could have had an impact on this investigation, you've gone behind my back to investigate me, and you've put a murder investigation in jeopardy through your actions. Marty, you've been dishonest, too. Pat's going to take this away from you, get someone else to investigate it. We'll just take some time to think about this, put a pause on everything. That's what we're going to do."

"You can't do that," I say. "It's got to be now. We can't wait or we'll lose him. We need to have Pat authorize roadblocks, a wide-scale operation."

Cooney turns to look at me. "Don't tell me what I can and can't do," he says. Alicia puts a hand on his arm again, but he shakes it off. His face is flushed a dangerous pink. He's raging. "Marty, I want you all out of my house. I'll decide what we're going to do. I'll call Pat! I'm in charge here, so you just get out and wait for me to decide how to handle this!"

We're all quiet, waiting. The house feels cold and cavernous. Sad.

Cooney's got six inches on him, but Marty draws himself up and points a finger at him. "You know what, Jay?" he says. "You can go to hell."

The snow swirls outside. We're almost back to the car when we hear Alicia calling to us. She's unsteady on her high heels on the snowy walkway. When she reaches us, she's out of breath. "I just wanted you to know," she says. "He didn't go back out. After Treacy left. I was . . . I was here, too." She looks away, defeated. "I know that's got to come out, too. I know what that means for both of us. But Jay didn't go anywhere. There was no argument in the street."

42

"What the fuck?" I ask them, holding my hands over the heater in the car. "Why did that guy say they were fighting if they weren't?"

"Maybe Alicia's wrong," Dave says. We all consider that. "She sounded pretty sure though."

"Can we go talk to the witness?" Marty asks. "He's right here, right?"

"His house is, but he doesn't live there yet. I have a number though." I find it in a note on my phone and dial. An automated message fills my ear. "Generic voice mail," I say.

Marty looks toward the water. The waves are high today, the Great South Bay agitated and rough. "Let's walk over and just see if he's there," he says. "Just for fun."

It starts snowing more as we walk toward the water, down to the construction site. Tara is huge and blank in the midmorning light, no one working there today. We knock on the door and check the garage, but the site is quiet. The next-door neighbor, an older guy in a long, puffy blue parka, is walking his dog and I say, "Have you seen the owner around lately? I think his name is Mr. Landers. It looks like things are pretty quiet here."

The man looks confused. "Mr. who?"

"The owner. Mr. Landers. I spoke to him here a few days ago."

He just stares at me.

"I don't know who you talked to," he says. "But the owner of that house is a Russian guy who lives in London. He has a contractor named Julio who manages everything. I don't think he's ever even seen the house. Once we realized he doesn't intend to live here we tried to get the homeowner's association to do something but he's got some kind of shell company that he's using to—"

I feel a chill wash over me. "The owner of the house isn't a guy from Boston?"

"No. He's a Russian guy. None of us has ever seen him. Why?"

"No reason. Thank you." The man walks on, the dog stepping gingerly through the snow.

I turn to look at Dave and Marty.

I'm remembering the guy we spoke to, his distinctive hair hidden underneath a baseball hat, his eyes hidden behind sunglasses, and I think of the driver of the white SUV, his thin face and pale hair, barely visible in the darkness.

"Oh my God! That was Marcus Weller we talked to," I tell them. "He stood right there and told me and Dave he saw Treacy and Cooney on the sixteenth!"

Dave's eyes are wide. "We had him. We were standing there talking to him! Fuck."

"He was stone-cold," I say. "He wasn't even afraid. He's toying with us. With me." I scan the road behind us. "He may be watching us right now." I call Heather back at my house and tell her that she and Paul should go down to my basement and lock the door behind them.

"This is crazy," Marty says, fumbling with his phone. "Pat's not picking up and I don't know what we're gonna do here." I've never seen him so upset. Usually Marty's pretty even, but he's swearing under his breath and I can see how stressed he is. "Call your friends over in Ireland and tell 'em what's going on," he says. "They can start tracing Weller's movements over there."

"Okay, but what are we going to do?"

"I don't know yet. I need to think about this. And then we gotta act quick."

We get back to my house at noon and I check in with Uncle Danny and Lilly. Without explaining why, Marty arranges for a patrol car to sit outside Uncle Danny's house. Heather and Paul tell us it's been quiet while we've been gone and Marty makes us all grilled cheese sandwiches while we figure out what to do.

"If we can go around Cooney and get the feds involved," Dave says, "then they can get his military records, they can have someone raid the Odyssey Group's headquarters in Maryland."

"You know how they work, Dave," I say. "If they take a week or two to do an investigation, he'll be long gone. We'll never get him. He's here now and there has to be a way to draw him out."

It's Heather Thornton who presents us with the solution.

I'm making coffee when she comes in from the living room, carrying her computer. "I thought you might like to see this," she says. "It must be . . . it must be from him, right? I'm assuming you didn't send this."

"What?" I look over her shoulder at her laptop.

There's a message in her inbox from Maggie D'arcy.

"What the fuck. I didn't send that."

"I know you didn't," she says. "Read it."

"'Dear Heather,'" I read aloud. "'I'm a police officer investigating the death of Gabriel Treacy. I know that you had some contact with him and I think you may be able to help me with my investigation. The matter is a bit sensitive though and I wonder if we could meet at the marina in Bay Shore, since I know you know where it is. Shall we say nine p.m. tonight? Thank you.'"

Dave and I look at each other.

"Marty?" I go to the entrance to the living room, where he's checking email. "I think we have something."

We spend the afternoon getting set up. We do it slowly, in pieces, so Weller won't see what we're doing if he's watching. Marty finally got Pat to agree to it and they put unmarked cars in the neighborhood, use the porta potties at the construction site and the shuttered snack bar to hide officers dressed as town employees, and park an old municipal road crew truck near the entrance and exit to box him in. I'm hoping he's not watching.

Marty says I have to wear a wire. He won't let me do it otherwise, and frankly, it's fine with me. Marcus Weller isn't going to get close enough to talk to me.

I eat light, a little tuna salad for protein and an energy bar Dave hands me. He gets me a single espresso, too, and I chug it in the car, then call Conor.

It's late in Dublin. "Hey," he says. "I was just thinking about you. Maggie, I'm so sorry about the other night."

"No, I'm sorry. I felt like you were judging me," I tell him. "I know you weren't, but I felt like you were."

"I know. I wasn't. I'm so sorry, Maggie. You're a great mother. I remember how it felt, when Adrien was having such a hard time. Everything feels like a judgment. I love you."

"I think I may get a solve on this case," I tell him. "I think I'm almost there."

"I knew you could do it."

"What are you doing right now?"

"I'm in bed, drinking a glass of wine and reading a biography of Indira Gandhi. The sun was out today. I went for a long walk on Sandymount Strand."

"Ahhh. That sounds so nice."

My voice must catch because he says, "Are you okay?"

"Yeah. I just . . . I love you."

"I love you too."

At eight forty-five, I drive toward the marina. It's a dark night, clouds obscuring the moon, and the parking lot at the marina is nearly empty. I let Heather's car idle for a minute, pretend to be checking my hair in the mirror, then get out, make a show of locking up, and walk over to the bench. Marty is worried about him setting up somewhere with a long-range rifle so we've discreetly cleared the area around the marina and picked a spot for me to sit where he can't line up a shot from anywhere else in the neighborhood. They still made me wear a bullet-proof vest, but luckily, Heather's jacket and orange scarf hide its bulk nicely. I'm wearing her hat and her boots, too, in case he's watching.

Marty and Dave and a few of the uniforms are in a car a block away, monitoring my wire. I'm armed, surrounded by guys who will jump out immediately to save me, and yet once I'm inside the marina, sitting alone on a bench, waiting, I'm terrified.

I wait.

It's nine ten, then it's nine fifteen. I whisper into the mike taped below my collarbone, "I don't know if he's coming."

The Great South Bay is still, little whitecaps here and there catching the moonlight. I think about Gabriel Treacy sitting right here, waiting for Heather Thornton to arrive.

What had he been feeling? How long had he waited before he realized she wasn't coming? Had he known Marcus Weller was there, watching and waiting, too? I look around, trying to figure out where Weller might be hidden.

He's been watching me from the empty house, I realize. But at some point he'll have to make his way here to meet me.

Unless he doesn't.

Something makes me uneasy, an idea lodged in my brain that doesn't get much time because my nose and feet are starting to go numb.

I wait five more minutes, then go back to the car and start it up. I can keep my vigil from here. I dial Dave's number, put him on the car system, and say, "I don't think he's coming, but I'm going to wait for another half hour or so in the car. It's fucking freezing."

"Okay," Dave says. "We've been keeping a close eye on all the approaches, but nothing so far."

"You guys mind staying on the phone? I'm a little freaked. It's so quiet out here. I know everyone's watching, but it's just . . . eerie." I watch the entrance to the marina, waiting for a car.

"Of course," Dave says. Then he laughs and I hear Marty says something and then Dave says, "Marty says he'll recite poetry to you. You seen any action at all?"

"Nothing. The parking lot's empty. I think that's why I'm freaked." My phone vibrates and I see a text from Lilly pop up.

Dave says something while I'm fumbling with my phone. "What, Dave?"

"No, it was just Marty asking if anyone was walking near the entrance, like anyone casing it, trying to suss out whether there's any surveillance . . ."

I've tuned him out because I've opened up Lilly's text and I'm reading it. *Mom? Did you send me this? Weird number.* There are three photos attached. One is a photo of me, sitting on the bench at the marina fifteen minutes ago, only twenty feet from where I'm sitting now.

The second one is of Marty and Dave sitting in the car just outside the marina entrance.

The other is of Lilly. My brain is scrambling to take in the details. It must have been taken today. She's sitting at Danny's kitchen table, wearing the black fleece hoodie she was wearing when I dropped her off this morning. She has no idea she's being photographed through the window. She has no idea she's being watched.

Everything goes blank for a minute.

"Oh my God," I say. "Dave, radio the car at my uncle Danny's house, right now! He was there. He took a picture of Lilly. He took a picture of me!"

"What? What are you talking about?" I hear voices. A pop. And then Dave screams.

The line goes silent for a moment and then I hear him shouting for help. "Shit, shit, Marty! Help me. Someone fucking help me. I think someone's shooting. Jesus, Marty, Jesus," and I start up the car and floor it out of the marina to the side street where they're parked. Somebody's already got the sirens on and Dave's pulling Marty out onto the street, Marty's body flopping past the door like a newborn, the blood already starting to pool beneath him on the pavement. I can see broken glass everywhere, blood everywhere.

"He shot him, he shot him!" Dave's screaming at me. "He must have a sniper rifle! Mags!"

He's doing chest compressions, saying, "Come on, Marty. Come on," and I yell at him, "Where did it come from? Where did it come from?" and he points to the houses on the water, the rooflines silver in the dark sky over the water, and then I'm telling him to send cars behind me and I'm running, running as fast as I can because I know exactly where he is.

My limbs are loose, moving easily. I don't even feel the exertion of it. The air is cold and clear and I can hear the sirens in the distance and I know they're coming for Marty, but I just keep running, my legs and arms pumping, my lungs working the way I've trained them to. All those early morning runs, all those days I pushed my body to keep going when I didn't think I could. It was all for this, my muscles propelling me through the chilled streets.

Cooney's neighborhood is quiet. Almost all the windows have lights in them and as I pass, I can see families watching television, parents putting kids to bed in upstairs windows, can hear music and doors slamming and the frantic bark of a dog. There's something surreal about these glimpses of normality while just yards away, a killer is waiting for me.

I can see the water ahead, silver white and shifting in the low light from the houses. The Russian businessman's house looms in front of me. I stay low, shielded by the bushes that circle the property and a giant dumpster for construction debris. I know he's in there, but I want to get a sense of where before I enter the building. He'll be armed, but I am, too. I should wait for backup to arrive, but I know everyone's focused on saving Marty's life right now, and this guy has made a career out of disappearing.

I look up at the second-floor windows, trying to find anything, a light, a flash of movement, but it seems completely still.

He may already be gone.

And yet—I try to think about what I know of him. He's a professional, he knows how to bide his time, how to watch and wait, but he's impulsive, too. He could have arrested or detained the guards who'd been keeping Gabriel Treacy and the others, delivered them to FOB Connelly, taken whatever credit he was going to take for the rescue, and been done with it.

But he didn't. Was he just impulsive, angry, or was there something he was trying to hide?

I try to think about what else I know of him.

He shot at Marty and Dave.

He didn't need to do it. It gave away his position. It turned this into something else, something with a lot of exposure, something that can only end in one way for him.

I keep my back pressed against the garage wall and put my hand on the doorknob. It turns and I slip into the dark garage, my ears tuned to any sounds in the emptiness. I turn on the flashlight on my phone and shine it into the space, holding my weapon out in front of me. The concrete floor is so new it still has the wet gray smell of creosote and dust. I slowly open the door leading into the house.

It's half-finished, the floors still covered with plastic, the walls drywall, the molding unpainted. The bank of windows on one side of the kitchen let some ambient light from the neighborhood in, and I can make out the outlines of the room. It feels empty; I don't think he's downstairs. I'm betting he has his sniper rig set up in one of the second-floor bedrooms, along with a camera and a long-range lens. I'm betting he still has the 92FS. I try to figure out the layout of the upstairs. I don't know how many rooms there are, but he must be at the front of the house, looking back toward the marina, in a room with another window looking out toward the street where Dave and Marty were parked.

Construction equipment is littered around the house, saws and hammers and buckets of paint and plaster. I pick up a smallish hammer and tuck it into my coat pocket. There's a staple gun and a small handsaw, but neither of them is both light enough and lethal enough to be worth it. My Glock and the hammer will have to be my arsenal.

I slowly clear the first floor, going room to room, checking closets and bathrooms, then take the stairs up to the second floor. The plastic on the stairs crackles as I climb. It sounds so loud I can't believe he isn't on me already.

I can feel his presence up there, feel him waiting for me, and it's only as I reach the landing and take in a low humming sound from the front of the house that I complete the thought I'd had downstairs. *He shot at Marty and Dave.*

He knows he's not getting out of here alive.

He knows I'm here.

He's waiting for me.

"Mr. Weller," I call out, trying to keep my voice strong and loud, in case I didn't detach my mike while I was running. "You are surrounded by Suffolk County Police. There's nowhere for you to go. Please come out with your hands up and let us resolve this peacefully." I move slowly toward the room to my right. The door is very slightly ajar and I can see a bit of light angling through the narrow opening and hear the low hum, louder now.

"Mr. Weller? Please come out with your hands up."

Silence. But he's there. I use my foot to push open the door and move into the room, my Glock out, the open door behind me in case I need to retreat. I already have my route planned: back across the landing and over the banister downstairs. I left the garage door open.

The humming is coming from a small electric heater plugged into the wall, and as I move into the room, I can see his equipment setup. He's got a sniper rig in the open window, which he's broken and wrapped with drop cloths. The heater is to keep the room temperate. I can still feel the frigid breeze coming in, though. The room's probably around sixty degrees. Not bad for most forms of physical activity. Weller and I will both have good control of our muscles, our hands will be able to grip our weapons well.

His camera setup, just as I thought, is in the window looking out at the marina. He has a tripod and a nice Canon DSLR with a long lens on it and a big flash. I need to step into the room to look out the window to see if the cars have arrived, and that's when he comes through what I thought was a closet door on the far wall, but is actually the door to the master bathroom. He's between me and the door back out to the landing and even though I get my Glock pointed at his head and my body into shooting stance, it only takes me a couple of seconds to realize I'm screwed: He's between me and the door. Behind me is a partially broken window, but it's a good drop to the ground and I don't know how much glass the drop cloths are covering.

"They'll be here any second," I say. We can both hear the sirens. He just smiles, in a way that makes me nervous. *Please let the wire be working. Please let them be listening.*

He's tall, muscular, his chest and arms straining the black sweatshirt he's wearing. His hair is gray, cut in a buzz cut. He looks like a soldier, like a cop.

"Did I kill your boss?" he asks. "I was going for your partner but he leaned forward to talk on his phone and I missed him. Your boss leaned into the shot. Practically a suicide."

In his right hand is the Beretta, the same one that killed Gabriel Treacy.

"Drop your weapon," I say. "Drop it now."

"I hope your boss didn't feel a thing." The floor behind him is littered with more equipment; I can see a pair of high-powered binoculars, a laptop, a sleeping bag, a couple of black gear bags he must have used to transport it all up here. There's a black backpack there, too, with a red leather luggage tag embossed with a gold "GT." Gabriel Treacy's backpack.

"Move forward," I say in a low, controlled voice. "I want you to lie down on the floor and drop your weapon. In about twenty seconds this place is going to be swarming with cops."

He just watches me.

"How'd you find me?" he asks. "Was it Paul Shouldice?"

Talking is good. Talking buys me time. Talking gives me a chance to figure out what he's doing, what he wants.

I force the anger from my voice and say, "No, we were trying to figure out the Renault in Ireland. They got a credit card receipt when you stopped for gas. You were . . . a bit of a ghost otherwise. But you applied for a permit in Vandenburgh, Maryland. Then later, I found something about Odyssey and Vandenburgh. We put it together."

"That fucking ATM," he says. "Shouldice told you why, I bet." His eyes are alert and interested, but there's something chilling about them, an emptiness I've seen before. I think about what Paul said. *He was some kind of psychopath, I'd swear it. The way he looked at me when he killed Ibrahim. He was controlling me and he was getting off on that control.*

"He told me a story," I say. "I don't know if it's the right one. I don't know if it's true."

He raises his eyebrows a little, intrigued. "Do you know what the Taliban did to the people it held captive? They tortured them. I heard stories about what they did to Gabriel Treacy. I'm sure you did, too. That's the story you should have heard."

"How did Heather Thornton get on your radar? I know you found the others through her, but what I can't figure out is how you got on to her."

There's something lizardlike about him, his eyes nearly unblinking, his gaze trying to make some sort of calculation, whether either of us is getting out of here, whether he'll hurt himself by telling me. Later, I'll realize I should have known by how quickly he starts talking.

"She called Darrell's office, looking for a comment on a story she was working on," he says. "Not *this* story, but the story about his name being floated for an appointment. That's it. She wanted to know if he had any comment on Odyssey's involvement in the killing of civilians in Iraq and Afghanistan. There was . . . an episode." He waves his hand dismissively. "Darrell grew up in Hauppauge, not far from here, so it's sort of a Long Island story, I guess."

Suddenly, I see how it happened. "You started monitoring her, didn't you? Just about the time that Gabriel Treacy contacted her because he finally wanted to tell his own story about what happened in Afghanistan. You recognized his name."

He shifts his feet, then puts his hands up. "I bet you think I'm some evil person who goes around killing innocent people. I'm not going to justify what I do to you," he says. "But I killed potential threats, is what I did. I saved a hundred other people."

"But the press wasn't going to see it that way, was it, when they started looking into Odyssey because the new administration wants to appoint Darrell Peterson to some post at the Department of Defense."

He doesn't say anything. "You hacked Heather Thornton's email," I say. "You had all kinds of tricks, didn't you? State-of-the-art malware. You were reading her messages and you saw one from Gabriel Treacy. You recognized his name."

"We keep files on Odyssey's exposure from different work we've been involved in. It's my job to know who's out there, to know what they're doing."

"To know whether they're talking?"

He dips his head just a bit and smiles at me.

"It was harder to hack into Treacy's email," I say. "He knew someone was trying to get into his work server and he redid the security. When he became suspicious about his personal email, he deleted the account. As it turned out, though, it didn't matter. Because he was meeting Heather Thornton and you knew exactly what she was up to. You must have planned to kill them both, make it look like a robbery, but when she didn't show up, you had to improvise. You killed him and then you realized he'd brought his backpack along to show her. And when you read his emails, you realized he'd been corresponding with his lawyer in Ireland. You realized he'd told Noel Thomason everything. Was he looking for legal advice about telling his story?"

Marcus Weller nods his head toward the window. "Back the fuck up," he says. I'm not sure why he wants me to, but I do as he says. We both still have our guns up, but my arm is starting to tire and I think his is, too, because he lets the Beretta drop just a bit and I do the same. "He'd deleted his email account, but he had some documents on his laptop that had everything in them, notes he'd written. He had letters on the laptop that the lawyer had sent him through a file storage account. He'd clearly told him everything. The lawyer had been researching the law for him, trying to figure out what kinds of protections he might have, what kinds of protections a reporter might have. I needed to deal with Thomason. It wasn't difficult, really. It's the kind of thing that you have to take care of from time to time."

"Like what you had to do to Pietro Griselli?" I want him to say it for the wire. If anyone's still listening.

The Beretta comes up again. I've made him mad. "Look, these are things that have to be done, for the greater goal. Odyssey does things no one else is willing to do. Things that make the world safer. Darrell will make the world safer, and these were just some things that needed to be cleaned up."

"Is that the 92FS?" I ask him. "That's the only part of this I can't figure out. Where did you get the gun?"

He smiles. The sirens are suddenly louder and I know they've rounded the corner into the neighborhood. He turns to the sniper rig, adjusts it. I think, *Dave.*

"You could have knocked me over with a feather when I saw that you got a match on the gun," he says, smiling. "We have dealers we use in DC, guys who get firearms from a whole variety of sources. I asked for something hot, something that would send you off in the wrong direction and I know they dealt with the gangs sometimes, but . . . the gods were smiling on me."

I meet his eyes. "I'm taking you in." Outside, the sirens stop below us. "They'll be inside soon," I tell him. "You don't have a lot of options.

If you let me arrest you, I can make a case for leniency, based on your cooperation."

"I think we both know that's not true," he says. "Now, I'd like you to drop your gun."

"How about you drop your gun? Then I'll drop mine and we can go downstairs." I say it as loud as I can, just in case someone is listening. I want them to know what the situation is. I want them to know where we are.

He just smiles. There's something about the look on his face that tells me everything I need to know. He knows he's not getting out of here. And that's what makes me shout, "They're here!" and drop to the ground, taking the hammer from my pocket and hurling it at his head, or at where his head was before he leaps across the room and gets his body on top of mine, his hands around my throat.

Pure adrenaline hits my veins and I try to fight back, my body sensing the seriousness of the situation. But I don't have a chance. He's three times my size and he's got his knee on my arm. He takes his hands off my throat, pries my gun out of my hand and tosses it across the room, and then he says, "Okay, we're going to go downstairs and explain the situation to your friends down there." And then he reaches behind him and picks up a small square object on the floor and he holds it up and says, "Do you know what this is?"

It's a garage door opener.

I look up at him.

"You've wired the house," I say. "When officers come in, you're going to detonate the explosives."

Please let someone be listening. Please let someone be listening.

He rolls to the side, keeping an arm around my upper body. He smells clean and spicy, with no undercurrent of fear. Most people would be sweating right now, the sharp scent of terror creeping into their pores. Fear has a particular smell, sweat with an edge, I always think. But this guy is so well trained to suppress all his human responses to danger that he's barely feeling it. "Let's go, Detective D'arcy," he says. "Let's walk." He lifts me up, frog-marches me in front of him to the stairs.

My mind is going fast, trying to find an angle. He hasn't had much time. I'm pretty sure he didn't wire the garage door, but he's probably installed explosives at the other entrances. He may have just placed them around the first floor. He'll wait until our officers have come in and then he'll activate the detonator.

Or maybe he'll make his escape and keep us from following him by keeping us trapped inside and threatening to detonate the house.

Maybe he'll detonate it anyway.

I need to tell Dave and everyone who's outside what's going on.

But I have no idea if they're even listening.

"Let's go," he says, nudging me onto the top stair. "Go slowly so you don't trip."

I don't turn to look at him, I just say, "Hang on," and then I hurl myself off the stair and down, taking him with me, and that's when I hear the boom, an explosion that seems to fill my head, fill the house, fill all of space.

And then I lose consciousness.

When I come to, the room is full of smoke. My head is throbbing and I can just barely lift it to look around.

Weller is lying on the ground next to me. I can see the Beretta lying past him, within a foot of his hand. I slide myself toward him, but the pain is so intense I have to stop. Outside, car alarms are sounding and there are sirens everywhere now. I take a deep breath and try again, sliding a few feet, then resting my head. I'm almost there when Weller groans and rolls toward me.

This is it. If he gets to the gun first, he'll kill me.

I say a silent prayer, for Marty, for Lilly, for me.

I roll over, ignoring the blinding pain in my head and, I now realize, my arm. I pull myself along the floor. There's glass, something sharp there, and I feel it pierce my skin but I keep going, moving toward the Beretta, and then I've got it in my hand and I'm up on my knees, pointing it at him.

"Get down," I say, in a voice that doesn't sound like my own.

I hear Dave's voice then, shouting, "That was a controlled detonation, Mags! We heard you. We've disarmed it," and I'm about to put down the gun when Weller reaches behind himself and swings something around, catapulting himself off the ground and in my direction. The hammer. It's in his hand and he's about to bring it down on my head.

I squeeze the trigger, aiming for his hand.

My shot is perfect. He yelps and drops the hammer and grabs his right hand with his left. "Get on the ground!" I yell at him. "Get on the ground! I'm placing you under arrest."

But he sits up and screams, "Shoot me!"

"No," I yell back.

He's still holding his hand, but he swings his body around and starts half crawling, half rolling toward me. Blood is dripping from his hand and he's shouting, "Fucking shoot me," as he advances and I want to so bad that I start squeezing the trigger.

I'm almost there, but then I hear Dave say, "I'll fucking shoot you.

Get on the ground!" and I leap forward and put the gun to Weller's head and Dave covers me while I cuff him and read him his rights, and when I look up at Dave and ask, "Marty?" and he shakes his head, I kick Marcus Weller hard, in the stomach, once, then twice, and then again, before we take him in.

43

Marty's funeral is on a gray Saturday a week later, at a Catholic church in Babylon that's packed with cops and court stenographers and newspaper reporters. The stained-glass windows filter the gray light, sending candy-colored confetti onto the floor around our feet. Marty's kids and grandkids and cousins, the whole great Croatian American extended family, pack the first three pews. His daughters cry the whole time. It starts raining during the burial and from across the gravesite, I watch Cooney trying to fashion a little umbrella out of the program for himself, to protect his precious hair, I guess, and he feels me watching him and looks away quickly, as though he's spotted something unpleasant.

Dave and I pay our respects at the graveside. I whisper, "Thank you, Marty," and Dave says a little murmured prayer and then we hug the daughters again and make our way back toward the cars.

Bill's there and he actually gives me a hug, tears gathering in the corners of his eyes. "I loved that guy," he says. "I loved him like a brother."

A couple of days ago, the day Conor arrived to take care of me, when my arm was still in a sling and I could barely walk from the pain in my back, it was Bill who came to the house to tell me Anthony Pugh was back on Long Island. He'd flown into LaGuardia the day of Marcus Weller's first hearing and gone straight to his house in Northport. "We don't think there's anything to worry about," he said. "But I'll make sure they keep track. You can relax, Maggie."

But of course, I can't. I know he's out there, waiting for something. *Waiting for me?*

When I told Roly and Griz about all of it on the phone from the hospital, I let them know we'd found Gabriel Treacy's laptop among Marcus Weller's things and that on it there was a letter Gabriel had written to Abena. "Can you print it out and take it to her?" I asked them.

Roly said they would. "You take care now, D'arcy," he said. "See if you can go a couple of weeks without getting shot at, mind."

Cooney's waiting by the Lexus and I catch sight of Alicia talking to someone across the road. Jenn Cooney is nowhere in sight.

He hasn't dropped out of the race yet, though there have been calls for him to do so, once he announced that he'd known Gabriel Treacy and hadn't told us. The Marcus Weller case, along with the revelations about Odyssey, and Marty's death, are sucking up a lot of oxygen and I'm betting Cooney thinks his role in the case will just get lost in the mess.

"Jay," I say, delighting a little in the scowl that comes over his face. Dave nods to him but doesn't say anything.

"Nice service," Cooney mutters. We agree, but I can tell from his face that he's got more to say.

Dave gets in the car and I'm walking around to the passenger side when Cooney says, "Maggie, I know you and I have had our issues. I hope you know that at one time I thought you were a good cop. But you withheld information in an investigation and, most important, you didn't come to me first, you didn't come to Marty first."

He's holding something, something that makes him smirk, just a little.

"That may have gotten him killed. I haven't done it yet out of respect for Pat, now that he's in hospice and it's nothing personal, but I'll be asking Pat's replacement to let you go once the smoke clears. You may find it better for your career if you resign and look for another job. Anyway, I thought it was the gentlemanly thing to do to let you know."

Dave's car roars to life. A line of mourners comes along the road. The rain is falling fast now. There's nothing Cooney can do about his hair.

I level my gaze at him, staring hard until he blinks and looks away.

"You can go to hell, Jay," I say, thinking of Marty. "You can fucking go to hell."

A week later, I'm curled into the corner of the couch with Conor. We're listening to Eartha Kitt, drinking wine. My face is mostly healed, but my arm still hurts; my doctor said it was one of the worst sprains he'd ever seen, but I didn't break any bones and it will get better eventually. Uncle Danny is out with Eileen. Dave is on a date with Heather Thornton, their second. He was the one who went back to my house to tell her she didn't have to be afraid anymore, who took her home and made sure she was okay. One thing led to another, I guess, and he told me that they'd talked for five hours on their first date, shutting down one of the new restaurants he likes so much.

Lilly is out with her friends.

Conor and I have the house to ourselves.

He's been telling me about Adrien. And his parents. The lambs started coming in earnest this week and he said that when he called to check on Adrien, his dad was asking when Lilly and I could come back, to help, and after he says it, the silence fills the whole room where I'm sitting, the house, the yard, the ocean, and for a moment we both wait. He has an arm around me and I'm leaning into his chest, listening to his heart.

"I was thinking," I say finally, not looking up at him, "I'm going to take a leave of absence before Cooney gets me fired, figure out what to do, use up all my vacation time. I'm done, starting the day Lilly gets out of school."

Conor waits.

"So, I was thinking."

Outside the windows, it's feeling a little like spring, slivers of blue sky showing between the clouds, a foolish bird singing somewhere. I'm looking for something from him, a sign, a gesture. I'm terrified. He's quiet, and then he says, "That sounds dangerous," and I can't stop myself grinning up at him. His eyes are brown, but green and gold, too, the edges crinkling when he smiles. He's here. He's one hundred percent here with me, ready for whatever I'm going to say.

"Yeah. I was thinking maybe Lilly and I could spend the summer in Ireland, maybe we could use your friend's house, the one you were telling me about, see how we like it, see if maybe we could, well, think about living there for a while."

"For a while?"

I can hear the laughter in his voice, can hear how he's teasing me, and I grin again, foolish and light all of a sudden, and I say, "Well, you know, we might not like it. So, yeah, for a while." I hold my breath. "For now."

Again I hear his heartbeat. "For now," he says. "For now."

The ocean was angry.

Gabriel stood on the beach, facing the Atlantic, letting the wind wash over him, depositing salt on his face and hair and coat. The beach stretched behind and around him, a band of wet sand, then ripples of dry running to the dunes. Shells and rocks dotted the creamy surface here and there. He bent to pick up a pink one for Abena, and tucked it into his hip pocket.

Robert Moses, the guy at the motel had called it. "Just drive over the causeway and you'll see the beach. It's nice this time of year." It was a state park, he'd discovered, with a huge tower and multiple parking lots with access to the beach. He'd driven to the farthest one, where he could see a lighthouse in the distance, and then walked down to the water. It was almost empty, just a few other walkers passing him on the beach, their heads down, protecting their necks from the wind.

Gabriel thought about the letter on the laptop, the letter he'd written to Abena. The letter told her everything, about his father, about how Stella had never let him talk about it, until the very end, when he'd told her what Gerry Murray had said to him, that day in the car. "I loved her. I still do," he'd said. He told Abena about how he had felt a shift in himself since Stella's death, how all the things he'd thought were true about himself were, maybe, no longer true.

He would send it. He would see if she could start again with him, if they could start again.

But first, there was this thing he needed to do. He'd written about that, too, about Paul and Heather Thornton, about what he was going to say, an account of those things that happened in Nangarhar in 2011. Already, he could feel the relief of it, of getting the whole story off his conscience. He would tell Heather Thornton and she would write the article and whatever happened next, chances were that Darrell Peterson wouldn't get the job and that psychopath wouldn't be able to keep killing people.

He breathed in the salt air and turned his face to the east, to Abena.

I have held myself back from you, Abena, he'd written in his letter, because of these terrible secrets, because of my fear. I love you, and I want to make a family with you, if you'll have me. That is everything I know, Abena, and tonight it is enough, much more than enough.

The wind stopped for a moment and he closed his eyes and listened to the roar of the waves.

Acknowledgments

In writing this book, I learned a lot about the vital efforts of humanitarian aid workers around the world. Ireland has always sent more than its fair share of people to do this work, and I emerged from my research in awe of the aid workers who risk their own safety every year to care for those fleeing war, persecution, and natural disasters.

I am appreciative of so many people for their support in this most unusual year:

Thank you to the incredibly innovative and creative booksellers, librarians, and reviewers who helped me launch *The Mountains Wild* virtually, and to my readers, and my pals in the crime writing world.

Huge, huge thanks to my agent, Esmond Harmsworth, for his hard work on my behalf and to the whole team at Aevitas Creative Management.

The folks at Minotaur Books couldn't be more amazing. I am grateful to everyone there and in particular to Kelley Ragland, Madeline Houpt, Sarah Melnyk, and Allison Ziegler. I am indebted to David Rotstein for his beautiful covers and to Ivy McFadden for her sharp eye. Thank you to Marisa Calin for her beautiful reading and to everyone at Macmillan Audio.

Gillian Fallon once again provided absolutely invaluable editing and perspective from Dublin.

I send huge thanks to the law enforcement professionals in Ireland and on Long Island who shared their expertise with me and answered my questions. As always, any mistakes or deviations from procedure or reality for the sake of story are mine and mine alone!

Even from a social distance, my early readers and my friends got me through. Thanks to beta readers Lisa Christie and Sarah Piel; the best book club ever; the Upper Valley *gaelgeoiri;* the Middlebury friends; the Rosary Terrace crew; and the neighbor lady walking support group.

Thank you to Dave and Sue Taylor, Tom Taylor, Vicki Kuskowksi, and Otis and Edie Taylor. I can't wait to hug you all!

And finally, a big, enormous thank-you to Matt, Judson, Abe, and Cora Dunne, the best pandemic podmates ever, for their love, support, understanding, and humor. I don't know how I got so lucky.

Turn the page for a sneak peek at
Sarah Stewart Taylor's new novel

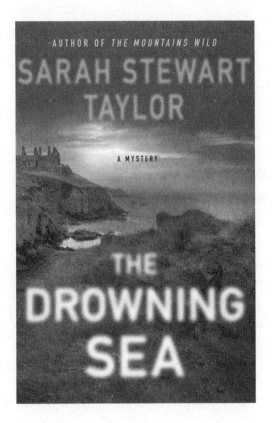

Available Summer 2022

One

....

The narrow trail disappears into the low grass, as though whoever or whatever walked there before us suddenly disappeared, or
turned around, or rose up into the sky like an angel. Far below the
path, the coastline curls and winds around the base of the cliffs, a
brilliant blue scarf of water, edged with lacy white surf.

Ahead of us, my boyfriend Conor's son, Adrien, and my daughter, Lilly, forge a path of their own, Conor and Adrien's corgi dash-
ing around their feet, barking and trying to herd them away from
the edge. Conor's hand is warm in mine. We can't stop smiling, at
the hot day—unusual for Ireland even in July—and at the summer
unspooling ahead of us, a whole two months on this gorgeous, remote West Cork peninsula in a rented vacation cottage. Lilly and
I flew to Dublin two weeks ago, right after school ended, and we
all drove down to West Cork the next day. The stretch of glorious
sunny weather has felt like a miracle, day after day of clear skies
and blue water.

A bird passes overhead, its gray wings and body a cross against
the paler sky, and Conor shields his eyes from the sun. "Peregrine
falcon!" he calls out. "If Beanie were a mouse he'd be in fear of his
life." Mr. Bean barks and we both laugh.

I first saw Ross Head from the passenger-side window of Conor's car as we turned off the narrow coast road in the nearby village and slowly crested the hill that leads to the peninsula. I felt my heart leap at the dramatic cliffs and the tall golden grass and the rocks dotted here and there with fuchsia and white wildflowers.

Ross Head is one of the smaller peninsulas along Ireland's southwest coastline; only two miles around the peninsula road that traces its outlines along the steep cliffs. At the mouth of the peninsula is a big gray stone manor house called Rosscliffe House, once grand, now disheveled-looking, though Conor has told me that it's in the process of being turned into a luxury hotel. The house was built on the ruins of a castle or stone fort and the over-grown gardens are dotted here and there with small stone struc-tures and the remnants of rampart walls and towers with views of the sea in almost every direction.

The same developer who's bought the house for a hotel has built five huge modern holiday houses along the cliffs and has started building more of them. At the construction sites, we can see steel girders shining in the sun; views of the ocean show through the skeletons of the huge structures.

Sheep dot the cropped green of the hills on another peninsula across the inlet, and where the peninsula meets what passes for a main road, there's a village called Rosscliffe with a smattering of houses and buildings, a horseshoe-shaped beach in a protected cove, a little harbor and sailing club, a few shops and two pubs, and holiday cottages and farmhouses strung along the roads.

"Our" place, as I've already come to think of it, is a cozy white-washed cottage perched at the edge of the cliffs across the penin-sula from Rosscliffe House and the new houses, with a hearth for turf fires, a cozy kitchen and sitting room, and three bedrooms in an extension that opens on to a stone patio looking out over the inlet. We've been here less than a week and I already feel attached to it in a way that makes me want to call our landlady, Mrs. Crawford, and make an offer. Conor says to wait until the stretch of fine weather we've enjoyed comes to an end.

We stop for a kiss, the sun hitting my cheek as I lift my face to Conor's, the wind swirling around us, rippling the grass. I'm full of that delicious feeling you get at the beginning of a vacation, everything still before you, the days not yet finite, the span of time not yet winding down. I formally resigned from my job as a detective on the homicide squad of the Suffolk County Police Department on Long Island in April, and for the first time in decades, I have no job to go back to, no calls or emails from my team building up, no one waiting for my return. The long-reaching implications of the case I worked in February, the one that led to me resigning from my job, have left me traumatized and anxious, though I can feel the sharp edges of the case's aftermath softening, as though they've been worn away by the wind.

Our cat died of old age in May. Lilly, Conor, and Adrien are all here with me. Only my uncle Danny is back on Long Island, but he moved in with his girlfriend, Eileen, in March and though he keeps sending me and Lilly texts about how much he misses us, I know he's just fine, better than fine actually, finally living again after twenty-three years of mourning his daughter without knowing that's what he was doing.

The sun is strong and direct at noon and I can feel it soaking into my body, giving me energy, warming me from the inside. There's a lone figure with long reddish hair on the path ahead of us, a birdwatcher, I realize when she lifts a pair of binoculars to her eyes and scans the sky over the ocean, and I wonder if she saw the falcon. I stretch my arm a little, testing my shoulder, which I sprained badly in March. I continue to have pain off and on, but it's mostly healed now. Conor is watching me and smiling, his worn green shirt bringing out specks of gold and olive in his brown eyes. His pale Irish skin is a little burned from all the sun and he looks windblown and handsome.

"What?" I ask.

"It's just nice to see you relaxed like this," he says. "It's very . . ."

"Unfamiliar?"

"Yes, but very nice. I worried, you know, that you wouldn't know how to be on holiday." His eyes crinkle a little at the edges, his mouth trying to hide the grin. His face still delights me, its novelty a legacy of the year we were long distance, I suppose, but also of the twenty-three years I didn't see him at all, years when I imagined his face and lived off memory and the few pictures of him online I was able to find. I feel a surge of love for him, a surge of gratitude for the circumstances, tragic as they were, that brought us to each other twenty-three years after we first met, after I first began to love him.

I smile at him. "Being on holiday? What's that? Is it a skill you can learn, like playing the recorder?"

"Oh, yes. I can give you pointers if you need them. I'm very, very skilled at being on holiday." It's true. Conor, a history professor, has a lot of work to do this summer on the book he's writing on Irish political history of the 1950s, '60s, and '70s, but he's doing it on the patio behind the cottage, surrounded by piles of reference works and notebooks and cups of tea. More than once, I've found him on the chaise longue, wrapped in a blanket, walled in by books on all sides, looking perfectly contented and pleased with the world. And when he puts his research aside to go for walks or swims or to sit on our patio and look at the view, he seems able to disconnect from his work in a way I've never been able to manage.

We turn around at the end of the peninsula, stopping for a moment to look at the visual spectacle of the five huge modern houses perched close to the cliffs like elegant seabirds, and then start back, Lilly and Adrien and Mr. Bean dawdling behind us, checking for whales or dolphins. Rosscliffe House looms ahead of us, and as they watch the water, Conor and I walk over to the house for a closer look.

It stands proudly and defiantly at the crest of the rise, a gray stone fortress with three stories of empty windows, an imposing columned facade, and what feels like a halfhearted attempt at decorative detail above the entrance. It's as though the architect took one look at the site and knew he'd have to trade beauty for stalwartness against winds political and meteorological. The house seems to be crouching there, bracing itself for the gusts sweeping across the peninsula.

When we walk closer we see a couple of No Trespassing signs and one reading NEVIN PROPERTIES, FUTURE SITE OF ROSSCLIFFE HOUSE HOTEL, A LUXURY RESORT AND WEDDING VENUE. I think someone has tried to tame the overrun gardens all around it a bit, but otherwise it doesn't look like they've started the renovation.

"How old is it?" I ask Conor.

"From the 1780s, I think I read. It's a good example of Georgian architecture, built by some ancestor of the painter Felix Crawford next to the ruins of what had been a thirteen-century Norman castle. We'll have to see what else we can learn about it."

"It's magnificent but ugly," I say. "You know what I mean?"

"Mmmm. They were meant to be imposing, these Anglo-Irish Big Houses. They had to be. Their builders were uneasy here, trying to cement their claim over a place they had no claim to."

We stand there for a minute, looking up at the house, then walk over to a floor-length window on the terrace and look inside the large, empty room on the other side of the glass. Suddenly I feel as though I'm being watched. The wind is snapping around us, doing funny things as it rounds the stone structure. The sound it makes is almost human, like a wailing baby, and I take Conor's arm as we walk around to the back, finding a stone terrace and covered portico. One of the floor-length windows is open a little, a rock wedged in the gap.

Something rustles and we both jump. "Just the wind," Conor says. The terrace is covered with dead grass and leaves and there's some trash there, too, and graffiti on the back wall of the house. "Well, someone's been here since the 1780s, anyway," he says, pointing to a blanket in one corner and a pile of empty bottles opposite.

"Not a bad place for teenagers to meet for romantic assignations."

"I don't know. I think I'd find it a bit creepy." We both take one final look up at the house and then he tucks my hand under his arm and says, "Let's go find the kids."

We catch up to Lilly and Adrien on the final stretch of the walking path and we all stand there for a few minutes looking back at the view. It's stunning, the almost turquoise blue water against the white of the waves and the vibrant green of the grass. Across the peninsula, the three white cottages, ours in the center, are tucked cozily into the landscape rather than defying it.

"We saw you up in the window of the mansion," Lilly says suddenly. "How'd you get up there? Is it open?" The wind whips her dark hair all around her face; she's impossibly vibrant, her cheeks pink, her body strong and upright against the wind.

"What?" Conor turns to look at her. "What do you mean?"

"We saw you up in one of the windows," Adrien says. "Just now. What's it like up there?"

Conor and I look at each other, confused. "We were looking at the house," I say finally. "We didn't go inside, though."

Lilly pushes her hair off her face. "Well, someone was up there," she says casually. "Right, Adrien? We thought it was you."

Adrien looks up and meets my eyes. "It looked like a woman, but maybe . . ." He turned seventeen in May and his face has thinned since the last time I saw him. Tall and gangly, he has his mother's blond hair and heavily lashed blue eyes, shy and intelligent behind his glasses, but there's something about the shape of his mouth and chin now that's all Conor and his gestures are Conor's, too. He's been so conscious of Lilly's feelings since we arrived, for which I'm eternally grateful. I can see him thinking, his eyes intent behind his glasses, trying to figure out if this is something we shouldn't talk about around Lilly.

"Maybe there was someone hiding up there," Lilly says. "You didn't hear anything, did you?"

Conor smiles. "I don't think so," he says. But now I'm thinking of the sense I had of being watched.

"Probably just the light," I say in what I hope is a reassuring way.

Conor nods. "Come on, Adrien, I'll race you back. We'll meet you two at the cottage," he tells me and he calls to Mr. Bean, who barks and chases after them.

"You ready to head back?" I ask Lilly. Before we went on the walk, she told me that she was tired because she didn't sleep well. "I'm going to stop at Mrs. Crawford's cottage to get eggs and bread. You want to come with me?"

"Sure. I like that bread we got from her."

Lilly and I walk in silence for a bit through the tall grass and then she says, "Mom, I was thinking I might want to run cross-country this fall."

"That's a good thought, Lill. We can talk about it. There's still a lot of time before then." I don't look at her.

"What?"

"Nothing, just . . . that's great. Maybe we can run together this summer. This is a gorgeous place to train. I saw there's a 10K in August in Bantry. Maybe we could do that." I try to make it sound breezy.

But she's alert to my hesitation. "What's wrong? We're going back, aren't we? We're going back to Long Island at the end of the summer?"

"Of course we are, sweetheart. And then we can talk about it."

"Talk about what?" She stops on the path, her hands on her hips, her legs long and lean in black leggings. Her thick brown hair is loose, rising all around her in the air.

"We can do this later, Lill. We're on vacation."

"*What?*"

The wind picks up again, whipping the tall grass back and forth. The ground beneath us is spongy, making me feel uncertain about my footing. "Well, part of us spending the summer here is to see if we might like to move here. You could go to school in Dublin and we could get some . . . some space from everything. You know, the past year has been—"

"What, and live with *Conor*?" Her face is incredulous.

"Well, yes, that's the idea. Their house in Dublin is big enough for all four of us and you liked the city when we spent those two weeks there in April."

She stops and stares at me for a long moment. Her eyes are dark, her face stony. "So what, you're just going to, like, become an Irish cop?"

"Well, I'd have to figure all of that out. Honestly, sweetie, nothing's been decided. It's all just—"

"What about school?"

"There's a really great school called St. Theresa's. It's right near Conor's house. They have room and you can walk and—"

"You talked to a *school*? Without telling me?"

I turn to her, my hands out, but she steps away. "No, we were just getting information, to be prepared. Nothing's been decided, sweetheart. We're here for the summer. That's all."

The wind shifts again. I'm furious with myself. Lilly's therapist said I should wait until later in the summer to talk to her about moving to Dublin. Lilly's been doing so much better, almost back to her old, sunny self the last month or so once we got past the one-year anniversary of Brian's death, but the therapist said that Lilly's biggest fear right now is not being in control of her life after her father's suicide. If her dad, if her whole idea of who he was, could be taken from her just like that, what else could be taken from her? I've fucked this up about fifty different ways.

"Why can't Conor and Adrien move to Long Island?" she asks. "Why do we have to move?"

"Well, sweetie, Conor's work is here. His area of research is Irish history after all, and you know, Adrien's mom is in Ireland, so they can't just—"

"Oh, so because I'm the one with a dead dad, I'm the one who has to move?" She's half crying, her hair whipping across her face in the stiff wind. Her cheeks are reddened now, her eyes dark and gleaming with anger. I want to reach out and lift her, bring her to me. I can feel her pain, her rage, her fear in the air between us. "You're so fucking selfish!" she throws out and runs back along the walking path toward the cottage. "It's all about you."

I stop myself from sprinting after her and let her go, telling myself she'll cool down. She disappears in the tall grass, so quickly it shakes me a little.

Letting the wind flow over my face, calming my heart rate, I stand there looking out at the view for a moment. It's stunning, all the visual elements combining to form a pleasing composition, but suddenly I'm aware of the sharp angles of the high cliffs, the treacherous distance down to the water. And when I look back at Rosscliffe House, checking the uppermost windows to see if I can figure out what optical illusion made Lilly and Adrien think there was someone up there, all I can see is the dark bulk of it, imposing and vaguely threatening against the endless ocean.

Sharona Jacobs

SARAH STEWART TAYLOR is the author of the Sweeney St. George series and the Maggie D'arcy Mysteries. She grew up on Long Island and was educated at Middlebury College and Trinity College, Dublin. A former journalist and teacher, she writes and lives with her family on a farm in Vermont, where they raise sheep and grow blueberries. Taylor spends as much time in Ireland as she can and loves to explore new corners of the island. You can visit her online at SarahStewartTaylor.com.